Other Books In This Series

Tesseracts 1
edited by Judith Merril

Tesseracts 2
edited by Phyllis Gotlieb & Douglas Barbour

Tesseracts 3
edited by Candas Jane Dorsey & Gerry Truscott

Tesseracts 4
edited by Lorna Toolis & Michael Skeet

Tesseracts 5
edited by Robert Runté & Yves Maynard

Tesseracts 6
edited by Robert J. Sawyer & Carolyn Clink

Tesseracts 7
edited by Paula Johanson & Jean-Louis Trudel

Tesseracts 8
edited by John Clute & Candas Jane Dorsey

Tesseracts Nine
edited by Nalo Hopkinson and Geoff Ryman

Tesseracts Ten
edited by Robert Charles Wilson and Edo van Belkom

Tesseracts Eleven
edited by Cory Doctorow and Holly Phillips

Tesseracts Twelve
edited by Claude Lalumière

TesseractsQ
edited by Élisabeth Vonarburg & Jane Brierley

CHILLING TALES FROM THE GREAT WHITE NORTH

TESSERACTS THIRTEEN

EDITED BY
NANCY KILPATRICK
& DAVID MORRELL

EDGE SCIENCE FICTION AND FANTASY PUBLISHING
AN IMPRINT OF HADES PUBLICATIONS, INC.
CALGARY

 EDGE

Edge Science Fiction and Fantasy Publishing
An Imprint of Hades Publications Inc.
P.O. Box 1714, Calgary, Alberta, T2P 2L7, Canada

In-house editing by Brian Hades
Interior design by Brian Hades
Cover Illustration by Chad Michael Ward
ISBN-13: 978-1-894063-25-8

EDGE Science Fiction and Fantasy Publishing and Hades Publications, Inc.
acknowledges the ongoing support of the Canada Council for the Arts and the
Alberta Foundation for the Arts for our publishing programme.

Alberta Foundation for the Arts

Canada Council for the Arts   Conseil des Arts du Canada

FIRST EDITION
(h-20090628)
Printed in Canada
www.edgewebsite.com

Contents

CHILLING TALES FROM THE GREAT WHITE NORTH

TESSERACTS THIRTEEN

Time Lapse
By David Morrell

In his valuable essay about horror elements in Canadian literature ("Out of the Barrens," included in this volume), Robert Knowlton has some kind words to say about my contributions to the genre. He notes that I'm a Canadian who headed south to the United States. What he doesn't add is that I also made contributions to the thriller genre, particularly with my 1972 novel, *First Blood*, in which Rambo was introduced. That statement might make some of you pause. A Canadian created one of the most quintessential American characters? Yep. The way that happened is worth describing in this anthology of Canadian writers — because my journey gave me a unique perspective on Canada.

I was born and raised in the twin city of Kitchener-Waterloo in southern Ontario. That's about an hour's drive from Toronto, and during the years I lived in Canada (1943-1966), Toronto was about as far as my adventures took me. Once to Ottawa. Once to Algonquin Park. Summer weekend drives through Guelph en route to the lake towns near Owen Sound. Back then, huge unpopulated areas occupied the distance between these places. The small town of Milton has halfway between Kitchener and Toronto, for example. Otherwise there was nothing except forests and farms. These days, that entire stretch of highway to Toronto is heavily populated. The road to Guelph — once rural — is crammed with homes and business. For that matter, so is most of southern Ontario.

I saw this change happen in the equivalent of time-lapse photography. In 1965, I was an undergraduate student at what was then St. Jerome's College at the University of Waterloo. My interest in Ernest Hemingway led me to the college's small library where I found the first scholarly work about him. Its author, Philip Young, wrote so wonderfully that I decided to apply for graduate work at the American university where Young taught — Penn State. To put this in context, in those days, you could look far and wide for a course in Canadian literature. A few Canadian authors might be included in a survey course. If so, they'd be tacked on after a multitude of British authors and a handful of American ones. It was perfectly natural for a Canadian to want to study American literature. After all, how could there be a sense of Canadian literature when Canadians were confused about their national identity? The country's form of government, a compilation of British and American mechanisms, symbolized the confusion. I recall numerous conversations in which Canadians tried to decide if they were more British than American or more American than British.

But paradoxically, as the forests and farms diminished, a sense of Canadian identity grew, and for me, this change also happened as if in time-lapse photography. I moved to the United States in 1966. I returned every three months to visit my family and friends. For a year, everything seemed the same, and then in June of 1967, I arrived back in Kitchener to learn about something called Expo '67, a World's Fair that was taking place in Montreal and celebrating Canada's centennial. The old debate about what it meant to be Canadian had been resurrected, but now it had passion. When I returned at the start of the fall, Expo '67 was still going strong, and the gorgeous television coverage of various World's Fair events related to Canada made everyone I talked to feel even more enthusiastic and proud. Canada's ethnic diversity, its abundance of natural resources, its beauty, its creative blend of various government models, its cleanliness (I've never seen a cleaner or more uncluttered country), its kind spirit, its vastness — these were celebrated rather than being taken for granted. As the years progressed, I visited less often and saw changes more dramatically. As populated areas grew inward, becoming denser, the national spirit expanded.

I can provide a very personal example. In 1966, when I made the long trek to Penn State to study Hemingway and specialize in American literature, I had every reason to expect that, after I received my doctorate, a Canadian university would hire me. In 1970, Ph.D. in hand, I applied to all of them, and not one would consider me. American literature? Hadn't I heard about Expo '67? Didn't I know that Canadians were finally gaining a sense of identity? Thus, as Canadian literature courses began being taught in Canadian universities, I remained in the United States, where I was accepted as a professor at the University of Iowa. *First Blood* and Rambo were the result, a Canadian's view of the Vietnam War and its tragic consequences.

But even though I write about American locales and subjects, I'm influenced by the attitudes and perceptions from my first 22 years, those formative decades spent in southern Ontario. I carry an American passport, but I also retain my Canadian citizenship. Thus, when noted Canadian author Nancy Kilpatrick contacted me to ask if I'd be interested in co-editing an anthology of Canadian horror fiction, I didn't hesitate. For one thing, I saw the project as an opportunity to learn more about that once elusive concept of Canadian literature. For another, horror is one of my favorite genres. I was a founding member of the Horror Writers Association. I received three Stoker awards and was nominated for two others. My novel, *The Totem*, is cited in *Horror: 100 Best Books*. When I was a kid, radio horror dramas addicted me, then E.C. comics like *The Vault of Horror* and *The Haunt of Fear*, then Poe's short stories, then Lovecraft, then.... Well, let's just say that I like a good scare, and some of the tales in this anthology are very scary indeed. Others make me see things in new ways. By taking me on a frightening voyage of imagination, they give me a better understanding of the so-called ordinary world and the horrors within it. All bring something fresh to the genre while at the same time displaying a remarkable skill with language. Perhaps the most impressive aspect that unifies them is the common identity of their authors: Canadians.

Canadian horror fiction? In 1966, when I moved to the United States, an anthology of this sort would have been impossible. Now it is part of the wave of national identity that continues to be the consequence of Expo '67, celebrating this distinctive, complex, justly proud country. All the influences I cited a moment ago were American. These days, an apprentice Canadian writer has every reason to expect the influences to be homegrown.

Time Capsule
By Nancy Kilpatrick

In 1970 I visited Canada for a weekend with my then-boyfriend. He left. I stayed. And immigrated.

Toronto, back then, was like a small town to me. It was quiet at night, there were few cars and people out on Sundays, the polite population kept their streets clean, and I felt for the first time in my life that I could walk anywhere, any time and be safe. And that feeling translated into an opportunity: I could pursue the vocation I'd always dreamed about — writing.

Over my nearly four decades in this country, I have lived mainly in Toronto, in Montreal twice (I live there now), Vancouver for half a year, and have traveled back and forth across Canada a dozen times, from Vancouver Island's west coast to P.E.I. I've come to love Canada. Who wouldn't?

I was born in Philadelphia, the first half of my salad days spent in both San Francisco and Chicago, and I dwelled for extended periods in both North Carolina and northern Louisiana. And while I discovered that the supermarkets in Canada had many similar products to those available in US supermarkets — although the writing on the boxes is, delightfully, in both English and French — I felt in 1970 as I feel now: Canada is nothing like the United States. For me, one of the easiest ways to see that difference is in the horror and dark fantasy writing genres.

A lot of Canadian writers have crept into the hearts of American, British and French-as-in-France publishers. Writers here are quiet, compared to Americans, barely tooting their own horns. The Brits, who frown on lining up your books at a convention panel you're participating on, adore Canadians. French publishing has embraced not just their simpler distant cousins in Quebec who share the same language, but have translated quite a few English-language authors from Canada as well. And of course both English and French writers in Canada have published in the Other Official Language. Many small and medium sized genre houses have sprung up in this country over the years that have embraced genre writers in both French and English: Éditions Alire in Québec translates English language writers, including yours truly. Hades Publications (EDGE imprint) in Calgary, the illustrious house that brings you the Tesseracts series, includes French language writers on their list.

All of the above is to say that Canadian writers of horror and dark fantasy get around. And they do so because of a unique voice. The stories in this one-of-a-kind Tesseracts, devoted to horror and dark fantasy exclusively, possess a chilling quality that doesn't so much focus on where they are set, but the subject matter about which they are written. These are human stories, with strong character development that involve readers, stories of a quality that reflect the world of literary fiction, but with an unnerving undercurrent, written in a tone that unearths the dark side of life.

Before I came to Canada I had written what is deemed 'literature'. I'd published a couple of stories, nothing exceptional. But it was always a strain. I love plot. I love characterization. I love story. The literary field had been shifting, turning minimalist, and I found myself having to contort and bend my writing to get in the emotions I wanted a story to hold and to pare back characters to a point where the reader could read anything at all into them, which left them a tad flat in my view. Essentially, I was never certain if the depth came through to the reader because the writing seemed too bare-bones in many ways.

I wrote my first horror novel in Canada, in 1975, in a small cottage on Huntley Street in downtown Toronto, which I shared with two women. One woman moved out. One went to Mexico for several months and returned. I didn't notice. I was hammering madly, obsessively, as writers do, on a portable manual typewriter. That book, a futuristic vampire novel, was set in 2006. It presented a lot of ideas the world would see come to pass: computers used in the travel business; moving sidewalks; old subway stations turned into shops; cryonic suspension evolved to the point where a body could be brought back from the dead — well, a vampire body anyway! It took until the year 2000 for a tiny Canadian press, Baskerville Books, to publish that novel, which became *Bloodlover*, the 4th book in my *Power of the Blood* vampire world, the 1st book of which was published in 1993 by Pocket Books (Simon & Schuster).

In Canada, I also made a firm decision to move away from literary writing when at the turn of the 1990s one of my short stories was selected as a runner-up in *The Toronto Star's* annual short story contest. As I perused my story in the paper, I though: this is really a horror tale! I revised it as such, and "Root Cellar" (the setting based on the farm outside Napanee where I lived for nine months) has since been published and reprinted several times over the years in horror magazines and anthologies and was selected for the prestigious *Year's Best Horror # 20* edited by the late Karl Wagner (DAW Publishing).

Canada has been good for me. If I hadn't been living in Canada, I doubt I would have had the opportunity to evolve as a writer. The nature of this country supports the arts. I've felt that support for the type of writing I do best, which is dark, and blends realities. I've made wonderful friends here, and feel part of the horror/dark fantasy/fantasy/science fiction/mystery communities. Federal, provincial and local governments provide some financial support for the arts as well, with Public Lending Rights; Access Copyright and Copibec; grants for writing projects and travel; programmes like writer-in-residence, library readings, school talks and workshops. And, of course, there is financial help for publishers, without which, many would not survive.

I can't say enough good things about Canada and its writing world. The only sad part of living here is that this country is a huge land mass, spread out over many thousands of often snow-covered kilometers. That makes it difficult for writers to get together. Fortunately, Canada has come to be a sought-after host for international genre writing conventions. To name just a few recent ones: World Horror Convention Toronto 2007 (where I was a Writer Guest of Honor); World Horror Convention 2009 Winnipeg; World Fantasy Convention 2001 Montreal and World Fantasy Convention 2008 Calgary (where David Morrell was a Writer Guest of Honor); World Science Fiction convention 2007 Toronto and World Science Fiction convention 2009 Montreal, where Tesseracts 13 was launched.

But apart from major events like these, local writers across the country find ways to congregate on a somewhat regular basis, providing support, encouragement, friendship, valuable criticism and oh yes, did I mention the beer?

Canada has come a long way since I moved here. Canadian dark genre writers have also come a long way. When you read the bios, you'll see some stars and some up-and-comers. When you read the stories, you'll discover what makes Canadian authors world renowned: love of story, development of characters, intriguingly dark plots, attention to detail, and a unique spin on story that's rarely seen elsewhere, all of which results in Canadian authors being sought-after outside our borders.

It's been my pleasure to live and work here. And most recently to edit this terrific anthology with the esteemed author — and super nice and generous man! — David Morrell. Brian Hades, publisher at Edge Science Fiction and Fantasy Publishing, dreamed up the clever idea for a special dark Tesseracts, number 13! He and his staff and his amazing wife Anita have made this volume possible.

Four decades in my adopted home and I have watched Canada become an innovator and leader in the realm of horror and dark fantasy fiction. I suspect that the best is yet to come!

YOUTH

Stone Cold

By Kevin Cockle

Sandy lays my clothes out the night before. I can still dress myself, so I insist upon it, even though it takes an hour and a half and leaves me exhausted. Slippers; sweat pants; loose t-shirt; housecoat; no socks. I get that together, then totter over to the wheelchair and sit down. I still wake up hours before everyone else — that much hasn't changed. I can sit by the window and watch morning light push its way through tree-leaves; hear the sounds of the neighborhood coming-to; listen to the Robins calling for food. All in all, I'm lucky. Things could be so much worse for me.

Around 7:30, I hear the house stirring: Sandy's up, making coffee. She peeks into my room — puffy-faced, but soccer-mom pretty — sees that I'm up. "Morning Jack," she says, her voice cheerful. She enters, takes control of my chair, wheels me into the living room. I can smell her mouth-wash in the air: minty. She turns on the TV, switching it to the business channel. They do that automatically — assuming I want to watch what I once was; assuming I'm still curious about it all. I'd be just as happy watching *Star Trek* or whatever else is on at this hour. But they have to do that kind of thing — make assumptions and decisions on my behalf — it's not like I can clearly tell them otherwise. Not worth the effort to complain.

I smell bacon, or some soy-derivative near-bacon, and eggs, toast, coffee. I love Sundays — just love them — for their pace and smells and sounds. It's almost as though the world is slowing down a little, trying to meet me half-way. Richie's up. I hear the murmur of his greeting to Sandy in the kitchen. My brother and his wife — looking after me: this is my world now.

I hear little Katie creeping up behind me. She moves in fast — still in her pjs — steps her slippered foot upon mine, then scampers away, tittering. Slowly, I make an imperious "how dare you" face — my features grinding into position — then I move my foot in retaliation, about 5 seconds too late to step on Katie. She giggles, covering her mouth from across the room as my reaction is hysterically slow, my rage comical.

"Katie?" Sandy's voice rises from the kitchen. "Are you bothering Uncle Jack?" Same question, all the time; they're always worried that Katie's somehow getting on my nerves. I manage what I think is a smile and I hope my eyes are twinkling.

"No!" Katie hollers back, wandering back over near my chair and sitting down beside me. I don't know why, but she watches the business channel with me in the mornings before school and CNN on the weekends. Look out Richie — got a little hedge fund manager in the making. I can't talk to her, but I feel she's on my wavelength — just taking things in by osmosis. Crazy kid.

Breakfast is the usual quiet, chattering affair. I can't chew the solid food properly — always choke when I try — so it's a special nutrient shake for me while everyone else eats the real food. But I like the sight of the breakfast plates and food — the collectivity of it — the homey odors of it. I always lived in the city, never ate breakfast, rarely had anyone stay long enough to eat it with me. If you had told me then that I'd be here now, I'd have thought you were insane and would've ordered security to remove you from the building.

I've never told Richard and Sandy about the cold — not since my first neurologist told me it was psychosomatic. I don't shiver, so there's no real way for them to know, and I've grown accustomed to it in a way, although it's always uncomfortable. I remember when it first hit — well before the general slowing-down — I was in the shower one morning, turning up the heat and unable to get warm. Wound up burning myself in the attempt. At night, I'd pile the blankets on, draw my knees up, hug myself into a fetal ball — but I could not shake the chill. It wasn't a freezing cold: I remember as a kid, taking the bus in the winter; it was that kind of cold. You're well protected, you're dressed for it, but you're still stamping and shuffling your feet, counting the seconds until the damn bus shows up. It was that particular kind of cold that settled in on me, and never left.

To this day, no one knows what's wrong with me. It's not a sclerosis; not ALS; not a brain tumor. There's a long — and growing incrementally longer — delay between my intention to act, and the ultimate movement of my body. I call it a "slowing down" because nothing else comes to mind, and because that's mostly what it feels like. I think they're getting the diagnosis wrong because of this cold thing, but there's no evidence of it, so there's no way to account for it. I'm fine — I mean — now, after all this time, there's muscle atrophy and other secondary problems creeping in — but as for the root cause of the slowing, there doesn't seem to be any physical reason for it. I'm healthy, I'm aware (though distracted these days), but I'm winding down. And I'm always, always cold, though not to the touch.

Breakfast burbles to conclusion. I get wheeled back to watch TV as the family goes about its various routines. We're driving to a baseball game this afternoon at the local park, but until then, there'll be the usual bustle of activity throughout the house. I settle in to daydream, watch the news. Not for the first time, I find myself loving the fact that cable news has provided a career path for beauty-pageant winners. Whoever would have thought that news-presentation would be the practical application for pageant-winning ability?

The break up of the private brokerages continues. Capitalism continues to grind to a halt, and governments everywhere look to lubricate the system with re-regulation and criminal prosecution of the executive class. The big fish this week is Don Dupre — head of risk management at Colman Ridgeway. Arrested — with cuffs no less — after charges had been laid. I know Don — good golfer. He's like all the guys that get caught: never thought they were doing anything wrong. Disconnected and unaware, they feel innocent and fault-free. Not like me. I'd come up through the bullpen — I'd been an unlicensed cold-caller at the start — I'd worked my way up and had no illusions about anything I was doing along the way. I'd known early on that something being legal didn't make it right, and that covering my ass would be a key career discipline. Don and the rest of the country clubbers had never had that anxiety, never felt themselves to be in jeopardy. As he walked out of the building on CNN, I could see the same denial and defiance on his face as everyone else had. I knew I'd be seeing it again in the trial, and in the conviction. Should've listened to me, Donnie; I got out with my parachute intact.

Reminds me of '98 — when the pac-rim currencies collapsed and Long Term Capital almost took us all down. That had been a terrible credit-crunch period as well — a time when the very gears of the international machine seemed to be gumming up and freezing solid. I actually had a dream about the whole thing three weeks before the events hit. In the dream, I had a view of the Pacific Ocean — very vivid — I could see the great, rolling green immensity of it from some airborne view point. Broad daylight, clear skies, hot and humid. Then, as I watched, a darkness seemed to grow under the water, and the center of it fell away, causing a gigantic vortex to turn. It was miles and miles across, and the vortex dropped down and down — and all I could hear was that deafening Niagara-like roar as the world's mightiest ocean turned in on itself.

When I awoke, I automatically interpreted the images as some sort of financial crisis centered in Asia — that's what I felt — and when the headlines began to howl in confirmation, I remember the crawling sensation on my spine. I was convinced that the dream had been a warning — almost as though my subconscious and nervous system were somehow jacked into the vast complexity of world finance, able to signal me in my sleep, when my waking mind could never have sorted things out in time.

"Did you ever think you might have CAUSED the crash?" Patricia Weller had asked me at the time, after I told her about the dream. She was typical of my women then: artsy; young; unemployed but going to school or making theatre work or just coaxing a little get-by cash out of yours truly. She lay with her chin on my chest in bed, golden ringlets damp and clinging to freckled cheeks. "You know— maybe you've got some latent psychic power, but you're totally unaware of it, so when it manifests, you see it in dreams and you THINK you're predicting things, but really you're causing them?"

"Uh... no," I said. "That hadn't occurred to me."

"Yeah," she continued sleepily, her voice throaty. "I've always felt it about you — the vibe. You've got... something, baby, something humming inside. But you can't see it, you know? It's all layered over and pounded down. You ever dream about airplane crashes or train wrecks? Maybe you're causing them too, reaching out with your mind and..."

"Maybe you should shut up now," I said, intending to be funny; coming across petulant instead. Patty was an astrologist and God knows what else: she was always coming up with alternative explanations for things, just to argue with me. Normally, I found it charming and challenging, but I hadn't taken this little observation of hers all that well. As I recall, I think I may have stopped seeing her shortly thereafter, though back then, I don't think I linked the break up to her playful little observation that night. Now that I have time on my hands, and I think about such things often, I see that she had definitely irritated me, at a period when I was already on edge because of the financial crisis.

Baseball in the suburbs is strange and wonderful — like most things out here. Sandy removes my housecoat and puts my windbreaker on — but it's mild out, and I won't need much more. The SUV has a sliding door and a wheelchair ramp so I can roll right in: I fit like a modular component of the thing — as though cripples come standard. Katie hops in the back with me, nattering. I imagine talking to me is like talking to her dolls — that's why it seems so natural to her.

The drive is a pleasant, brief, tree-lined affair. Richie and Sandy moved to the gated community when they'd had Katie, and I can see why. It IS idyllic, as advertised. The people ARE friendly; the houses large and well kept. The place does have a small-town feel, and with the man-made lake, golf course, parks and so on, it's almost as though you aren't part of the city at all. As we pass one of the outer gates, I get a glimpse of the beefed up security — all Iraq and Afghanistan war vets who cannot be messed with — and a funny thought occurs to me. Soldiers return to lucrative guard positions in these communities the way beauty pageant winners found a home in cable news. I laugh — silently of course, really more of a twitching in my chest — but I enjoy the premise all the same. I'm still considering the parallel when I hear the SUV's tires crunching on gravel and I know we've turned into the ballpark parking lot.

I love this place. Attached to the golf course, I can smell putting-green must and freshly turned soil in the air. Sandy and Rich call out to folks they know as I'm wheeled down my ramp, and together we head into the ballpark. It's small, but it's a carefully crafted replica of nineteenth century ballparks: it also serves as a place to hear live music on warm Friday nights throughout the summer. The canopies and the railings are all exquisite and transporting: if not for the modern chairs and modern people, you'd swear Ty Cobb was about to step out onto the pitch at any moment.

The game itself is good, played by our community team against the team of some other gated place, the name of which escapes me. Technically, it's A-ball, with some of these kids actually destined for the big leagues, but it's not A-ball affiliated with the minor leagues *per se*. Those leagues are dying and being reorganized around the new communities that can afford them. I'm aware of this stuff on a level that escapes Richie and the rest, but God love them: they're keeping baseball alive at the grass roots level.

The sun is warm. I can tell because I'm squinting in the light, but I'm cold inside my windbreaker. I know from experience that a sweater or another jacket won't make any difference, but the funny thing is, I'm sweating. On some level, my body knows it's hot, knows it's July, knows it's a summer Sunday afternoon. Only the rest of me refuses to accept those facts. The rest of me is thirteen years old, waiting for a November bus to arrive while I'm trying to stamp blood into my toes.

It's the change of scenery I like. All my time is idle, and my mind wanders as it would if I was home, but there's a pitcher with a three-quarters sidearm delivery that's so gangly and beautiful to watch that it momentarily holds my attention. Then I'm off again — thinking of Focke-Wulfs strafing the golf course; ogling someone's daughter a few rows down from us; sipping cola through a straw as Sandy holds the can. Here and there, I see other invalids — mostly seniors, but not all — enjoying being out with their families in the same detached way as I am. I like being at the window at home; I like being here in the sunlight with these people; I like hearing Katie chatter about imaginary things and events. At one time, I know this — all of it — would have driven me absolutely batshit. But now, it's almost as if the slowing down has taken root in my mind and sensibility as well as my limbs. I don't feel trapped by this; there's a calmness to this state of being. A patience.

I never reflect upon whether I deserve the love I'm getting: I don't. It's just that simple. Had it been Richie struck down with this disease, I'd have paid to have him looked after, but there's no way he could've stayed with me. When Richie found out I was hospitalized, he came to my room, looked me right in the eyes, and said in that quiet voice of his, "You're coming home with me and Sandy, Jack. You're staying with us, and that's all there is to it." Just like that, he was once again my kid brother who had done all my playground fighting for me and never once questioned his role. All our lives, Richie would've taken a bullet for me, and I'd have let him.

So I'm lucky, I know it, and I'm grateful. And, some small part of me reminds myself, Richie and Sandy are my beneficiaries, and that means they're set for life. I sit and mull over that nasty little thought and all its implications. It's like a fragment of my old self, punching through the fogginess — a style of cognition I thought I'd left behind me. The way I used to have of recognizing the material reality of things, of seeing the way things worked, of recognizing everyone's interests and motivations. I feel muscles in my mouth firing, though I'm not sure if I'm smiling. You can take the man out of finance, but you can't take finance out of the man, apparently.

The ballgame ends as ballgames will: I forget to check the score. Everyone files out of the park in orderly fashion, back to their hybrids and SUVs. I doze a little in my chair as Katie does her best to lobby for an ice-cream stop en route. There will be a little TV in our future; Richie will read while Sandy and I watch something of interest to Sandy. There will be a quick, shallow bath for me when my nurse comes over. Sandy had initially protested this "waste of money," but sometimes her can-do attitude crowds my shrinking sense of dignity. It's better to have a nurse look after some things — better for all of us. I've got toe nails that need clipping and an ass that needs wiping. Sandy's like a frontier wife: so unflappable, so thrifty, so willing to roll up her shirtsleeves and slop out the stables. Really, it's not necessary.

Just like that, Sunday will drift to the finish line, and we'll all retire to our various rooms for the night. I couldn't ask for more.

Monday morning, I'm up at five — hours before the rest — years of waking up on New York time having left their imprint on my nervous system. Sandy's laid my clothes out: I start the journey towards being dressed. Eventually, I'm able to make it to my chair — anything more than a few steps and I can't make the micro-adjustments necessary for true walking balance. And once again, I sit at the window, half dozing, watching the light come up.

Eventually, I hear kitchen-puttering; a toilet flushing; a faucet running; a kettle boiling. I hear Katie complaining, which is odd, so I focus enough to make out her voice saying, "I'm cold, mum. Feel my hands."

"Katie, your hands feel fine, go wash up."

"But mum..."

"Go on now, Katie."

My heart pounds against my ribs; I feel the roar of blood in my ears and a terrible plunging sensation in my stomach.

The bottom has fallen out of the Pacific Ocean, and the whole world is going to be sucked down and down into the swirling vortex.

I'm slowing down; the world is slowing down; gears are grinding. There's a sympathetic resonance here, a harmony, but I am not causal.

I am not causal.

● ●

Kevin Cockle lives in Calgary, Alberta, and often incorporates Calgary-style boom-town themes in his work. A frequent contributor to *On Spec* magazine, Kevin has dabbled in screen writing, sports journalism, and technical writing to fill out what would otherwise be a purely finance-centric resume.

● ●

Striges

By Daniel Sernine

Translated by Sheryl Curtis

As her coffee cooled between her dirty fingers, she watched the coaches for an hour, maybe more. The yellow bands on the bus terminal marquee fractured into fragments on the surface of puddles, shattered every now and then as vehicles drove by, their headlights gleaming.

They bore images of highways, the coaches, images of wet cities, interchanges and refineries, steel bridges and cement ramps, endless suburbs, sodium vapor streetlights in the purple twilight.

The Greyhounds, particularly, captivated Rosamund, the sleek dog vainly chasing after a dream — or maybe fleeing from it — like some of the young people she imagined on the rear seat, weary, jeans torn, eyes shining with sleeplessness, a boy and girl seeking adventure, a teen-aged runaway, Regina or Omaha left far behind, lost.

On the bay window that separated her from all that and kept her dry, Rosamund made out the pale splash of her own face, hair ragged. It had been some time since any make-up had touched that face.

She took a liquor store bottle from her pocket and poured a few drops into her coffee, which had already been thoroughly spiked, then drained her cup with a grimace.

The snack bar was empty. The waitress was talking listlessly on the telephone, bored with her mother or sister. Rosamund left.

As she walked past the Hôtel Gouverneur Place Dupuis, she thought about her last night with Paul-André, what had it been, almost a year ago? Their final attempt had failed, a pathetic effort to weave the threads of their lives that had once, ever so briefly, been entwined, back together — a rapprochement more like the static electricity that makes two mismatched socks cling as they're pulled from a dryer. Their relationship had grown out of a sense of "better this than nothing," but they had finally come to see — Paul-André first, no doubt — that nothing was actually better.

Now, Rosamund *was* nothing, and Paul-André would probably ignore her if he crossed her path — if he recognized her, that is. That evening, she barely looked up at the building as she walked past.

She walked down to Old Montreal, past the enclosed parking areas and the rooming houses, past the construction sites and burnt out ruins, past the leprous concrete of the overpass, past the graffiti of distress.

⋇⋅⊹⋅⊹⋅⋇

At St. Paul Street in front of the Bonsecours market, she stumbled over the cobblestones, vulnerable ankles twisting. Even though she wasn't that old, her joints pained her at times, particularly when she'd been drinking. The surface of the narrow streets became smoother as her feet carried her west. Those same streets where once, wearing the latest fashions, a touch of purple in her hair, she would walk by the beggars, giving them no alms, just a brief glance.

STRIGES
BY LAMIA

The poster was still stuck to the dirty shop window, collapsing under the weight of the humidity. The "Marquettinge" sign had disappeared from the front of the building, but a few relics remained in the empty offices. Rosamund stopped. Striges had been her concept: the poison green flask, all curves and rounded claws, the

silver stopper, pointed like a beak or spur. The pale woman
on the poster was supposed to be Lilith, demon of the night.
On the side of her face, her skin morphed into scales and
her hair into feathers.

Audacious and persuasive... that had definitely been
Rosamund. She had won over her colleagues, sold the
concept to the perfume manufacturer Lamy, and had even
convinced them to change the spelling of their company
name. Which didn't prevent her from being laid off a few
weeks later when a major client had withdrawn its account
and work had become scarce.

She had no idea if Lilith had made the perfume company a fortune, but the Marquettinge agency no longer
existed and its empty offices had not been leased since.
There were so many advertising firms — and so many
perfumes.

Rosamund caught sight of a movement in the shadows,
at the back of the office. Perhaps a squatter. It was going
to be a cold night.

She left the small dilapidated building behind her, after
one final glance at Lilith's transparent image. "Striges used
to eat children," she had explained to her friend Rolande
when talking about the new perfume. "Use just a little and
you'll catch all the boys you want. Then you can just eat
them up." Rolande was a PR agent for the same agency.
In her late thirties, she devoured all the young men in the
business neighborhood with her eyes: the waiters at *La
Sorosa* or the *Saint-Amable*, the court messengers, the graphic
artists, the photocopier technicians, the university graduates
slaving away in architects' offices. She'd comment on a
taught thigh, firm little cheeks, a well-filled crotch, and
she hated the baggy pants that had been in fashion for so
many years.

Meanwhile, Rolande's own son, Marc, had played hooky
every other day. It wasn't long before he dropped out for
good and his butt was being judged by potential johns.

Rosamund had seen him a few times since, wandering
down St. Denis Street or panhandling near a subway
entrance. The last time, no later than the day before. He

had to have been sixteen. Driven by a remnant of pride, she had decided against approaching him and asking about Rolande, who had been laid off a few months after Rosamund. No notice for her either.

Rolande and Rosamund. Another time, another world.

>+I+I+I+<

The drizzle was unrelenting. The neighborhood was deserted, the dusty shop windows inhabited solely by the reflection of lights on the wet road. A few streets over, a car hissed as it drove past. Then the silent lights changed from red to green.

Rosamund stepped out from an alley where she had squatted down. In the dark, she had found it impossible not to wet her jeans a bit. Like perfume, she sometimes wore the scent of her own urine, as she roused from the stupor in which rubbing alcohol had plunged her for ten or twelve hours.

She shivered. Some distance off, on the sidewalk on the other side of the street, a child walked toward her, silently. Definitely a child, dainty, in a black or dark green raincoat, made shiny by the rain, head down under the drizzle.

A child at this time of night? Rosamund and her kind were used to seeing them fairly often. Little girls wandering in the night, apparently unconcerned, as if nothing worse could happen to them than being abandoned by their whore of a mother or kicked out by a stepfather for refusing his advances.

Another time, Rosamund would have felt something — pity, compassion. She had even used to write letters to the editor after watching news stories that she had found particularly upsetting. That evening, she went on her way.

After a few steps, she stopped under a streetlight and buttoned her collar. She took the bottle from her pocket. Shaking it produced a thin sound. She gulped down what remained of the alcohol, her breath fogging under the icy light. She threw the empty bottle into an alley, its fall obviously cushioned by a pile of rubbish. No sound of breaking glass.

Where had the little girl in the oversized raincoat gone? Rosamund walked more cautiously, a little slower. The cross streets provided glimpses of the city, standing beyond the trench of the highway, blurred, fragmented into small squares of light. An indistinct murmur wafted through the air, the city's breath.

After taking a hundred steps or so, along a not-quite-straight line, Rosamund stopped again, alarmed by a wave of silence. She turned her head. Shivers ran up and down her back. In a shop window, lackluster reflections slept on bronze or copper instruments, vaguely nautical.

With a buzz and a splutter, a neon light came back to life above Rosamund's head. She jumped and looked up. She stared, dazzled for a moment, at the meaningless letters that filled the air with a reassuring hum.

The silence dispelled, she set out again. She had walked down the short Cours Le Royer and now the nave of the Notre-Dame Basilica loomed before her, black in the drizzle, bristling with pinnacles, dominated by its towers, gargoyles perched on its arched buttresses. But, no, this was not Paris, and gargoyles had never set foot on this continent. Was it possible that she once had the means to travel to Paris?

She wondered what had happened to Bleuette, whom she hadn't seen in several weeks and who had usually spent her nights with two or three bums in a nook under the cathedral. Occasionally, she'd walked the same route as Rosamund, haunting the underground network at Square Victoria. She wasn't even 20 and came from Lac Saint-Jean where her family, or so she claimed, owned the best blueberry patches in all Quebec. Perhaps she'd returned to her ever so wealthy father. Perhaps she'd encountered some guy who had roughed her up a little.

The warmth in her chest washed away the malaise that had overwhelmed her as she thought about the little girl she had seen in the night and Bleuette who had disappeared from the circuit. Now, a given thought never stayed long in Rosamund's head. It was like a draft of air where the waste from the present and past floated, circling about for a moment, then drifting off into the fog of her memory.

She walked back down toward St. Paul Street. Farther off, someone else walking in her direction brought her to a stop once again. But she identified him, wide man's coat with shoulders that were too broad, battered hat, Adidas gym bag in place of a shopping bag. It was herself, reflected in the glassed wall of an entrance. Yes, she recognized herself, that mouth, a straight, joyless line, that sullen double wrinkle emphasizing the bitterness, dark eyes like two accusations, a mug no one could ever love, although she had once used make-up to give it some style.

Behind that...? A child, the wet wings of her raincoat almost dragging on the ground.

Rosamund turned around. The kid was no longer there. Nothing but a beer sign, red, blue and white, casting a cold presence on the wet sidewalk.

Had it been the same girl? Her coat was dark, with deep folds. But she wasn't really there.

That face, though, sharp and pale, almost gray?

She had just dreamed her up. Like she had dreamed up the medieval stone creatures when she thought about Notre-Dame de Paris, a moment earlier, the monkeys, imps and petrels, their grins petrified. She was used to it. She didn't always have good liquor store booze to whet her whistle.

❖❖❖❖❖

Farther along, as she arrived at a deserted McGill Street, she walked around a building twice before finding the opening in the fencing. A sheet of plywood, with a nail loose at the bottom. Fingers white with the effort, she managed to pry it aside. A dreamy graffitist had written "neon god" on the boards in fluorescent letters; an angry one asked "who's listening?"

The nails caught on her coat, forcing her to turn around. Rosamund's last vision of the street was once again, briefly, inhabited by a thin gray child, wearing a sort of thread-bare cape, shining with the rain. Gray cloak, clasped at the neck by two hands hidden beneath it. Gray face with sharp features. And her eyes, in two zones of shadow, revealed only the twin reflect of a streetlight. Were the lips at the bottom of the face smiling?

The plywood swung back, cruelly pinching Rosamund's fingers.

The pain rose to her heart, and she reeled. A tall, thin plant, venomously green, rose out of the ground, looming over her, a large, hard, pod waving at the end of its stem. It struck Rosamund on her head, fracturing her skull, then opened to sow seeds in the furrows of her brain.

A minute later, there was no plant, and no light that would have let Rosamund see one. She walked into the sheltering concrete structure, where the air was barely less damp than the drizzle. She wandered about for a moment, almost blind, until her eyes adjusted to the dark and she saw a staircase. The rubble cracked under the soles of her shoes, her feet striking bits of brick with a hollow scraping.

One floor, another, then another.

There were no longer any walls, only floors or ceilings cutting the space into layers and the urban skyline into slices. Skyscrapers smoked under the clouds lit by their spotlights, silver or amber, their antennas truncated under a too low sky.

She walked over to the edge. A solitary taxi was driving up McGill Street, tires hissing. A flash of lightning and she saw a crowd, ten thousand people maybe more. The avenue had become an esplanade and the silence a clamor, ten thousand heads swarming under the spotlights, dominated by the large billboards with giant perfume flasks in green and white neon.

Then the crowd disappeared, devoured by the void in an instant, and silence once again filled the deserted street.

Rosamund wavered, leaned against a column for support. A cold gust of wind caressed her face, clearing her mind.

She took a few steps, walked to the other side, no wall there either.

Flames, the sky was burning, red clouds jostled above the fiery city, like a bed of coals, buildings wavering in the inferno. Giant ladles poured molten metal through rips in the clouds. Then flames and coals merged into dark masses, leaving only the warehouses and the cranes in the port, the diamonds of the streetlights in place of embers, the sky colorless.

Rosamund stumbled. That vision had been even shorter than the previous one, but this time her hands reached blindly for the column. She grabbed onto it and turned her back to the void.

What her soothed eyes eventually revealed was more commonplace. Huddled together towards the middle of the floor, as on the other stories, two dozen vagrants slept on cardboard, or in the open, bags clutched in their hands. They were all there — the jobless, the forgotten, the unemployed — all the city's lost children.

She climbed up another flight of stairs, to the last floor with a roof, a floor inhabited essentially by pigeons.

No one was there. But maybe there was. A sole squatter, laying in a threadbare sleeping bag... a few steps from the edge, young from what she could make out of his beardless face and his curly hair. It was Marc, Rolande's son. She recognized the white polka-dotted bandana he always wore. An emotion swirled through her, like a breath, ever so brief. Then she prepared to settle down for the night.

The sound of hasty steps shuffled along the concrete. One of the street girls was walking across the floor, in front of Rosamund, her coat waving behind her. The woman froze for a moment.

A commotion of muffled flapping outside. Large birds landed on the ledge of the floor, slender creatures with long feet stretched down, vast wings pointed up. Then their membranes folded up like wet leather along their flanks, as they bent over the young sleeper, no larger than children.

A wave of heat overwhelmed Rosamund. When the discomfort dissipated, the little girl was standing in front of her — a young woman, perhaps, after all, very short and slim, wan in the pale urban light. Her skin looked gray, the color of the city, her beauty cruel and her chin sharp. She was smiling, that was true, a thin, knowing, derisive smile.

She stared at her, stared at Rosamund with her cat's eyes.

Shivers ran up and down Rosamund's back, a true spasm this time.

Over there, the nylon sleeping bag was torn between powerful claws, the stuffing tossed about in a turmoil of wings that covered Marc's exclamations. Fleshless heads all plunged at the same time. They bickered. Some pulled up suddenly, with a tearing sound. The boy's shrieks rose above the melee.

Rosamund wanted to race over, but a sharp pain ran through her wrist. The first creature had taken her hand, as if to kiss it, digging its needle-sharp teeth between the bones instead. Rosamund cried out, and in her mind, a winged creature flew over the steeple at Notre-Dame where she was perched. Rosamund fell to her knees. Everything wavered, the city, the ceiling, the floor. One of the striges circling the boy stepped back towards the void, flapping its wings, pulling or stretching something caught in its mouth.

A deep darkness spread its veil in front of Rosamund, and the concrete rose up, striking her in the face.

➵╍╂╍╂╍╂╍➵

When Rosamund woke in the gray dawn, the city was gradually revving all of its motors, transformers, compressors and fans.

Wrist humming with pain in a crust of dried blood, Rosamund stood and took a few steps toward the edge of the floor. Near the void lay a sleeping bag torn into ribbons, sprayed with purple, next to a threadbare sneaker.

The sky above the city was gray, empty of any trace. Yet Rosamund believed she saw an after-image burned on her retina, as if the clouds had retained the picture, a body writhing in a flurry of wings, spread-eagled between claws and mouths bickering over its limbs, its blood raining down over the deaf, silent city.

• •

Though less known to Canadian readers than some of his fellow Québécois F&SF writers, Daniel Sernine's career has spanned more than 30 years, with 37 books published. His works have repeatedly garnered prizes, including the *Grand prix de la science-fiction et du fantastique québécois* in 1992 and 1996.

With undergraduate and graduate degrees in translation and a doctorate in interdisciplinary studies, Sheryl Curtis is a professional and literary translator. Since 1998, her translations have appeared in *Interzone; On Spec;* various *Tesseracts; Year's Best Science Fiction 4; Year's Best Fantasy and Horror 15* and elsewhere.

• •

Kids These Days

By Rebecca Bradley

Moira adjusts the needle in her son's arm, wipes a dribble of formula from her daughter's chin, shakes the sweat from her own forehead. "Swallow, Amy," she says. "Swallow, Timmy. Come on, guys, it's good for you, okay?" Patiently she alternates between son and daughter: inserts nozzle into mouth, squeezes, wipes, instructs to swallow. And again. And again. Not very efficiently, they obey.

Jeff hurries through the kitchen in his overalls, carrying his toolbox. He pats Amy and Timmy on their heads in passing. "Be good for your mother, kids. You okay, Moira?"

What can they do, but be good? What can she be, but okay? She puts the feeder down long enough to stand up and kiss Jeff goodbye. He looks tired. The plant has lost another technician, the sixth this year. That's how life goes, in these days after the world has ended. When he's gone, Moira disconnects the IVs, sponges her children off, and starts getting them ready for school. Obediently they walk where she aims them, stand and sit when told to, hold up their arms, insert foot or hand or head into whatever garment is held open for them. Amy can even manage buttons on good days, and this is a good day. Moira hugs her — "*Clever* girl, Amy!" — then feels obliged to praise and hug Timmy as well, in fairness. Who knows what they see and hear?

→•I•I•I•←

This is a bright September morning, but unseasonably chilly, a broad hint that winter may come early this year. Moira bundles her children into warm jackets and wraps scarves around their throats — nobody wants to be nursing head-colds on top of everything else. She tows them along by their empty-glove hands, around the upheavals in the pavement, past the shuttered convenience store, across leaf-littered streets lined with sagging cars. This is the sort of greenbelt suburb where the young and prosperous had clustered for breeding purposes. Bainbridge's Disease, therefore, hit it very hard. On the Baker family's route to school, a dozen or more expensive swing-sets are rusting in overgrown back yards, squeaking in the light fall wind. Scattered toys make patches of colour deep in the yellowing grass. Moira and her children walk past the burnt-out Fraser house, the Aquino house with its boarded windows; the Zelitsky house, home of Amy's best friend, Madison. Alas, the Zelitskys gave up hope some time ago. The glass-less windows stare at Moira across a jungle of old lawn, as blank as the eyes of a latter-day child. The glimpse of faded pink near the sidewalk is Cortney's tricycle, right where she left it.

Sukey Chang is waiting on the next corner with Davey, Donny, and Mark, all three of them swaying like captive balloons on the ends of their leashes. Davey has a bandage tied around his head like a tennis-player's sweatband, and Sukey looks faintly defiant as she greets Moira. Moira does not ask. She has long suspected that Sukey loses control now and then. The boys frequently sport bruises or ban-dages, and Moira has actually seen Sukey whip Donny with his own leather leash when he is being more lumpen than usual. But three children must be so much more exhausting than two. Anyway, to whom would Moira report the abuse? As long as Sukey manages to keep feeding and wiping and leading them to school, her boys are better off than the Swanson twins, or the Clemms, or poor little Madison Zelitsky with her slashed throat.

Indeed, they're passing the Swanson house now, and out of habit Moira averts her eyes. She is the one who followed her nose into that house to find Sarah Swanson lying in the kitchen while the twins caromed aimlessly off the family-room walls. Moira was shocked, though not at Sarah shooting herself.

No, the shocker was that Sarah had left the twins dependent on the kind offices of the Commission for Orphaned and Abandoned Children. In the dry-eyed social morality that emerged in the wake of Bainbridge's Disease, you are expected to take your children with you when you give up hope. That is what euthypacks are for. Moira often wonders what she herself will do if Jeff ever dies accidentally, as Tom Swanson did. She knows that whatever happens, she will never stop hoping. Never.

⟶⟨•⟩⟨•⟩⟨•⟩⟵

Terrance Street, the most direct route to school, has been impassable since the gas main exploded. How lucky they were that the undermanned fire trucks could keep the blaze from crossing Memorial Park. Moira and Sukey tow their children along the detour, past the charred beams and brick piles of the little strip mall and the townhouse complex, and into the schoolyard. This is only the second week of school, and attendance is still good.

Moira leads Amy and Timmy to the fenced play area, where twenty or so of their playmates are milling around the monkey bars and the sandbox in slow time Brownian motion. She opens the gate and pushes them gently inside. They shuffle straight on for a few steps, until Timmy collides softly with Alison Tanner and bounces sideways into Amy. No harm is done. On they go, shuffling and milling, milling and shuffling. Moira shuts the gate and joins the mothers conversing by the door.

School is where the hopes of the parent generation are most clearly expressed. Keeping the bodies going is one matter. Working towards a brighter future is quite another. Yes, Bainbridge's prion heads straight to the frontal lobes, and yes, it multiplies disastrously there, in any brain not mature enough to block it, severing connections, scrambling neurons, eating souls. Adults, with their fully ripened frontal lobes, are largely immune to the effects. When the pandemic first broke, the oldest victims were in their late teens. The youngest were those conceived after the pandemic's main hammerblow, those whose births were the worst possible news for the human race: a cohort of babies who never *ever* cried, even as they starved to death because they could not be taught to suckle. After a while, nobody had babies any more.

But that was then, and this is now, and still there is hope. As long as the mothers and fathers of the world can keep their children's bodies functioning, there is hope. Brain damage be damned! Gene therapy is the name of the game, the magic bullet being forged by the scientists, the test-tube sorcery that someday soon will make the surviving children well again. Moira's faith in the scientists is absolute. She does her part by tending the shells of her son and daughter, just as a housekeeper will air, polish and clean an empty house in the expectation that its owners will return. The IV supplies antibiotics to keep them well, vitamins and minerals to nourish them, meds to keep them docile. Unsedated, the limbic system tends to kick in a little too primally and the behaviour can turn awkward. The solid food is necessary to keep the gut from closing down, and to keep the children from eating *other things*.

Meantime, hopeful parents do their best to nurture minds as well as bodies, just in case. Even the scientists cannot say definitely whether some tiny flame of conscious-ness does not burn deep in the children's ravaged brains. *Talk to them. Read to them. Educate them. Assume they can hear you.* Moira, taking the government pamphlets as her gospel, is tireless in her post-Bainbridgian maternal duties.

→◦|◦|◦|◦←

The school door swings wide. Stooped, greying and entirely unshakeable, Miss Arthur greets the mothers and signals to the volunteers to set the children walking in her direction. Moira has no duties on this week's roster, though she is down for playground supervision next week and classroom assistance the week after. How lucky they are to have Miss Arthur still willing to serve — so many teach-ers have simply given up. Moira waves to Amy and Timmy as they pass, thinking wryly what a joyful surprise it will be if someday they wave back. And what she wouldn't give to hear them quarrelling again!

"I don't see Lisa Murray," Sukey says beside her. "I wonder if Joshie came down with a bug on the weekend. He was a little feverish on Friday."

"Well, then, it's a good thing if she's kept him home. Coming to Safeway?"

Sukey shakes her head and moves towards the school steps, speaking over her shoulder. "Sorry, Moy, I'm on the roster today. But could you pick me up some candles and balloons for Davey's birthday party? I won't have time before tomorrow. See you at twelve."

"Okay." Twelve o'clock is feeding time. Every mother has to come and do her own. Walking towards the school gate, Moira kicks away a little picture-memory: Amy, Grade One, two months before Bainbridge's and the end of the world, waving goodbye from the same school steps. In her hand is a lunchbox with a cartoon princess pictured on both sides. Inside the lunchbox are a tuna sandwich, an apple, carrot sticks, a box of raisins, a small carton of juice. Timmy, stumping along beside Moira, argues ingeniously for a lunchbox too, but Moira tells him to wait until next year — next year he'll be old enough for kindergarten, and she'll buy him a lunchbox for his midmorning snack, even though he'll still be coming home for lunch....

Moira blinks rapidly, and after a few seconds she has the tears under control. She looks at her watch. There is more than enough time to get to Safeway, buy birthday things for Sukey and formula for the kids and a bit of real food for the grownups' dinner, and perhaps to go down Sixth to see if there's any sign of the library reopening. And it will be a kindness to stop in at Lisa Murray's on the way, to see if Joshie does have the flu, and if Lisa needs anything from the store. Single mothers have a tough time of it in this age of the world. Moira goes out the school gates and down the street, bears left past the ruins of the Well Baby Clinic, and carries on up the hill towards Lisa's upscale condo complex.

Moira would not care to live there herself. The complex is a little isolated, set off by ruins on one side and the upper edge of Memorial Park on the other, and Lisa and her son Joshie are almost the only tenants left. It's probably safe enough, but it is no longer pleasant. Moira follows the cracked sidewalk past the dry swimming pool and deserted playground, along a laneway flanked by graffiti-spattered garden walls. More windowpanes have fallen away since the last time Moira dropped in, and the grass runs riot in all the postage-stamp yards except Lisa's.

The smell hits her as she passes Lisa's open window, a desperately familiar smell. Moira's pace slows for a step or two, then quickens. The outer door is open, but the door to the living room is shut, and she can hear movement behind it. She stops in the hallway, nerving herself. She has a shrewd idea what she will find.

"No, Joshie, *bad boy*," she says firmly as she steps into the living room. It is clear his meds have worn off, and that he is, or was, very hungry. Lisa's body, except for the arm that Joshie has been able to chew off, is in a tangle between the couch and the coffee table. Keeping a careful eye on Joshie, Moira bends over to inspect the remains. Suicide looks unlikely, she notes; almost certainly natural causes, perhaps a heart attack or a stroke while lying on the couch. And judging by the stink and by Joshie's level of limbic distress, death must have occurred as early as last Friday.

Joshie approaches, growling deep in his throat, dangling his mother's arm by the wrist. He drops the arm and reaches for Moira, but oh! kids these days are so terribly slow! Evading him easily, Moira backs out of the room. She shuts the door behind her and wedges the handle. Joshie will be safe enough until the Commission's van comes for him, and Lisa is beyond needing protection.

Between having to stop at the Commission to report an orphaned child, and finding a long lineup at the one manned checkout counter at Safeway, Moira barely makes it back to school in time for lunch. The other mothers shake their heads at the news of Lisa's death, but the shakes are perfunctory. What's another death? Everyone's affect has been hammered flat.

But that evening, Moira is surprised. She mentions Lisa's death to Jeff in passing as he helps bathe and diaper the children for bed. He has been gloomy all evening, indeed for the last week or so, and now his mouth goes tight. He drops the IV hookup on Timmy's bed and flops down beside it, closing his hands like shutters over his face. Moira, taken aback, finishes the IV for him, tucks Timmy into bed, and kisses the children goodnight. Then she takes Jeff by the elbow and leads him into the kitchen. His hands are still over his face. She sits both of them down at the table.

"What's up?" she asks.

Jeff drops his hands and stares at her. "I can't go on, Moira."

She stares back. "I didn't know you were so fond of Lisa."

"This isn't about Lisa. Hell, I hardly knew her."

"What, then?"

"Nothing. Everything. The whole damn thing." He leans back in the chair, his eyes screwed shut. "Listen, Moy. Al Burket's putting his affairs in order. I found out today. Though I don't know what he's waiting for, myself. They're taking the kids with them anyway, so what's the point of tying up loose ends?"

"They're just trying to do it right, Jeff. It's such a shame, though, when parents give up hope like that."

He opens his eyes and stares at the floor. "That's not all. Emily Grissom had a stroke last night — dead by morning. Ben was at work today, but he's pretty cut up. And I bet he'll be reaching for the euthypacks himself before long, since he can't look after that daughter of theirs on his own, and his heart's bad to begin with."

"Don't think about it, Jeff. All we can do is keep on hoping. I know it's sad, but that sort of thing happens all the time."

"That's just the point, damn it!"

"Poor old Jeff," she says, unruffled, "you've had a bad day. Get yourself a drink, and I'll put the steaks on. Just remember, any day now we could get good news from the scientists." She starts to rise, but he leans forward to catch her shoulder and pushes her back into the chair.

"I've been thinking."

"Don't you want your drink?"

"I don't want anything. Moy, we can't go on."

"Stop it," she says. He is starting to worry her.

"We're dropping in our tracks. We're—"

"Stop it," Moira repeats, more sharply. "It almost sounds like you're giving up hope on me. As long as there's life, there's hope."

He looks at her wearily. "You call this life?"

"Of course it is!" she says, swallowing irritation, making the effort to smile wide, wider, widest. "We can't give up now. What if we give up, and the very next day the scientists find the cure? Think of the children."

"Children." He laughs at that, bitterly and mirthlessly, and then he begins to cry. "There's not going to be a cure, Moira. I doubt anyone's even working on it any more. Do you really want to leave Amy and Timmy behind in a world like this?"

"You're talking crazy."

"It's the truth. We've got to do it while we still can."

Moira's lips are dry. She licks them. "What do you mean?"

"You know what I mean, Moy." He tries to take her hand, but she bats his fingers away.

"You want us to kill ourselves," she says icily, "and murder the children."

"Children! Children!" He laughs again, through his tears, and then he gets up from the table, already laid for dinner, and crosses the room to the meds drawer. He opens it as far as it will go because the four euthypacks which the law insists be kept on the premises have been stashed at the very back. "I think we should do it now, tonight, unless you want a couple days to set things in order. But it's urgent to take care of Amy and Timmy, because think what will happen to them if we suddenly drop dead. They'll be in the same fix as that woman's son you found today."

"You *have* gone crazy," she says.

"No, Moira, I've stopped fooling myself." But he does seem more than a little manic, shoving the table settings out of his way with a forearm as he sits down, clearing a place where he can get the doses ready. Moira realizes she should have seen this crisis coming, but the children keep her so tired. He breaks open the first euthypack and starts assembling the guaranteed painless applicator.

"Stop that."

"It's for the best, Moy." He fumbles in his eagerness, but the euthypacks are designed to be user-friendly, forgiving of clumsiness. The first is ready, the second snaps together easily in his hands.

"Stop it."

"I mean, half the guys at the plant are already gaga, honey, I don't want—"

He stops talking because Moira has sunk one of the steak knives deep into his back. He dies as he hits the floor. Moira falls to her knees beside him, sincerely grieving, but knowing she has done the right thing. Weeping softly, she pulls the knife out and turns Jeff on to his back. She arranges his floss of hair across the liver-spotted dome of his head, bends over to kiss his papery cheek. Then, still weeping, but with undamaged hope, she goes to check on her children. Tomorrow is Davey Chang's forty-third birthday party, and she needs Amy and Timmy to get a good night's sleep.

● ●

Rebecca Bradley, a product of Calgary and Vancouver, is an archaeologist by training and also the author of five novels and three volumes of short stories. She currently lives in Calgary, but is in the process of a very slow move to the interior of British Columbia.

● ●

Quints

by Edo van Belkom

Doctor Jean Dupuis drove south on Highway 11 and turned east at Callander heading toward Corbeil. He'd gotten the call from Mme Leduc at three in the morning and was in his car and on his way to the Geroux farmhouse less than thirty minutes later.

Yvette Geroux was delivering her baby two months ahead of schedule. But while Mme Leduc was as much a champion midwife as her more famous great aunt, Benoit Labelle, and had delivered hundreds of babies over the years, there were complications which she felt required the attention of a doctor. That, and the mother-to-be refused to deliver in hospital. And since Jean Dupuis was *le docteur* in the area, the honor of rising from his bed in the middle of the night to deliver a baby in a farmhouse with no central heating fell squarely onto his shoulders.

As he drove east along the road to Corbeil, Dr. Dupuis realized that he'd be passing by the Dionne Homestead and the former site of "Quintland" where five of the most famous babies in the world had been born and raised.

The Dionne quintuplets were born more than seventy-five years before, on May 28, 1934, to a poor farmer named Oliva Dionne and his wife Elzire. They'd already had five children at the time and the incredible birth of five identical baby girls, while causing a sensation around the world, initially brought misery to an already poverty-stricken family. In the years that followed however, the quints appeared in movies and newsreels, on the cover of countless magazines, and hawked every product imaginable from Lysol Disinfectant to Colgate Dental Cream, from Quaker

Oats to Palmolive soap. The five girls: Yvonne, Annette, Cécile, Émilie, and Marie, had saved Northern Ontario from bankruptcy, earned many individuals untold riches, and brought good news to a world that was in desperate need of it.

But at what cost?

Doctor Dupuis slowed as he passed the site of the old Quintland and remembered the ruins of it he'd seen as a child — a collection of more than a dozen wooden buildings in the middle of a large hayfield surrounded on all sides by thick forest. On the right had been the Dionne farmhouse where the Quints were born. Then there were the two souvenir shops owned by the Quints' father, Oliva Dionne. Across the road on the left were the nurses' residence, a police sentry box for the provincial police who had guarded the compound, a U-shaped public observation playground, a second more private playground, and the Dafoe Hospital and Nursery — named after A.R. Dafoe who had helped bring the Quints into the world — and another souvenir shop run by the two midwives who had assisted Dr. Dafoe, Mme Labelle and Mme Legros. Further back from the road had been the "big house" that the Quints had moved into in 1943, ending Oliva Dionne's nine-year struggle to reunite his five girls with the rest of their family.

It was all pretty desolate now, even more so beneath the haunting light of the moon. Following the death of their sister Émilie two months after their twentieth birthday, the four surviving Quints had all moved away. Two of them had gone into convents, while the other two studied to become nurses.

The thought of nurses reminded Dr. Dupuis of the reason he was out on this warm July night. He pressed a little harder on the gas pedal and his Lexus surged forward, rolling down the road toward Bonfield, a small town about five miles east of Corbeil.

He arrived at the Dupuis farmhouse ten minutes later and was greeted on the dilapidated front porch by Mme Joanne Thibault, Yvette Geroux's sister-in-law, who'd been helping the midwife. She held a black bead rosary in her right hand.

"How is she doing?"

Mme Thibault shook her head.

Doctor Dupuis stepped past her and entered the house to find Bertrand Geroux, the husband, just inside the door. He was putting a pot of water on the wood-burning stove in the kitchen to boil.

That was good.

Doctor Dupuis nodded to the young man.

"Thank you for coming, doctor," he said. His voice was shaky and his skin appeared pale. He looked scared, and probably with good reason. This was Yvette Geroux's first delivery and Bertrand was in danger of gaining a child and losing a wife all in the course of a single night.

"She's in here," said Mme Thibault, opening the door to the bedroom just off the kitchen.

Yvette Geroux lay in the middle of a big wooden bed. To the right of the bed on her knees was the midwife who had roused him from his sleep, Mme Leduc. The two women were praying. The midwife's voice was a low rumble while the mother's lips were barely moving.

Dr. Dupuis set down his bag and put a hand on Yvette Geroux's forehead. She was ice cold.

"Stop that now," he said to Mme Leduc. "Get some more blankets in here."

Mme Leduc nodded and left the room, but before she returned Yvette Geroux had instinctively begun to push and Dr. Dupuis had to hurry to prepare to receive the baby.

The child was born just a few minutes later, the tiniest baby the doctor had ever seen. It had a large head with a wisp of hair on top, long and thin arms and legs, almost like an insect's, and an overall blue tinge to its body.

The infant struggled for breath. Dr. Dupuis held it carefully in his palm and massaged its back. Then he turned it over and blew air into its lungs. Suddenly, the baby coughed and a bubble of mucus escaped its lips. Miraculously, it started to breathe on its own.

Dr. Dupuis handed the baby over to Mme Thibault who wiped it clean and wrapped it in a warm blanket.

"Oh my God," said Mme Leduc. "There's another one coming."

Dr. Dupuis wasn't surprised by the second baby. The premature delivery and the tiny size of the first — he guessed it weighed less than two pounds — meant there was a strong possibility of a multiple birth.

"Yvette, you really should be in a hospital," he said, but the new mother shook her head adamantly.

This baby emerged as easily as the first, and like the first it was not breathing. Dr. Dupuis began massaging it and blowing into its lungs, but couldn't waste time trying to completely revive the baby.

There was another on the way.

He handed the second child to Mme Leduc, who continued the job of breathing life into the infant's underdeveloped lungs.

After the first and second child had passed through the birth canal, passage for the third was quick and easy. As Dr. Dupuis was busy tying off the baby's umbilical cord. He noticed it was already breathing on its own. That was a good sign, and meant that this one would have the best chance of surviving.

He handed the third baby to Mme Leduc.

Mme Thibault was elsewhere in the house looking for more blankets to wrap the babies in.

Dr. Dupuis waited for the afterbirth, but to his surprise, another baby was on its way out. Still inside the protective shroud of its amniotic sac, the fourth hardly bore any resemblance to a human baby and appeared almost spiderlike as it slowly moved beneath the translucent walls of the sac.

Mme Thibault began praying under her breath as she wrapped the third baby in a blanket and hurriedly began preparing for the next one.

Dr. Dupuis ruptured the amniotic sac, removed the fourth baby from inside it and tied off its cord. Again he handed it to Mme Leduc. He turned back to Yvette, hoping that the afterbirth would be next.

But it was not.

The tiny head of another child appeared, still wrapped in its amniotic sac just like the others had been. He gently cradled the baby in his hands, ruptured and removed the sac and tied off the umbilical cord. When he handed it to Mme Leduc the full weight of what had happened hit him like a punch in the gut.

He had just delivered five identical baby boys, all developed from a single egg.

Incredible.

The odds of giving birth to fraternal quintuplets was somewhere in the region of fifty-four million to one, but the odds of giving birth to identical quintuplets was so small as to be incalculable. There had only been a handful of naturally-occurring cases in all of medical history, the most recent being the Dionne Quintuplets born seventy-five years earlier just five miles down the road.

Was there something in the water?

In the air?

Perhaps the DNA in the gene pool of this area that had been passed down from generation to generation made multiple births more likely.

Whatever the reason, an impossible act of nature had occurred virtually in the same place for the second time in a couple of generations.

It was a miracle.

"God has blessed you five times," Mme Thibault said to her niece, who appeared to be doing marginally better now that the babies had been birthed.

Were they blessed?

Or cursed?

What might happen to these babies if they lived? Would they be treated as thoughtlessly as the Dionne Quintuplets had?

Bertrand and Yvette were simple farmers with a small patch of rocky land and a few cows to their name. Would the provincial government step in and simply take over guardianship of the quintuplets, separating them from their parents so that they could be cared for by people who all shared a piece of the quintuplets' financial pie? Would Yvette and Bertrand Geroux have to entrust the care of their five young boys to a council of guardians and a team of nurses — all of them strangers? Or would they become stars of a reality television show without a private moment of their own and the whole world scrutinizing the children's care and development.

Early in his medical career, Doctor Dupuis had treated a reluctant Elzire Dionne several times for minor things relating to her old age, and each time he met her he couldn't help but get the feeling that the woman was tormented by deep-rooted feelings of guilt and anger. Truly, she had been a sad and pitiable figure.

Here was a woman who had at one time loved children dearly, but instead of being allowed to hold her new babies in her arms as she had done so many times before, she and her husband were only permitted to see their girls through a bay window for the first two years of their lives. Meanwhile, the quintuplets' official news photographer was allowed to spend as much time with the girls as he wanted.

Elzire Dionne had been heart-broken by the tearing apart of her family by people who would do or say anything to earn money from the exploitation of her Quints. Sure, the girls were returned to the family at the age of nine, but by then the damage had already been done. How could they be expected to just step out of the fish-bowl that was Quintland — a kingdom in which they were five princesses — into a house where they were just one of twelve brothers and sisters. The family and the Quints never adjusted to their new situation, and as a result none lived a semblance of a normal life.

Never even had a chance.

Mme Leduc had gone out to tell Bertrand of his good fortune. In the course of less than an hour his family had gone from two to seven. He came into the bedroom, his face white as candle wax.

Clearly, he wasn't looking upon the birth of quintuplets as a blessing from God.

While Mme Thibault knelt by her sister-in-law's bedside and wiped her forehead with a warm, damp cloth, Bertrand went to the other side of her bed, sat on its edge and took his wife's hand in his.

"Five babies," he said to her. His voice had a tone that suggested he still couldn't believe it.

"Like Oliva and Elzire Dionne," said Yvette. Her words were barely more than a whisper. Obviously, she was still very weak.

Dr. Dupuis, tending to the five babies, looked curiously over at Yvette. There seemed to be no joy on the new mother's face in response to the news — none at all.

"Yes, like the Dionnes," said Bertrand with a nod.

God, thought Dr. Dupuis, the press was going to have a field day with this. Quintland, or some manifestation of it, would be re-opened and the circus would start all over again, only now there would be television and the internet to add to the horde of paparazzi: cameramen, news photographers, and magazine and newspaper reporters.

"Doctor!" called Mme Leduc. "One of the babies is not breathing."

Dr. Dupuis rushed over to the bassinet where the five babies lay wrapped in blankets. The second one from the left had turned a deep shade of blue. Quickly, he un-wrapped the baby and began massaging its back to stimu-late its lungs and heart. Then he turned it over and blew warm air into its mouth to encourage the lungs to start up once more.

"Do you have any brandy?" asked the doctor.

"Yes," answered Bertrand.

"Go and get it."

In 1934, Dr. Dafoe, the famed country doctor who had delivered and cared for the Dionne Quintuplets, had often given the smallest babies a couple of drops of rum diluted in ten drops of warm water. The little trick had never failed to revive them then, perhaps it would work now.

Bertrand returned with a bottle of brandy. Dr. Dupuis mixed up the tonic and used an eye dropper to place the drops onto the tongue of the tiny blue baby.

As he counted out the drops, Dr. Dupuis thought of Dr. Dafoe doing the very same thing seventy-five years before. Dafoe had been a simple man, moving north to escape his well-to-do family in Toronto and live in anonymity among the simple people of the region. But after the Quints were born he had changed, and not necessarily for the better. He had taken over control of the quintuplets, calling them "my girls" and referring to himself as "Boss Number One," and the head nurse, "Boss Number Two." Such arrogance and blatant disregard for the family was utterly shameful.

And while Oliva Dionne had been chastised in the media for profiting in even the smallest ways from the birth of his daughters, Dr. Dafoe profited enormously from the numerous personal appearances, newspaper columns and radio shows he did each year. All of his fame and fortune was a result of the Dionne quints, yet he exhibited a general contempt for the parents. Likewise, Oliva and Elzire Dionne had developed an absolute hatred of the man, and a general mistrust of all mankind.

Would the same thing happen to him? Part of Dr. Dupuis wanted to answer with an emphatic No! But another part of him wasn't so sure he would be able to resist the temptation. It would begin with an interview with the local newspaper and radio station, then the CBC... a Newsworld special hosted by Dr. David Suzuki, followed by appearances on Dr. Phil and Oprah...

Dr. Dupuis took a deep breath, exhaling slowly. He placed the final drop onto the baby's tongue and massaged its chest. It was breathing again on its own, but if it and the others weren't moved to the hospital in North Bay within the hour, it was unlikely that all of them would survive.

"This one is not breathing now, doctor!" said Mme Leduc.

Dr. Dupuis examined the child, unwrapped it and began to massage its chest. Mme Leduc mixed the brandy and water and handed the eyedropper to the doctor. As he'd done with the first, he placed the drops onto the baby's tongue. When he was done, the baby seemed to have responded. It was breathing again, but just barely.

He handed the baby to Mme Leduc and she wrapped it again in its blanket.

It would be a continuous struggle to save all five of the infants, thought Dr. Dupuis. If he remembered correctly, nine out of every eleven babies born under three pounds at birth failed to survive. Especially born at home like this.

And even if all five did survive to adulthood, what kind of life would they have? A tragic life, full of distrust, guilt, misery and frustration. They would never be able to have what others would consider a normal existence.

Never.

Unless something could be done about it now.

Before it was too late.

Dr. Dupuis went to Yvette's bedside and saw that her condition had deteriorated slightly. Like her five children she too was close to death. Her lips were white and the tips of her fingers had turned black. He gave her two injections, one to raise her blood pressure and another to prevent post-natal hemorrhaging.

"Mme Thibault," said Dr. Dupuis, his cellphone at his ear as he called for an ambulance regardless of what anyone in this house wanted. "Get the brandy..."

"Yes."

"Then take Bertrand to the kitchen and pour him a drink."

"Yes, doctor," said Mme Thibault, leading Bertrand out of the room.

"Mme Leduc," he said. "Heat more water... and see what you can do to get some fresh air into the house."

Mme Leduc nodded and exited the bedroom.

Leaving Dr. Dupuis alone in the room except for Yvette, who was barely conscious,...and the five babies.

He went over to the bassinet containing the five babies and stood there looking at them. The two that had been struggling for life had turned an ever darker shade of blue.

Dr. Dupuis took a moment to consider what he was about to do. He wasn't an especially religious man, but all of his patients were devout Catholics. They would see the birth of quintuplets as a blessing, a miracle of God. But, how might they interpret God's persistent efforts to take back two of the babies?

As he looked at the two blue babies, struggling for every breath, he couldn't help but think that God had changed his mind on the miracle.

It was then that Dr. Dupuis knew for certain that what he intended to do was the right thing.

God's will.

He placed one hand over each of the blue baby's mouths and pinched off their noses with his fingers.

Already short of breath, the two babies passed quickly and without sound or struggle.

Three babies remained.

Enough children to create some interest, perhaps generate some financial support for the family, but not enough to tear it apart.

Dr. Dupuis pulled up the blankets so the faces of the two babies were hidden from view.

Mme Leduc came back into the room.

She looked at the bassinet and saw the two covered faces. "Are they dead?" she asked.

"Yes."

"Thank God the other three are all right."

Nodding, Dr. Dupuis looked at his hands and thought about God.

• •

Edo van Belkom is the Bram Stoker, Aurora and Silver Birch Award winning author of more than 30 books and 200 shorts stories of horror, fantasy, science fiction and mystery. Among his novels are *Blood Road*, *Scream Queen*, *Teeth* and *Martyrs*. Some of his best short fiction can be found in the collection *Death Drives a Semi* and *Six-Inch Spikes*. As an editor, he is responsible for the young adult horror anthologies *Be Afraid!* and *Be Very Afraid!* and his young adult novels include the Wolf Pack series, *Wolf Pack, Lone Wolf, Cry Wolf* and *Wolf Man*. He is also the author of the ongoing adventure serial Mark Dalton: Owner/Operator which has been published monthly in *Truck News* magazine and has spawned two novels published by Natural Resources Canada to teach long-haul truck drivers fuel-efficient driving practices, and two audiobooks from Graphic Audio. Edo lives in Brampton, Ontario with his wife Roberta and son Luke. Visit: *www.vanbelkom.com*

• •

An Abandoned Baby Carriage

by Kevin Kvas

In my little world, under the shady maple tree beside the bench at the playground where the three paths of our suburban parklands intersect, there stands black and still and fully upright an old-fashioned baby carriage, silent and abandoned. It stands tall on large and spoked wooden wheels rimmed with steel, its ornate frame grasping a velvet nest below an accordion canopy that flails on a windy day like a sorcerer's cowl fashioned from the tattered wings of a hundred bats. It looks perhaps one hundred years old, yet shows no signs of dying. Indeed, all but the velvet interior, which appears magically soft and untouched, is weathered to the point of having achieved some perverted homeostasis with Nature. In the domain of the carriage, it is *Nature* who seems the parasite.

This is the playground by which I pass every day on my afternoon walk. Since the day I moved to this suburb over two years ago, for as long as my habits here have existed, the carriage has existed also, and busily so — not fading, but only darkening by the hour. Except today is winter — one of the worst this city has seen, I am told — and in a phenomenon as of yet unseen, the carriage has disappeared completely under the snow that still falls even now in the excessive blankets of the land's overbearing mother. Nonetheless, I am not in the least discouraged to keep to my routine and trudge through this wasteland only in boots, for I am a student abroad with neither dollars nor patience for snowshoes. But understand — one need not see the carriage physically to experience its presence: the carriage casts its own snows over one's mind. Snows of ash. As though reversing to their source, they fall as smoke to the fires of my thoughts, to burn there for a while before withering away again and dousing those embers along with them and congealing into yet another paradoxical, lacquered lump of coal, invisible tumour of obsession. It is the carcass of a cow, dangling heavy from the hook of my mind; an optical blemish unseen in its ubiquity. Yes: in these blankets of winter, when like everything else the carriage is this whitewash of nothingness — that is when my yearning calls strongest. But when spring comes — and how the time dies quickly! — it is nonetheless shocking to watch the object rise from the slush and salt and foam untainted in place and state and as natural as a tree or beggar's filth, yet as synthetic and false and jarring as the pitiful, scarcely frequented children's play-structure beside it. For that is how this all plays out: in fast motion the wasteland wastes away, a mirror to all my life's excursions, which beside the carriage lie fruitless. And as the carriage rises from that muck, all thoughts are only further submerged.

⊷⊶⊷⊶⊷

Such is my curiosity about the object that I do not return home for the summer but register for two courses — one on the occult, the other on E.A. Poe — and secure an evening shift at a nearby video-rental store.

One day, one walk, I come across one of those paradoxical, diminutive embellishments mothers find so irresistible — a child's running shoe, fit for perhaps a six-month-old. It lies lost not on the paths near the abandoned carriage, but at least a mile away on the sidewalk of a busy street down which I sometimes go to access the plaza for lunch. Of course, my immediate reaction is to believe — to *hope* — that this juvenile object bears some connection to the other. For one thing, the shoe does look antiquated. It is red high-buttoned leather. I lean down and pick it up, with the intention of bringing it — as an offering, if you like — to the carriage, as though dropping it gently into that tantalizing velvet might, as in a spell, combine the powers of those two reagents to lure the owner — or baby, now grown up — back to its lost possessions (which seem more like limbs). But I can only lift the shoe an inch from the ground before a spider of nausea clenches my belly and creeps up my spine. I wince and bring a hand to my dizzy brow, dropping the shoe — only to see something bounce out from it and onto the sidewalk.

Taking deep breaths, blinking the spots from my eyes, I lean down again and find what I think is a pebble. Then the gears of reality — or of my visual cortex — grind together, and I recoil at the sight of what suddenly clicks into place, transforms in my very hand. There is no pebble. It is the tooth of a human baby.

→┼•┼•┼←

I am back home. My stomach is filled with cheap Vietnamese food, and my mind is knotted with regret: should have taken the shoe — and the tooth. Instead, I kicked the tooth down a sewer and fled from the shoe as one might a rattlesnake. Were these items not keys to this mystery? The answers I was looking for? Though I wonder if really I would have been able to take them. Like the carriage, would my interest in them have become asymptotic?

Time slides on, my walks double in frequency, and my hand hovers ever closer to that sacred velvet interior; but "closer" is as close as ever I come: close yet infinitely far. For surely my greatest desire is to rid myself of this distraction, the carriage, and retrieve the reins of my life. But how might I do this, without investigating the object further, satisfying my curiosity?

It is absurd, this hope I bear, to have the mystery someday unveiled before me. But even more absurd is that I recognize this hope as such, and yet remain powerless to its truth. It is external, the force of this shrine's mystery, and I know not whether a solution exists. All I know is the suffering reality that the object is, though abandoned and antiquated and inexplicable, ultimately just a baby carriage.

The next day, the shoe is gone.

≫•❧•❧•≪

I have purchased a full outfit of baby clothes — socks and all — as a possible substitute for the lost shoe from which I ignorantly fled.

I lay the clothes carefully inside the velvet nest, taking equal care never to even graze my hands against the edges of the carriage. I lay these clothes in the shape of a baby.

I do not know what I expect.

≫•❧•❧•≪

A week later and nothing has happened. But I think I know why. The baby clothes I bought were modern. The shoe I found, however, like the carriage, was antiquated, perhaps Victorian. So I pay visits to a thrift store, costume shop, museum, and touristy nineteenth-century village reproduction, and gather enough Victorian-looking (if not Victorian) baby clothes for two full outfits. I return to the carriage and lay out one of the outfits accordingly.

≫•❧•❧•≪

I wake past midnight to the sound of a baby crying. There is no baby in my house, and all my housemates are in the city-core burning brain cells. I take a walk into the night without hesitation. My obedient legs carry me automatically to the carriage's domain. As I approach, the crying becomes louder. But when I get to the playground, I stop.

I am afraid to approach the carriage itself; afraid to see what might be inside, waiting for me. Or what won't be inside. I stand there for fifteen minutes, my sweat-shivering gaze shifting between the carriage and the path home. Then the crying stops — abruptly — as though the baby, invisible or ubiquitous, has been soothed, if not absorbed into thin air. So, bravely, I then approach the carriage and peek inside the velvet nest. At first, there appears nothing unordinary; there are only the white lace booties, the long embroidered gown, the flannel under-shirt. There is certainly no crying child.

Then something — not the brass buttons, but some-thing else — catches a glint of moonlight. And I see that there are teeth, a full *set* of baby teeth this time, arranged in an ellipse just above the miniature petticoat's collar. But there is more. Above these lies a tuft of black hair. It reminds me of the dislodged fur of a dog, or the fur that remains of a trampled squirrel.

I abruptly run home, where I lie in bed for hours, trem-bling myself to exhaustion.

❖❖❖❖

I wake in the morning, no longer trembling, but not without worms in my stomach. My heart rate is too quick also, as though I have been awake all night without knowing it, alive in some other world. My head hurts. It is like a hangover, but affecting every part of my body; and not a hangover of drunkenness, of course, but of fear. Horrible fear. I am pale and lethargic all day; I follow my work routine hypnotically, avoiding people whenever possible. I find that I cannot bear to speak even one word to people; cannot bear to sit or walk or be awake at all — but nor could I sleep. It is only later that night, when I visit the carriage after my shift, that despite last night's experience, despite the carriage's blame in all of this, the sight of it immediately calms me — as though now *I* am the baby being soothed.

Heartbeat stabilized, face back to its usual colour (pale), fears blanketed, I take a quick glance inside the carriage to find the clothes and paraphernalia gone. Then, with an ambiguous smile, I return home and continue, more or less, the tainted routine that is my life.

❖❖❖❖

There was a time when I went on walks for the exercise, for the time to gather thoughts. Now those things, and all others, have ceased to matter. All thoughts, all routines, now converge upon this single monolith of interest. My walking routes have adopted increasingly circular designs, as to permit a second or third passing of the object in a single outing. Thus it is a lie to say I go for "walks" at all anymore. I go for *orbits*. This is my daily engagement: to view this object as a tourist might once in his lifetime travel miles to view a monument or World Wonder. The tourist's giddiness never leaves me. It is a glass of vitality that never empties, but a glass reserved for but one empty purpose. I find myself walking at night more often now, in hopes the odd hours might provide better answers. The night frightens me — it still seems filled with the echoes of infantile cries — but still I venture, for still I yearn.

And still I do not understand. Why does it attract me so, but seemingly repel everything else? What does it want?

This city where I exist (and occasionally try to live) is integrated. Such is the case in the newest suburbs, anyway. This means you find low-rental houses behind those of the upper middle-class. On one side, the dividing fences are stained hazelnut; on the other, defaced with orange and green neon graffiti. On one side, the lawns are large, flush, fertilized, and appropriately vegetated; on the other, weedy and cluttered with toys and old pieces of wood with nails sticking out of them. The idea is to keep the oils and waters of society astir, to maintain an illusion of polarities dissolved as one, rather than to allow one to congregate below or atop the other, intact with all its like-minded molecular brethren. As a result, both sides are diluted, depersonalized and compromised for the sake of a collective integrity.

But that is why I am continually surprised — especially when one considers that the already graffiti-defaced "playground" here consists merely of one playhouse of a size suitable only for very small children, and is thus scarcely occupied — that neither hoodlum nor common teenaged troublemaker has ever come along and stolen or desecrated this baby carriage. Perhaps to ride around in it a little, before smashing it into a tree and then stomping flat its loosened parts. I am no hoodlum, but as a teenager I was certainly a troublemaker, and would not — as exemplified by the numerous times my friends and I hijacked shopping carts — have hesitated to find something stupid to use it for.

Or would I have? There is something too strange, too illogical, about a baby carriage abandoned in suburbia. The mind creates answers for it, casts a shield about it, convinces you that you must simply let it rest, let it remain a blemish to your vision, a scar of unanswered curiosity. Day after day. For there is no sin greater than to meddle in the affairs of the perfect human larva. The baby bears a shield of emotion only surpassable by the hands of the addicted or disturbed. It is this emotion which, by association, shields also the carriage, lends to it that aura of untouchable cosmic unity. Such is the power of infancy. Such is the power of vacancy.

With any other object, I would not put it past any resident — low-rental or otherwise — to "repossess" it without hesitation. But in the carriage's case, it is this very dispossession which marks it so possessively. It is this very *emptiness*. Emptiness can contain anything. An emptiness as permanent as this is infinitely capable of changing.

And that is the best rationale I can devise for why it remains here. But these suburbs represent the modern housing establishment, and this carriage is antique — almost latter-day Victorian. Did it exist here among trees and moss in the earlier days of this city? Did it remain untouched, invisible, as deforesters and builders walked and worked unconsciously around it as one might squirm from a cold current?

If this is the case, then my life is a summer in which cold currents are always welcome.

I wonder if the city groundskeeper comes here every couple of weeks to check if the garbage can is full (it never is). I wonder if *he* wonders about the carriage as well. But I have never seen a groundskeeper.

I have never seen children, or anyone, at this playground. But now I am noticing that even the surrounding paths are empty. I no longer see the bikers, the dog-walkers, the... Who else did I see? It seems the more I look for people, the less there are, as though, like my curiosity, the act of looking is asymptotic. But still — why repel everyone else and not *me*?

Since my curiosity can only be called an unstoppable bullet, I can only assume the answer I seek is an indestructible wall. But knowledge of this fact does nothing to divert my obsession.

I tell myself it is not the carriage itself that compels me, but the enigma, the story *behind* the carriage. So what is that story, then? What is that hidden *essence*? What is this carriage but the exoskeleton of a demon?

❖·❧·❖·❧·❖

Summer comes to a close, and life is the same; there are still no answers. I cannot win the battle against my own mind: I want the carriage to be both preserved and destroyed. I want myself to be both enslaved and liberated.

The new term begins, but school means nothing to me. I find myself doodling a picture of the carriage in class, completely unconscious of the lecture. I am already skipping classes.

But the carriage has infected my perception in ways far worse. Through association, its curse has spread to all other children-related objects, including children themselves.

Canadian Thanksgiving comes round, and I return for the first time since Christmas to my parents' house in my quaint hometown — an odd sight, because there is no suburbia there. Some cousins are down for the weekend. One of them is eleven months old, beginning to walk, and I cannot bear the sight of him. I find his soft skin, his miniature body, his high-pitched gurgles — all the markings of "cuteness" — utterly repelling.

As my family members lounge around the living room, laughing and watching the baby, I sneak away into

my father's office, overcome by nausea — only to be met
by babies hanging from the wall: pictures of my brother
and myself.

I especially cannot bear to look upon the latter. My
younger version seems to stare into my heart and say, "I
am you no longer, and no longer are you me. Go away from
here. Find your own child."

>•‡•‡•‡•<

Today I awake not in my bedroom, but in an outside
field. I have fallen asleep staring at the carriage. I check
my pocket-watch: almost midday. Yawning, I rise slowly
and then notice something peculiar. Two women — mothers
or day-care guardians, perhaps — and their five children
are approaching from the northern path.

Quickly, I retreat down the western path and find a large
pine under which to hide. To my amazement, the group
stops at the playground. As the children go to the play
structure, the two mothers notice the carriage. I watch as
they converse, undoubtedly remarking upon the object's
strangeness, all the predictable curiosities cycling through
their minds. I see shrugs of shoulders, swerving of heads
searching for traces of an owner. Then the more portly of
the two women does effortlessly what in two years has been
for me impossible: she lays a hand on the carriage.

She tries to push it, but the carriage won't budge. The
other woman bends down after her and examines the
wheels. More talking, then one more pushing attempt, but
still the carriage goes nowhere. The women seem to come
to some agreement on the matter: I imagine they decide
that the wheels are jammed. Their interest extends no
further. They gather their children and leave.

Why may some pass by here, and others not? Why may
some touch the object, unaffected, and others not?

Empowered by the women's demonstration, I approach
the carriage and try to lay hands on it for the thousandth
time.

But — for the thousandth time — "approach" is still only
as far as my legs will take me. Close, but infinitely far. I
no longer believe that fear is the cause — I feel no fear now.

No, it is something else that freezes my mind, compels my arms to lock up within a hair of the carriage's grasp. Strangely, I feel not even frustrated. It is not like something forcing against my will; it is rather as though I have no will at all; as though, when within a certain perimeter of the carriage, the idea of touching it passes from my mind unnoticeably. I stand mesmerized for a moment with that vacant feeling of having gone to my bedroom to retrieve something, only to forget what it was. Then at last I turn away, wondering if that *was* the reason I came here: to forget why I came here.

As I exit the perimeter, perhaps I remember that I had intended to touch the carriage — but now I no longer want to. Until next time, I think.

And so on to infinity.

❖❖❖

I have decided to perform a full day's vigil. There is something, I know, that I am missing. Something, perhaps, that requires a seamless twenty-four hours' attention.

There must be something that visits this place. Something that visits here at least once a day, but which, through its trickery, always comes at the time when I do not. Yes. I believe so.

So I sit in the bushes on a blanket with a carton of milk and a basket full of waxy-skinned fruit and poorly structured peanut-butter and corned beef sandwiches, and I watch and wait for the Visitor.

❖❖❖

I fall asleep, nine hours in. I wake to find that it has rained and that the bushes have provided little shelter. I am wet, and there are worms about me.

I slam my fist into the basket of sandwiches. I get to my feet, tearing worms off my skin. I roll up the muddy blanket and the remaining sandwiches and disperse them with great tosses across the field. Then I stomp over to the playground.

It begins to rain again. Softly at first, then in absurd splashes, and suddenly I am half-walking, half-swimming, half-breathing, half-drinking through this mold of water in which I am a two-legged spider, engulfed, the muddy grass below me a sticky and beckoning web of jutting broken fingers.

Did I tell you that the grass never grows around here? There is grass, yes, but it never grows; it just stays at this nicely groomed height, despite that I have never seen nor heard an industrial lawnmower roaming the area. It is the dark-green of spinach, as though frightened sick into not growing. Except for the tips. The tips of the blades are so dark as to appear charred, and in a night such as this, the whole park appears as the rotted, burnt remains of a microbial forest. These are the dead-lands.

I can see scarcely inches through this lost monsoon. I direct myself towards the playground only by natural magnetism. Every so often the thunder roars, but even so, I think I hear again a baby crying, louder than anything — like the world's tears, omnipresent. I cannot see, I cannot hear; I can barely even *feel*. I am one with the water and muck around me. The water seems to fall right through me, so easily does it slip over its skin-stuck brethren. And then the carriage and the old woman appear from nowhere.

The woman wears a scanty white nightgown. Soaked, it might as well be invisible. But the features of her nakedness are not so obvious, as her skin seems soaked to almost the same effect: she is so thin it might be that she's wearing her bones on the outside.

She turns to me, unsmiling, and says in a tired, timid voice that still somehow carries through the weather: "Do you remember me?"

I ponder this. Her eyes are a faded blue, and her flesh, rain or no rain, resembles the tear-streaked grime of bathtub enamel. She bears a black birthmark on her fuzzy upper lip.

But no, I do not remember her, and before I can voice this, she turns away into the rain, as though knowing my answer. I reach out after her, but my reaction comes a second too late. I fall only through mist, and there is nothing to be seen nor felt: the woman is gone.

Something else has occurred, however.

When I reached for the woman, my shoulder brushed the side of the carriage — and I *touched* it.

I stand for a moment in contorted tableau, digesting what I have done. But I feel neither relieved nor fearful. I am merely expecting something to happen.

I stand there for the longest time, the rain never stopping. The dark clouds above have slowed the dawn. But nothing happens.

Nothing to my knowledge.

⇢⊹⟊⊹⟊⊹⟊⇠

Everyone I ask says the same thing.

They all know about the carriage in the park; they all know it's there.

And they all think they know what it means.

The only thing they do not — *can*not — admit is how they unconsciously avoid it.

Well, there are other things they do not know or admit as well.

But this is what they tell me; they, the people of my neighbourhood with whom I have, until recently, neither talked nor expressed the slightest care in all my time here:

It's a memorial. The memorial of a mother and her baby of ten months who were struck by a car while crossing Yorson Road. Actually, I heard a few variations on the story, but it doesn't matter. What fascinates me is that a memorial such as this, simple and unmarked and movable, has gone untouched. I never thought a suburb could be so tightly knit that everyone might come to know the meaning of one object and respect that object accordingly. Then again, as shown from my own experience, the feeling that the carriage evokes — the pure *sense* of it — is alone enough to inform a passerby of what it represents. It is a meaning that still lives, to this day, in the feast of my mind.

Nor has anyone ever seen an old woman come by the carriage. Nor did any of the old women I spoke with look familiar. Maybe she only comes out at night, when it rains; maybe that's why they don't see her. That's what I believe — until I see her again that very day.

She is dressed the same, except that her garment is dry now, not as translucent. She turns from me and begins to walk away. I open my mouth to call after her, but no sounds come out.

Then the carriage begins wheeling after her, slowly. It is unmanned, without propulsion, and has a supposedly bad wheel.

Nevertheless, there it goes. I watch it go. And watch it go. I am transfixed, imagining that I push it, walking behind it, at the same time lying within it, everywhere with it.

● ●

Kevin Kvas lives in Ottawa, Ontario, where he is a musician, videographer, unruly tele-surveyor, and student of literature at the University of Ottawa. His fiction has appeared online in such publications as *Dog Versus Sandwich* and *Cezanne's Carrot*. Read more at *www.kissofkvass.blogspot.com*

● ●

Silence

By Stephanie Short

Karl didn't cry as Liesel dug at his bleeding foot with the nail. It hurt terribly while she tried to dislodge the dirt and small twigs tamped into the wounds, but he had learned over the last few days how little could be accomplished by crying.

The other children, those that were left, seemed to have learned the same lesson. The cave where they huddled was silent except for the laboured breathing of those who had fallen into a twitching, exhausted sleep. The others sat and stared, their eyes as blank and dry as Karl's, the eyes of dead things.

A final sharp poke at the sole of his foot, and then the nail was withdrawn. "There," Liesel whispered, not daring anything louder. "At least it won't fester." Her mother was the village midwife and knew about such things.

Karl nodded. "Thank y—"

But he had spoken too loudly. It had often been a criticism of his mother's that he was an inexplicably loud boy who could not control his voice, especially in church. She would often wait until she got him home before reminding him that silence was golden.

The Piper didn't wait. He swept across the cave, moving even now with that uncanny grace, and struck Karl hard, knocking him to the floor. "Did I tell you to speak, rat?" he snarled between his uneven teeth. "Did I? No. I did not." He grabbed Karl by the rags that were all that remained of his best Sunday clothes. "I ordered you to be quiet. And you will be quiet, rat, unless you would like to dance again.

Bad children need to dance." He shook the boy and then let him drop back to the floor. The Piper looked around at the huddled children, all the staring eyes watching them blankly in the dimness. "You know where bad children go, don't you?"

They knew.

"So, shut up," the Piper snarled, kicking Karl hard in the ribs. The man's expression looked even more unpleasant because of the visible swelling around one eye. "Or you'll go the same way."

The children remained silent, watching the scene expressionlessly, none of them willing to look the Piper in the eye. They didn't need to be reminded about the price of misbehaving.

Nor did Karl. He lay where the Piper had thrown him, even though a sharp piece of stone was cutting into his back. Once, he thought dimly as another kick landed, he would have yelled, screamed, even swore. But now he had learned the value of silence. He wondered if his mother would have been proud.

He kept his eyes lowered submissively until the Piper, deeming them all properly cowed, gave a snort and, with one last kick, moved back to his fire at the cave entrance.

Karl watched the man for a moment or two, his brightly coloured clothes catching the firelight, but his tormentor did not seem inclined to make an example of Karl as he had with some of the others. Instead, the Piper just sat and stared into the flames, one hand always on his pipe. The brass glinted in the red light.

The children sat as far away from the man as was possible in the cramped cave. They remained in small groups, huddled together against the cold, but not daring to approach the fire. A few, like Liesel, spoke in soft whispers, but most were silent. No one wanted to get beaten. Or worse.

Karl had wondered what the Piper planned on doing with all the children he'd led away. At first, he had feared that they would all be guided into the river to drown like the rats. He would always remember the tide of grey and black and brown bodies, tumbling and clawing as they were dragged to their doom by the haunting sound of the Piper's music. Their terrified squeaking had almost drowned out the noise of the water. He remembered their eyes the most, tiny black pools, searching for an escape, and he had been shocked to know that an animal could feel so much fear.

Now he thought that the rats might have been the lucky ones. Sometimes, in the night, while the children caught a few hours of restless and whimpering sleep, one of their number would vanish. First Henri, then Adela. Had they disappeared because they cried too much? Or because they were among the youngest of the surviving children? No one knew, and no one would dare ask questions about it in case they were the next to go.

But Karl thought about the Piper and how he never needed to sleep, and about the magic in the music. Once, he had half-wakened to the sound of the pipe being played very softly, although it might have been a dream; the sound haunted him even there. But the next morning Adela was gone and the Piper looked stronger, wilder than ever in his motley clothing, as he led them further away.

Karl glanced toward Liesel and saw, under the hunger and exhaustion, the quiet desperation in her eyes. She knew. They all did, on some level. Around them, the other children looked at each other, their eyes like those of the rats as they'd plunged into the water. They didn't dare speak, but the desperation didn't need words. The feeling of it echoed louder than mere noise. Surely someone had a plan, someone could get them out of this.

But no one did. Their fear of the Piper was too great. He held them as helpless as he had held the rats, and the rats had been far more dangerous.

Since the great plague of rats had begun, the people of the village had never known a moment's peace. The rats, huge and glossy, had slunk through the shadows and into houses and barns, spoiling where they went. Cats, knowing when they were outmatched, ran and hid. Dogs, being either braver or less intelligent, attacked the rats, and if they were lucky, came away whimpering. The blacksmith's terrier was killed outright, prompting the man to tell everybody that the rats were the agents of the Devil. He'd started giving everyone nails to carry in their pockets, the iron a charm against evil. The children were kept close and warned, because enough rats could kill a human. Their parents had whispered, and worried. And then the Piper had come.

They really should have known better. They should have realized that the man in the colourful clothing was no backwoods conjurer, skilled only at charming people out of their money. There was something strange and sinister in his music. The trick with the rats proved that. But when he demanded his extortionate fee, what were they to do? There wasn't that much money in the entire village. So they'd refused to pay.

Most of the villagers, while uneasy, had been sure they made the right decision. After all, the rats were dead. The Piper couldn't bring them back. And they weren't sure it was right to be consorting with someone who had such obviously dark powers.

Yes, Karl thought grimly, they really should have known better.

Nevertheless, the adults had seemed pleased with this solution. Some of them looked very smug that Sunday as they sat in church, listening to the priest, who could read his congregation well and deliver a thunderous sermon on the punishments due to those who practiced witchcraft. They had continued to look smug, nodding sagely at the descriptions of hellfire and torment, until the music began to play. Until the children, scrubbed and neat in their Sunday best, had risen jerkily to their feet as if pulled by strings. The adults had watched helplessly, frozen to their seats by the music, as the children began to dance, following the sound of the pipe.

Karl remembered little about the days since then. The music had led them to the mountains, and after that, everything blurred into grey rocks and grey skies, the scrape of their feet over the path, the crying of the children, and, always, the music of the Piper.

Only a few moments stood out clearly, as bright and sharp in the grayness as the musician's clothes. He remembered Ilsa falling after a few hours. She was small and tired easily. He and the older children had frequently left her behind, complaining, when they played in the village, not wanting the little crybaby slowing them down.

Apparently, the Piper hadn't wanted her to slow them down, either. Or he simply hadn't cared that she couldn't keep up. She had cried weakly when she fell, her limbs twitching as she tried to keep dancing, or at least move out of the way. But she couldn't move, and the other children couldn't stop. They heard her screaming for a long time after they left her behind, trampled and crushed by their own feet.

The first night they'd stopped in another cave near the edge of a cliff, where Wilhelm, Jakob, and a couple of the older boys tried to attack their tormentor. They were big boys, almost men, and they knew how to hunt and how to fight. And there had been four of them, and only one of the Piper.

They never stood a chance.

Wilhelm, tall and strong, with the young ladies already sighing after him, had landed one punch on the Piper before the man had reached for his pipes. The melody he played was quite different from the dancing music. It was a frenzied, harsh tune that tore the air, that scratched and bit. And Wilhelm and his friends, instead of destroying the Piper, began to destroy themselves.

Otto had slit his wrists with a piece of jagged stone. Jurgen had taken the piece of bloody rock from his friend's suddenly nerveless hand and used it on his own neck. Jakob had walked calmly to the stone wall of the cave and started smashing his head into it.

It was the look on all their faces that haunted Karl the most. The helplessness, overlaid by a deep concentration, as if they were making sure they performed a difficult task correctly.

The violence had gone on for a long time, especially with Jakob. The other children had stared in horror, transfixed by the spectacle and the music.

At last Wilhelm was the only one left. He stood motion-less, having watched his friends drop, one by one, into twitching bloody heaps on the cave floor. Karl had seen that look, the rat's look, in his eyes as he struggled to free himself from the music's clutches.

The Piper, on the other hand, had looked peaceful. Serene. While he played, his face shone with beatitude, like the pictures of the saints. He had looked at Wilhelm, eyes like still water, and nodded gravely at the cliff.

In spite of the long drop, and the noises they had heard as Wilhelm hit the rocks, the children still didn't make a sound. They were learning.

Now it seemed they had learned too well. They stared around at each other, helplessly quiet, unable to make even the most desperate of plans. Some had slumped to the ground in despair, closing their eyes as if they were already dead. One or two had started to cry again, silent tears running down their faces, cutting tracks through the dirt. A few looked at each other, their eyes stony and grim. Most just stared.

Karl eased himself back into a sitting position, moving as quietly as possible. He supposed his father would have said that it would be better to die here in a pointless fight with the Piper than to wait and fall to the musician's unspeakable needs. But Karl didn't want to die at all. He just wanted to go home.

He absently turned the nail over and over in his hand as he tried to think of a plan. They were only children, weak and small. Wilhelm had been one of the strongest, and it hadn't done him much good. But there had to be some-thing they could do. Small things were strong in large numbers. Enough rats could kill a dog, kill a human. Or could have, before the Piper led them away to die.

Karl's hand clenched around the nail, his hands over his ears. He wouldn't die like Wilhelm and the others, the haunting music filling his ears, dragging him along like a leaf in the river. He wondered if the music followed them into death, tainting heaven with its poisonous sound. He wondered if a part of them still danced, or if they were free in blissful silence.

Silence. Karl opened his hand and looked at the nail. Black iron, and sharp. A charm against evil. It hadn't worked so far. Maybe it was time to find a new use for it.

He raised his eyes and saw Liesel looking back at him. The fierce light in her icy blue eyes made her look like one of the warrior maidens from the old legends. She reached into the pocket of her apron and brought out her own nail, its black surface glinting dully in the distant firelight. Around them, other children, the grim-eyed silent ones, drew out theirs. They looked at each other, communicating silently, the only way they could. Then they all looked at Karl.

He nodded, just once, not breaking the silence.

Nor did they break it when they rose, after their work was done and the fire had died down, and went for the Piper. They moved silently, ignoring their pain, gliding through the shadows like rats, bloody nails clenched in their hands.

Their tormentor was not sleeping, but he had been staring into the fire for too long to be able to see into the darkness. Moving carefully, they fanned out, picking up heavy stones.

The rocks must have made some noise, some scrape or rattle, although Karl couldn't hear it. But something alerted the Piper and, as he spun quickly, he saw them close to him, saw the fire glittering feverishly in their eyes. He reached for his pipes immediately. Putting them to his mouth, he moved his fingers, but Karl and the others couldn't hear the tune he played. They saw the confusion in his face as they continued to advance, holding rocks or nails or with just their small hands curled into claws. As they moved closer to the dying fire, the blood streaming from their ears caught the light, red and bright as the Piper's scarf.

The musician tried to scramble to his feet, but Liesel, moving quickly, threw a rock that caught him in the mouth. The blood that sprayed across their faces as he fell was warm and comforting. Before the Piper could rise again, Hans and Frieda, hoisting a heavy stone between them, dropped it on his leg. Karl felt the impact, a sort of heavy crunch, through the soles of his wounded feet, and smiled. The Piper writhed, but could not rise.

Their enemy trapped, the children drew closer, their small hands clutching nails and rocks. Karl paused only to kick the brass pipe into the fire before moving in, his own nail, his charm, held like a knife.

The Piper's mouth opened wide, and Karl knew he was screaming. But all he heard was the blessed, perfect silence.

• •

Stephanie Short was born in Newfoundland and has lived in three other provinces since. Currently, she lives in Sydney, Nova Scotia with her fiancé John and three enormous cats. She divides her time between writing, knitting, and convincing the neighbourhood children that she is actually a witch.

• •

The Weak Son

By Matthew Moore

Am I dead? I must be.

I think I've been in this house for a couple of days now, but I can't remember where I am or how I got here. Funny, I should be bothered by all this, but I'm not because this place seems familiar.

I always end up down here in the basement, looking at one of the floor joists. It has a bunch of wires and pipes snaking through a hole drilled in it. Something tells me it's important.

The front door just opened. In an instant — with just a thought — I'm there.

Two men are coming in, dressed in jeans, t-shirts and windbreakers. One is in his late teens or early twenties, the other old enough to be his father. Behind them, in the gravel driveway, is a pick-up truck.

I think they've been here before.

The older one surveys the room while my brother—

My brother.

They're my brother and father.

"Dad?" I ask, moving to him. "Dad, what happened to me?"

A chill washes over me, full of fear, anger, and regret. It's my father's emotions.

No, more than that. Memories. I see them — *feel* them — all around me.

He was surprised and angry as he read—

He forces the memory away, telling himself he's almost done. After this, he'll never need to come back.

He's afraid.

He's afraid his guilt will keep building every time he comes here until he cracks and confesses what he did. But more than that, he's scared there's some evidence he's missed. He's checked everywhere he can think of, but what if, when he left me, I wrote another note describing what he'd done and hid it for Ken in some secret hiding spot?

Ken. My brother's name is Ken.

"I think we can get all this in one last trip," my father says.

All this?

Last trip?

Ken is still for a moment, then picks up a cardboard box. I move to his side. "Ken! What's going on? What happened to me? What did Dad do?"

Ken heads out the front door, thinking how much he hates this.

My dad grabs a bundle of blankets and follows.

The floor.

It's covered with boxes full of books, plates and cups, old board games. Blankets and sheets are folded in neat piles. There's an old coffee table, some folding chairs and a small shelf.

This stuff has been here the whole time.

Ken and my dad return from outside, their boots echoing sharply.

The echo. It's wrong for this room.

I see why: the hideous green carpet is gone. So are the couches and chairs, the tables, the paintings on the wall. All that's left is what's on the floor.

What about the other rooms?

With a thought I'm in the bedroom Ken and I used to share. Empty. No pictures or posters on the wall. Our bunk beds are gone. The books and games and trophies that filled the shelves my grandfather built when he bought this place are missing.

The main bedroom. Nothing. I move into the closet. Empty except for a few hangers.

The kitchen. Nothing in the cupboard. The microwave, toaster, coffee maker — the pale green countertop is bare.

This is our cottage. It's almost empty and I hadn't noticed.

I couldn't even remember where I was.

The living room. I'm at Ken's side as he and my father carry out the coffee table. "Ken, why are you moving everything out? Is it because I died here?"

Memories, sick and putrid:

—a phone call—

—screaming his rage—

—a frantic three-hour drive—

Ken slams his mind shut as he walks backwards to the truck. He can't stand how the memories bombard him when he's here.

I've done this before.

Every time they come here, I ask them what happened, but they can't hear me. They work in silence, only speaking to ask for help carrying something or how to arrange things in the truck.

But in their silence, they remember. Their memories scatter and ricochet around me, their quiet a storm of thoughts and regrets. I try to get them to remember what happened to me so *I* can remember.

And then they leave, and I forget again.

"Dad, what are you scared of?" I ask as he enters the room again, knocking a dead leaf from his boot.

I was standing on the workbench—

He scratches the back of his head, digging fingernails so deep the pain obliterates the memories.

"Ken," I say as he passes through the front door. "How did I die?"

A hospital. As the doctor talked, my father — a stoic man whose only emotions are anger and disappointment — held back tears. Ken couldn't hear what they said, but saw our father's grief as a performance and began to suspect our dad was covering something up. That maybe he was to blame.

"I don't understand," I say. "What did Dad do?"

Ken thinks about standing in the basement weeks later — silent, shocked — Dad watching from few steps away.

He rubs his eyes and picks up a box full of old plates. Memories spark to life:

—Mom in the kitchen cooking Thanksgiving dinner—

—Ken and I quickly doing the dishes so we could go back outside to play before dark—

—Ken bringing a plate of leftover pie down to the dock as we fished in the early morning—

As Ken tries to hold these back, I remember more:

Ken and I catching fireflies in the dusk of hot summer evenings...

Watching shooting stars on cool autumn nights...

Ken teaching me to fish — teasing but patient, laughing but kind...

"But why are you leaving?" I ask.

He promises himself he'll return. They just need to shut the place down for while. When he can deal with the pain that I'll never be there, he'll be back.

"But I *am* here!"

Ken lifts another box, grunting to cover what could become a sob, as he realizes the future he thought he would have — where we would share this place and bring our kids here — is gone.

My father looks up from re-arranging a box of pots and pans, and asks "What?", a threatening edge in his voice. Immediately, he regrets speaking. He wants to keep the silence of the last few trips. He's been able to deflect Ken's questions and doesn't want to get him talking again, but his instinct is to see the sound as some kind of protest or exaggeration. Some kind of *challenge*. And his immediate reaction is, and always has been, to deal with *anyone* who challenges him.

Words swell inside Ken...just like they have before. He wants to turn and demand to know what really happened. But he's already done that and every time he's asked for details, my father reacts with anger or dodges the question. "Dad, we've been through this," he replies, headed for the pick-up.

"I guess we have," my dad responds, willing himself to be calm. Let Ken have his little rebellion.

"Don't let him shove you aside like that," I say to Ken, tree branches overhanging the driveway crisscrossing him in dark shadows, as he sets the box in the back of the truck. He goes cold and jagged, looking back inside the house. "What question *haven't* you asked?" I demand.

Random snatches of conversations with my friends shoot through Ken's memory.

My friends.

I used to have a lot of friends.

And I was on a team. A sports team.

Memories of my friends' tears and regrets and anger about missing the warning signs coalesce into a single idea. As Ken comes back inside the house, he asks, "How did you not see it coming?"

Something — like a memory but not a memory — surfaces in my father. He stays focused on the box of pans as he gives it voice. "We *all* missed it, Ken."

It's a rehearsed answer.

Rage blooms within Ken, sharp and scalding. "I was at school, Dad! Don't give me this 'we all missed it' crap when *you* were here."

He has another reply ready, fighting to control the fury at being challenged once again. "What could I have seen?" He stands. "That his grades were slipping? High school was almost over, so he backed off a little bit. You did the same thing at his age."

He's lying. I didn't back off. I just didn't care. But my father did. This rage he can barely control is the same he unleashed when I starting bringing home F's.

"Slipping, maybe," Ken says, "but he was *failing*, Dad! And skipping school. And he quit the track team. Did you know I talked to Coach Abernathy? Do you know what he said?"

The track team. I ran track.

Ken continues. "Coach said he quit because he thought he wasn't good enough. Coach almost dropped dead when he heard that. Second best kid on the squad thinks he's not good enough. Now where do you think he got that idea?"

Fear of what else Ken might know twists deep in my dad's gut. He knew Ken had suspicions, and he kept a close eye on him to see if he went looking for some hidden note the one time he was here, but had no idea Ken was asking around about me. Where I was weak and a disappointment, Ken is strong — a worthy son. Is he so strong, my dad wonders, that he came here to accuse his own father of having a hand in his brother's death? Could he even be considering avenging his brother?

"Well?" Ken demands.

My father's rage and fear coil around each other. He takes a deep breath, telling himself he is in control and Ken is grasping at straws. Still, my dad notices the handle of a heavy iron skillet within easy reach in the box at his feet. "If he wanted to quit track, that's his business. He was always weaker than you, Kenny. He was the one who would quit."

Mike, my captain on the track team, jumps into Ken's mind. "It wasn't just his grades or track, Dad. Mike Fitzgibbons told me how he started pulling away from everybody, that he was tired all the time, he never talked anymore. You didn't see *any* of that?"

Mike. I lied to him so many times. Told him I was fine and could handle how hard my dad rode me.

My dad thinks of the basement again, and guilt rises, but he pushes it away. It's not his fault. But it *is* his fault, even though he believes he did nothing wrong, and now for Ken to question him. To doubt him. "He's a teenager, Ken!" my father shouts, his rage starting to break lose. "He—"

"He *was* a teenager, Dad," Ken says. "Was."

"Do not correct me!" my father bellows, his voice echoing in the empty, darkening room. He looks down again at the skillet's handle, anger blooming into violence, wanting to strike out, the desire to break and bloody, the need to show he is in control.

He thinks of the basement, his fingers working a knot.

I want to ask about that knot, but his wrath vibrates around me — through me — familiar and terrifying. But Ken is the focus of his rage this time.

Ken holds his ground. His mind is empty — waiting, expecting a blow. Almost wanting one. Wanting the excuse to unleash years of pent up anger for everything he — we — went through after our mom died and our dad twisted into the man he is now.

As they stare at each other, a small bit of my father's mind realizes that if he lashes out, he could be the one getting hurt. Ken is taller, leaner, younger, faster. Ken can beat him and there's no way in hell my father would suffer that humiliation. Finding out just how weak I was — how I wouldn't even fight back — had been disgraceful enough.

I find my voice and ask, "What happened in the basement?"

My dad turned from me and headed up the cellar stairs, disgusted, knowing I'm too much of coward to—

He squeezes his eyes shut.

He has to get out of here.

I need to keep pressing him. I won't be weak. Not this time. "If you didn't do anything wrong, then tell him. Did you kill me because I was weak?"

His guilt and certainty collide. He pushed too hard, but he needed to push me.

He breaks Ken's stare, picks up the box, angles around him and heads to the truck.

Ken just watches him pass. Again he flashes on a future without me, but now I see more: plans to get a job at school, find an apartment and never come home. It's more than resentment — Ken is scared what he thinks happened to me might happen to him.

"Ken," I say, "he's scared of *you*. He almost remembered. Don't stop."

My father returns, his mind whirling with something new. Something he's holding back to use to distract Ken from asking about me. "Look, I don't want to talk about

this. Next week I sign the papers, and this will be over."
He picks up two folding chairs, waiting for Ken's response.

Surprise and dread — cool and deep — creep from him.
"What papers?" Ken asks, suspecting what I just learned:
My father is selling the cottage.

"Don't let him distract you," I say. "Find out what
happened to me!"

My father replies, "With the new owner."

"You sold this place?" Ken asks. Emotions spiral from
him: anger, surprise, revulsion.

"We both made the decision to sell." A lie.

"No, bullshit," Ken replies. "That's not what we talked
about." Ken's memory is a shattered mirror. Strained phone
calls about if he could enjoy being here...Coming here only
once after I was dead and Dad never leaving him alone
for a moment.... The pain of my absence...

"We gave it three months."

Three months?

"And you said you didn't want to come here anymore."

I've been here for three months?

"Yeah, but I never said I wanted you to sell the place."

"What else am I supposed to think?"

Ken is speechless.

"Think about the basement, Dad," I say.

He came down the stairs after getting back from town
and saw my feet—

He shakes his head at Ken and heads back outside.

"He's lying," I say to Ken, and Ken knows it. "Stay on
him. He'll crack. He'll confess. And then you can keep this
place and not leave me here alone again."

But Ken is disgusted. He feels like the world has fallen
away and he is alone to face it.

With nothing else he can do, Ken picks up the shelves
and heads for the truck.

This can't happen. If this is the last time they'll be here,
what will happen to me?

I think of when Ken and I were kids, and those memories fill Ken. He pauses, the shelves almost forgotten, unable
to hold back tears. Random memories tumble from him,

filling the space around me. I snatch one — Grandpa teaching Ken to fish when he was a little boy — and hold it, twining it with the memory of him teaching me to fish. "This was *mom's* cottage," I say. "Dad has no right to sell it."

Ken's sadness solidifies, turning to sharp-edged anger. He slams the shelves down and says, "Ya know, maybe you could think — maybe hope — maybe fucking realize — that I would want to come back some day! Bring my kids here. Keep this place in the family."

My dad swallows his rage. "You never said you wanted to own this place."

"I didn't think it needed to be said."

"It's too late." My father remembers relief at the buyer's offer, and enthusiasm a few weeks earlier as he gave the buyer a tour of the cottage. During everything, my father never mentioned me, even as I followed him, peppering him with questions. But the memories those questions brought up only strengthened his determination to sell.

"You didn't think to ask me what I thought before you sell it to some stranger?" Ken asks.

The buyer asked about spending a weekend here, and my dad agreed. "I thought I knew."

Some time ago, there *were* sounds and movement here, but I ignored them. Was that him? Did someone spend a weekend here and I didn't even notice?

"Well, Dad, you didn't."

"There is nothing I can do."

"Ken, don't let it end here!" For the first time in my— for the first time ever, I shout at my father: "Tell him what you did if you're so fucking certain it was the right thing to do!"

As he came down the cellar stairs, he saw my shoes on the workbench and realized I was standing on it. Then he noticed a piece of notebook paper on the steps—

Satisfied he's won the argument, my dad grabs the shelves from Ken.

"He almost remembered!" I shout at Ken. His mind is a deep-red cyclone of thoughtless anger. "Nothing is signed yet!"

The cyclone evaporates. "Just tell the guy you changed your mind," he says. "If nothing is signed, it's not too late."

My father spins and fixes Ken with a stare, furious that Ken has found a new point to argue. He's in charge, he makes the decisions. He's not some coward who needs to be told what to do.

My father thinks of that floor joist in the basement. I'm down there, looking up at the large hole in it.

Upstairs, my dad says, "Your brother died here! I cannot stay here anymore!"

There are small strands of something caught in the hole's rough edges.

"Then don't sell. I thought you were going to rent it or let it sit empty. Do that. But don't sell it!"

They look like fibres from a rope.

"It's done, Ken. The paperwork is a formality, but it's done."

I don't remember my dad ever stringing a rope down here.

"You know," Ken says, "you talk about quitters, Dad, and it seems like you're the one who's quitting now."

In my father's memory, was he tying a knot... or untying one?

"Don't *ever* talk to me like that."

But there's a laundry line outside. Why—?

"Or what?"

Oh God.

"What are you going to do, Dad?" Ken continues. "Ignore me like you ignored—"

Oh God no.

"I did not ignore your brother!" my father bellows. His unbound fury slashes dark crimson, but beneath it is the truth: he didn't ignore me. He focused too much on me. "He was a selfish quitter! Don't lay his bad decisions on me!"

"He needed help! God, how could you have been so blind? Did everyone see it but you? Did you *want* it to happen?"

"Kenneth—" my dad begins, but can't say anymore. His will breaks and memories surge up. I'm pulled upstairs into the deepening darkness of the room.

He was headed into town for groceries and figured he should get a new seal for the hot-water tank while there, but needed to measure it. He came in the side door and down the cellar stairs, finding me standing on the workbench, motionless, one end of a rope around my neck, the other through that hole in the joist.

"He loved this place," Ken continues, his voice breaking. "Loved it so much he chose to die here. And I love this place. But none of that matters because you're going to give up on something that belongs to the family. Or what's left of it."

My dad, pulled back from the memory, says "We. Are. Done." He heads for the truck.

"Ken!" I scream. "He could have stopped me."

I thought he had gone into town and I was alone. As I stood there, I wasn't sure if I was going to do it. I couldn't stand him anymore, couldn't stand being such a disappointment, but was this the only way? I wondered if Ken could help me. Maybe get an apartment together.

Then I heard the side door open. I froze, terrified, unable to move even as he came down the cellar stairs.

He just stared at me.

"You quitter," he finally said. "Are you really that weak? I've see you moping around and this is your solution?" He picked up the note. The note where I explained how angry I was, how he made me feel like a failure. He read it and said, "Well, if you're going to do this, then *do* it. For the first time in your life, do something right. But no one's going to see this." He crumbled my note — a note I spent weeks writing — and stuck it in his pocket.

"And then he turned around and went upstairs!" I scream.

My father appears in the doorway, his face a kaleidoscope of shadows in the gloom. His mind is all right-angles with the certainty he has won. He will sell this place, and Ken knows nothing.

"Ken, don't let him go!" I scream. But Ken is done, his mind on someplace beyond here. "Don't give up."

My father says, "You coming?"

"You let me do it!" I scream at him. I stood for hours before stepping off the workbench, my heart empty, my mind filled with my father's words. "Tell Ken what you did, you coward!"

When he returned from town, he'd expected me to be sobbing in the living room. Not finding me there, he put away the groceries and went into the cellar, new rubber seal in hand, certain I would be down there, crying. He first saw my feet again, but this time they were swinging freely in the air.

Seeing this through his eyes, I remember. I circled him, asking him questions, wanting to know what had happened. But all I did was build his anger — anger that I gave up, that I didn't stand up to him.

He cut my body down, untied the knot, and checked for a pulse. Not finding one, he put the rubber seal on his workbench and then called 911.

"Yeah," Ken replies.

"Don't leave!" I scream as Ken walks out into the fading light. "Don't leave me here alone!" I think of us as kids again, but it makes Ken feel ill. "Don't let him sell the cottage!" The door swings shut, leaving me in darkness. "Don't be weak and give up!" A key slides into the lock, the tumblers turn, the bolt clicks home. "Or just kill him!" I move to a window and see the pick-up head along the narrow, tree-lined driveway. It reaches the end, turns, and disappears up a forest road.

They have to come back. They've got to. Then I'll get my father to admit what he did. I was so close. They must have forgotten something, or forgotten to *do* something. At the end of the summer, we used to have a ton of things to do to close this place, like turning off the water pump or... something. We had a list of chores, but I can't remember them. I guess that's why we had the list.

But they were moving things, so they need to come back for more, right? Sure. Even though the living room is empty, there are other rooms in this place. They must have stuff in them.

They'll be back. Whoever they were, they'll be back. And that'll be good because, when they were here, I could remember things. Like where I am and...

I go down into the basement and look at that joist again. The one with the hole in it. I think it's important. I just wish I knew why.

Am I dead? I must be.

● ●

By day, Matthew Moore is an online communication specialist. By night, he's a science fiction and horror writer. Later at night, he's the publicist for ChiZine Publications, a small Canadian publisher. He lives in Ottawa, Ontario with his wife and two beagles.

● ●

Billy and the Mountain
By Jason Ridler

My best friend waits outside, vigilant and curious. Today is the deadline I've been avoiding since Issue #1. Pinned to my drafting table are the last two pages of the very last issue of *Billy the Pict and the Mountain*. On the left half are dry ink renderings of Billy. I gave him three long, thin panels: the reader will jump the gutter from one to the other and land in the heart of the story.

Jump. See his southpaw blunderbuss pistol, raised high. *"You did it, Mountain! You smote Big Nasty and his army all by your lonesome! Two Huzzahs, I say. Two Huzzahs at least!"*

Jump. See the razor-thin silver saber shining in Billy's right fist, his eyes wide. *"And I've bested Mack Gnasher's head to a bloody, ruined pulp and no fooling!"*

Jump. See Billy's indigo-tattooed face, stunned. *"Why, Mountain! What are you doing with him? Speak at last, my silent partner!"*

I jump, reaching for the last panel, the mighty splash page on the right. Here, the silent Mountain will speak at last. My neck and wrist ache, wanting to fill that virgin page with the violent behemoth's last appearance, the one I'd planned since the beginning of the series.

The dead-white gutter hooks my eye. I can't make it. It drags me down, deeper.

※·※·※·※

I was doodling ninjas and vampires bashing Andy Cohen's head, when Mom shrank time. "Don't wait until next Sunday to do all that homework, Case. Christmas

break will be over before you know it, and then it's back
to the grind."

The Christmas spirit vanished, and my mind filled with
the image of Brock P.S. and the hallways I tried to wade
through in silence. I grabbed my parka, told Mom I was
heading to the library to study, and entered the crisp Janu-
ary darkness.

I trudged though crunchy snow to *Bruce's Smoke and
Magazine Shop*. The air was blue, and the floors had stains
that pre-dated Atlantis, but there was no clock, and loitering
was routine. A perfect hiding spot from reality.

I bought five chocolate bars, ate four in eight bites, and
headed to the magazine shelf to read *The Savage Sword of
Conan*. I had yet to enjoy Robert E. Howard's books, but
the massive Marvel magazine was stuffed with my own
daydreams: one monstrous outsider, through pure and
bottomless rage, can crush his cackling enemies, no matter
their number, and win. Time slowed whenever I visited
the mighty Cimmerian.

There it sat, on the bottom shelf, the cover screaming
for my attention. Conan slashed through a legion of skeletons in a Stygian temple. I almost saw him *move* off the
page when the doorbell chimed.

Andy Cohen, new ski-jacket tight on his trim build,
walked in. He looked around before speaking. "Hey, Casey,
man. Merry Christmas."

"Happy Hanukah, Andy."

He smiled, but stared at the black slush floor. "What
are you doing?" The doorbell interrupted us. A kid ran
inside, straight to the pop fridge at the back.

"Reading comics," I smiled. "You still collect Super-
man?"

"Nah, not really." He scanned the ceiling. "You still, uh,
drawing that stuff?"

My jaw clenched. "Yup. I'm making a comic for art class.
The ninja versus vampire idea we came up with last summer."

"Oh," Andy said. "That's awesome." His smile flickered.

"How was your Bar Mitzvah?"

His smile faded. "Oh, that? No biggie. Kinda fun. My Dad even let me have some grape wine." He shoved his hands in his slick coat pockets. "Sorry about the invitation. I guess it got lost in the mail or something."

"Yup. Sure. Whatever." Even that two-faced shitheel Trey Gorim had gone. Andy left the store without buying a thing. I ate my last chocolate bar and returned to Cimmeria.

I lifted the giant-sized issue from the bottom rack.

"Conan rules!" said a high, nasally voice.

The magazine smacked the skuzzy floor. "Whoa!" A needle-thin kid, in a massive sheep skin coat and scarf, snatched the magazine. I'd never seen him before. He had a hockey player smile and shaggy brown hair. He handed the filthy Conan to me. "It ain't in mint condition, but you could tell folks you dragged it through the corpse swamps of the Black River."

"Ok. Thanks." I went to the cashier, bought the comic, and left the poor kid behind.

Halfway home, he was at my heels.

"I'm Jimmy Brude." His voice was high and nasal. A Scottish accent trailed his words.

"Casey Belfort." He stuck out his bare hand and I shook it, feeling silly. He looked at least two years younger than me.

"Good to meet ya, Casey." He told me he was new to Kingston, just moved from Scotland. "What school do you go to?"

"Brock P.S."

"That's where I'm starting. After the holiday, that is. What luck!" He rambled about all his favorite comics as we drifted between yellow streetlight and winter darkness. "Oh, you're gonna love that issue of Conan, mate. It's an early one, about when he's a king of all Aquilonia. I must have read the original a million times. I'll let you see it, if you want."

"Cool." I had barely said three words in total. The kid couldn't take a hint. I picked up my pace and was about to say goodbye.

"Did you say you draw comics?" Jimmy said. "Superheroes and the like?"

I slowed. "Well, kinda. I've never actually finished one. I was working on this spooky ninja comic, but I don't think it'll work."

"Oh?"

I sucked nougat from my teeth. "My partner quit."

Jimmy's face lit up in the blue moonlight. "Did you need a new one? Because I've loved comics my whole life, but I couldn't draw a polar bear in a blizzard drinking a vanilla shake out of a white Dixie cup for all the tea in China. But I got a million ideas for stories, maybe a billion. Oh, it would be brilliant! We could even do it for school, like you told your old mate in the store."

I flinched.

"Oh, sorry about the listening, but I couldn't help it — that store is mighty wee. Please, Casey. I've never passed art class. Partners?" Goofy grin on his face, Jimmy extended his hand again. I suddenly didn't want to walk alone anymore.

I shook it again. "Partners."

"Brilliant!" He pulled a Dr. Pepper from his pocket, cracked it open, and took a long sip. "Ah!" He passed me the pop, and I took a swig. "Any story ideas you want me to think about? We are partners, after all."

I snorted. "So long as I never draw a ninja or a vampire again, I'm happy."

He nodded. "Understood. Let's have our first meeting tomorrow. Hmm, can we do it at your house? Folks are still unpacking."

I laughed. "My mom will freak. Doing homework on a Monday." He wrote my phone number and address on his pale hand.

"Brilliant! This is gonna be wild!"

Two snowballs punched the back of Jimmy's head, and he hit the sidewalk knees first. Laughter followed. Then a voice. "How could you faggots miss Fat Ass?"

Three thin shadows were behind us, refusing to step into the streetlight.

"But we got the shrimp," one said.

"Yeah," said another, a girl. "That's gotta count for something."

Jimmy picked the snow out of his eye. "Phew! You gotta declare war before firing the first shot," he said as I helped him up. "They cheated. They're bloody villains."

"Let's go," I whispered, pulling Jimmy with me.

"Don't move, Fat Ass, or by Christ, you'll get a snow-job every day until Easter."

I'd managed, until that moment, to be a very fat ghost to Trey Gorim. For a class president, he had a mean streak the size of Jupiter. Flanking him had to be Keith Fisker, strong like a bull and half as smart, and Jan Shipton, the toughest and ugliest thing in school. She worshipped pretty Trey like a god.

Trey crossed his arms, his bomber jacket creaking in the cold. "Let's see how many shots it takes to bring Belfort and his boyfriend down. Fire!"

A salvo cut through the air. I shielded Jimmy, my Gortex hide absorbing the barrage. Water, dirt, and salt ran down my neck, seeping into my sweater. Each shot got colder and hurt deeper as they zeroed in on my head.

"Run," I said. My ears burned.

Jimmy's face bunched. He grabbed the Dr. Pepper can and dropped to his knees. "Never. Let's smite 'em!"

Jimmy's hands darted into the snow bank and in rapid order produced three perfectly round snowballs filled with sidewalk grit and dirt. He dowsed each with Dr. Pepper.

"Move in!" Trey said.

Jimmy handed me one. The thump-thump of Cougar-boots chomping through snow got closer. "I'll get the bozos on the sides," Jimmy said. "You nail the ringleader!"

Shaking, not thinking, I nodded.

"Charge!"

Jimmy jumped back and launched both snowballs like comets. I pivoted and saw Keith and Jan run face first into Jimmy's brownball specials. Trey, leading from the rear, halted a few yards behind.

His face went stern. "Fat Ass, don't even— " My own cannonball was already in the air, fueled by rage and pain. But the limber son-of-a-bitch dropped and cheated fate. My brownball smacked a fourth kid, standing behind Trey, in the shadows. He walked into the light revealing a freshly ruined ski jacket. Andy Cohen wiped the sludge off his front, gave me a stink face, and then drilled a snowball into my throat.

✦┅┅┅┅✦

Jimmy called me the next day at noon, yelling over the static from wherever he was.

"You make it home ok?"

"Yup." They'd descended on us like jackals until I was Casey the Snowman and Jimmy was a large snowball. They would have made it yellow snow if a guy walking his dog hadn't scared them off.

"Hey, what's wrong with your voice?"

"Snowball. Throat. Remember?"

"Right." His voice went reedy. "Look, I'm sorry, Casey. I am. I wish I was big, like you. I fought like a devil, but that one you nailed had me pinned. God, he got me seeing red. Next time we cross, Casey, I'll do him in for both of us. I swear."

"Whatever."

"Can I still come over? I'll bring you that Conan book, the one that was in the comic." That issue had been torn apart and left on me like Cimmerian confetti. "Borrow it as long as you like. It'll be fun. I promise." Mom had pestered me all morning to go to the doctor, but I didn't feel like a lecture about my weight and the rise of teen diabetes.

"Yup."

"Brilliant!"

The sore throat and anger towards Jimmy both vanished during that week of creation. By Friday, we'd devoured mountains of calorie-wise popcorn, drank oceans of diet cocoa, and constructed the hexagon-planet Fantabular, a world of Samurai gorillas, werewolf magicians, and other mishmash stolen from every source we could find. Fantabular was ruled by the iron fist of Big Nasty and his brood-army of robot Jockmen. Fiercest of Nasty's agents were the evil twins Dingus and Dangus, the vilest boy and girl duo on the planet.

"But Big Nasty's right hand is a human weapon who throws deadly shots of lead, quick as gunfire," Jimmy said, nodding to himself, lost in his own thoughts. "He'll be called... Mack Gnasher. And he'll get smotted. You bet."

I'd sketched out each one in uniforms stolen from Star Wars, GI Joe, and Thor comics. I gave Mack Gnasher a pronounced absence of male genitalia.

"What about the hero?" I said.

Jimmy smacked his head. "Almost forgot! Why have just one? Great heroes work together. Captain American and Bucky, Batman and Robin, Tarzan and Cheetah. Let's make one each. I'll go first." He scratched his scruffy head, his mind searching somewhere beyond my kitchen and the stink of diet junk food. "Eureka!" He shot up his arm. "The last king of the Picts!"

"The what?"

"Wee Scottish warriors, fierce and tougher than a sack full of wolverines. I'm part Pict, you know?"

"Sure."

"I am! The name Brude stretches back ages. They even covered themselves in woad."

"Now you're just making crap up."

"No I'm not!"

"Fine, what the hell is woad?"

He smiled. "War paint. They tattoo themselves with it. Makes 'em even deadlier. Can fight a hundred men and not feel a bloody thing!" My hand cramped, wishing I had some woad. He shoved popcorn in his mouth and kept going. "My hero will be the last king of Picts, like Bran Mak Morn, wandering the wastelands of the world, smiting enemies and crushing evil. He's wee but tough and faster than a chased rat, and no one can match him with blade or pistol. Yeah, he'll have both, one in each hand! And he's tattooed in blue from head to toe in woad! His name will be..." He closed his eyes. "Billy the Pict!" He crossed his arms. "Now you, Casey."

I tapped my pencil, knowing full well Jimmy had just written himself into our comic. "How about a giant. Big, strong, deadly. Maybe he can't be knocked down."

"That's brilliant! He'll be the strong man, to go with the wee man. That's classic!"

I coughed. "And he won't speak."

Jimmy's face bunched. "Why not?"

I lifted my meaty hands. "He speaks with his fists."

Jimmy slapped my back. "Brilliant, Casey, just brilliant. Now pick a name that can't fall down."

I doodled a giant with small, thick legs and massive arms. "I always liked Man Mountain Moore, the monster of Stampede Wrestling. How about, 'The Mountain?'"

"Brilliant!"

Mom took the empty popcorn bowl from the table and lifted Jimmy's shaggy coat from the floor where he'd dropped it. I saw her reaction to its condition and winced.

"Maybe that's enough homework for today" she said. "Why not go to the town hall rink? Get some exercise?"

I pictured it: Trey and his gang. In armour. Armed with sticks. "Nah," I said.

"Well, maybe you little heroes could go to Jimmy's house for a while? I think I need a break from kung-fu monkeys."

"Samurai gorillas!" we said, crossing our arms.

Mom laughed and stared at the ceiling. "Oh god, my mistake. Jimmy, would that be okay with your parents?"

He held his cocoa. "The folks are kinda picky about guests and the like."

"Well, we've done our bit at the Belfort mansion to feed your imaginations and bellies. They can at least take an afternoon." She grabbed the phone. "What's your number?"

Jimmy's face went bluish-white. "We don't have a phone."

"Oh," Mom said, putting ours down. "Well, then, maybe you boys should just head over and ask. If they say no, come on back. I should have regained my sanity by then."

Jimmy led me through a winding path, north of the main drag, close to the Heights. Keith and Jan lived in this ghetto, unchained, but I didn't know where. It wasn't cold enough to lose an ear, but the farther we went meant a longer walk back, and the sun was fading fast.

"How much farther?"

"Not long. You read that Conan book yet?" His sneakers poked a hole through the iced snow. I followed, leaving deeper crevices.

"Just the first story, 'The Phoenix and the Sword.' I never knew Conan had been a king. It was cool, but I kinda like it better with the pictures."

Jimmy stabbed the ice with a kick. "I used to have the original story, bought it when I was a kid. Could have bought a mansion if I'd kept it in good condition. But I keep losing things with every move." He jumped and cracked the snow under his small weight. "Even when I stand still." He bit his lip, and we carried on.

An hour later, my throat burning, we stopped.

"Let me run in and see what the folks say," Jimmy darted into the dark mouth of a dilapidated bungalow one day away from collapse. He closed the door hard, and I watched the structure shimmy with snowdrift. Everyone knew the Heights were the dregs, but until you stand in throwing distance, you never feel it.

Jimmy appeared in the front door and cupped his mouth like a horn. "Sorry, Casey. Got some chores to do. I'll come over tomorrow. We can start on the first Fantabular adventure. Holler if you get lost!" He waved, then shut the door.

I was deadly far from home.

The wind bit through my ears about halfway back to civilization. I held them with my gloved hands for the rest of the way, yelling at myself for not bringing a toque. I never heard them coming.

Sheer force tackled my legs and my chest. My back snapped across the iced snow, and I sank an inch. A weight dropped on my chest, and three snowballs pounded my face.

I was blind, but I could hear Trey.

"Time for a yellow snow cone, Fat Ass. Open wide!"

Frozen fingers grabbed my jaw. I clenched everything.

"Bust his ribs!"

Boots hammered into me. I gasped and swallowed ice. Another snowball rammed into my face. Then another. I was drowning, but I could still hear Trey.

"Now! Do it!"

I gagged and waited for the hot stream of piss. When nothing happened, I coughed bile and snow.

"What the fuck? Do it!"

The weight lifted off me. I rolled over, wiping my eyes.

Above me, Andy Cohen zipped up his fly, face tight, head low. "No."

"You goddamn Jew!" Trey swung hard and fast, but Andy dodged it. I pulled myself up as Keith and Jan tangled Andy's limbs. I pounded through the snow.

"Trey!" Jan yelled. "Behind— "

I rammed Trey Gorim, landing on him with a violent crunch. He gasped once, then screamed. "Get off!" He kneed my stomach with such force that I accept no blame for what happened next.

A steady stream of black cocoa and kernels spewed from my mouth to his. He thrashed, but I had him pinned as I emptied a day's gorging into his screaming face.

Swinging wild, I drilled Trey's head over and over, my heartbeat doubling with each shot. "Bastard!" Lefts and rights broke through his guard, and I felt the sweet, terrible shock of his head snapping back and forth from my blows, as quick and deadly as Jimmy's snowballs but hard as hate. I just kept hammering Trey until his pretty face was a red and white mush with two swollen eyes. From a dark hole in me, a scream burst out that forced his eyes to open and see me in the talon grip of rage. I pulled back my fist, eager to knock him out of this world.

Keith and Jan shoved me off and dragged their leader away into the Heights. Both had fresh bruises and red-drip noses. I sat on my knees, exhausted, Andy before me. His face was swollen with shame and disgust. He held himself.

"Casey," he said, spitting. His lip was cut. Bruises were forming on his left eye. "God, man, I'm so sorry." He extended his hand to me. It was pale, with red cuts where he'd hit Keith and Jan. I lifted my own, knowing I couldn't get up by myself, when something hit Andy like a train.

I scrambled to my feet by sheer will, pain eating through every nerve. A hazy, brown-blue cloud was pounding

Andy's head with something big. I knew it was Jimmy before he spoke.

"Not this time! You won't win this time, you bloody cheat!"

I stumbled. I crawled. I lunged and pulled at Jimmy's coat. It came off in shards. My throat was shaved ice, raw and wrecked. Andy rolled on to his belly and pulled himself away. A red trail flowed from his head.

For a second, the blizzard of Jimmy could be seen. His face was ice blue, teeth seething. "You can crawl, but you can nay hide!" He lifted a thick branch high above his head, splattering me with blood. "Villain, yer smoted!"

I caught the branch, and he dragged me to him; he was that strong. He snapped at me, his teeth bared, but then his growl dropped.

"Casey?" He pulled the stick. I held on. "But... he's one of the bad guys! We have to crush 'em. Finish 'em!"

I shook my head, but the words wouldn't come from my injured throat. Andy twitched in the snow, gripping his head but not saying anything. Jimmy stepped back from me as if I'd grown another head. My rage was empty, but I held on to the branch as Jimmy kept pulling.

"But we have to win! We have to beat them! That's what heroes do!"

I held on, even though there was a big part of me that wanted Andy crippled and broken. Like Trey. Under my fists. Knuckle to skull. Skin torn. Eyes peeled back with terror. Crushing him. Damn near snuffing him out in the snow.

A word choked out of me. "No."

Jimmy released his grip, eyes shaking, face tight. "No. We let him live. Because *he's* your mate. Even though he pounded your throat with ice and snow and damn near choked me in a headlock." Jimmy spat. "Fine. He's all yours, Casey. Yours and yours alone."

He grabbed the remains of his jacket and left us.

⋙⋅I⋅•⋅I⋅•⋅I⋅⋘

I was in bed all that Saturday. I refused to tell Mom what happened or go to the doctor, leaving her in hysterics. My throat was raw and scratchy, my sides were killing me, and

I could barely eat anything tougher than pea soup. I slept most of the day.

A foul, earthy smell woke me at 3 a.m. that night. The moonlight made it easy to see the shape in the door, a thin shadow with a blue face. Then came the nasally voice.

"Casey?"

Pain shimmered in my throat.

"Still can't speak, huh? Kinda like the Mountain, which is pretty brilliant."

I gripped my covers, thinking of Andy, his silence, the blood, that lost look in his eyes. I'd practically dragged him to his house and then watched as his Dad took him and stormed off in their BMW toward Kingston General. I had no idea if he was ok, dead, or worse.

"I'm leaving, mate," Jimmy said. "I thought, maybe this time I could stay. I mean, you liked Conan and comics. And I thought since even big folk make them I could stick around, stay still." He sniffed then sighed. "But you changed. I could see it, in the snow. You looked at me like big folk. And when things change, I hurt folk. Especially mates." His wet eyes blinked at me. "I'm sorry."

Flashes of that week, of Jimmy's bravery, his wild mind and machine-gun mouth, crashed into a picture of Andy's bloody face and dead stare.

"Me too," I grunted.

Jimmy nodded. "But I wanted to say, before I run, that you were a good mate, Casey. Making Fantabular was brilliant, and I hope you'll draw it up someday. I'm keen to know how Billy and the Mountain end up. You can have that Conan book, too. No worries.

"I guess you don't need me, Casey. You got bigger things to worry about. No hard-luck feelings, ok? Oh, right, sore throat. Don't speak." He giggled. "Just like the Mountain. Brilliant." He left as I struggled for a word, but none that I had were up for the task. Talking was Jimmy's strength.

I never saw him again.

✦◦I◦I◦I◦✦

I pull my eyes out of the gutter and settle on the last page. Lead scratches paper.

I'm done. A mid shot. The Mountain's craggy face is worn. His titan brow slumps. Rusty daggers and broken arrows fill his oak beard. Tears swell in those blue orbs as he stares at his brave friend, but they have not fallen. His scarred hand waves. Mack Gnasher, the once mighty right hand of Big Nasty, waits for him on the warwagon, face battered, eyes frozen in a zillion-yard stare.

Finally, after years of silence, The Mountain speaks. "Goodbye. Billy."

The last panel: *Victorious arms dropped, Billy watches the Mountain and Mack head down the hill from the battlefield as a new dawn breaks in Fantabular.*

The sun is up. My deadline is here. The ink is going from bright to dark. And my best friend is still outside the door, still vigilant, still curious.

"Good morning," I say.

The door opens a crack.

"Come on in. It's all done."

Andy shuffles in, slow and tired, blanket in hand. His face is the same as his last visit, like every visit, expressionless but just as youthful as the day Jimmy Brude tried to save me.

"Have a seat," I tell him. "But we need to be careful with the pages, just like last time. So I'll turn them, ok?"

Andy takes my stool, drops his blanket, his voice toneless. "I remember."

I put down the first page and wonder if it's true, if he really can remember. I sniff away a sob as Andy starts to read.

● ●

     A former cemetery groundskeeper and punk rock musician, Jason S. Ridler's poetry and fiction have appeared in such venues as *ChiZine, Nossa Morte,* and *Dark Recesses.* He is a graduate of the Odyssey Writing Workshop and holds a Ph.D. in War Studies from the Royal Military College of Canada. Visit him at Ridlerville: *http://jsridler.livejournal.com/*
● ●

The Tear Closet

by Suzanne Church

My father was a thief who stole my mother's soul.

The larceny began one night behind the soda shop. Mom thought herself ugly, so when he sweet-talked her, she shut her mind and allowed her heart to sop up the whimsy, her future pilfered by the foreign delights of lust.

They were married in a private ceremony. Grandpa Randall might as well have signed the papers himself. His faith forbade an unwed daughter becoming a mother.

My entrance into the world nearly killed her. I fussed in the nursery while Mom recovered. She begged to hold me, but the nurses pronounced her too weak. My father worked, but not in the sales office like he told Mom. No, he worked his baby maker inside one warm hole after another on the bed with the iron-bar headboard in our basement apartment. His mother washed the sheets for him before Mom and I arrived home.

Within a year, my father abandoned the secrecy of his sinful wanderings. Mom cursed his name and he beat her for it. I screamed continuously. Some people don't remember being babies, but I cannot forget how the salty smell of tears filled my nose like the putrid stink of brackish pools on a derelict beach.

→⊷⊹⊶⊹⊶←

On my first day of kindergarten, my father accompanied me to school. I remember he handed me a paper bag with a bread-and-butter sandwich and an overripe banana inside. He tilted his head and smiled.

"Mabel," he said.

"Yes?"

"You're going to meet plenty of boys in school. But I want you to remember that I'm your man."

The bell rang and the parents hugged their children. My father got down on one knee and kissed my ear. It made a loud slapping sound, and the suction from his mouth tugged on my eardrum with a painful pop. I heard his breathing, fast like he had been running. As the teacher called us in, he whispered, "Forever."

The smell of his breath, coffee and sugar, lingered in my nose. I tried to erase him from my mind, but he seemed to hover behind me.

I threw up that first day, right after Miss Gage brought us to the carpet for story time. The pungent odour of vomit chased my father's stink away. The custodian cleaned the mess and Miss Gage sent me to the office. The secretary called home. Mom picked me up.

"Does your stomach hurt?" she asked.

I shook my head.

"Were you scared of the teacher?"

"Miss Gage is nice."

"Oh."

I thought she would say more, perhaps ask about my fear, but she tugged my hand and led me home. She cooked pancakes from a mix, using water instead of milk because the milk truck skipped our apartment when we couldn't pay. We didn't have syrup, only butter. Grandpa Randall brought us butter on Sundays on his way home from church where he prayed for us.

Before my father returned home that evening, Mom cradled me close and wrapped a soft blanket around us — a pink one with ribbon sewn on two sides. "I want to show you a secret," she said.

She took me inside the broom closet beside the fridge. "Here," she pointed at the far wall. With a hard nudge of her shoulder she pushed and the wall opened inward.

I stood with my mouth open.

"Sit," she said.

I crawled into the small space and settled on the floor with my blanket around my shoulders. It smelled of her. She snuck in beside me and closed the door.

In the menacing darkness, she said, "Watch."

Slowly, hundreds of pinpricks of amber light glowed and brightened. When they burned vibrantly enough for me to see Mom's face, they began to fall, inching to the floor where they trickled into a pile around us.

She reached out and cupped a tiny handful of amber brilliance. The light reflected on her cheeks and in her eyes. She was crying. I rarely saw her cry.

"These are my tears," she said. "I keep them safe here, in my tear closet, so that your father won't find them. Would you like to share them?"

I nodded.

"Take a few in your hand."

I grabbed for the pile and the lights scattered.

"Slowly, Mabel. Be gentle."

She guided my hand to the floor. I breathed slowly and tried not to wiggle. A few lights skimmed down, nudged at my fingertips, and then moved away.

"Easy," she said.

The lights snuck close once more and moved into my palm. I felt sadness, as though my world had filled with sorrow and I had to cough it out of me. Tears filled my eyes and I encouraged them, crying and sobbing. My entire body shook.

Mom hugged me, still holding the blanket over my shoulders. She cried too, not vehemently, but more than I had ever seen.

I don't know how long we wept, but when the two of us stopped, my body drooped with relief. All around me, amber lights sparkled, pulsing bright, then dim, then bright again. So many tears that the closet warmed from their brilliance.

"Mom?"

"Yes?"

"Do you come here a lot?"

"Not much."

"It's beautiful."

She nodded. I held her and closed my eyes. When I finally opened them, the lights had all faded away.

"We'd best get back," she said.

⊹⊱•⊰•⊱•⊰⊹

Mom walked me to school for the next two months. But when the pancakes thinned and my lunch turned into a slice of bread, she took a job with the phone company. She reported at half past seven, so my father had morning duty. He would hug me and rub his unshaven face against mine to awaken me. The whiskers burned, scratching my skin like hundreds of dirty needles. The first time he did it, I told him it hurt.

"Love hurts," he said.

"Why?"

"Because men are strong and women are weak."

"Mom's strong."

He glared at me while he chose a skirt and blouse from my closet, sniffing them before he tossed them on the bed. "Get dressed."

I changed while he made my lunch. Then he brushed my hair, yanking out the tangles and swearing while I bit my lip. After he finished my second pigtail, he sniffed my hair.

I hated his nose most of all.

⊹⊱•⊰•⊱•⊰⊹

I lived for Sunday mornings because I would wake with Mom snuggled next to me. We would take our time rising and talk about what I had learned in school during the past week. I considered telling her about my father's sniffing, but I didn't want to waste our time together with sad thoughts.

Most Sundays, my father slept late and spent the afternoon bossing Mom around. She would bring him his coffee and aspirins, and make as nice a Sunday dinner as she could afford.

One Sunday in June, we woke early and Mom showed me how to make pancakes. My father wasn't home yet, so we giggled and played. Mom put red food color in the batter so we would have pink pancakes for our girl-time.

We sat down to eat them, heaping extra butter on, when he arrived.

"My head is splitting," he said. "Where's my coffee?"

"I'll put it on," said Mom. "The pancakes are ready."

"I'm sick of pancakes." He slapped her hard across the cheek. She fell from her chair at the kitchen table, her elbow catching a glass on the way past. It smashed on the floor.

"Clean your mess," he said.

When she stood, the broken glass cut her feet. She didn't cry out. Her feet left blood-stains on the floor.

"Now you're making it worse." He slapped her again. When she fell backward, the glass cut her hands.

He pointed a finger at her. "Don't *cry*. I can't stand your crying. You're so weak."

She shook her head and reached for a cloth to clean up the shards.

I hurried to the broom closet and brought Mom the dustpan.

She took it from me. "Go to your room. Stay there. I don't want you cut."

Stepping carefully in my slippers around the glass, I did as she said. I left my bedroom door open a crack and watched her sweep the glass and dump it in the garbage. When the floor was clean, she rinsed her hands and feet in a basin, vigilantly checking for shards. My father paced in the living room, complaining that she was taking too long with his coffee.

She needed to cry. I could feel it filling my head. The tears waited. I added my own fear to their power and willed her to sneak into her tear closet.

The coffee percolator hissed and gurgled as Mom poured the steaming liquid into a mug. She hurried it to my father.

"Finally," he said. After taking a sip, he looked up from the couch and caught me watching.

"Shut your door."

I did. I considered sliding the bolt lock, but feared his anger. Tears tingled under my fingers. I pressed my ear against the door and listened. Between his slurps, I heard the gentle clunk of the tear closet's secret door.

"Where's the cream?" He slammed the cup down. "Woman?" His footsteps moved towards the closet. "What are you doing in there?"

A slam.

Millions of tearpricks jabbed all over my body. Mom begged him for mercy. I didn't dare open the door. Instead, I sat in the far corner of my room, hugged my knees to my chest, and sucked on my pink blanket while I rocked back and forth. He yelled and he hit, but he never once mentioned the tears. Their pain kept worsening all over me until, exhausted, I collapsed and slept.

Mom left for work before I woke the next morning. While I dressed, my father sniffed my discarded clothes, including my underpants. I couldn't understand why anyone would want to smell something that had touched my bum.

I looked up at him and he smiled. But it wasn't a happy smile. I wanted to cry, but the tears wouldn't come.

As he yanked a comb through my hair, I asked, "How long will Mom work for the phone company?"

"Until the day she dies."

⊹⊱•⊰•⊱•⊰⊹

In November of the same year, Sean Pensky arrived in our grade-two class. He was about an inch taller than me, skinny, and he had a bad mouth. It always said stuff he didn't mean, or so he told Miss Howard.

One day at recess, he ran up to me on the playground. I was skipping by myself, and he yanked the pink rope out of my hand and said, "You stink."

"Do not."

He threw the rope over the fence onto the baseball diamond where the big kids played. "Do too."

"Get it back."

"No way."

One of the big kids grabbed my rope, then another joined in, until they were playing tug-of-war. The game ended when it broke.

"Thief!" I shouted at Sean.

"I didn't steal anything. Your stupid rope's right there."

I shoved him. When he shoved me back hard, I fell down and scraped my knee. A teacher took me to the nurse's office to slap on green goo that smelled like the dark hallway at the hospital where Mom would get stitches. The office called home.

My father picked me up. He stared at my knee. "Looks sore."

I nodded.

"I'll kiss it better."

"It doesn't hurt that bad."

He signed me out and smiled at the secretary. She smiled back. He covered the wedding ring on his finger.

As the school doors clanked closed behind us, he said, "I'll kiss it better at home."

He kissed more than my knee. He touched my private places and smelled them too. His whiskers scratched and scraped me. His tongue dirtied me. I wanted to cry, but I couldn't. He had stolen my tears, just like Sean had stolen the skip rope.

The next day at school, I hunted for Sean at recess. Before he spoke, I punched him. He collapsed like an old shoe. I kicked him. He screamed and cried, begging me to stop.

"I'll steal your tears," I shouted at him.

The principal dragged me into the office and made me tell my story. He said that stealing my skip rope was wrong, but hurting Sean was worse.

"Is there anything wrong at home?" he asked.

"My father loves me."

"Your Mother's on her way from work."

"Mom?"

He nodded.

I waited in the office. When she arrived, she stared at her shoes and apologized to the principal. They called Sean down from class. I apologized to him in front of everyone. Mom signed me out and handed me a rectangular, yellow ticket.

"We're going for a ride," she said.

We walked from the school in the opposite direction of home. Mom took me to a stop where a red bus picked us up and took us downtown. From there, we walked to the phone company.

"You can stay here for the rest of the day."

"Really?"

She nodded.

I sat on a stool beside Mom. She wore a headset and answered all sorts of questions. Her voice sounded full of hope. Not sad or hurt like at home. When she had a break, we walked to the ladies' room holding hands. For the rest of the day I felt elated. On the bus ride home, a tear slipped down her cheek.

"You found your tears?" I said.

She nodded. "Your father didn't steal them. They're safe."

She cried and hugged me and I cried too. We wept so much that a lady sitting a few rows up came over and asked if she could help.

"We're more happy than sad," said Mom. "Glad to be together."

The lady gave us a funny look, but left us alone. Mom and I stayed on past our stop. After a while, the driver parked the bus. He opened the front and back doors, and then approached us.

"End of the line. You have to get off or pay again."

"Oh," said Mom.

I thought she would pay our fares, but she didn't. Instead, we exited by the back doors and started walking, but not towards home.

"Where are we going?" I asked.

"Away."

"For how long?"

"Forever."

I asked her if that was the same as how my father had said *he* was my man. Forever. She stopped walking and sank to the ground. Her skirt slipped up, showing her panties. I leaned forward to smell them.

"What are you doing?" she asked.

"He sniffs my underpants, to make sure they're right."

Her face turned white, like the chalk they painted on the grass at school for the baseball diamond. Her hand shook as she stood and pulled me beside her.

"Come on," she said. "Hurry."

I wanted to ask her where we were going, but I didn't think she knew.

The sun dropped low in the sky. We continued walking. Mom limped and said her shoes hurt her feet. I told her to take them off, but she wouldn't.

The street lights came on, illuminating the bridge over the valley. Brown water, the color of Mom's high-heeled shoes, flowed far below. Miss Howard had taught us the name of the river at school, but I couldn't remember it. Mom walked us right to the center of the long bridge. We were up so high, I felt like a bird. The wind roared in my ears. Cars sped past on the road beside us. She stopped, gripped the railing, and looked down.

"Isn't it beautiful, Mabel?"

I nodded.

"It's a long way down," she said.

"I'm scared."

She sat down with her back against the railing and said, "Me too."

The cold made me shiver, so she wrapped her arms around me. "I wish I had my pink blanket," I said.

"Sorry, sweetie. There wasn't time to get it." We sat in the middle of the bridge, shaking and silent.

"I'm done," she said. "I can't go back."

"Home?"

She nodded. She had her tears and I had mine and she didn't want anyone to take them.

I started crying. "Why does love have to hurt?"

She wiped the tears from my cheeks with her fingers and dried them on her skirt. Her hand felt as cold as the basement cement floor.

"Love only hurts when you don't deserve it." She stood and leaned over the railing. "I'm too ugly to deserve love."

"*I* love you, Mom."

"You deserve better. We've come here to hide our tears. Climb up here and I'll show you where we'll keep them."

I stood. The wind hit me hard, and I almost fell into the traffic.

She put one leg over the railing. "Come on, Mabel. The tear box is right here." She pointed past the railing, where I couldn't see.

I stood on my tiptoes and leaned over. Hovering below the railing, a swarm of her tears drifted together, their amber light glowing.

She swung her other leg over the railing. "Come on."

I grabbed her hand, but I couldn't will myself to climb. I shook my head.

"It's okay," she said.

"No, Mom. Please."

She pulled on my hand. I dug my feet in and held on. She swayed in the wind, twisting my arm until I thought it would pull off. My hands were sweating, and her grip slid.

The cloud of tears enveloped her. Poised for a heartbeat, our eyes locked. Then she and the amber lights disappeared over the side. She didn't scream on the way down. I knew she had found the bottom when I heard a faint thud on the wind.

I sat. On something. I pulled it out from under me. She had lost one of her brown shoes. The thin heel reminded me of Sean and his skinny legs. It smelled of the stockings Mom hung in the bathroom on Sunday afternoons.

For a long while I shivered and waited. For what, I didn't know. My father had stolen her from me sure as he had stolen her soul. He had taken all that we had.

Three times, I stood and leaned over the railing.

I thought about throwing her shoe over. She needed both shoes. It was too dark to see to the bottom of the ravine, but I thought I could see a dim orange patch of light below. Her wide eyes kept flashing in my mind, afraid, determined, alone. My teeth chattered in my mouth. Maybe the tears had helped her fly away? I tried to lift my leg to climb over, but I lost my balance and fell backwards. Strong hands grabbed me.

A man.

"What are you doing out here alone?"

I stared up at his broad shoulders and smooth face. "Nothing."

"Where do you live?"

I should have lied, should have run and never looked back. Instead, I recited my address as I had learned to do at school. The man walked me home. My father was there, with liquor on his breath and anger in his eyes.

"Ran away, did you?" he said. "The principal phoned."

The man said, "I'll leave you to it, then." He left us, taking hope with him.

>+I+I+I+<

The night after the funeral, where we said goodbye to Mom, I had a terrible nightmare. I was falling and falling for what seemed like forever. When I woke, I could barely catch my breath.

My father's snores drifted into my room. Mom used to make me a snack whenever I woke from a nightmare, so I tiptoed across the cold basement floor into the kitchen. When I opened the fridge, I feared the light would wake him.

It didn't.

Inside was a cake the neighbour had baked to help us through our loss. The last time I had had cake, Mom had baked it for my birthday. She had stuck candles in the middle and told me to make a wish and then blow them out. The first wish that had popped into my head was for a puppy. But I never got a puppy.

I set the cake on the counter and took out a knife. With all of my heart, I closed my eyes and wished for tears. The knife slid easily through the rich chocolate frosting. It was brown, the color of the river and my Mom's shoe. As I glided the knife free of the cake, I stared at the goo clinging to the steel blade. Inhaling deeply, the chocolate smelled as rich as cream and as pungent as a grave.

I lifted the slice of cake onto a plate, found a fork, and approached the broom closet. I had wanted to sneak into the secret part since mom had left us, but my father had always been watching, touching, sniffing. The back wall squeaked as I shoved it inward. I stopped and listened.

My father snored on.

I crawled into the closet, sat, and tasted the heavy frosting while the cake melted on my tongue. As I raised a second forkful, amber lights began to arrive. The chocolate tasted salty; I found tears on my face.

I licked my fingertips, one at a time, tasting salt and chocolate together. As I pulled each finger free of my mouth, the lights scurried out of the way.

"No," I said to them. "Don't leave me."

They did the opposite. They doubled and doubled again, adding more light to the small space. I remembered how my mother had held me here, how her love had comforted me. I missed her so much.

"Mom?" I said to the tears.

Some hung silent in the air around me, others pooled in my lap and on the floor nearby. Though they warmed the small space, I still felt chilled.

"I miss you."

On and on the tears arrived, and with each new volley I wept. I cried as quietly as I could so my father wouldn't hear. "Please come back to me, Mom. I need you."

I could almost hear her voice, the way she would say, "I love you, my sweet Mabel," right before she tucked my sheets tightly around me for sleeping. I think the tears missed her, too.

For a long time I lingered in the tear closet, sobbing alone until I thought I would dry up like a shrunken apple. "Why does forever have to be so long?" I asked the lights.

They gathered around, hovering closer, until they seemed to fade inside of me. I lost sight of many of them. My sadness lingered, but my crying lessened, turning to whimpers and then shuddery sighs.

Exhausted, with my empty plate in hand, I crawled out of the closet. The clang of the dish in the sink seemed louder than a glass shattering. The knife, still covered with cake and frosting, lay on the counter where I had left it. The shape of it appealed to me so I picked it up.

Determined and armed with the dirty knife, I walked into my father's room. He was still asleep, sprawled half in and half out of his blankets. His head lay on an angle against the iron bars of the headboard. Without thinking, I held the blade above his nose. Would it slide as easily through him as it had through the cake?

He awoke and looked from me, to the knife, to me. His eyes opened so wide I thought they might get stuck like the glass eyes on a doll. For the first time in my life, I saw fear there, as though my father was actually afraid of me.

"What're you doing, Mabel?"

I couldn't answer, couldn't move. As the seconds ticked past, fear left his face. The contempt he had always shown for Mom took its place. With a sneer, he slapped at my hand. The knife flew across the room. It sprayed bits of icing and cake on his clothes as it tumbled into a pile of them on the floor. In that moment, I understood my mom's years of terror.

Afraid, I stood there, staring at him. He sat up and drew his hand back, readying a violent, backhanded slap.

The tears began to drift out of me, swarming and advancing towards my father. In huge clumps they landed on him, making the faintest of plunking sounds as they hit. He swatted at them, swiped them, scratched them, but they eluded his every effort. I watched his hands with fascination, stunned that such a big, strong man couldn't hurt these tiny lights.

When I looked back at his face, he was crying. Huge tears streaked his face. His nose, that horrible, awful nose, dripped snot in two matching ribbons over his lip.

He whimpered.

I knew how much he hated crying. I couldn't help but stare at him as he did.

"Get 'em off. Get 'em off me." He kept repeating it, over and over, while he cried and swatted at the tears; his eyes as wide as Mom's had been when she learned to fly.

I found my voice. "Love hurts. But not because men are stronger than women."

I took a step back and then another. When I was far enough away that he couldn't touch me, the tears around him began to fade. My father continued to scrape and swat at them, even when I couldn't see them any longer. A small army of tears stayed around me, on my arms, my legs, my hair, ready to defend me if he got too close.

I turned my back on him and started for my room, but stopped to face him once more. "Love hurts because you don't deserve it."

*•I•I•I•<

The next day, when he walked me to school, my father kept his distance. The few times that he ventured too near, or tried to sniff me or touch me or grab my hand, he would start to cry. Though I couldn't see any tears on him, my father continued to brush and swipe at his arms and legs and scratch his skin raw. I wore the tears like a blanket, my amber blanket, bigger and brighter than the pink one my mother had shared with me.

When Miss Howard saw us, she came over.

"I'm so sorry for your loss," she said to him.

He nodded and wiped another tear with his sleeve. Without answering, he started for home.

The bell rang, but when I tried to hurry for the line, Miss Howard said, "Wait, Mabel."

She knelt down in front of me. "If you need time alone, or to call home, just ask."

"Okay."

She nodded. "Your father is so sad. He must have really loved your mother."

"I don't think so," I said.

"Why would you say such a thing?"

I shrugged. "Because they aren't his tears."

"Whose tears are they?"

"They used to be Mom's, but now they're mine."

• •

When Suzanne Church isn't chasing characters through other realms, she's hanging with her two children in Kitchener, Ontario. She is a graduate of the Clarion South Science Fiction Writers' Workshop. Her short fiction has appeared in *Cicada*, *On Spec*, and *Neo-Opsis*, and in several anthologies. Read more at: *www.suzannechurch.com*

• •

RELATIONSHIPS

Little Deaths
By Ivan Dorin

On the night of your conception, Death leaned against my doorframe like a tilted S beneath the drape of his black silk robes. One forearm and hand curled to frame his hooded face, while his other robed hand rested on a cocked hip, holding the handle of his inverted scythe, its blade propped on my threshold like an afterthought.

"Hey, babe," he cooed. "Fancy a date?"

"I'm far past the point of fancying much of anything, and didn't take kindly to being called 'babe' even when it might have suited me," I retorted.

"I wouldn't have either of us take me too seriously, but I don't see you merely as advanced age allows you to appear," he told me. "I see you as you were and could be. I've come to offer a form of rebirth, as difficult as it may be to accept."

"No doubt because of the cost." I'd had two sets of clients in my day. The first ones wanted the second ones killed. The second ones wanted pleasure. If both agreed to pay, I provided both services and collected both fees. The second ones weren't informed of my arrangements with the first, of course, and paid with both their money and their lives, but at least part of the experience was consensual.

"I require only what would be paid in any event," he said, pushing himself away from the frame and standing straight. "Two coins that would be placed over the eyes of a corpse to pay for passage into the next world."

I still kept a bag of such coins as souvenirs. I'd never left them on the eyes of my dead clients. As far as faith in the existence of an afterlife was concerned, I had even less to lose than life or money. "I hope your other employer pays better," I muttered, regretting my words almost instantly. It was unprofessional to ask who wanted me killed, or what the price was, but I'd been in secluded retirement for decades, and no longer thought of myself as worth hunting. My etiquette was as withered as my flesh.

"There is no other employer," he told me, "but I do offer extra services. If, after my work is done, you're so transformed that you no longer consider yourself to be the same person, then your afterself could enjoy me. The first two coins buy you an ecstatic exit from this world, two more buy your afterself a place in the next world, and two more after that will get your afterself a transcendent arrival celebration. Of course, collecting from someone who currently doesn't exist can be problematic. It's best to get payment in advance, and sometimes people don't get along sufficiently well with their afterselves to buy them anything at all, no matter how much both selves may need the extra services during the transformation. Dying alone is bad enough on this side, but continuing the process on the other side with nothing but a nascent and despised afterself for company is not an experience I'd recommend to anyone. Of course, the people who need the extra services are too afraid to believe or understand what I'm saying, and don't purchase them, and no matter what your inclinations, I've made a terrible pitch and probably talked myself out of any bonuses already."

I was indeed a pragmatic, two-coin sort of customer, and absorbed little of this rambling speech beyond the first sentence. It sounded to me like I could pay extra for my own assassination and the defilement of my corpse, neither of which seemed very appealing. "So this is what it is to be Death?" I asked him. "Magical powers far beyond those of mortals, and business skills far beneath them?"

"It's a labor of love," he said with a shrug.

If and when you read this, you may believe that I accepted Death either too quickly or not quickly enough. You may read from a world in which beautiful young men freely and eagerly offer their supple, sculpted bodies to withered old women. You may study my history and wonder why I was so quick to accept such an offer, when my world was so corrupt that I must have suspected Death of being less than honest.

Whatever you imagine, though, you probably won't remember how tiresome my world was. Every word was a halfhearted stab, every social exchange a veiled attempt to assassinate. For all the lies I expected him to tell to make my passage pleasant, he still seemed the most honest that anyone had ever been with me. As strange as it may seem to you, I also identified with him as a professional and wanted to see him succeed. His job was more difficult than mine in many ways, and that intrigued me, since the clients I made love to had never known in advance that they would get more than they paid for. I'd often wondered what it might be like to have no conflicts of interest when I entered a bedroom, and have a single client who wanted both the love and the death.

"It must be difficult to make a living when you love to kill so much," I said.

"I see myself as a Tarot card sort of Death. I don't think of what I do as killing."

I folded my arms and let a little puff of air out of my nose, a faint snuffing sound. "You're new at this, aren't you?"

"You could say that I change. I renew myself by renewing others. I'm not jaded, but that doesn't mean I'm inexperienced. I'm quite prepared for you."

"What if I'm not ready to be 'renewed'?" I asked.

"I believe you've been ready for me for years," he answered. "I've merely waited for the time that would be most enjoyable for us."

"Us? What's in it for you?"

"The pleasure of watching your transformation, as well as the usual physical dimensions of the act. Or usual for me, at least. Amplified for you."

I rolled my eyes. People had spent years searching for ways to make the little death bigger. I'd done quite well enough in my day without the aid of any such charlatans.

"I can prove it, of course," he said. "What do you have to lose? Before the end, why not feel what it's like to be young once more?"

I let my forehead slump to the doorframe, making the faintest of thuds. "Haven't you come a little late?" I grumbled.

"I could wait until you're a corpse, but now you can play an active part. You also smell better."

I wanted to change the subject. Unfortunately, a new one didn't spring to mind.

"I won't interpret the gesture as acceptance," he added, "but you could let me in. My work requires a body of flesh, and though the night is warm enough for those in motion, I'm not wearing anything under these robes."

A whore, or one who would imitate her, must make her client feel as credibly desired as possible. When entering a man's room, I always made a point of complimenting him, on his looks if he had some moderately attractive feature, on his clothes if he knew how to conceal his bodily flaws, on his possessions if he had nothing else.

He didn't even glance at my surroundings. When I was no longer backlit by the fireplace, he propped his scythe on his shoulder and gave me a long hooded look.

"Perhaps it's because your breasts were some of the last things your clients ever saw," he said, "but they described them to me in elaborate detail. It's a pity that you used such disruptive means to impress customers with the memory of your beauty. I think your breasts stand on their own merits."

It would be easy for a fraud to invent such a response as one my dead clients would give, and that annoyed me, but my dead clients could also have concentrated on the physical to keep the other aspects of our exchange private, and that threatened to disarm me. "Yes, I'm quite enamored of them myself," I shot back. "I'm especially fond of the way they 'stand' against my stomach."

"Then enjoy them while you can," he said with a chuckle. "You'll soon see them as I do."

I continued to stand there, calling his bluff, even posing a little, daring him to look at me. He didn't look away, though. He gazed for so long, in fact, that I began to wonder if he were daring me not to enjoy it.

"I've been remiss," he said.

"Excuse me?"

"I've talked to many people who knew you and were the subjects of your art. I've asked them in detail how you might like to be the subject of that same art. Perhaps I should have paid more attention to other forms."

I was glad of the firelight, because I was starting to feel somewhat flushed.

"Your work demanded discretion, of course. Perhaps no one ever made a sculpture of you, or painted your portrait?"

I cast my gaze at the floor.

"Very well," he huffed, sending a ripple through the fabric that hooded his face. "Patience is part of my role, after all."

You might wonder why I wouldn't have sought to be immortalized earlier in my life. As far as I was concerned, I'd already done so. When I came to collect my assassination payment, those who paid for the killing sensed that I'd been unbearably intimate with my physical victims, and envied them. I was feared, lusted after, imagined; I eventually had my trade name sung, spun into tales, and repeated in hushed whispers. My mystique grew because no one who paid to experience my beauty in its entirety could live to tell of it. On that night, of course, there was nothing left to tell. I'd also spent my life giving others what I wanted, wondering if the night would ever come when someone might guess where my desires lay and satisfy me in turn. Of course, since I was hired to kill those who might have so pleased me, this made it difficult. Now I was being served by Death himself, or at least, someone who had gone to the trouble of imitating him.

Death took the time to understand me. Death took a packet of powder from his robes and emptied it into my tub, expanded it by magic so that I could lie down, poured water in and stirred it until it was of a consistency between jelly and plaster. Death delayed satisfying his desires, restrained himself as he told me to strip naked, watched as I climbed into the goo, and pressed down on me as I slowly sank beneath it.

The fluid was as warm as the womb, and as attentive as a multitude of lovers. I'd never felt so completely and intimately caressed. It was as if he could dip a finger beneath the surface and touch me everywhere at once. At first, he gave me a straw to breathe through, but as the mold began to harden, he withdrew it. I imagined that my spirit would leave my body under its thin concealing shell, as some like to believe, and return one day to find its old container displayed as a statue of an anonymous withered old woman with an inexpressibly beautiful expression of bliss on her face.

I was ready to die then, but he wasn't finished with me. I felt myself lifted, and set down again. He split the mold open, and pulled it away, and I blinked at the firelight in my own room from my own bed.

I tried to sink into the blankets. The loss of touch was difficult to bear at first, but he took out a miniature canvas, easel and paints, then took his place behind them as they enlarged to full size, and I felt as if caressed again as he began to paint. "The mold was only a crude literal rendering, of course," he told me. "I hope this will show more of what you felt during your life."

"My soul, rather than my body?" I asked.

"Oh, no, nothing so nebulous as that. You're about to leave your previous experiences behind, like a snake shedding its skin, and you may want every sort of record you can get. The body is a canvas with only so much space."

"Does no one paint where I'm going?"

"The people of the underworld are fascinated by the things they couldn't afford to do in their previous lives, but repelled by the subject matter of those same lives," he said, a little sadness creeping into his voice. "They even hesitate to refer to what they did before as living. Many could paint better than anyone you've ever known, but they'd be uninterested in painting you as you appear now." He glanced up again, but without moving his brush. "I'm sorry," he said. "I shouldn't bias you against them."

I'd been lying on my side, but I found the energy to raise myself on one elbow, assuming a sidelong version of the pose he'd struck when I first answered the door. "And what about them?" I asked. "Are they biased against me?"

"Well, you did send some of them there a little early. I think you could make amends, though. The underworlders don't value status or wealth, but they crave companionship, and the dying can't reach their realm without the help of guides, people with the skills of an— I mean, a—"

"An assassin-whore?" I was quite flattered that Death wanted me to share in his work. It could be a way to have me all to himself.

"I prefer the title 'New Life Escort'," he muttered, lowering his hood to the canvas. His brush stokes grew faster and faster, until he was painting at many times normal speed. His magic, demonstrated or promised, seemed to have a common and simple root principle.

"You increase things," I said.

"Yes. Understanding the basic thing is the hardest part. If you manage that, then you can enlarge a thing, or apply what you've learned to other properties like speed, intensity— "

"Parts of the body—" I interjected.

"No," he said, "the most interesting things happen when one increases pleasure itself, not any part or parts associated with it. But I should warn you that if you continue to expand your inquiries, this work may be a less accurate rendition than you might have hoped for."

I didn't interrupt again. I didn't want him to think like a young man painting a young woman. I'd never been able to separate youth and beauty from the cycle of anticipation, ecstasy, and revulsion I went through each time I offered my insides for sale. In my lust to live on in the only way I thought possible, to become a legend, I inflamed clients with my open, vulnerable, and mutable youth, the readiness with which I found, became, and revealed what they wanted. I withheld nothing that was asked of me, not even open-mouthed kisses, intimate secrets, brutal truths.

That was why they had to die.

When he'd finished and I stood so close to Death myself, I saw the struggles, frustrations and pains of my life painted across the canvas, burying my youth so deeply that only he and I could see it. I felt that even in nakedness, I could choose how close I wished to be to the viewer. Because of that, my likeness showed more warmth and desire in her expression than I could have imagined possible.

Before he could ask for payment in advance, I pried up a floorboard, undisturbed for many years, and drew out my bag of coins, some of which I'd placed over the eyes of my own clients before taking them back. I held the bag out to him.

He reached in, scooped up some coins, and slipped them away inside his robes with the hand of a practiced thief, accustomed to knowing their number and weight without looking.

"Keep the tip," he said, his voice growing more breathy and hoarse. "This has been, and will be, my pleasure."

It was like my first time. I'd all but forgotten what desire was, having felt it ebb for so many years. I rediscovered the wave of transformation that seemed to pass where a hand met my skin with intent to arouse. The skin not yet touched could never be the same as that in the wake of a hand or a tongue, yet it craved the ripple and shimmer that couldn't be sustained without consuming more and more of the untouched parts of me. I'd never forgotten that first ecstatic violation, and the nameless, ever-hungering thing it created within me. I'd fought and feared it all my life, and it sought new outlets as quickly as I contained it, poisoning all my once innocent pleasures until I withdrew and feared everyone and everything but that which now made love to me.

I struggle to record, now, a joy that may be too small for you to remember. You will no doubt come to know pleasure beyond anything I could imagine, pleasure like what he spoke of and I ignored, pleasure to which even dead flesh answers. There was magic in him, of course. He'd hidden the ritual steps of a spell among our preliminary posturings, and the spell gave me the mechanical responses of a younger body. Yet the pleasure my mind allowed me to feel for the first and last time couldn't have come without my aches and droops and wrinkles, and the freeing certainty that I could experience fully, desire completely, hold back nothing, and be consumed at last.

When I was satisfied and sleepy, with my arms around him, I pitied him the most. Someone with no qualms about killing would have done so at the climactic moment. I prompted him to pretend one last time.

"If I sleep now, will I wake in the next world?" I asked him. I'd looked for it myself, too many times, in the dying light of a client's eyes.

"You won't quite be there," he said, as kindly as possible. "You'll wake with everything you need to find the next world, or to make it yourself."

"If I find it, what will it be like?" I asked again.

"You'll be able to go where I go and do what I do. For companionship, you'll have all the people who ever lived to choose from, and all of them will be better than they were in their first lives. There'll be no fear of aging or death, and none of the evils caused by those fears. People will learn, trust, enjoy and love more than anyone you've ever known. They'll have everything that they've ever wanted or could have achieved given enough time, and they'll have all the time they ever wanted."

I wasn't quite satisfied with this. I couldn't see why such people would want to have anything to do with me. "Could I still visit this world?"

"Whenever you like, although the dying will usually resent you if they know what you are. You'll be more content than they, given time, and you should feel less need to leave a legacy or call attention to yourself, so you won't be immediately conspicuous. If sometimes you do wish to stand out, it's usually best to visit the dying at times steeped in mystery and superstition, when you're most likely to be considered a figment of the imagination, and to dress and behave as outrageously as possible. It's easy to be dismissed, actually. The dying can't comprehend the idea of seeing a truly live person, much less being one."

So, soothed by this promise of deniability, I fell asleep, imagining myself playing the part of a fairy on leave from the underworld, dancing around a fire beneath the stars.

As the old joke goes, I slept like a baby. I slept for two hours, and woke up screaming.

"Ah, you're awake," said Death. I heard the slap of his bare feet as he crossed the floor of the kitchen. He poked his hooded head through the doorway and then stepped into full view. One hand was pulled up into one sleeve of his robes, which was wrapped around the handle of my frying pan. The other held his scythe, which he was using to scramble some eggs. "You were out of bread, but I made a fresh loaf from a crumb I found under the table."

I was shackled to my bed. My surroundings hadn't changed at all. I was beside myself. It certainly wasn't the first time I, soon to be you, had fallen asleep after a job and awakened next to a corpse. It was the first time that I was the client and the corpse looked like me. My companion had made use of the mold as I slept, so that his client could leave the fake corpse in her place and begin her new life unobtrusively. Already the aged, fleshy duplicate bore little resemblance to the woman lying next to it. The living woman had been transformed by the pleasure that she had always thought of as deathlike, but which actually makes one younger, a pleasure whose effects had been magnified by magic which had passed to her, and which she already desired to pass on to others.

"I'm sorry about the restraints, but people can get very hostile when they realize that I'm not going to kill them," Death said. "I try to tell people that I actually bring them to life, but the part of them that could accept such an idea is underdeveloped. It's like individuals contain two selves, the 'I' or primary self they can see, and the buried, secondary 'you' which they can glimpse only in people the second self resembles. The first wants to take life and die, while the second wants to give life and live. In your case, the first always suppressed the second, but that's changing now."

His "underworld" was just a community of people who had to keep their eternal youth hidden from those who didn't share it. Physically, there was no next world, but there were next people, and I was turning into one. I'd been distracted because the experience had been big, not little. I hadn't realized that he was making me young rather than killing me. Too furious to speak, I wondered what services he'd actually provided, and looked for the bag of coins I'd held out to him.

"I took four coins, but I put them back again," he told me. "The choice of prices was just to determine your attitude toward your second self."

He'd taken four coins and delivered twice the service agreed upon. He'd emulated me, the infamous assassin-whore of decades past, the shadowy figure known as La Petit Mort, who was always paid twice and always gave the customer more than what was asked for.

"I'll stay with you while you become young again," he said, "and, if rejuvenation is the same as death to you, both of your selves will get what they wanted. I can't stop the transformation, but I'll help you in any other way I can. You won't start your new life alone."

He really had talked to my old clients; they'd been brought back to life. In a world of ageless and resurrected people, nothing I'd done or said could stay buried or mysterious, and all the deaths I'd caused would be of little consequence. The mystique that I'd built over so many years was gone from my mind in an instant.

I wanted to kill him for what he made me realize about myself. All my killings had been in vain, not just because my clients hadn't stayed dead, but because I never killed the person I wanted to kill the most. That person would be you, the version of myself that would give life rather than take it, the version that I could have been without the killing, the version that in spite of the killing seemed bound to emerge anyway. I hadn't wanted a child, half me and half victim, and I'd prevented any child of mine from ever being sired, even by Death. But you I hadn't seen, understood, or dared to consider possible. Even as I felt you taking over my body, your emergence seemed inconceivable to me. I cursed you blindly, ineffectively, and pathetically in the end, as I screamed at the increased strength in my muscles, the further firming of my breasts, and the fresh wetness between my legs. I told him to write these words to ever young you, my future, better, second self, the one I'd so perversely feared and hated all along. I dictated to pretend to myself that I could remain apart from you, safe from my own potential, to control and contain, one last time, the one I sought behind the eyes of everyone I ever killed.

●●●●●●●●●●●●●●●●●●●●●●●●●●●●●●●

Ivan Dorin is a third generation Albertan. He grew up in Bentley, Calgary, and Didsbury. His most 'Canadian' story was anthologized under five different titles containing the words 'Home', 'Alberta', 'Saskatchewan', or 'Canada'. His work has also appeared on CBC radio, and in *On Spec*, *GUD*, and *VOX*.

●●●●●●●●●●●●●●●●●●●●●●●●●●●●●●●

His One True Love
By Catherine MacLeod

Lorena Kirby checked the rearview mirror as she turned off the main road. She wouldn't have been surprised if someone had followed her from the graveyard, but no, there was no one back there. She supposed at this hour — and the funeral really *had* been held too early for decency — most of the neighbours were either at work or still at the church talking about her.

She'd caused a minor scandal by driving herself, but at least the talk would keep the mourners entertained. George had been disagreeable for the whole of their marriage, and downright miserable for the three years of his illness. She didn't want him back any more than she wanted to be stuck at the church until someone else said she could leave.

She pulled up to her driveway as the mail truck stopped across the road.

"Morning, Henry."

"Morning, Lori. How are you?"

"I've been better."

"No doubt." She liked Henry, always had. He left the mail every morning at ten, worked his way up the road, drove back at three like clockwork. He was the steadiest person she knew in this town. She especially liked him for not offering his condolences. She'd had four days of it, and it was getting old fast.

"Is there anything you need?" he said.

She drew breath to answer and yelped as a bluejay screamed above her. She squinted up into the tree as it shrieked three times.

"Calling for its mate," Henry said.

"Is that what it is?"

"Yup. Bluejay doesn't let anything get between him and his one true love. He shouldn't be here, though — you mostly don't see them on Friday." She saw him start to say more, and catch himself. He looked embarrassed.

"Is this another one of your superstitions?" she asked.

"Bluejays pick up ghosts. Friday is the day they carry them to the afterlife."

"Right, I remember hearing my mother say that once." Of course, she'd also said she was happy, and Lorena didn't believe that, either, any more than she believed the local folklore. "Don't you ever hear any cheerful superstitions?"

"Not about bluejays," he said. "I know you don't like birds. I guess this doesn't help."

"It's okay." She took the sympathy cards and stepped back from the truck.

"You need me, you know where I am."

"Thanks, Henry."

She waited until he was out of sight, then, for the first time in she-forgot-how-many years, pulled the wooden gate across the end of the driveway. She hadn't invited anyone back to the house — another breach of etiquette — but there were always a few who were selectively deaf, and she wanted to be alone. She drove around the back of the old house, parking where the car wouldn't be seen from the road.

She leaned against the hood, dropping the keys in her pocket, listening to the leaves chatter. It was a lovely morning, really. She'd imagined the day they buried George would be different somehow, but it was just like any other.

Still, there was something she'd wanted to do for years, and a day like any other was as good a time as any.

Around the house, every fifteen feet, were wooden poles hung with ornate birdhouses. Building them had been George's hobby. She hated them. Two or three she could've lived with, maybe, but not all these. The poles tore up the lawn; the hangers squeaked in the wind. Worse, she had a fear of birds. Ornithiphobia, it was called. A mild case, her mother always explained anxiously. Manageable. Her daughter didn't have heart flutters or panic attacks, or any such nonsense; she was simply a very sensitive girl.

"Freak," Lorena's father muttered under his breath, still loud enough for her to hear. She knew he wasn't just talking about her phobia. She lived with his disgust like she did with her fear of birds — as well as she could. She'd gone to school with George, and he knew about both.

And when they married, he ringed their home with birdhouses to keep her inside.

Just touching them was hard, but Lorena took them down and hurled them into the woods.

She unlocked the porch door and jumped as a bluejay flew over her head. The same one? She thought so as it shrieked three times, calling for its mate. She took her sweater off and waved it to shoo it out, but it hopped into the rafters and settled down. She left the door open so it could fly out on its own.

It screamed again as she went inside.

She dropped her sweater in the kitchen, her shoes on the stairs, her black dress on the bedroom floor. She set her purse on George's bureau and studied her reflection in the mirror. There were dark circles under her green eyes. They'd been there so long she wondered if they could be permanent, like tattoos. She hadn't been in the bedroom since George died, not from superstition, but because she'd spent too much time here already. His painkillers were still on the nightstand, his pajamas under the pillow. The warm, jaundiced smell of him lingered.

There was something else she'd wanted to do for years. She took off her wedding ring.

Lorena stripped to her underwear and padded down the hall to the guestroom. She smiled gratefully as she slid between clean sheets and thought there might not be enough sleep in the whole world for her. But she'd take what she could get.

As she drifted off, she heard the bluejay scream in the porch and recalled the old saying, *A bird in the house means a death in the house.*

Too late for that, she thought, and slept.

⊱•⊰•⊱•⊰

She woke an hour later and wept. These past three years, she hadn't slept more than an hour at a time — it seemed as if George was always wanting something. She wondered if what he'd really wanted was to keep her close. He could've just said so, couldn't he?

Well, no, apparently not.

She'd hoped now that she had time to sleep she would, but apparently old habits were going to die even harder than George.

"Once more with feeling," she mumbled, and got up. Her ballet teacher always said that when Lorena missed a step, and it stuck.

The quiet was exquisite. No coughs or moans, no tasks invented to keep her running. No need to pretend she didn't resent him taking her care as only his due, not even worth a thank-you.

But then, she couldn't remember the last time he'd said please, either.

She leaned her forehead against the window and watched the wind sway the trees. As a girl she'd wished she could be so graceful.

Whaack! Whaack! Whaack!

She skipped back as the bluejay hit the glass in front of her face. It couldn't get in, she told herself, and retreated anyway, trembling.

God, she hated birds. She guessed even if she *had* become a ballerina she wouldn't have been dancing any swans.

She went downstairs, stepped into her shoes, and went out to the porch. She thought about putting something on over her underwear, and didn't. It was her house, now; she could do what she liked. The jay was back in the rafters. She eyed it warily. It returned the look. It wasn't so frightening when she knew it was there, but she hated surprises.

She went through the porch into George's built-on workshop and confronted the junk-half-finished furniture covered in tarps like sheetified ghosts, tools rusted with disuse, blueprints yellow and curled at the corners. He never got rid of anything. If it was ever his, it was always his, and he kept it close. The walls were covered in bird-houses. It was almost too bad she wouldn't be here come winter; she'd have enjoyed stuffing them in the stove. The place was filthy — he didn't clean, and he didn't allow her out here.

There were a lot of things he didn't allow her. She thought she'd spent her whole life in this house, just hoping to get out of it alive.

She kicked his workbench over with a satisfying crash. *Take that.* A pot of old nails went flying. A cloud of dust puffed up like something poisonous.

Whaacck! The bluejay dropped through the smog, its wing brushing her face. Lorena did a startled *pas de chat* and ran for the kitchen door.

A sharp pain in her ankle tripped her on the steps. Then she was inside, the bird beating against the window. When she smacked her hand on the glass, it flew off.

A line of blood dripped into her shoe. Probably a nail sticking out somewhere — what a mess out there. It was a wonder George hadn't blundered over something and broken his neck.

Lorena snorted softly. It would've been a kinder way for him to go. And it would've saved them both some time.

❖❖❖

That afternoon the phone rang forever. She let the messages go to voice mail.

"Lori, it's Jane, call if there's anything I can do."

"Lori, it's Paul, call if there's anything I can do."

"Lori, it's Anne, call if—"

She turned the phone off. The fridge was full of casse-roles and dainty sandwiches brought by the neighbours. She brewed a pot of coffee, sniffing the aroma like perfume. She hadn't made it in the last year; the smell sickened

George, or so he said. It was easier to do without than listen to him complain.

The bluejay screamed as she ate asparagus rolls and chicken salad. A bird in the house, a death in the house. Could you die from having your nerves rubbed raw? She doubted it; she would've died long ago.

Tomorrow, she'd have to deal with the world again. There'd be insurance forms to sign and thank-you cards to mail. There'd be tiresome conversations with friends who meant well and well-wishers who didn't. And banking, which she would've preferred to do today. But no — until she could sell the house, she still had to live with these people, and to some extent it mattered what they thought about her.

"Poor George not cold in the ground, and her marching into the bank demanding his money. Plain to be seen what *she* cares about."

It was true, but she didn't need the ill will. Tomorrow was time enough. Today she'd finish putting George to rest. She ate her last sandwich, put her favourite plate in the sink, and dropped his in the trash. His favourite dish, mug, and glass followed. He might be with her forever, but it was time for him to back off.

She took a handful of garbage bags upstairs, emptied his closet into four, and his bureau into two more. His pills went down the toilet like toxic confetti. The jay screamed three times in the porch, another selfish creature forever wanting its mate. She didn't believe in ghosts, but it sure acted like George. She tied the bags shut, dragged them to the head of the stairs, and rolled them down.

During those last months at his bedside, she'd made lists, organizing, preparing for freedom if, oh God please, it ever came. When he ranted at her for neglecting him, not even pretending she cared, she replied, "It's just a grocery list," or "I'm sorting out my recipe box."

She'd written, *Put clothes out for pickup. Buy garbage bags. Write thank-yous for cards and food. Funeral — black dress w/ grey sweater. Pearl earrings. Polish shoes. Buy black pantyhose.*

She'd started asking for her groceries in boxes instead of bags. She'd stacked them outside George's workshop and wrote, *Sell tools.* Some of them, she saw now, weren't worth selling. Maybe she should just call the garbage collector to make a special trip.

The bird screamed again. Maybe it was angry because she'd thrown out the bird houses, she thought, and shrugged. She wouldn't miss George pounding away out there, tracking sawdust into the house and yelling at her when she offered to sweep it out of his workshop. It was *his* place and she could damn well stay out of it. She didn't see him in her sewing room, did she?

No, but she knew he would've made a point of going in if she'd asked him not to.

There'd been a time when he was civil enough, back when auditions were few and paying jobs fewer, when her father was making noise about her so-called dance career not paying the bills and why was she still living at home at her age?

At twenty-three she was supposed to be married and someone else's problem.

She wanted to move to the city, someplace she'd fit in and make friends, because she never had here. Where did some girl from the sticks get off, thinking she could become a ballerina? Dreams weren't a big commodity in these parts. Finally she realized she wasn't going to get out of town without help, and that wasn't going to happen. She was on her own, flailing.

George's parents were dead. He had their house. He had a job, and Lorena knew he'd never quit — as a child he'd gone hungry too often to risk it again. She wasn't surprised when he proposed; she knew the boys were looking. She read too much, but she could cook. Except for her crazy ambitions, she wasn't too wild.

She wanted out of her father's house. She didn't mind working, but damned if she'd give him the money. She remembered hearing him curse her mother out once, and finding her in the kitchen later, still crying as she laughed.

"What's so funny?"

"Nothing."

"Then why are you laughing?"

"Oh, Lori, what else am I supposed to do?"

Lori pondered that for a week and then married George. What else was she supposed to do? Others had asked her; she was never sure why she chose him. Maybe because he was clean about himself, or because his eyes were the same colour as hers. She didn't wonder about it when she had her own house to run. She was glad he didn't expect her to socialize. She didn't see the birdhouses coming, but at least he got her out of her father's house.

She tried to remember that when he railed at her from his bed. She was uncaring, he said. Unthinking, insensitive. He brought up the one time she'd gone to an audition after they'd married, and Lorena wrote, *Life insurance. Empty bank account.*

She bathed him and dressed him in clean pajamas. When she washed his face, he tried to bite her. His doctor said the illness was affecting his mind. But he was still wily enough to hide his bankbook. She found it anyway.

He has money hidden — where?

How much there might be she couldn't imagine. He'd earned a good wage all those years with the trucking company, but there was less in the bank than there should be. He wasn't one to drink or play cards, and with the amount of time he spent home vexing her there couldn't have been another woman. He was reasonable about household expenses, and they ate well, but Lorena went without a lot. The dance lessons went first.

She put the garbage bags against the workshop door and waited to feel something. She didn't. George had been there when she'd needed him, once. She hadn't expected him to love her. She did expect he'd be kind.

But they hadn't even danced at their wedding.

⇥·I·I·I·⇤

Lorena sipped sweet coffee and watched the day. The sunlight was pale, pale gold, the color of almost-autumn, the sky even bluer than that fiend in the porch.

She was starting to feel the change of season and pressed her hand to the small of her back. She did a deep *plie* to work out the kinks, and froze, mid-stretch.

He has money hidden — where?

Where was the one place she wasn't allowed to go?

His workshop. It would be just like him to stash it in the birdhouses. Or no, he wouldn't put it someplace the mice could get in. There were glass jars of nuts and bolts, his metal tool box, thick plastic storage crates stacked against the far wall. Any of those would be safe.

"Oh, George." No wonder he had so many unfinished projects; he was too busy communing with his money. He wasn't a *bad* man, not really. But he was scared and angry and weak, and that was bad enough if you had to live with it.

What would be considered a decent mourning period for a woman who wasn't mourning? she wondered. She'd already had an offer on the property, some tourist wanting a summerhouse. It was almost what she'd hoped for. Just enough to get out. But she'd spent half her life wanting more than just enough. With George's money, she could have a small city apartment and the occasional evening out; time to watch those old movies she liked — and dance classes. She wasn't going to be a ballerina now, but she liked the look of ballroom, and she still had some moves.

If there wasn't another offer on the house in the next week she'd take this one anyway. She couldn't think of anyone she'd miss except Henry.

She slipped into her sweater, knotting the belt as the phone rang again. She waited a moment, then checked the voice mail.

"Lori, it's Marion, call if there's anything I can do."

She supposed the callers meant well, but today was the first time any of them had ever offered to help her with *anything*.

She shoved the phone in her pocket and toed the door shut behind her. She didn't see the bird. Maybe he'd finally flown off.

It was a clever hiding place, in a way — if someone broke in, they'd think there was nothing worth stealing. She considered the shelves under the shop window. They were lined two and three deep, glass jars and plastic tubs full of nuts and bolts, screws and brads. If pickled mice had been in them, she wouldn't have been surprised; she didn't know half of what George did out here. She set a cardboard box on a backless chair and started opening jars, dumping them slowly. She hit paydirt on the third try. In the bottom of the jar, folded neatly and covered by metal washers, was a plastic sandwich bag full of fifty-dollar bills. Two thousand dollars or so, she judged.

There was more in the other jars, mostly fifties and hundreds. What would George ever have done with it? Not travel, she knew. Not dress better. Certainly not spend it on her. Likely keep it just to know it was there. He was always so scared of having to do without. But she never would have allowed that to happen; she could still work. She would've taken care of him like she promised and he expected. She was the bastard's wife, after all, even if neither of them was happy about it.

She pulled another bag of hundreds out of a mason jar. If George hadn't already been dead, this would've killed him. Or at least he'd have been more cantankerous than usual. Too bad — the money was hers now.

The pain was as sharp as it was unexpected.

Lorena dropped the jar as the bluejay's claws slashed her face. Glass shards rained up from the floor. Roofing nails and money went flying. She whirled as the bird bounced off the back of her head, raking her neck. She swatted at it, covering her head with her arms.

Whaacck! A claw sliced her hand, and blood ran from her torn cheek into her mouth as she screamed.

The jay screamed back three times, demanding to be given his one true love.

⇥⊹⊹⊹⇤

Lorena spit blood into the sink as the bluejay rattled the kitchen window. She picked a glass splinter out of her cheek and another out of her forearm. *Stupid bird. Stupid, miserable* — oh, she couldn't get out of here fast enough. Just take the money and run.

But taking the money was the problem, wasn't it? And she did want it. There was great comfort in knowing she didn't have to settle for another life of just enough.

A hot shower washed away the dirt, revealing more cuts and punctures than she'd realized.

Okay, she wasn't beaten, just slowed down. Eventually the bluejay would get hungry and leave the porch. She'd out-waited George. She could out-wait the bird.

Even so, it galled her to wait at all. Hadn't she already done her time? All these years, life could have been easier if he'd pried open his wallet once in a while.

But if it was ever his, it was always his, and he kept it close.

Not me. Not anymore.

The bird was still fluttering at the kitchen window. Whaack! Whaack! Whaack!

Bluejay doesn't let anything get between him and his one true love. Well, if it was calling for its mate, it had a lot in common with George. She remembered two weeks back, the day he'd rained terror on the nurse she'd hired. He knew where Lorena had gone, what errands she had to run, and when she'd be back — but she was supposed to be *here*. The poor nurse was almost running when she got to the door.

That was the day Lorena got the padlock keys copied. She didn't count on being able to get them after he died; she figured he'd find a way to flush them first. She sneaked them off his nightstand in a handful of dirty tissues. Now that she thought about it, their absence could've been his reason for terrorizing the nurse.

She "found" the keys under the magazines he'd knocked on the floor.

"Hey, look what you dropped," she said, setting them on the stand.

"Well, isn't *that* just a kick in the head?" he gasped.

"Yup. You want your pill now?"

Poor George, always calling for his mate. Forever hoarding his one true love. He'd tried to keep them both hidden away, like something sealed under glass.

But glass shatters, Lorena thought. She wouldn't. She *wouldn't*.

❖❖❖

She opened the door a crack. She didn't see the bird, which didn't mean it was gone. But there was no rush of spiky feathers, at least.

She found George's old corn broom and swept the spilled nails under the bench. She sorted delicately through the broken glass, fishing out loose money and finding several more bags. She rolled the money up in a scrap of burlap and shoved it inside her sweater.

There was forty thousand, give or take. She picked up the last bottle, a jelly jar amazingly unbroken. Through a sprinkling of carpet tacks she could see more hundreds. Her eyes filled with tears.

It was more than enough.

Whaaacck!

She stumbled over a paint can as the bluejay dive-bombed her. She grabbed the top shelf for support and heard the old wood snap. She screamed as she fell forward over the chair, pulling the box of nails with her. Old ice cream tubs fell off the shelf, their contents lethal hail. She barely knew which was worse, hardware cutting new orifices or the jay coming at her again.

Getting to her feet was more than misery. The bird flew at her face, slashing her arms as she covered it. She slapped at it, getting bloody pecks for her trouble. She tripped back a step, and felt the gash across her calf as she hit George's old band saw. She turned and lurched for the porch.

Whaaacck!

It was right in front of her. She ducked, grabbing the first thing she touched. She hefted the jar full of hundreds and pitched blindly. She didn't look back as glass shattered. She staggered into the house and slumped against the door.

Whaaacck!

She spun. The bird was inches from her face. She struck out, connecting hard enough to drive it against the wall. It fell to the floor, dazed, ruffling through the remains of the jelly jar and the smashed kitchen window.

She could already feel little bones crunching under her shoes, smell feathers singeing in the stove. She lifted her foot, and hesitated just a second, squeamish at the thought of handling it.

The jay pecked her ankle. She yanked her foot back, then caught herself and kicked at it.

She kicked empty air. The jay was up, sailing over the stove into the diningroom. Lorena grabbed the broom and limped after it. She knocked it off the top of the china cabinet, swiping down her mother's china tea service. She swung as it skimmed the front window, tearing down the lace sheers she'd sewn by hand.

In a moment, the room was a shambles, and the broom handle was too slippery to hold. Her hands were too bloody. She broke and ran, the jay shrieking as she reeled upstairs, falling into the first room with a door. She sprawled on the floor, listening to the sinister brush of feathers on the other side.

✢✦✦✢

It was George's room, and wasn't *that* just a kick in the head? Carpet tacks trickled through her hair. There were nails in her back. Blood soaked through her sweater, sticking it to her stomach. She decided not to look inside.

Her mouth was dry. She felt sick. There was a brass screw nailing her shoe to her foot, and another gouge down the side of her leg. She thought there was a finishing nail stuck in there somewhere.

She shook her head. It hurt. Going into the workshop in bare legs wasn't the dumbest thing she'd ever done, but she ranked it in the top ten. The world was starting to feel distant. She didn't want to go into shock; she was scared she wouldn't come back. Her fingertips were studded with tacks. They snagged as she put her hand in her pocket. The phone was gone. The keys weren't there.

She thought for a minute. It wasn't easy. The phone was most likely out in the workshop, and she wasn't going back after it. Keys in the workshop, too? Maybe. Or maybe they fell out when she tried to shoo the bluejay away.

Stupid bird.

The clock on George's bureau said 2:21. Dear God, had the funeral really only been five hours ago? She thought it would be later. She thought it would be peaceful.

She thought about Henry.

If she could get to the road by three, Henry would take her to the hospital.

Her funeral dress was puddled on the floor beside her. She didn't think she could get her sweater off to put it on. She closed her mouth over her fingers, tugging the tacks out with her teeth, biting down to numb the pain.

The bluejay was still scraping the door.

She rummaged George's alcohol off the bureau and sloshed it over her cuts, screaming through her teeth. She pulled her purse down and looped the strap around her neck. She had the money. She had bank books and ID and everything that would let her just keep going once she left the hospital. She never wanted to come back. The new owners could worry about the local wildlife. Let them clean up the battlefield.

It all came down to this — one last stand in the bedroom she'd spent her whole marriage wanting out of. The day they buried George was indeed a day like any other — she was just trying to get out of here alive.

The notion made her laugh, a sound that startled her as much as it did the suddenly-silent thing in the hall. Really, what else was she supposed to do?

Once more with feeling, Lorena thought. And opened the door.

● ●

Nova Scotian Catherine MacLeod actually likes birds. Her publications include short fiction in *On Spec*, *Solaris*, *TaleBones* and several anthologies, including *Tesseracts 6*. She's currently watching *30 Days of Night* five minutes at a time.

● ●

Eurydice in the World of Light

by Andrea Schlecht

I did not look back.

Several times I was almost overpowered by temptation. I heard the crunch of my footsteps as I walked over the ashes and shards of hell's pathways, my fingers dancing on the taut lyre-strings. But I heard no footsteps behind me.

She is light of step, I thought.

I stopped suddenly and paused in my music. I listened for that one footstep that would continue after my sandaled feet came to a halt.

She is not following me. The gods play cruel games.

But a small kernel of my hope remained, and I did not look back. I played my lyre as never before, summoning all my grief and hope and longing into the dance of my fingers. The notes echoed from the damp cavern walls with a singular beauty of sound, sound that only the gods and I can make.

A sickly spirit, no more than faint spots of luminosity arranged in a human shape, walked beside me for a time. Or floated, rather. The shape — of a huge, broad-shouldered warrior — dissolved to nothingness below the waist, and his footsteps, if such there were, remained silent.

Eurydice is one of these yet, I thought, and when we reach the surface, she will become fully as before.

Or will she? Will she perhaps remain with no more substance than a wisp of smoke to haunt my days and nights, and wring my heart until it turns to stone? The gods play cruel games.

I passed — I could not say *we* passed — skulls and bones and bits of pottery and metal, the debris of the dead. My music drew more of the spirit things. They drifted in complete silence, weak glimmers of sorrowful aspect, sometimes only for a few heartbeats, before Death's realm pulled them back into its bowels. One spirit hovered over a broken skull and shed drops of dim light on the bleached bones.

A low heap of sludge lay in my path, smelling foully of sulphur. I stepped around it, and then turned my head to one side. In the lurid hell-light, I saw crudely engraved figures — of animals, of warriors — in the rock of the cavern wall. Patches of slime lent them a garish colour. Rivulets of water dripped over them into stinking, stagnant pools.

I stopped that turn of the head before it was too late.

On the other side of the heap, after a bend in the tunnel, I saw a new kind of light. Sunlight from the reaches of the upper world. True light.

Soon, I thought, soon I will be able to look over my shoulder and then what trick of the gods will I see?

I did not dare hope with all my heart and soul.

The true light grew brighter. In a moment I felt its warmth. Hell's mouth, agape, framed a patch of blue sky with a curl of cloud, a tiny sail, traversing it, and the green tops of slim poplar trees against that perfect blue. In another moment, I heard the whispers of the poplar leaves.

The temptation was at its greatest then. How I wanted to turn around and say, "Look, Eurydice, do you see it? Do you see the sky?"

But I held firm.

When my feet touched grass, I took several more steps beyond hell's mouth to leave no doubt that I had observed all the conditions. Then—

"Eurydice," I said, still facing the poplars.

"I am here, Orpheus."

And it was her voice, close to my ear. She was free of hell.

At last, I turned around.

It was indeed Eurydice. Her skin, young smooth skin. Her hair, long lustrous hair. Her form, her beautiful, graceful form. The lights of heaven shone in her eyes.

When I took her in my arms, *her* arms coiled around my neck. We kissed. My lyre lay forgotten in the grass.

A faint sulphurous smell reached my nostrils. Perhaps a speck of the foul-smelling sludge we had passed clung to the shrouds that still clothed her.

❖❘❖❘❖❘❖

We went home to our cottage. Eurydice ran from room to room to see if all was as she had left it, then out into the garden where she hurried from bush to tree to flower, her shrouds billowing behind her. I captured her in the grass as one would a delicate butterfly.

An unfathomed time later, she emerged from my love as if from a gentle dream and turned her thoughts to our little plot of land. "The vegetable patch is overgrown with weeds," she said. "I can't even see the chickpeas."

I had not entered the garden since the day I lost her. "We'll tidy it up tomorrow," I told her.

But she insisted that we make a start before the close of day, and we worked until the chickpeas and leeks were clear of weeds.

In the evening, she inspected the pomegranate tree near our cottage, and frowned. "This tree is diseased." She ran her hands over the bark.

I had not looked at it closely since the year before. There were now black discolourations on the trunk, and a fungal growth had taken root in a gap near the base. Decay was consuming the trunk. The little tree, however, was decked in blood-red blossoms.

"This tree isn't so old," I said, "but I can see that its end is near. Let it bear fruit one more time. Then I'll cut it down."

❖❘❖❘❖❘❖

So our life together resumed.

The world was in its springtime, as was Eurydice. Her smiles held love and promise and happiness. Every day I prayed to Apollo and thanked him for his rare gifts.

Eurydice gave her garden the closest attention, having been cruelly parted from it in the early spring, and it flourished. She treated me with the same care to small things, with always a squeeze of the hand while we took our meals, a pause in household duties for kisses, and her head lay on my shoulder during the day's last light.

Yet all was not as before.

The night the summer heat took hold of our valley, I woke with a start and felt a coldness in the room. I touched Eurydice. Cold as stone. She stirred slightly and said something soft and sweet-sounding and incoherent.

The next morning her skin was warm, her love for me undiminished. The shock of her death is still with me, I concluded. My mind is overwrought.

I did not always come to such a conclusion.

That summer, the blooms on Eurydice's flowers were the biggest I had ever seen. One evening she did not hear me coming up behind her as she picked an armful of lilies. She straightened suddenly, startled. Then her smile surfaced.

I knit my brows. Hints of slyness darted around that smile, strange twitches in the corners of her mouth.

That look remained before my mind's eye, causing me to wake several times in the night. A faint but distinct smell of decay rose from the pillow next to mine. I imagined some infected flesh inside Eurydice, some token of hell, slowly spreading.

She seemed unaware of any contamination and sang to the next dawn with notes that birds might envy.

I never doubted that this was my Eurydice. It could be no one else.

While playing the lyre in praise of Apollo, I glanced up and saw Eurydice under the dying pomegranate tree, inspecting what were to be its last fruits. She cherished them all the more for being the last, and brushed the unripe pomegranates against her cheeks.

But Death had left its mark on her, and my dark dreams multiplied.

During the full moon at the height of the summer, a shaft of moonlight fell on a fleshless skull in my bed, fell on huge hollows in the place of eyes.

The fever in my mind did not abate with time but raged all the more as those summer days unfolded. Eurydice had been in Death's hands once. She was tainted.

Irrevocably.

Tainted.

When I kissed her uncontrollably on those summer nights, I knew that I sucked disease and death from her lips, sucked them into my own body. I rutted blindly with release but no joy.

Still, she left beauty wherever she went. I often admired the huge flowers she cultivated that season. I sat in the grass and gazed at them in the setting sun to watch their petals close by imperceptible degrees.

At intervals, I played slow evening tunes on my lyre, and a small flock of birds came to listen and peck at the grass. A deer with a fawn at its side emerged from the trees; they stood and listened mere steps from me, mere steps from the birds, and the instinctual animal fears of one another were cast aside.

The back door of the cottage flew open. Eurydice stepped out. For the first time within memory, I struck a false note on the lyre. The birds took flight. The deer fled to the trees.

She no longer belonged in the upper world.

I became afraid to eat the meals Eurydice set before me. She remarked with concern on my loss of appetite. And sleep came seldom to me as that summer entered its final moon.

Why did I not look back?

We harvested the pomegranates from the sickly tree when they were ripe. Not many, of course. A number of branches were dead. But we did fill two baskets.

Afterwards, I went to the grindstone and spent a long time sharpening the axe.

From the garden, I picked gladioli for our bedside. I noticed that grubs had established themselves among the flowers, eating through the lower leaves.

That night, I saw Eurydice rise from our bed in the darkest hour. Careful not to knock over the gladioli, she flung a light cloak over her shoulders, slipped out and danced in the moonlight, her nimble form silhouetted against a red-gold, horizon-grazing moon.

She is embracing the darkness, she longs to return to its realm — I can see it in her dance, I thought.

It was no dream. I swear that it was no dream.

She carries Death inside her like a child, a piece of carrion awaiting its gestation. But she will never lose her beauty.

The gods play cruel games.

As soon as the sun rose, I took the axe to the grindstone one more time and spent the first light of the day honing its edge. Warm drops, my tears, fell on my hands as I worked.

When done, I slid a finger over the edge. It was not quite sharp enough, and I found a whetstone for it. Eurydice remained in our bed as I slowly applied the whetstone to the bronze axehead.

She sleeps by day and wakes by night.

My tears flowed unceasingly.

When I had honed the edge until it was the thinnest and finest I had ever seen, I ran my finger over it once again. A line of blood appeared.

It was sharp enough.

● ●

Andrea Schlecht was born in Germany, but grew up in Hamilton, Ontario. She later moved to Ottawa with her husband where they raised a family. She has now retired early from her day job as an archivist — but not from writing. Her stories and poems have appeared in *Realms of Fantasy, Prairie Fire, Dreams and Nightmares, Bywords* and other magazines, both genre and literary.

● ●

Bed of Scorpions
by Silvia Moreno-Garcia

The maid brushed the two scorpions off the bed and crushed them under the heavy heel of her shoe when they fell to the floor.

"You have to check the bed every morning," the maid said. "Check your boots. They tend to get in there too. And give a good shake to your clothes. The dangerous scorpions are not the black ones. The pale ones are the ones you can miss if you're too hasty."

Beatriz stared at the white sheets.

"Have a good night."

The maid closed the door, and Beatriz was alone. She approached the large bed in the centre of the room very slowly. She peeked under the covers, afraid the maid had missed an arachnid.

Beatriz went to sleep fearing she would wake up to the sharp sting of the scorpion.

⊹┊⊹┊⊹

Beatriz rose early and found Ramon in the dining room. He seemed happy and untroubled, picking at some eggs. A shaggy, ugly dog roamed around the table. It made her nervous.

"Good morning. You want some chocolate? I can recommend it. But stay away from the solids. The cook has no talent and the..."

"I thought he'd be here this morning."

Ramon shrugged and lifted his fork. A piece of egg fell to the ground, and the dog gobbled it up.

"It's rude."

"There's plenty of time to meet and greet."

"Well, of course. Why should you care?"

"Beatriz, don't start with that. It'll spoil breakfast. Sit down."

"He didn't send an automobile like he promised, and the house is old and ugly and shabby, and there are scorpions in the beds."

"Fine," Ramon said, his hands falling on the table, making the cutlery rattle. "We'll get on the train and to hell with everything. We spent all that time and money for nothing. All those dresses and hats and now we're back worse than where we started."

She didn't tell him they were always worse off. They would swindle and cheat and steal, but money evaporated from their hands, and then it was time to start over again.

Beatriz bit her lip and was silent.

"Come on, sit."

"I'm not hungry."

"Beatriz," he began.

She did not pause for his apology.

✦•✦•✦•✦

In Mexico City, they had a little courtyard with pretty potted flowers, a fountain and canaries in their cages. But that was long ago and far away. In Durango, there was nothing. Or rather, there was a sea of weeds growing as high as her knee all around the property and insects buzzing next to her ear. A dirt trail led her towards some trees and a makeshift family cemetery with small headstones.

From there, she could get a good look at the two-storey house which seemed more unattractive in the morning light than the previous evening when they had arrived. This is not, she decided, a proper hacienda.

Her childish fantasies had conjured a magnificent mansion at the height of fashion with Parisian furnishings and a handsome husband. She ought to have known better.

Movement in the grass startled Beatriz. Looking closer, she saw a huge snake scurrying behind a tombstone. She rushed into the house and sat in her room all day long.

⊹⊶⊱⊶⊰⊶⊰

She heard him slip under the covers, but she did not turn around, her eyes fixed on the wall.

"You're still angry?"

She felt his breath against her neck and did not move, her body coiled tight.

"Come on. Don't be mad. Don't you want to...?"

"No."

"Beatriz."

"We are in his house."

"And so what? I don't care."

"No."

Ramon fell back with a heavy sigh.

"You are insufferable."

"Leave me alone."

"Beatriz, look at me."

"I want to be alone."

She turned and stared at Ramon, but he only shrugged in the way he always did, dismissing her words. She'd found his constant shrugs charming when they were younger.

"Come, kiss me," he said.

She did, and then bit his lips so hard they bled.

When he buried his face against the crook of her neck, Beatriz stared at the ceiling and wondered if scorpions would fall upon them, like the maid said they sometimes did. She thought they might blanket their bodies during the night, and when dawn arrived, they would be dead.

But in the morning she still lived, and Ramon was gone.

⊹⊶⊱⊶⊰⊶⊰

The next day, they ate mole, and the chicken was dry and unsavoury. After the meal, the maid said that Mr. Villanueva was still sick and would not come downstairs. As a result, Ramon and Beatriz sat in the lounge by themselves and whispered to each other.

"He'll be dead in six months," Ramon muttered.

"You think so?"

"I hope so. He's thin as a stick. At least he was when I met him at The Victoria. He never got up before noon, and when he did, he was cold or burning hot all the time, and his hands shook."

"But it's not contagious."

"I told you, no. Something in his blood."

"But what if..."

"It's fine. Don't worry. Go around the house and see if there's any interesting stuff."

She did worry. She was supposed to marry that sick man. But Ramon had concluded their conversation. He unfolded the same paper he had carried under his arm during the train ride and pretended to read it.

Beatriz left the lounge. She wandered through the hallways, noticing cracks on the chequered azulejos. Finally, she slipped into what the maid described as the library. It was disappointingly small. She didn't see any "interesting" stuff, which meant anything worth pocketing. If Villanueva proved to be more difficult than Ramon had anticipated, they could steal some items to justify their trip.

She glanced at the paintings on the walls, her hands brushing the spines of the books.

They had a great library once. In a corner, there had been a large terrestrial globe, and Ramon and Beatriz used to spin it and giggle, and their fingers would fall randomly over the places in the world they would visit. But their father had been a gambler and a fool, and now they would never go anywhere.

She turned away from the books.

Something on a desk caught her eye.

It was a mechanical bird. It had glass wings and bright glass eyes and sat in a golden cage. When she wound it up, it began to sing, moving its tail and beak. The bird turned its head, stared at Beatriz and fell silent. The melody had concluded.

"Do you like it?"

She turned, knowing it must be him. The groom Ramon had picked for her. Some naïve fellow to marry and cheat.

He had black hair, dark eyes and a plain face. He was younger than she had expected. Very young. Perhaps twenty to her eighteen years.

"It's extremely pretty," she replied.

"It belonged to my mother. It sings twenty-five different melodies."

He walked towards her, leaning on a black cane and limping slightly.

"I'm Justiniano Villanueva."

The limp, like his age, was a surprise. Her brother had said her groom was a fine gentleman, but he had not mentioned much else. Neither Villanueva nor his clothes looked very fine, though. Still, she smiled.

›•]•]•]•‹

She changed into the blue dress with the floral accents and the mother of pearl buttons, the nicest and newest one she had. The seamstress had assured her it was the style they were wearing in France. If she married Villanueva, Ramon had promised her, they would go to France, and there she would be a great lady in silks and diamonds.

For now France was a vague dream, far from the ugly little house and its shabby lounge where they congregated. Villanueva's mongrel dog sat by his feet, and the clockwork bird, now dusted for them to admire, played a short melody.

"I'm sorry I couldn't come down earlier. I was indisposed."

"We understand."

Beatriz sat quietly as they spoke. She wondered what Ramon might have told Villanueva when they first met. She tried to picture him speaking his business talk, all fake deals and imaginary tales, and then in the midst of it leaning forward and saying, very casually of course, how he happened to have a sister.

"How do you like it? I know it's not as grand as The Victoria."

"I find it charming."

A beautiful sister who played the piano very well. A sister of marriageable age. Then some other bits of conversation, all steering him in the right direction: their father had died recently, Beatriz was very sad, Ramon worried that his business kept him away from Beatriz, she was all alone in that big house. And Villanueva probably leaned forward and wondered if both of them might not like to pay him a visit during the summer.

"Well, hopefully you're not too bored. It's a quiet house."

"We enjoy quiet, don't we?"

A trap, of course. Calculated. They had played that game before. But it had been the opposite way around: it was Ramon who married or promised marriage.

"Yes," Beatriz said, monosyllables the only form of communication she could manage at the moment.

The bird stopped playing the melody, but Villanueva did not wind it up again.

⇢⊹⊹⊹⇠

Later, hidden in the sea of grass, Ramon and Beatriz sat together.

"Do you remember all those years I spent learning how to play the piano?" she asked. "Father said I simply had to learn that. Look now, there's no piano."

She pulled bits of grass and let them fall onto the ground.

"It scares me," she said finally.

"What?"

"That he's dying."

"Who cares?"

She turned to look at him.

"He's filthy rich, you know," Ramon said as he smoked a cigarette. Normally he wore gloves to avoid staining his fingers, but he had foregone such formalities in this remote corner of the state.

"I don't want to marry him."

"I said he was rich."

"Maybe he will not want to marry me."

"He better, and you better please him. There's more money here than we've ever had."

"Then *you* please him."

Ramon grabbed her by the jaw, fingers digging into her flesh, and pulled her forward.

"I've had my share of old, ugly bitches in my bed. Sores and wrinkles and grey hair. All to keep you fed and dressed."

"To keep *us* fed and dressed," she muttered.

He squeezed her tighter and clenched the cigarette between his teeth.

"Don't be an ungrateful little whore. You know what happens to ungrateful whores."

She blinked. She knew.

"If you bruise me, he'll notice," she whispered.

Ramon removed his hand.

"It's your turn this time," he muttered.

He thrust his hands into his pockets, hurrying back towards the house. It was difficult to walk with her fine blue dress and her nice shoes, but Beatriz picked up the edge of her skirt and ran behind him.

"Don't try to come into my room again," she said. "I don't want you to ever come back again."

She tripped and fell, but he did not stop. She lay in the middle of the narrow dirt road. The fine new dress was now smudged and dusty.

⋄⊹I⋄I⋄I⊹⋄

She sat next to a dry fountain and did not turn when she heard Ramon approaching. But then the great ugly dog appeared at her side, wagging its tail, and she knew it was not Ramon standing behind her.

"Dinner is in an hour," Villanueva said.

"Thank you."

That was all. She did not offer him any polite conversation. Perhaps her silence would inspire him to leave. He stayed, leaning on his cane as the sun set.

She saw then, or perhaps noticed for the first time, a scorpion a few inches from her foot.

"Oh my God," Beatriz said.

He also saw it and sweeping down, grabbed the scorpion by the tail and held it up.

"Oh my God! Get rid of it!" she yelled.

So he did, tossing it away, and she rushed inside the house. Justiniano joined her at a more leisurely pace.

"How could you do that?" she asked.

"I've been catching scorpions since I was a child. I used to collect them."

"You did?"

"I still have a few specimens lying around."

"That's very... odd."

"Not in Durango."

"I think it's disgusting," she said.

Justiniano shrugged, and she frowned, biting her lip.

"So how do you grab one without letting it sting you?"

⊁⊹⊹⊰

She looked at a jar filled with alcohol and tiny baby scorpions floating in it. There was also a wooden frame with several specimens carefully pinned and displayed on black velvet.

"How can you collect them? How can you bear to touch them?"

"You shouldn't be afraid of them. Careful, but not afraid. I had a big black one sting me when I was a boy, but I'm not scared."

"If a scorpion had stung me, I would never get near one again."

"Do you want to hear an interesting story?"

She closed the armoire that contained his specimens and books and sat in one of the rattan chairs across from him. His cane was propped against the wall; the dog lay at his feet.

"A long time ago, a man was taking a stroll when suddenly he saw a white scorpion. He prepared to kill it, but then the scorpion yelled to the man. 'Spare me, spare me,' said the scorpion. 'I must kill you,' said the man. 'Let us make a trade,' cried the scorpion.

"The scorpion asked the man to take him to his home and let him live there upon a cushion of red velvet and feed him insects. If he did this, the scorpion said, he would be very lucky and gain much wealth. So the man did this, and the man became wealthy and well-known. The scorpion in turn grew big and fat. He grew so big the man began to distrust it. 'Why, that scorpion is nearly the size of a cat,' the man thought. 'If it ever got angry it could sting me and kill me. Maybe I should kill it first.'

"So the man fed the scorpion its daily ration of insects on a poisoned dish. Immediately the scorpion realized it had been betrayed. 'I am dying, but I will not die alone. You poisoned me, and I shall poison you. Let my poison live in your blood and claim the sons of your body. Let them all live short, painful lives.' And then the scorpion stung the man and died.

"Since then all the sons of the man have died young, but they have been immune to the venom of scorpions because they already carry the venom in their body. That is why I am never afraid of scorpions."

It was getting dark outside, and the library grew thick with shadows. The mechanical bird, sitting on the desk, reflected the sun's dying rays.

Beatriz leaned back.

"You really think I'm going to believe that story?"

"Would you believe when scorpions mate they perform a dance?"

"No," she said chuckling.

"And sometimes they devour each other."

"As they dance? Why would they do that?" she asked with a smile.

"I suppose it is in their nature."

❖❖❖

The days passed and then the weeks and Ramon grew anxious. They had been invited to spend the summer there, and now the summer was coming to an end. Beatriz used to think of Paris often, but now it was a blurry dream, and the thoughts of wealth and marriage had also faded. All that remained around her was the stolid reality of the small house, the fields kissing the orange sky, and Justiniano's slow steps at her side.

"When you are alone, what do you do?" Ramon asked, pacing around the lounge.

Beatriz rode with Justiniano beyond the cemetery, so far that the house disappeared, and farther still with the ugly dog by their side. Afterwards they sat in the library, and she made the mechanical bird play its melodies.

Beatriz shrugged and did not answer.

"Has he touched you?" Ramon asked, his nails running down her left arm.

"He has not."

"He should. If he had you, then maybe he would feel obliged to marry you."

Beatriz shrugged again and caressed the head of the great dog, which sat at her side in the lounge.

"Maybe he does not care for marriage, and it would not matter if you dangled me naked in front of him. Have you thought of that?"

Ramon leaned forward, meaning to strike her. She recoiled. The dog growled, and Ramon stopped, his arm frozen in mid-air. He stepped back, staring at her in silence, and then went towards the door.

"Make it happen," he warned her. "You must make it happen."

∻⊹∘⊹∘⊹∘⊹<

Ramon was good with women. He could lie effortlessly to them. He had swindled half a dozen widows with a few words, a few smiles and his youthful charm. Marriages happened quickly for him. Three, four weeks of courtship and they were before the priest, and just as quickly Ramon and Beatriz had disappeared, taking with them jewels, money, anything they could.

It was the easiest way to make money, he said. Easier than fake business deals or some of his other shady endeavours.

But what was simple for Ramon became complicated for Beatriz. Because she liked Justiniano. Because he was a nice man, open and kind. Unlike them. They were the deceivers, the scorpions lurking between the bed sheets.

So she sat in the library while the mechanical bird sang and Justiniano read his book and her fingers fell upon the chair's arm, marking the melody. She did not dare to speak, afraid some untruths might curl around her tongue; she was of the lineage of betrayers and thieves, both she and Ramon shameless liars since birth.

"Why do you like the bird so much?" he asked.

Sometimes he asked her things like that. Questions springing like water from his mouth. Facts, tidbits of information about scorpions, butterflies, dogs, horses, escaped him all of a sudden, for no reason. He talked suddenly of the animals he adored and then of a story he had heard as a child, turning next to a poem in a book he had been reading.

She did not mind. She'd grown accustomed to this, just as she had grown used to the great dog that always followed him or that sometimes he had to pause for air when they were walking, like an old man even though he was young.

"It's beautiful," she said.

"I think you should have it," he said.

"It was your mother's."

"Now it is yours."

He looked at her, his face happy and ablaze with a question.

"Thank you," she said

She felt the lies welling inside her and excused herself before he could speak.

→•I•I•I•←

The next morning, Justiniano did not come out of his room, and she heard the maids whispering that he was ill again. The doctor arrived.

The house was very quiet. Everybody crept around, talking in low voices, and Beatriz realized as the days bled into one another that they were all awaiting Justiniano's death.

She locked herself in her room. The mechanical bird played its songs. Sitting in the middle of the bed, she could not think, or speak, or move. She only listened to the bird.

Ramon sneaked in late one night and sat next to her.

"It's all ruined," he said. "He'll be dead in a few days. That's what the doctor says."

She did not reply.

"It's your fault. He would have been easy to handle. You mucked it up. Now what'll we do?"

"What we always do," she whispered.

"What *I* always do. You are useless."

He headed towards the vanity and looked at the mechanical bird. The songs had all become the same, and she had not wound it up.

"We'll sell this. And some other things. I've taken a few items. We'll go back to..."

"You can't sell the bird."

"It's got to be worth something."

"But it's mine. He gave it to me."

Ramon turned towards her and slapped her face.

"You'll do as I say."

"No."

"Come here," he said, and pushed her against the bed.

"No," she said

But she knew this melody. She'd danced this dance before. She did not rouse the house with her screams. This was who they were and what they were, entwined in anger and desperation and pain. *Promenade a deux*. Ramon and Beatriz. This dance had no beginning and no end.

⇥•┃•┃•⇤

She awoke before dawn. The room was dark and quiet. Ramon had left. He always left before morning broke.

Beatriz rose and combed her hair. She dressed slowly, pulling each button with care. Then she grabbed one of her shoes and looked at it as she did every day. That morning, a blinding white scorpion nestled inside one shoe.

Rather than crushing it, rather than yelling and breaking it into a thousand pieces, she whispered to the scorpion.

"Let us make a trade," she said.

She shook the shoe, and the scorpion fell to the floor. From the floor, it crawled onto her flattened hand. It sat there, as docile as a kitten.

Beatriz went to Ramon's room.

❖❖❖❖❖

The curtains were pulled tight, shielding him from the sun's harsh glare. He lay under the blankets, smelling of salves and sweat.

"It's just a fever," she said.

"Beatriz. My chest hurts."

"Hush."

"I can't get up."

Ramon's skin was waxy, and his lips were chapped as though he had been out in the sun for many hours, but he had spent the whole morning in bed.

"You aren't going to leave me, are you?" he asked, trying to hold her hands. "You're going to sit here and stay with me until I get better."

Beatriz did not reply but only smiled.

"Bita,"

He had not called her that in years. Not since she was eight. She remembered a studio, a portrait of the children. While the photographer fiddled with the camera, their father had said they must remain still. She held her breath and clutched Ramon. It seemed to her that a decade after she still remained in the same pose, a little girl in her prim dress motionless against a theatrical backdrop.

"Bita, answer me!" he demanded, his nails digging against her skin. But the nails were brittle and tore like silk paper.

Beatriz unlaced her hands from his.

❖❖❖❖❖

Beatriz changed her clothes for dinner, moulting into a bright yellow gown Ramon had disliked. On the vanity, the mechanical bird sang a tune she had not heard before. As she swept her hair up, she heard a knock at her door.

Justiniano stood there, a flimsy phantom suddenly made solid. He looked tired, with dark circles under his eyes, but he did not carry his cane, and Beatriz knew very soon he would be fine. Perfectly fine.

"How do you feel?" she asked.

"Better," he replied, but there were questions in his eyes.

She touched his face, straightened, and kissed him, brushing away his questions with her hands.

• •

Silvia Moreno-Garcia lives in Vancouver with her family and two cats. Her fiction has appeared in *Futurismic* and *Shimmer*. She writes a regular column for *Fantasy Magazine* and is currently working on her first novel. You can find her online at: *www.silviamoreno-garcia.com*

• •

Overtoun Bridge
by Bev Vincent

Emma clutched her arms with her bare hands and leaned into the brisk wind, chiding herself for not wearing a coat over her snug cardigan. Cold penetrated her bones. Leaves and dust swirled at her feet as she climbed the gravel footpath leading to the road across Overtoun Bridge. The part of her journey she always dreaded.

Beyond the bridge and nearly a mile of pavement awaited a warm pub, and the warm embrace of a man willing to pay her to do what she would gladly have done for free. She couldn't very well attract a man's attention wearing a fleece-lined parka and a wool muffler. Still, she wore sensible walking shoes, not stilettos like some tart in an American film. The men around here would burst out laughing if she staggered into the pub on heels.

Her goal was to spend the night in the arms of someone like Constable John Cafferty or Callum McPhee, the greengrocer — or any of the other men who had welcomed her in the past. If the man tucked twenty quid into her purse the next morning, she wouldn't argue. She had bills to pay like anyone else. But it wasn't about the money — it was about not spending the night by herself in a bed made for two.

At the end of the path, she turned left toward the stone bridge. Its single lane arched over a deep ravine carved out by a tributary of the River Clyde. The rush of water cascading over the falls far below the bridge was barely audible above the howling wind.

A border collie stood motionless on the bridge, staring at the waist-high, eighteen-inch thick stone wall that kept vehicles — and people, Emma supposed — from tumbling into the ravine. The dog was on the far side of a semicircular alcove that jutted from the wall so pedestrians could get out of the way of passing cars.

Emma froze. She wasn't scared of the dog, which looked like Bob Murchie's. Rather she was afraid of what it might do. *Don't listen*, she wanted to yell at the animal, but she couldn't make her throat work. *Go on home like a good doggie.*

The collie twisted its head one way then the other, as if it heard something confusing. Emma's dog used to react the same way to the theme music from a daytime soap — back in the days before her husband left, taking both the dog and her dignity, leaving her only memories she didn't particularly want.

She recalled the story the pale, thin stranger from Aberdeen had told her about the bridge two years ago, after they made love. That had been during the week when Milton became the center of media attention, before the ever-wandering eye turned elsewhere. Emma had fantasized briefly that the man would take her away from here, but the price would have been too high. He saw too much.

The collie suddenly crouched and leapt over the thick wall as neatly as a champion show dog clears a hurdle. It made no sound Emma could hear. There was only the wind.

Released from her momentary fugue, Emma rushed to the spot where the dog went over. Planting her hands firmly atop the cold stone, she leaned over the wall and stared into the brambles near the river below, trying to spot the dog. Hoping it had somehow survived and was now scampering along the bank, lapping at the water or chasing a mink in the scrub.

A strong gust pressed her against the wall. Her arms stiffened in response. Then she glimpsed the black and white collie, lying at the edge of the rushing water, its head twisted at an unnatural angle, its mouth open as if in amazement.

She caught her breath, unexpectedly overcome. A tear formed at the corner of her eye — she brushed it away before more joined it. *It's just a dog*, she told herself. Her sorrow was tinged with regret, a fleeting sensation that threatened to overwhelm her before vanishing as quickly as it materialized. She blinked rapidly while trying to figure out the origins of the intense sensation, but it had passed.

She had to tell someone what she'd seen. Trembling, she pushed away from the wall and glanced toward Overtoun Manor, with its baronial cupolas, stone parapets and a peaked tower that looked like it was meant as the last refuge if angry villagers ever stormed the estate. Lord Overtoun had died twenty years ago and the castle-like building had fallen into disrepair. For a while, the grounds were used as a wildlife refuge, and some society was supposedly raising funds to convert the manor into a youth center, but it was currently unoccupied.

The next closest place in that direction belonged to Jimmy MacMillan, but he was eighty years old, nearly blind and had no telephone. She might as well continue on to Milton. If John Cafferty was at the pub, he'd know what to do.

As she walked along the tarmac, once again hugging herself against the wind, she thought about all the evenings over the past two years — closer to three, now — when she'd taken the shortcut through Overtoun Estate, and how seldom she'd returned home until the following morning.

The women in Milton hated her — or was it envy that made their eyes burn like coals when they saw her? If a woman couldn't hold onto her man, that wasn't Emma's fault. She had suffered the same fate, picked herself up and moved on. More or less.

In town, the buildings took some of the bite out of the wind. The sidewalks were empty as usual on a Saturday evening. With all the shops closed, most people were either at home in front of the television or at the pub. Cars and bicycles huddled in front of the Fox and Hound. When Emma got close, she heard laughter permeating the inn's thick windows. Flickering light and the musky aroma of smoke told her Alex had the fireplace going.

Emma paused outside the heavy oak door, patting her hair into place and pulling down on her sweater. Her arrival usually put a temporary halt to conversation, as if everyone had been talking about her. She considered asking one of her lovers about it some evening, but she wasn't apt to get much out of any of them. They didn't seek her company for conversation. Talk was likely what they were trying to escape, given the chattiness of Milton women.

A bubble of warmth emerged from the inn when she pulled the door toward her, as if the heat meant to ward her away. Or maybe it was just the furrowed brows and narrowed eyes within the pub that made her feel unwelcome.

She stepped over the threshold. To the right, couples sat at small tables in front of the hearth. The men regarded her with curiosity and the women with disdain. Emma couldn't resist taking a tally of the men who had forsaken their wives to be with her. Those who hadn't done so yet looked at her with the highest degree of interest.

Her business lay, as always, with the men lining the long oak bar to her left. John Cafferty was there, of course. Milton didn't have much crime and everyone knew where to find the constable if some crisis arose. As good here as at the station, he often said. Callum McPhee was there, too, along with Angus McDowell, Roddy McAllister and Vernon Fearon. Her regulars.

They all looked up when she came in, their glances lingering on the curves they remembered beneath her cardigan or on her long, bare legs. Any other night, she would have taken a seat at a table against the window behind them and waited for one to break away from the pack and join her. Tonight, however, she marched straight up to the bar.

Most of the men found something else to do when she approached. Vernon pretended interest in a rugby match on the TV, and Angus plucked a coin from a stack and inserted it in the video lottery terminal at the end of the bar. Maybe they were afraid she was about to tell them she was pregnant, or that she had acquired something contagious.

Only John looked her straight in the eyes, his eyebrows raised, his face open and welcoming. "Evening, Em," he said in his gravely voice.

Suddenly Emma didn't know what to say. She pointed toward the door. "The bridge," she said at last. "It happened again."

That caught everyone's attention, even Alex Miller, who owned the pub. He flung a tattered rag over his shoulder, put down the mug he'd been wiping dry, and came over to join the others.

"Bob Murchie's collie, I'm sure." A shiver traversed her body. "Right in front of me."

"That's five in the last five months," Vernon said.

"At least," Angus said, the gambling machine now forgotten. "Lord knows how many before that."

"If people kept their dogs on the leash this wouldn't happen," Callum said. He offered the same opinion every time the subject came up.

Roddy McAllister swivelled on his stool. "Are you certain she's... I mean, did you check?"

"Aye, sure, Roddy. I risked my neck on those craggy rocks and brambles to see if a stupid dog survived falling, what, sixty feet."

"Just asking," Roddy said and turned back to his pitcher of ale.

Emma shook her head. If there was a lazier man in Milton than Roddy McAllister, she hadn't met him yet. Most of the time he couldn't even be bothered to get on top in bed.

"We should check, all the same," John said. He pushed away his half-finished pint, got off his stool and grabbed a coat from a peg near the dartboard.

"I'll come, too," Angus said, casting a rueful glance at the video terminal. Emma wondered how much money he'd shoved through that slot over the years, fifty pence at a time. What satisfaction could a man derive from pushing a button and watching the wheels spin, hoping the big prize would come up? Better to spend his money on ale. At least then he'd get something in return, if only a paunch and a pounding headache the next day.

Angus had proposed marriage early one morning in the narrow bed in his house two blocks off High Street. He'd never quite forgiven her for turning him down, but that hadn't stopped him coming back to her once every couple of weeks, before he wasted his paycheck on lost causes. Or maybe she was just the first in a line of lost causes that led steadily downhill to the poker machine.

"Me, too," Emma said. She would rather face the cold again than be left behind to tell and retell what had happened on the bridge as word spread among the pub's patrons. Even those who despised her would get over themselves long enough to hear her story. Emma would hate every second she spent talking to their carefully assembled façades, just as the people behind those façades would hate every moment they had to listen to her. But another story about Overtoun Bridge would be too good to miss, so people would bite their lips and listen and ask questions. In small towns it didn't take much to cause a stir, but even in a bigger place than Milton a bridge where dogs regularly committed suicide would have been cause for talk.

"Are you sure?" John asked. "It's mighty cold."

Emma nodded.

John ran his hand along the pegs. It came to rest on a coat she recognized as Vernon's. "You don't mind if Emma borrows this, do you?" he asked. "Since you've got the game to watch, and all."

Vernon blushed. Emma thought he was probably ashamed he hadn't offered to join the constable, but it was too late now. Or maybe it was the idea of Emma being seen in his coat — the same one he'd been wearing around town for years — that embarrassed him.

"Sure. Mind you don't snag it on something is all," he said. "It's my best." He couldn't find it in himself to look at Emma as he said this.

"Thanks, Vern," Emma said. She could smell him on the coat when she accepted it from John. She had to push up the sleeves to get her hands out, and the shoulders pooled around her upper arms, but it would help keep her warm.

Outside, she had to walk fast to keep up with John and
Angus, both of them over six feet tall and with long strides
to match. She twisted her head into the wind to catch their
words, though they weren't directed at her. Men often
talked to each other as if she weren't there.

"I tell you, that place is cursed," Angus said. "On account of Kevin Malloy."

The incident with Malloy had occurred when Emma was
eighteen. Convinced his two-week-old son was the devil,
Malloy had thrown the infant off the bridge. As far as she
knew, he was still in a mental hospital in Glasgow.

Emma couldn't see John shrug in his heavy coat, but
she knew him well enough to sense his reaction to Angus's
statement. "That was only thirteen years ago," he said.
"Dogs have been going over that wall since I was a lad.
They're attracted by the smell of squirrels or mink living
under the bridge, that's all. Or by the rustle of tree branches
down by the waterfall."

"Those acoustics experts from Edinburgh tested for
sounds only a dog might hear and found nothing." Angus
said. "And what about those psychics that came the other
summer? They didn't know about Malloy."

Emma felt a pang at the mention of the psychics and
looked away from the men. John only stared at Angus for
a second before continuing down the road.

"One said he felt children grabbing his legs," Angus
said. "Another sensed a Victorian woman in a shawl. People
around here have always talked about the white lady who
haunts Overtoun." He paused for breath. Getting no response he continued, undaunted. "Every one of them said
they felt anxious and depressed. Especially at the far end
of the bridge."

"Claptrap," John said without turning.

Angus spun around to Emma, probably hoping for a
more receptive audience. "You remember, don't you Em?"

Emma nodded. Newspapers as far away as America and
Japan had covered the story, she'd heard. She recalled the
grim man in a threadbare suit clasping his hands together
as he delivered his verdict. "A workman fell to his death

when the bridge was built," he'd said. "His ghost lingers in the gully, calling out to whoever crosses. The dogs are answering his summons." Unlike the others, he hadn't qualified his statements by saying "I feel" or "perhaps." He'd spoken with an air of certainty that made him seem more substantial than he was.

In her bed later that night, the man — whose name she no longer recalled — had regarded her with wide, sorrowful eyes. Emma had pretended she wasn't interested in his psychic insights, but in truth she'd been terrified that he would peer inside her soul and see how empty she was.

"How else do you account for Gilbert Ferguson's dog?" Angus asked. "Survived the first time, got better and jumped again four months later. Cursed, I tell you."

He stared at Emma until she nodded. All she knew was that the dogs — mostly Labradors, collies and retrievers — always leaped over the east side of the bridge, usually during clear weather. She'd heard all the theories, but none felt right — except for what the sad psychic said. Every time she crossed the bridge, she tried to blank her mind so as not to imagine that poor, lonely workman, trapped in the gulley for a hundred and fifty years, desperate to be heard. Maybe Kevin Malloy had heard him, too.

By the time they reached the estate, darkness was beginning to fall. They paused at the verge of the narrow bridge. John turned to Emma. "Show me where."

He knew the spot, but Emma led him to it all the same, stopping beside the alcove. "Right here."

John nodded and leaned over the wall to look into the ravine.

Emma moved to his side. Her hand brushed his atop the cold stone. She appreciated that he hadn't questioned her memory. Hadn't so much as asked, "You're sure?" He seemed to have more faith in her than anyone else she knew.

The sun was setting over their shoulders, so the bridge cast an elongated shadow before them. Emma could make out little more than the silvery ripple of flowing water below. Maybe the dog had only been injured, like Gilbert's retriever. Or perhaps the water had carried it away.

"See anything?" Angus asked.

"Too dark," John said. He backed up several steps and knelt. "From here, you can't tell what's on the other side. Maybe they're just trying to jump on top of the wall to satisfy their curiosity."

"Except it's always the same place, isn't it?" Emma said. "And he didn't even graze the wall going over. Like he was jumping a hurdle."

John stood up and brushed dirt from his pants. "I'll go down and take a look," he said. He pulled a pair of work gloves from his pockets and strode to the end of the bridge.

"Be careful," she said.

"I'll stay with Emma," Angus said. She wasn't surprised. Angus wouldn't risk tearing his clothes on the brambles covering the steep bank that led to the tributary. New trousers meant less money for the slot machine.

Emma watched John inch his way down the incline, clutching at shrubs and roots with gloved hands to keep from falling. She became aware of Angus standing beside her. From the corner of her eye she saw him shifting his weight from one foot to the other and braced herself for what was coming.

"Listen, Em. I was wondering if maybe later..."

Emma offered her sincerest smile, a look she had perfected over the years. "Another time, Angus. Okay?"

"Sure, sure. Right. Another time." He made an awkward half-bow as he spoke, then drifted away a few steps and stared over the side of the bridge.

"Do you think the dogs are deliberately killing themselves?" she asked.

"Goes against instinct," Angus said. "Dogs are born survivors. If they know they're dying, they might slink off and hide. Nah, it's like those psychics said. Something lures them over the wall. Overtoun is haunted."

"Someone should put mesh on top of the wall," Emma said.

Angus shrugged. "There's no one to look after the old place—"

John called out from below. Emma leaned over to see what he wanted. She didn't like the note of urgency she detected in his voice. He was a man who rarely revealed emotion.

The wind had started up again, whipping at her borrowed coat and lifting her skirt. She concentrated on the place where she'd seen the collie's inert body, trying to catch a glimpse of John in the fading light.

She called his name, but the wind carried her voice downstream.

Angus yelled too, his baritone rolling out of him like a boulder. No response. His brow was furrowed, his obvious concern matching her own deepening dread. She pictured the desperate construction worker's hands clutching at John, dragging him into the earth.

"What do we do?" she asked.

"He might have fallen." Angus shook his head. "I'll have to go down."

"It's too dark," Emma said. "Wait here. I'll run to my place and get a flashlight. Keep calling, to let him know we haven't abandoned him."

"Maybe I should just... " Angus made a feeble gesture, as if he meant to head toward the embankment.

"Not until I get back," she said. She took him by the shoulders and looked him square in the face. "Promise."

"All right, Em. I'll wait."

"I'll be quick."

She jogged to the end of the bridge and turned onto the trail toward the break in the stone wall surrounding Overtoun Estate. The road on the other side led to a small group of houses the locals called the village.

After Jimmy MacMillan's, she passed Bob Murchie's house and saw lights on inside. She wondered if he'd missed his collie yet. Through her mind flickered the image of a grizzled man sitting in an easy chair facing the television, hoping any moment now his dog — his companion — would scratch at the door to be let in.

If not for the urgency of John's situation, she would have taken a moment to stop and break the news. Bob had always been kind, even if he disapproved of her. Later, she promised. She would knock on his door and sit with him while she explained what had happened. No one else in town would think to bother.

She spent longer at her house than she wanted. Finally she turned up a battered flashlight in the old cabinets in the back porch, placed there no doubt by her husband — before he left her for a woman from work and moved to Inverness.

When she re-emerged into the cold night, the half moon was obscured behind clouds. She walked as fast as she could, back to the broken wall and up the path beyond. Even with the flashlight, she picked her steps carefully on the uneven ground. As she approached the bridge, she resisted calling Angus to find out if he'd heard anything from John. She didn't want her voice to betray how worried she was. To keep the men of Milton coming back, she had constructed an arsenal of false emotions — so much so that she barely knew which ones were real any more.

The flashlight's conical amber beam struggled to keep darkness at bay. Still, she should have been able to see Angus near the alcove twenty feet away. She swept the light back and forth, surprised he hadn't said anything when he saw the light approaching.

"Angus? Ang?"

The whistling wind was her only response.

"Silly bugger," she muttered. He must have gone down the embankment without waiting for her. That or he'd gotten impatient and returned to town for help. Either way, she'd wring his neck when she got her hands on him.

She aimed her flashlight at the ravine. Here, darkness won the battle. The beam failed to penetrate as far as the riverbank or even to the bramble-covered slope. Sixty feet, she thought. A long way to go when it's steep and dark.

"Angus?" she called, louder this time to make herself heard over the wind. "John?" The black night swallowed her words.

She couldn't imagine Angus dragging John up the bank alone. Maybe John had recovered from his fall but had been hurt badly enough that they couldn't wait for her. She trained her flashlight on the road, looking for footprints, splashes of blood, anything that might reveal what had happened. At the end of the bridge, her beam played across the long grass, but she went no farther. If she tried to climb down to the river she risked falling or getting stuck at the bottom.

Returning to the alcove, she turned off the flashlight and sat on the cold concrete. She pulled Vernon's jacket down over her bent legs, tugged the sleeves over her hands, propped her elbows on her knees and lowered her face into her covered hands. She listened to see if she could hear anything — the call of an injured man, a broken dog, or a workman trapped between heaven and earth, lonely, wanting only to cross the chasm — but there was only the wind.

Her heart ached, thinking about what might have happened to John. Angus, too, but it was John she was most concerned about. Whenever she needed comfort, she'd catch John's eye at the bar. He'd order her a vodka tonic, carry his beer to her table, sit quietly and listen. He never seemed embarrassed to be seen with her. The other men in town paled in comparison. They scratched an itch. She believed John actually liked her. If only she had kept quiet about the dog, none of this would have happened. She and John would be having a drink while waiting for one or the other to make the first, inevitable overture.

If the two men were found dead beneath the bridge in the morning, she knew what people would think. They would say the men got into a fight over her and had fallen to their deaths. Stories about phantom Victorian women or clutching children notwithstanding, everyone in Milton would believe she'd lured the men here, like a siren foundering ships on the rocks.

Angus should be back by now if he'd gone into town. Emma couldn't just sit in the darkness and do nothing. John and Angus needed help. This time she'd enlist as many men as she could, and make sure they brought with them lights and ropes, and any other tools necessary to ensure no one else was lost.

She squared her shoulders, lifted her head from her hands and sighed. Part of her hoped that when she got back to the Fox and Hound, the two men would be at the bar laughing with the others over pints of ale. She'd be pissed if that were the case. Pissed and disappointed that they'd displayed so little concern for her feelings. But John wouldn't do that to her — would he?

Still, it would be so easy to stay here until morning. Thanks to Vern's coat, she wouldn't freeze. If she didn't return to the pub, the others would assume she'd gone home with one of the men — or even both. How long before anyone cared enough to come looking for her?

She thought about her dog, a golden retriever she'd gotten as a puppy shortly after her wedding. Why her husband had taken the dog when he left, she never understood. Probably just to be mean. It might as well have dashed its brains out on the rocks below, like the others. For all she knew, her husband might have thrown it over the edge, one final ugly act while leaving town on his way toward a new life. At this very minute, he was probably tucked in a warm bed in a cute little house in Inverness with what's-her-name.

Emma wasn't going to cry, though, not even here in the darkness where no one could see her. Not about any of it. She was fooling herself if she thought she held any power over the people of Milton. The women probably laughed behind her back. And the men? What did they say about her when she wasn't around?

This wasn't how her life was supposed to turn out. There were supposed to be children. A cozy home, with a husband she sent off to work in the morning with his lunch after a hearty fry-up breakfast. A husband who came home every evening and told her how special she was. What had made her think she deserved any of that?

Every regrettable thing she'd ever done cascaded through her mind. The lies she'd told her parents as a teenager. The boyfriends she'd dropped in favour of someone better. Trying so hard to please her husband while his heart secretly turned black against her. Turning herself into the whore of Milton while deluding herself she was something special — even to a man like John Cafferty, just because he treated her kindly.

Emma heard a chuffing sound nearby, like a dog offering a half-hearted bark. She freed one hand from her sleeve and groped on the ground until she came up with the flashlight. When she illuminated a border collie sitting in the middle of the bridge, she slowly got to her feet, keeping the light aimed at the dog. It lowered its nose, poked at something on the road and woofed softly again.

"What?" she asked. "What do you want?"

The dog stood and shuffled its feet. Emma couldn't be sure, but it looked like the animal she'd seen earlier. Bob Murchie's collie. It didn't seem injured. *Wouldn't that be ironic*, she thought. *All this fuss and the dog wasn't hurt after all.*

But that couldn't be. She'd seen it with her own eyes, lying broken at the bottom of the ravine.

The dog growled, nosed the object again, pawed the tarmac, and then suddenly leapt at her. Emma dropped the flashlight and put up her hands to ward off the attack. Time seemed to stand still. Her heart froze. It took her several seconds to realize nothing had happened. How had the dog missed her? Had it been her imagination? Or the doomed workman appearing to her in the form of the bridge's latest victim?

Trembling, she dropped to her knees and located the flashlight, but the bulb had broken. She tossed it aside and crawled to the spot in the road where the dog had been sitting. Pebbles cut into her hands and bare knees. She groped around until she found the object the dog had been prodding. She held it in the air, trying to catch as much moonlight as possible, to confirm what she suspected.

A glove, like the one John had been wearing when he climbed down the slope. John wasn't at the pub. The only person who truly cared for her was gone. In that moment, the clouds cleared and the half moon emerged, bathing her in its cold light.

She turned, intending to look down into the ravine, but stopped. If she did look, she might not be able to go through with it. She took off Vern's coat, draped it over the stone wall where he would see it, and backed up to the spot where John had knelt earlier to gain a dog's perspective. She wanted to feel his presence one last time.

Another cloud passed in front of the moon, stealing away the silvery light. Clutching the glove in her hand, Emma expelled all the air from her lungs and ran toward the edge of Overtoun Bridge. When she was close enough, she launched herself into the air, imagining herself as a champion collie facing a hurdle.

In the darkness, as she plummeted, a chorus of mournful howls arose to greet her.

• •

Bev Vincent grew up in Charlo, New Brunswick and received his PhD in chemistry from Dalhousie University in 1987. His first book, *The Road to the Dark Tower*, was nominated for a 2004 Bram Stoker award. His short stories have appeared in *Cemetery Dance*, *Ellery Queen's Mystery Magazine*, *The Blue Religion*, *Doctor Who: Destination Prague* and elsewhere. He is a regular contributor to *Storytellers Unplugged* and *Cemetery Dance*. His website is: www.bevvincent.com
• •

Dead to Me

By Kelley Armstrong

I sat on the sofa and watched my dead ex-husband take the last pizza slice from the box. I suppose I should say, "My dead ex-husband's ghost," but he didn't look like a ghost. Or act like one. I'd think he wasn't dead at all if it wasn't for the way his head lolled to the side, neck broken.

I suppose, too, that I shouldn't call him my ex when the divorce hadn't been finalized. And, no, that impending divorce had nothing to do with his accident. I'd been there, but I hadn't killed him.

"You know what would go great with this?" he said, lifting the dripping pizza slice. "A cold beer. Any chance, babe?"

"You don't need a beer. You're dead."

He shrugged and leaned back into the couch, feet propped on the coffee table. "That's a matter of opinion."

"Well, you're dead to me."

He met my gaze. "Am I?"

I got up and went to bed.

⊰•I••I••I•⊱

As I tried to sleep, I could hear him downstairs. Not giving me a moment's rest. Selfish bastard.

My mother had warned me not to marry him. With my mother, though, there were few things in life she hadn't warned me against, from learning to ride a bike to buying my own business. She had her reasons — I was her only child, and she'd been an invalid since the accident that killed my father, so it was in her best interests to keep me safe and close. Whenever I suggested getting my own place, she'd peer at me over her glasses, cold eyes glittering, and say, "Go on, but remember this: If you walk out that door, you're dead to me."

Those were the last words she'd said to me, when I finally did leave to get married. Six months later, she was dead, and the house was mine. I'd rented it out until, sadly, her predictions on my marriage proved all too accurate.

Despite her dire prophesies, it hadn't ended badly. We separated by mutual agreement. I returned to my mother's house. He kept the condo, which he'd had before we married. As a lawyer, he made more money, but I pulled in enough not to bother with alimony. No kids, no pets, no fuss, no muss. He'd even given me a convertible as a parting gift... and to make sure my bedroom door stayed open.

⇢⊶⊷⊶⊷⇠

I walked into the bathroom the next morning and found him in the shower. I tried to pass by, but he threw open the door and leaned out.

"Wanna join me?" he asked, waggling his brows.

"No, thanks."

He only grinned. "Then I guess I'll have to take care of it myself."

He wrapped his fingers around his cock and met my gaze, his grin inviting me to watch. There'd been a time when I would have — a lot of times when I *had*. But there was nothing sexy about a dead guy whacking off in my shower.

I turned away and started brushing my teeth. A couple of minutes later, the door squeaked open again.

"Grab me a towel, babe?"

"You're dead," I said, not looking up from the sink.

"Matter of opinion."

I turned then. "You want an apology, don't you? That's what this is all about. Yes, I'm sorry you're dead. But I have no reason to apologize."

"No?"

"No. Now go away."

"Til death do us part, babe," he said, grinning. "And you're not—"

I strode out and slammed the door behind me.

→·]••]••]·←

I spent the morning in my home office, trying to balance the bar's books and ignore the noise from downstairs. Demanding my attention, as usual. That's the misleading thing about strong-willed people. You figure if they're so capable, they won't need you. Bullshit. First my mother, then my husband, always demanding, always expecting, always needing. Death didn't change that.

At first, he'd liked my independence, liked what I'd done with my life. He'd been tired of dating lawyers and doctors and PhDs. A bar owner with a high school education better suited his bad boy self-image.

After we married, though, he started expecting more. More of my time, more of my attention. Why couldn't I host dinner for his colleagues? Why wouldn't I join the other wives at the charity luncheons? Why didn't I try harder to fit in? Why didn't I make more of an effort to better inform myself, better educate myself, just *better* myself?

He began to notice my deficiencies. Not that he ever said so outright, but he got in his little digs, always joking that he might not have the smartest wife in a room, but he always had the best-looking one. Eventually I decided I was more mistress material than wife. He didn't disagree. So we split. He got the stuck-up, straight-laced lawyer girlfriend, and I was the woman he came to when he wanted to hang out and kick back, to talk and screw until morning.

That was fine by me. I got as much out of it as he did... until two days ago, when I told him it was over. He didn't like that, and he died because of it. But I didn't kill him.

→·]••]••]·←

When I went downstairs to head out to work, he was there, crouched at the bottom of the stairs, fingering a dent in the baluster.

"Seems I left a mark," he said.

"Yes. A year ago, when you ripped out my mother's chair-lift for me. Remember?"

"Are you sure?"

"Of course I'm sure. You fell—" I pointed "—over there."

He looked at me. His eyes had started sinking into his skull. I glanced away and tried walking past him, but he stepped into my path. Tried again. Blocked again.

"What?" I said.

No answer.

"I didn't push you down those stairs, and you know it."

He didn't argue, only slid his gaze to the side, conceding my point.

"So why are you—? Oh, I know. You wanted a proper burial — big funeral, fancy headstone, scenic plot." I crossed my arms and looked up at him. "You know I couldn't do that. How would it look? You break your neck on my stairs three days before our divorce is finalized? The cops would have ripped me apart, and your bitch girlfriend would have led the charge."

He didn't argue, which was as good as agreement. Didn't get out of my way either, though.

"What if I was one of your clients?" I said. "What if I'd called with the same story? My soon-to-be-ex died from a fall down my stairs after an argument. You would have told me — off the record, of course — to do exactly what I did."

Again he said nothing. This time, when I tried to get past, he let me.

→•I•I•I•←

After work, I lay in bed, listening to him downstairs. He seemed to be getting quieter, but I could still hear him. Damn him. Tenacity was a fine trait, but there comes a time when one needs to accept the inevitable. He never could, and that's what had gotten him killed.

He'd come over Thursday night, as he always did, telling his girlfriend he liked to work late and wrap everything up before the weekend. We had our routine down pat. He'd bring takeout. We'd watch TV, maybe a movie. Then we'd adjourn to the bedroom, euphemistically speaking. There were rarely beds involved.

That day, over Chinese takeout, I'd told him there would be no more Thursday nights after the divorce. I'd had enough of his jealous girlfriend, always sending her friends to my bar to check up on me, driving past my house when he didn't come home on time, cornering me in grocery stores to warn me that once the divorce was final, I'd have no reason for contact with him, so I'd damned well better not have any. At first, I'd been amused. After a year, I was sick of it. Besides, I'd met someone, a firefighter who came into the bar now and then, and we'd hit it off and, well, you know.... Point was, it was time for us both to move on.

He hadn't liked that.

We'd argued. When it was obvious he wasn't listening to me, I'd retreated up the stairs. He followed. At the top, he'd grabbed my arm. I'd wrenched away. He'd fallen. The end. Not my fault.

It was over, and he couldn't accept that now any more than he could on Thursday. It was time for another chat. So I went downstairs.

He wasn't grinning and teasing now. Again, nothing new. His grins had always been quick to turn to scowls when charm didn't get him what he wanted.

"Get over it," I said.

He glowered at me, sunken eyes narrowing.

"Don't give me that look. Remember Tim from your softball team? Paralyzed in that ski accident? What did you say?"

He only glared, his shriveled lips tightening.

"You said you wouldn't want to live like that. So now you've changed your mind?" I snorted. "Great. And who did you think would have looked after you? That girlfriend of yours? Give up her hotshot lawyer job to play

nursemaid to her drooling boyfriend? Not a chance. You
know exactly who'd have been stuck with it. Your not-yet-
ex wife. Well, no way. No fucking way."

His lips parted in something I didn't catch, but I knew
it wasn't complimentary.

"You would have been miserable. Just like her." I waved
at my mother. "On her death bed and she calls me home,
begs me to take care of her. I look after her for a month,
and what were her last words? Told me I was still cut out
of her will. Vindictive bitch. So I did what I had to do. But
I'm not a murderer. I didn't kill her, and I didn't kill you."

"I'm not dead," he rasped.

I ripped off a piece of duct tape, then leaned into the
basement crawlspace, where he lay beside the decomposed
body of my mother. He thrashed his head from side to side,
feebly protesting. I slapped on the tape.

"You're dead to me," I said.

I rose, relocked the hatch, and went upstairs.

Peace and quiet, at last.

● ●

Kelley Armstrong is the author of the "Women of
the Otherworld" (paranormal suspense), "Darkest
Powers" (YA fantasy) and Nadia Stafford (crime)
series. She grew up in Southwestern Ontario, where
she still lives with her family. Her website is:
www.KelleyArmstrong.com

● ●

MYTHOLOGY

Viaticum
By Katie Harse

Dai thought he saw Elam rise, thought he saw his master's soul speed upward in a streak of shining light, just like they'd said it would, when they left him here. "Two weeks," they'd said, "until his soul leaves his body." Two weeks to guard his master from scavengers and grave robbers who might desecrate this holy ground and impede Elam's passage to the world above.

Surely it had been that long. Surely tomorrow they would come and get him, as they'd promised, whatever their promise to a slave might be worth. Dai shivered in the damp and drew his thin tunic closer around him. A faint light shone through the cracks in the seal around the mound's entrance, and if he lay back, he could see a sliver of blue sky. Even so, it was cold here, under the ground. He pressed his face against a crack. Warm air teased him, the spring winds blowing across the plain, the smell of thawing earth and grass.

Eyes long unused to light recoiled from the sun, and Dai backed deeper into the tomb again. The lamp they'd left him still glowed in its niche, gentler than the glare from outside. "Be blind when I get out of here," he muttered in the general direction of the ornate sarcophagus that was his only companion. "I hope you appreciate it." His voice sounded strange in his ears, echoing in the silence of the tomb like a cough in a temple, or slaves whispering among themselves while their masters slept.

Even so, Dai spoke again, wondering at how the words rasped in his throat, as if reluctant to come out. "Not that

I'm not happy to serve — haven't I always been?" Perhaps
because he knew the answer, he added quickly, "It's an
honour, isn't it, to guard your—" He couldn't say it: to
guard his master's body through the soul's last days in
this world. Although why Elam should need a guard
down here, in this tomb covered with its mound of earth,
he didn't know. Not for him to question, but surely that
was enough to conceal Elam's resting place from robbers.
The very idea of burying the dead—

In her country, Dai's mother had told him — in *their*
country — they consigned corpses to clean fire, and their
souls ascended with the smoke. He hadn't said it then,
but Dai remembered wondering how many fires had
burned after the battle that had ended with a people
enslaved, his mother in chains, her husband dead. He
shivered again.

Surely tomorrow they would come to unseal the tomb
and take him back. There might even be a reward for such
service. For defending his master even in death. That was
something else to think about, Dai realized, wondering
why it hadn't occurred to him before. Because he didn't
want it to, he supposed. With Elam dead, he was
nobody's — he knew *she* wouldn't want him. A slave was
nothing, but a slave without a master was less than
nothing.

He felt weak, but told himself it was just hunger. An
earthen jar lay beside him, its mouth gaping wide, and
he reached inside with little hope. It had contained dried
meat, by the smell of it, but it was long since empty. He
licked his fingers, remembering the food they'd left here.
Good food, better than the daily fare of slaves, certainly.
But now all gone, save for a few grains of salt that burned
his tongue and raised a thirst more severe than the hunger
had been. The water was gone, too, and the wine they'd
left for Elam's journey.

Dai fumbled along the wall of earth, feeling the damp
coolness of it under his fingers, his cracking lips. His
tongue scraped along the face of it, tasted a trickle of
water. It wasn't enough, but after several mouthfuls of

sticky mud, he could convince himself he'd had something to drink. Food was a different matter. His mouth
tasted of ashes. Funeral ashes, he thought, and would
have laughed if he'd had the strength. The ashes of a
good, clean fire that make it unnecessary to defend the
dead from scavengers and thieves. He thought he heard
Elam's answering laugh, turned his head to the sarcophagus and saw nothing but a carved stone box.

At first it had bothered him, eating the food, drinking
the wine they'd left here for his master's journey to the
other world. But then, if the soul was going to leave his
body, what need had it for earthly food? Perhaps the
food's spirit had flown upwards as well, leaving the base
substance behind for those that really needed it. All too
complicated — he shouldn't even be thinking like this.
Shouldn't be thinking at all. But there was nothing else
to do, alone in the gloom. He could feel the closeness of
the walls, the weight of the earth above him.

Idly, Dai ran his hands over the empty jars, the rich
fabrics and polished metal mirrors, the silver cups and
the jewels — for all the good they did. He couldn't eat
them. He amused himself by closing his eyes and trying to guess what each piece was — anything to keep
his mind off the ache in his belly, the darkness, the growing cold.

He was afraid to sleep.

Something sharp pricked his hand. He drew back, and
then inched forward again. His fingers found the blade,
gently this time, then wrapped around the dagger's hilt.
He couldn't see it well in the dim light, but he didn't need
to. He knew this knife as though it were his own, for Elam
had carried it since Dai had known him.

It fit his hand surprisingly well — that still amazed
him, though he'd played this game for days. Elam had
been bigger, stronger than Dai, but his hands were small,
with graceful, slim fingers that moved constantly when
he talked, writing the words, it had always seemed to
Dai, in the air around him. Dai closed his eyes and pictured the dagger's jewelled hilt, crowned with topaz as

dark and brilliant as his master's eyes. The fine chased
metal showed his crest, the hawk with outstretched
wings familiar to Dai as the seal on Elam's letters.
Finally, he stroked the hard, polished steel of the blade.
The metal warmed under his touch, until it felt as if
he'd just taken it from Elam's living hand.

Unbidden, a voice echoed in Dai's ears, shattering
the vision. The words of a child, but with all the authority of the prince he was. "Don't touch it! Weapons
aren't for slaves, boy."

"You're younger than I am." He couldn't help it; he'd
been a child then, too, and didn't understand.

"But I'll be a man someday. You'll always be a slave.
And *I* have a dagger of my own, and you never can."
Dai was smart enough not to say that *his* father had
been a nobleman as well, if not a prince. Selas pulled
the smaller knife from its sheath and brandished it at
Dai. "I'll cut your ears off, boy, for your insolence."

He might have done it, too, but Elam came through
the door then, and pulled his brother away. "Let him
alone, Selas. Are you all right, boy?" It sounded
different when he said it, gentler. Dai had nodded,
unable to take his eyes off the older prince's face, to
tear himself away from the kindness there. Then Elam
broke the spell, snatching up his dagger from where
he'd left it on the table, and turning coldly on Selas.
"What kind of courage does it take to threaten a slave?
He has no power to hurt you, any more than a dog
does." Elam laughed, and tears prickled in Dai's eyes.

Elam paused. "Besides, Mother gave him to *me*,
remember. He's mine." And from that moment on, he
was.

And look what came of it. Dai opened his eyes,
raised the dagger towards the sarcophagus. "Better I
should cut my throat with this. Of course, with my luck,
they'd come back two hours after I bled to death. Is this
amusing you?"

Then it occurred to him that Selas would take the
throne, and he didn't know whether to laugh or cry.

Discarding the dagger, Dai crawled towards the sarcophagus, scraping his palms on the pottery, and knelt
beside the box that held Elam's body. Reaching up, he
traced the inscription round the rim. He couldn't read
the symbols, but he knew the letters of his master's
name, well enough to forge them. "Not that I would
have," he told the corpse inside. "But I could have issued
orders in your name, signed letters, deeds, anything."
In another life, he thought, in another world, I could
have been you.

The words mocked him. How do you sign an order
you can't read? As well as being Elam's page, his at-
tendant, his sometimes confidant, Dai had been his
copyist, spent years duplicating the shapes of letters,
words, sentences without ever knowing what they
meant. It hadn't occurred to him to ask — Elam might
even have told him, might have taught him... no, that
was impossible.

Dai ran his fingers lightly over the carved effigy on
the box's lid, the coloured plaster image of Elam's face,
not much older than his own, and far too young to die.
He studied it as his fingertips explored the strong,
straight nose, high cheekbones, full lips, as if he didn't
know that face by heart. The plaster was flawless and
smooth as skin, but cold. Dead.

Dead. Dai's throat tightened, and tears burned in his
eyes — a waste of water, he told himself, trying to hold
them back. He didn't know if they were for Elam, or
for himself. He tried to think of happier times, but the
memories wouldn't come, and the pain in his stomach
was growing stronger, as if rats were nesting there. There
were wasps in his mouth, as well, and when he tried
to stand the chamber whirled. Dai sank to the floor
again, his head in his hands.

He thought again of the last time he'd seen Elam,
gone to him after hearing the rumour that the woman
who was to be his master's wife had dozens of slaves,
that her father would provide them with an entire
household. That Elam wouldn't need him any more.

Dai had told himself that slaves weren't supposed to feel like this — it was illegal, immoral, by every tenet of law, impossible, but still the feelings grew until they almost choked him, until he burst into his master's study that afternoon, demanding to know how Elam could even consider it, by all the gods. "How could you choose her over me, when I've been with you since — since the beginning? I wasn't *alive* until I met you! How *dare* you—"

"How dare *I*?" Now his master sounded like *her*, the way she ordered her slaves around. The fine brows rose over bright dark eyes. Then he sighed. "Leave me, Dai — I've got work to do."

Work? What do you know of work? He wanted to say, wanted to scream that it was only an accident of birth, the lusts of a nobleman unsatisfied with his lawful wife, a war lost, a husband dead — but slaves weren't supposed to have those thoughts, either. Instead he met Elam's blazing eyes and shook his head. "Not until you throw me out." He hated the way his voice shook, the way his breath caught in his chest.

Elam stood, stepped back from the desk. "Go. Or I'll—" It could have been Selas speaking, the voice from that long-ago memory, the hand raised in fury.

"Do it!" *Act like my master for once, even if you beat me, even if you sell me*— Thoughts pounded inside Dai's skull, a tangle of emotions he couldn't understand. *Give me a reason to hate you.*

Elam swore, then turned and strode towards the door, slamming it violently and leaving Dai standing in the now-empty room, tears streaming down his face. If Elam had hit him, had screamed and threatened to send him away, to sell him to the mines, or the galleys, it would have been easier. At least then Dai would have known what to think, how to think. How to be a slave again. That Elam never gave him a reason for it made his hate the strangest of all, and he cursed his master to all the gods before going out the door after him, but by then Elam was nowhere to be found.

When the Old Man — for the life of him he couldn't remember the overseer's name — had come into the slaves' quarters that evening, his face pale, looking as if he'd come to order an execution, or at the very least a flogging, that was what Dai had thought it was. He'd come here after a day spent wandering the grounds, rather than to his own bed outside Elam's door, because he couldn't bear the thought of *her* sleeping behind it as well. The kitchen was already abuzz with rumours, but he managed to ignore them until the Old Man told them. "The young master's had a fall. His horse came home without him — they say he's..."

"No," Dai whispered. "No. There's not a horse in the world that would throw him. Everybody knows that." He pleaded with them, but no one would meet his eyes. The buzz grew again. Everyone knew someone who had heard from someone who had seen the young master riding away like a mad thing, putting his horse at impossible fences. Angry, they said the groom said, and the horse returning half dead with running.

They were talking to calm their own fears, to come up with an explanation, to make it an accident. "For if it hadn't been, they'd have killed us all," Dai told the effigy. "And instead—"

Instead. He raised his head and looked around at the shadows cast by the pitiful lamp. The streaks of light around the seal had long since faded, without even the suggestion of stars. "Instead I'm shut in here with you...." He tried to think if he'd heard of anyone else guarding the dead for those all-important two weeks. He couldn't remember, but there are things slaves don't talk about, for fear of inviting bad luck. If one disappeared, he might have been sold, or killed, or—

"They're not coming back, are they, Elam?" The effigy stared at him with blank eyes. No, why would they? They'd been trying to get rid of him since the beginning, Selas, and the woman, and this was the easiest way of all. But Elam?

The walls rushed towards him, the shadows, and the smell of earth and death and his own body, suddenly suffocating, like a wet velvet cloth held over his face. He was going to die here.

Now the cold was sharper than before, and coming from somewhere deep inside him, so that he shook with it, and with the great panting sobs that tore from his throat. He pictured himself lying here, unable to move, to stand, watching his body waste into nothing. Anger rose from his hollow stomach and boiled into his throat. "You *knew*!" The wave of it carried him upward, screaming at the sarcophagus. He snatched up a heavy brass urn and smashed it down upon the effigy's smiling, mocking face. Chips of plaster stung his skin, and his hand throbbed warm and wet. Blood spattered Elam's ruined features.

Dai leaned against the box, exhausted. "Maybe I *deserve* to die." That afternoon, he had cursed his master, wished him dead. The gossips in the kitchens and slave cells would have thought nothing of it, of course. "All slaves curse their masters, and they curse us, you know. That's the way things are."

But I meant it.

He wondered if Elam had planned it as revenge, that Dai might share his fate. "Your good and faithful servant. Gods! I'm going to starve to death, and I haven't killed myself." The absurdity of the words struck him, and he laughed, a raw, painful sound that rang dully from the chamber walls.

No. It was ridiculous. And surely the gods — their gods — would take no notice of a slave, and if the gods of his mother's people had heard his curse and killed Elam, then why would they leave him here as well, doomed to share his master's grave? Unless he wasn't going to die, unless there was some escape. He struggled the few steps to the entrance and the seal, felt eagerly for purchase, thinking he might dig his way out, but it was hopeless. When they'd first shut him in here, he might have done it, but now he barely had the strength to stand, especially after that last outburst.

Dai turned back to the sarcophagus, bent over the effigy's maimed face, tears mixing with blood on the shattered plaster and cracked stone. "I didn't mean it. And I don't hate you."

He imagined that Elam reached out to touch his cheek with gentle fingers, and heard the soft, familiar voice. "I know." Then he was gone, and Dai was back in the cold, damp darkness of the tomb.

When he leaned on the sarcophagus this time, it made a grinding sound like bones being set, and a new, foul smell, stronger than those he now knew well, filled air already thick with the stench of dissolution. He must have breached the coffin's seal, and now the lid lay balanced at an angle, his master exposed. Curiosity overcame disgust, and he bent closer, reaching for the lamp. Shadows danced across Elam's face, the flickering light giving it a distorted kind of life, so he could almost imagine that the skin moved, that the face bore some expression beyond the ugly blankness that he saw when he looked closer, the once-full lips shrivelled and old-looking, Elam's features obscured and discoloured like a giant bruise. Dai's stomach heaved, then settled to the dull ache he could pretend he didn't notice any more.

He forced himself to look again, not to see the split and mottled skin, but to imagine Elam there. He pictured his master as he had once been, smiling and kind as the sun on a warm day, and reached out to touch the beautiful face, to smooth the thick, dark hair out of his eyes. But the eyes were flat and sunken, and the hair, when he touched it, came away in his hand. If the plaster face had been too cold, too perfect, this was too much of the earth. He hated this thing, for all it bore Elam's name and wore his jewels — his topaz earring glinting in the lamplight, beautiful against the horror.

In despair, Dai raised his fist to smash the hateful, warped face of the thing that should have been Elam, to pound it into a pulpy mess. He didn't have much strength, but his hand drove through the loose, swollen flesh, came away wet, stinking bits of meat clinging to his fingers. Still sobbing, he brought the hand up to his eyes, then to his lips, choking. "Elam, I'm sorry." His master's face, cheerful and alive, stared out at him from the sarcophagus, then faded when he looked too long.

Dai bent, pressed his lips against the cold, soft hands folded across Elam's chest. "I'm sorry." Then he took his master's fingers in his mouth, took Elam's very substance into his body, and smiled at the shadows.

• •

Katie Harse is currently working on a Ph.D. in Victorian literature and culture at Indiana University, Bloomington, but still thinks of herself as a Calgary writer. Her fiction has appeared in *Tesseracts 6* and on CBC Radio, and she is a long-time member of the Imaginative Fiction Writers' Association.

• •

A Patch of Bamboo

by Jill Snider Lum

Patrick Carter couldn't see Yokohama; the branches were too dense. He felt disoriented — the whining roar of a million cicadas and the damp, exotic smell of the forest had its usual effect, making him drunk with sensation. He held on to the wooden railing, breathing in the humidity. *In the past,* he thought, *when they lived with this ghastly noise all summer, they must have just been able to tune it out. The same way they deliberately ignored each other's private conversations, for the sake of politeness.*

He resumed his climb up the hillside steps, slowly in the stifling heat. There were tourists at Sankeien Garden today, in spite of the oppressive weather. Old Mrs. Saito, his acquaintance who ran the admission gate, had let him in for half price. She joked that his devotion to the Garden was only matched by his tolerance for Japan's summer weather.

He saw the tunnel ahead and above. Its mouth gaped, deliciously mysterious, too dark to show that it only led to a little seventeenth-century tea-house. After seven visits, he was still drawn to it.

He looked away for a moment as a descending tourist jostled him. When he looked back he saw a woman, hurrying into the tunnel in a flash of green-and-yellow kimono.

There was another small path through the woods, so she must have come up that way. Suddenly he felt a strange urgency, an irrational need to follow her. He hurried up the steps, sweating and breathing hard.

He entered the tunnel and saw her rounding the bend. Oddly, she seemed somehow out of focus — sweat in his eyes? — but her jerky movements had a look of desperation, and her face in profile seemed stretched in a grimace of terror. She had no feet.

Patrick choked on his own breath as he realized what he was seeing. She moved as other humans move, running as fast as she could in the long, restricting kimono. But her ankles ended before the ground, and he couldn't see her feet.

Patrick charged forward with an incoherent cry, not caring if passing visitors noticed — had no one else seen her? But when he rounded the corner, she wasn't there.

No one was there.

Patrick stood shivering in the close heat, the scream of the cicadas like a knife through his head. *I must be completely insane,* he thought. *Only a bloody nutcase runs* toward *a ghost.*

⇥•⊹•⊹•⊹•⇤

The next day was Sunday. His tutorial student, Ito-san, came for lessons in the morning, but he had trouble paying attention to the young man's progress. It didn't help that Ito-san was himself a part-time employee at Sankeien Garden. He'd been the one to introduce Patrick to the place, to its addictive calm and its fascinating historical buildings, its hundreds of years of history.

And, evidently, its ghosts. Patrick's mind churned, replaying the vision of the ghost-woman. *They say Japan is a land of ghosts,* he thought, *but I figured that was just the cultural context of Shintoism. Ghosts can't be real, can they? And Japanese ghosts have invisible feet, in all the stories, but I'm not Japanese. So if I were crazy, wouldn't I see a ghost with feet? An insane Westerner would see his own kind of ghost, wouldn't he? But what about an insane Westerner who knows a lot about Japan, who's lived in Japan for months, who knows the language fairly well? I feel like I blend in here. Did I see a real Japanese ghost? Or am I just insane, hallucinating one?*

The air-conditioner's laboured whine reminded him of the cicadas. His head hurt.

Toward the end of the lesson his student asked, in Japanese, "Sensei-san, is anything bothering you?"

Patrick shook his head politely. "I'm fine," he said. Then on impulse, he added, "Ito-san, do you believe in ghosts?"

Ito knit his brow, very slightly. "Do you mean spirits?" he said. "I am a Shintoist. Of course I believe in spirits. There are spirits in everything, everywhere. We say there's even a spirit in every single grain of rice."

Patrick nodded. Ito waited politely.

"I know a lot about Shintoism, and how it affects Japanese culture," said Patrick, carefully. "Do people here... would you say that people in Japan see ghosts fairly often?"

Ito raised his brows. "Depends on the people," he said.

Patrick sighed inwardly. "Pardon me for that personal question," he said. Ito looked a little baffled.

Patrick switched back to teacher mode. "Well, now," he said, "before you go, we will begin your lesson on Articles. They are the part of English grammar that Japanese speakers find hardest to adapt to. They come in Definite and Indefinite, and they might seem ridiculous at first, but the English language would not make sense without them."

Ito smiled — a real smile, in the corners of his eyes. "Like spirits," he said. "As a foreigner, you might think they're ridiculous at first, or crazy. But to us Japanese, Japan wouldn't make sense without them. I told you I was a Shintoist, and I am... the way all Japanese are Shintoists, even the ones who have other religious beliefs, or no beliefs. Most of us really aren't religious, but spirits, the idea of spirits, even the reality of spirits... it's part of us. It is something that you will experience as you live here."

"I know," said Patrick. Ito looked at him, and lifted his eyebrows, slightly.

❖❖❖❖❖

The sign on the admission booth at Sankeien Garden had a dozen things you weren't supposed to do, listed with pictograms so that everyone could understand them. You weren't supposed to eat or drink in Sankeien Garden, or bring dogs, or vandalize the buildings, or carry weapons, or be rude to others, or detonate explosive devices. Patrick had often chuckled at it — it was such a characteristically Japanese sign. *But*, he thought as he climbed quietly over the fence, *it doesn't say you can't sneak in after closing, so I'm following the rules. What a good thing.*

His stomach was jumping — fear at the prospect of being caught and thrown in a Yokohama jail; and fear of what he had come here to examine, to face in the dark.

The security guards at the Garden took their work seriously. Twice they passed closely by him, almost near enough to touch, but he hid in the bushes beside the pathways, and they didn't see him in the gathering dusk. He wondered, stumbling a little as he finally reached the hillside steps, what old Mrs. Saito would say if she knew he'd snuck in after closing. He choked back a hysterical little giggle, and began to climb the stairs.

The cicadas were still screaming. The damp heat was worse.

He waited at the tunnel's mouth, and that strange sense of urgency crept over him. Here in the dark, with no one around to distract him, it grew in strength until it almost overpowered him.

When he saw her this time, she glowed like a movie, every detail in sharp clarity against the darkness. He was too frightened to feel any triumph that he'd been right about that.

She ran awkwardly in the kimono, feet invisible, green-and-yellow sleeves flying, and horror clear in her face. Patrick ran close behind her, gasping, stumbling over rocks and the roots of trees. She came to the turn and looked backward. He heard her shriek — or was it the cicadas? — and then she turned and ran again, with him in close pursuit.

He wasn't prepared for the glowing, footless figure that rushed past him. It was a man, wearing the traditional garb of a samurai, with his hair gathered in a queue. There was blood on the sword the man carried — and blood on both his hands.

Patrick put on a burst of speed, trying to keep the samurai from catching the woman, and knowing he was an idiot, since both were long dead.

In front of the little tea-house she lost her balance, falling into a patch of bamboo in one corner beside a fence. Then the samurai was on top of her.

She screamed, beating at him with her fists, and this time Patrick knew it was not the cicadas he heard. Their roar sounded like a dim recording, a backdrop of static behind her screams of rage and terror.

The samurai reared back and swung his sword, and her head came off in a fountain of blood. Some small object she had been holding in her hand fell to the ground, her blood puddling over it. The image was so clear as to be no longer an image at all.

Patrick turned away, his stomach heaving with terror, and convulsed until he vomited. When he turned back, the figures had gone.

✦•I•I•I•✦

He came back the next day after teaching his classes, an hour before Sankeien Garden was due to close. He got off the bus in the pleasant, expensive neighbourhood near the Garden, in a shower of emphatic Japanese rain. He wished for his umbrella, left behind on a bus three days before. The air wasn't any cooler after the rain.

He walked ten minutes past nice old houses, with courtyards, and driveways, and space enough for a little landscaping. He tried to keep his mind occupied by estimating how long ago each house had been built. There was no line-up at the Garden's admissions gate, this near to closing time.

He said, "Konnichi-wa, Saito-san," and bowed correctly to the old lady. She was wearing pink and dark plum. She smiled, bowing back, and her eyes had their usual twinkle.

"Are you going to jog around the Garden, Carter-san?" she asked, teasingly, but with the formality he expected of an elderly Japanese. "We're closing soon, you know."

"I came to talk to you," Patrick said. "Do you have a few minutes, please?"

"Certainly," she said, and he saw that she was curious behind her politeness.

"I saw a ghost here, two days ago," he said, slowly. "Yesterday I saw two of them."

Her face became guarded, and Patrick assumed she was restraining her reaction for politeness's sake. "Really?" she said.

He told her about everything he'd seen, including the decapitation, mentally crossing his fingers and hoping she wouldn't call the cops to throw him in the nut-house.

She didn't.

"Oh," she said, in a flat voice. Her eyes were no longer cheerful. "I've seen that woman's ghost, too."

Patrick bit his lip, almost disappointed. "You have?"

"Yes. But I have never seen *him*."

Patrick didn't know what to say. Mrs. Saito just nodded.

"The samurai ghost doesn't surprise me," she said. "He's part of her story. The woman — her name was Michiko, in fact — her father found out about that samurai's disloyal dealings with their clan's enemies, so the samurai killed the old man, and Michiko saw him do it. The story goes that Michiko had just dressed, and was putting on her jewellery when she heard the commotion, and came to the front reception-room in time to see that Samurai murder her father. She ran away to a neighbour's home, but he came after her, caught her in front of the neighbour's tea-house, and cut off her head. It's the same tea-house we have here at Sankeien; it was moved here twenty-two years ago. The ghosts... well, they moved here, too. I came to work here myself, around that time."

Patrick frowned, at a loss. "How do you know all this, Saito-san? Are you interested in ghost stories?"

She shook her head. "No, no," she said, with strange deliberation. "I do not like ghost stories at all. But the woman you saw is my direct ancestor — my grandmother, many generations back. Her full name was Saito Michiko-san. The man you saw was her cousin by marriage, Kandagawa Hideo. He was a very shameful, disloyal person."

Patrick managed not to gape at her. "I — I didn't realize, Saito-san," he said. "Please forgive me if I have caused you pain, or upset you. It was shocking and — crazy, what I saw. I had to tell someone about it, and — from the talks we've had before, I thought you might... understand? I know you love this place, you've told me so, and I know that most Japanese people believe in spirits...." He groped for words, wishing his Japanese vocabulary were better.

"I do understand, Carter-san," said Mrs. Saito, and smiled at him, warmly now. "Thank you for telling me about this."

"Thank you for listening," he said. He was about to bow and wish her a good evening, when something else occurred to him. "Saito-san, when she... before Saito Michiko-san disappeared, I saw her drop something on the ground. Some little thing that was in her hand. Do you know what it could have been?"

Mrs. Saito thought for a long moment. "Oh, yes," she said, nodding to herself. "That would be her ring. Kandagawa Hideo robbed her corpse of the jewellery she had — adding insult to injury, but he was that kind of man, apparently. When their clan members caught him, he had all of her jewellery except the gold ring her father had given her when she married. No one ever found it."

Patrick nodded. "I see," he said, feeling drained, numb. "Well, thank you, Saito-san. I hope you have a pleasant evening."

She looked suddenly uncomfortable. "See you again, Carter-san," she said, bowing.

Maybe, thought Patrick. *And maybe not. Maybe I should leave well enough alone.*

→·⟨·⟩·⟨·←

But after two weeks with his days and nights haunted by screams and cicadas and decapitated heads, he realized it was hopeless. He wanted desperately to leave it alone, but it wasn't leaving *him* alone. *It's because I'm foreign, but I know the Japanese culture,* he thought. *The spirits — her spirit — must be reaching out to me for help, because no one has helped before.*

He devoted a number of evenings to research, and after a few false starts and incorrect assumptions he eventually located the original site of the tea-house.

The next evening he took the subway to Tokyo, and then a bus, and then a cab. The driver had trouble finding the address in the late-night urban maze, and Patrick wasn't sure what would be there, so he couldn't help. It frustrated him no end.

Eventually he got out at the address and paid off the cab-driver. Four hundred years earlier, the tea-house had stood on the grounds of a substantial house outside of Edo. Now the spot was a pub-restaurant in Ikebukuro. The English sign said "Drunk Squids," and had a drawing of a goofy-looking cephalopod holding a beer mug in one of its tentacles.

Patrick went inside, sweat running down his back. The air conditioning was set at Japanese-normal, the dim interior warm rather than furnace-hot. Three or four tables were still occupied, businessmen having obligatory after-work drinks with their colleagues and bosses. One or two of them were sweating as badly as Patrick was.

The now-familiar sense of urgency rushed over him. It made him shiver.

The waitress was young and wore a frilly apron. Patrick ordered hashed beef rice and a mug of beer. "Special discount if you get the large mug," the girl said, smiling politely. He nodded. In this weather he could drink a litre of beer at once and barely feel it.

After the food came, he ate it slowly, savouring the thinly sliced beef and onions and the sharp taste of the sauce. The mug of beer helped him relax a little. What could they charge him with, anyway? Trespassing, of course. Maybe vandalism. But likely he wouldn't get caught; it wouldn't play out that way. Before he'd arrived, the idea had still seemed ridiculous; but now that he was here, he knew just what to do, and where to do it. That urgent gut-feeling told him — or *something* told him. He could practically hear the cicadas.

Patrick ordered dessert, one of the crazy Japanese ice-cream sundaes with green tea sauce and chocolate syrup and mochi balls and sweet black beans and whipped cream. He ate that slowly too; it killed time. He knew he should have come later, but he had felt unbearably restless at his apartment and eventually couldn't stand the waiting.

He finished his sundae and left, eyeing the bar's exterior one more time. Then he walked around the neighbourhood for an hour, watching the crowds and marveling at the neon. Casually he made his way back to Drunk Squids and saw that it was shut.

No longer being careful, he strode to their side door at the street corner. There was a neat little patch of ground there, unpaved, the kind of spot for guerilla gardeners to strike in the night.

The side-street was deserted. Patrick squatted and thought, suppressing giggles, that this might be his defense. *I was gardening. I was going to plant some sunflower seeds. You can't send me to prison for that.*

He knew just where to dig: in that spot, that patch of ground, curiously unpaved as though some agency had kept the earth open. That frightened him.

❖❖❖

He made the trip to Sankeien Garden again the next evening, feeling a wry urge to chuckle when the bus-driver recognized him. He got off as the sun was lowering in the sky, and went up to the admission-gate once more.

"Carter-san?" Mrs. Saito didn't mask her surprise. "Here again at closing time? Is something wrong?"

"Um," he said. He wasn't sure how to start. It would have been difficult even in English.

"Do you have more questions about... the matter we spoke of earlier?" she asked.

He blinked a few times. "Not exactly, Saito-san," he said. "I... I went to the place where the tea-house used to stand. In Tokyo. It's a bar. I found a patch of ground, and I dug. I found this."

He opened his palm, and showed her the ring. He'd polished it up a little, so it shone dully.

She looked down at it, and then up at him, her wide-eyed surprise giving way to a disapproving frown.

"I don't understand how I knew it was there, Saito-san." Patrick knew he was awkward, babbling. "I felt this feeling, like when I saw the ghosts. Kind of an urgency, the pressure to *do* something. I know it all happened a long time ago, but they're still here, and I had to do something. It was like they were haunting me, I couldn't forget them, I thought about them day and night. I know spirits are part of life here in Japan... and I think this is what they wanted me to do."

She shook her head, very slowly. "You should not have done this, Carter-san," she said. "Saito Michiko-san... you've brought her ring to me, her descendant. That was why she came here, I am sure, because she wanted her ring back, her ring from her father; and now, because I have it, she has it too. I lived near the tea-house that was on my ancestors' land, before I had to sell it, and I used to see her ghost. When I donated the tea-house to Sankeien Garden, I moved to Yokohama and came to work here, too. I used to see her after closing at the mouth of the tunnel, or sometimes during the day when I'd wander up there on my lunch break. It was a comfort to me. I am alone in the world, you see, I have no family and no real friends, but at least I had my foremother, I could see her. I knew where I came from. I had people in my past. Now I have... nothing. I wish you had not done this."

Patrick frowned. "But surely you can't mean you *wanted* your own ancestor to be tied to the earth this way." He knew, even as he spoke the words, that they would have sounded insane to him two weeks before. "Saito Michiko-san must have haunted the place because of her unfinished business, maybe the way she died... maybe because she wanted this ring back, like you say. Well, if finding the ring releases her from hundreds of years being tied here and not getting to the afterlife, don't you think that's a good thing?"

The old lady blinked. Patrick saw, to his horror, that tears were running down her face. "I'm so sorry to have upset you, Saito-san," he said, hurriedly. "I'll take the ring back and bury it again. I didn't mean to — to..."

"No, no," said Mrs. Saito, lifting a wrinkled hand, and shaking her head. "You meant well, Carter-san. But you have brought it here to me, so it is too late."

She held out her palm to him, and he gave her the ring, watching her papery fingers curl around it. "Will you put it in your kamidana?" he asked, knowing she would have a shrine to her family's spirits.

"I will do what must be done," she said, very politely. She gave him a closed smile and bowed, with great formality. But she did not say, "See you again," as she usually did.

Patrick hoped he hadn't offended her too badly.

✦✧✦✧✦

Ito-san came for a tutoring lesson two days later. Articles, he said, were certainly strange, but he was trying to absorb them. He thought he was perhaps on the verge of seeing why English would be much harder to understand without them.

"And you, Sensei-san?" Ito added, in Japanese now. "Are you understanding spirits a little more, since we talked? Do you begin to see why Japan makes no sense without spirits?"

Patrick nodded. "Oh, yes," he said. "I do. Definitely."

Ito smiled, with a touch of irony. "A good start," he said. "Oh, by the way, did you hear what happened at Sankeien Garden yesterday?"

Patrick's stomach tightened. "No," he said. "What happened?"

"Well, you know old Mrs. Saito who runs the admission gate, don't you? I know she's told me that you and she have had several discussions when you've visited."

Patrick nodded, trying to keep his breathing normal. "Yes, I know her," he said.

"Well, I'm afraid I have bad news about her, Sensei-san. She was found dead yesterday morning at Sankeien in front of the tea-house. The one at the end of that tunnel. You know the one I mean."

Patrick stared at the young man. "Dead?" he said. "How? What did she die of?"

"She killed herself," said Ito, his voice flat. "Stabbed herself in the throat, like a samurai woman. She did it in that patch of bamboo that grows in front of the tea-house. Left a note. They found it in her pocket. It said she had nothing to live for, now that her last link to her family was gone."

Patrick's stomach heaved. He shook his head. "Ito-san, I don't feel well," he said. "We can continue this lesson another time. I'm sorry. Please go now."

"Do you think it had anything to do with the ghost she used to see?" Ito said, ignoring him. "She used to tell me it was like her last family member. What do you think happened, Carter-san? Do you think it had anything to do with that?"

"Please go now, Ito-san," said Patrick, trembling. He stood up.

Ito rose, too. He moved to the door of the flat, never taking his eyes from Patrick. "You think you know more than you do, Carter-san," said Ito. "But you are a foreigner. Never forget that — or you'll do even more harm."

Ito shut the door behind him, quietly.

Patrick buried his face in his hands.

• •

Jill Snider Lum, a native of Toronto, is the author of *Maggie's Luck and Other Stories*, a fantasy/SF/dark fantasy adult-literacy reader. Her fiction has recently appeared in *Shimmer* magazine's Pirate Issue, and in *Tesseracts Twelve* (with Michael Skeet).

• •

The Radejastians

By David Nickle

We three ate lunch outside in the springtime. There was a picnic table under a small tree, well out of sight of the loading docks, and it was there we met: Viktor and Ruman and I. We had all come from the old country, the same old country, and I suppose that marked us... not in the same way, but as the same, all the same.

Viktor had not been there since he was a child, which was forty years ago, and had worked the warehouse for a decade. The mark was faint on him. Although I had been back more recently — a year earlier — for the solstice festival, I had felt like the alien there, walking the cobbled streets of Radejast alone, among the dancing virgins and the yowling monks in their woven-straw masks... the vendors who sold the long, blackened apple dolls of saints I could no longer name.

Ruman, now.

For him, the mark was fresh, for he had just arrived a year and some months ago. His family still lived at home in the smelting town in the southern mountains, waiting for word that he was established enough that they might also make their escape — and profitably join him here.

Maybe he shared his mark; infected us too with it. Maybe that mark pushed the others away from us: or drew us together, and so away from the others.

Maybe this, maybe that. We had a half hour for lunch, and on those fine days that were neither humid nor frigid, the sun only so high at noon, we spent it out of doors. We talked only a little. For truly, we had little in common between us, save our mother tongue and dimming recollections. The conversations we had during that time stand out like horsemen on a plain.

"I am thinking that I am going to be saved," said Ruman one Tuesday in April. The sky was clouded over us. But Ruman was the greyer.

"What do you mean?" I asked, and Viktor interjected: "He means he's going back to that church."

Ruman shrugged and stirred his soup so the color of beets deepened in it. "I must think of my soul," he said.

"Shit, Ruman," I said. "Don't do it. Those ones will only rob you."

"No, no," said Viktor, "they will not rob you. When I came here, I tried a church like that one. No one robbed me. What I gave, I gave. How it went, it went. But I don't think it saved me."

Ruman looked up. "You are here, aren't you?"

"Not because it saved me," said Viktor.

"Well this is a different church," said Ruman. "They have a great cross, visible from the motor-way. The building is shaped five-sided. And they are all virgins, the women there. The unmarried ones, of course."

"Ha! Now we come to it!" I said, and Ruman's grey flesh went a deep red.

"Wife at home," said Viktor, finger wagging, "wife at home."

"I just think it's time to be saved," said Ruman. And that was the end of that conversation.

⋆⋅I⋅∘⋅I⋅⋆

Ruman went back to the church.

Did that place save him? I saw no evidence that it had, as we gathered each day in the growing shade of our tree, at our table. Perhaps that is because he did not speak of it. But that was not the only thing. Ruman brought a little pamphlet that he set out one day — it had a painting of a brown-haired, blue-eyed Jesus, spreading his hands over a multitude of sinners, the light spreading around him as though it had substance.

But he displayed it almost with embarrassment, and when Viktor and I spared it only a glance before setting in to our sandwiches, he pulled it back to his lap with something like shame.

After that, the pamphlet was gone. And so we would eat, and sometimes Viktor would talk, I would answer, and in the end we would return to the shadow of the loading bay doors.

And as the days went by, I found I wondered with rather more urgency: did the church save Ruman?

He came to us a thin man, with the long face and dark brows of our kind, pale of flesh and bent of back. Was his color any deeper, was there more certainty in his eyes as the days went on? Had he put flesh on in his time there? If anything, he seemed the opposite: thinner, his outer layers honed away.

But could I say? And as I considered that, I considered this: could I say how it was that I wondered so, after the health of Ruman's frail soul?

As the summer deepened, we left the bench to the women from the front office who appreciated the sun more than we. Viktor was so unappreciative that he took the night shift, which he said he preferred in the heat of high summer. As for me — I hefted crates from shelf to belt, and soaked in the heat as it soaked me, and watched Ruman, as he did the same — thin, and bent, and strangely resolute.

And so it was one Thursday afternoon in July that I quietly spoke to Ruman, and the following Sunday, drove with him to church.

⚜⚜⚜

Ruman lived in a house in the eastern suburbs, where he rented a room of his own and shared a bathroom and kitchen with five other men. Too many men in the house, and everyone knew it. Ordinarily, he would take a bus from there, after walking ten minutes through twists of the subdivision to the bus stop at the main road — the neighbours eyes burning his back as he came and went. His very home was an affront to them.

I didn't pity him. Three years ago, I lived in a place just as bad, and these days, I lived in an apartment only a little better. I had a car but it was old and forever breaking down; and I'm not sure my life was much improved by having it. But I could tell he was grateful for the lift.

"I thought you might not come," he said as we pulled away from the house.

"Why not?"

"I thought you were afraid," he said.

"Afraid?"

"Like Viktor," he said. "Men from dark places... they fear the Light."

"Men from dark places fear the dark," I said, and he snorted.

The church was fifteen minutes away from Ruman's house, in an industrial park like the one in which we worked. And Ruman was right; you could see the cross from the highway. It climbed over the structure on a steel lattice, and at night you could see it would light up. It would glow blue, Ruman explained as I shifted lanes to get off the highway. Why was it called the Good News Happening Congregation? I wondered as we drove past the driveway, looking for a spot on the road. GOOD NEWS HAPPENING CONGREGATION was stamped out in moveable letters on a sign-board mounted on wheels. Ruman had no proper answer for that.

We crossed a wide parking lot and approached a large bank of glass doors. There were a great many people clustered inside, and more moving in and out. When the doors opened, a burble of music and conversation and laughter drifted out. I speculated that we might be late and worried at the consequences.

"Will the virgins be angry?" I asked, but Ruman straight-facedly reassured me: "This is how it always is."

He took me through the door and led me inside.

→•]•[••]•[•←

There is a cathedral in the middle of Radejast. It addresses the approaching pilgrim as a fist of granite and slate and limestone, lifting black iron bells and arches and gargoyles to touch the dangled teat of the soot-cloud that ever hangs low over the land. Within: a forest of stone pillars, some carved with the likenesses of Radejast's saints, some simply chiseled with the mark of its venerable religion — all surrounding the dome, so high and wide that when emerging from the pillars I stumbled beneath it, madly fearful that gravity might suddenly reverse, fling me from the floor, and smash me against the curved mosaics above the whispering gallery.

The Good News Happening Congregation's hall was larger than Radejast's cathedral by half again: a great circular space beneath a peaked roof, lit from high, clear windows on every side. Behind the pulpit stood a crucifix with a painted sculpture of Jesus Christ bound to it, bright lines of blood trickling down his slender limbs, from the crown of thorns he wore. Altogether, it was half-again taller than any similar icon in Radejast.

Surrounding the pulpit, curved rows of folding chairs radiated outward across a floor of polished concrete. Ruman craned his neck in a certain direction and waved. When I looked there, I saw a woman with short blond hair, a deep tan, beckoning us over. We moved to join her and what turned out to be a group of five more.

"That," explained Ruman as we made our way down the aisle, "is Cheryl and her friends. But I do not know all their names still," he added, embarrassed.

"I will introduce myself, then."

"Thank you."

"Are they—?"

Ruman cut in. "Stop talking about the virgins. I don't know."

But Ruman was wrong. I was not set to mock him, make implications about his wandering attentions, remind him of his wife, as Viktor had that day. Stepping into this vast space, breathing the fresh-scrubbed scent of these pilgrims, I only thought to ask: Are they good people? Because looking across their faces, all of their faces — they seemed like good people to me.

"Well hello there, sleepyhead," said Cheryl, as we moved to the seats that she and her friends were saving. "Is this your friend?"

I introduced myself and held out my hand, and Cheryl took it in both of hers. "I am sorry we are late," I said. "My fault."

"Oh goodness," said Cheryl. "You're not late at all. You got Ruman here early."

"Cheryl's just saying that Ruman could use some sleep," said one of the others — black hair and heavy-set in a print dress. "Look at the rings under his eyes." Ruman snorted, half-smiled and looked away.

"I'm Rose," she said, and added: "God Bless."

Ruman said "God Bless," and I said so too, and for the first time of many that morning, we all eight of us joined hands and said it again together.

⇥⊹⊹⊹⊹⇤

The morning service went on for some hours. There was singing and some talk from the tall, dark-haired pastor of the congregation, and of course some reading from the Bible. And then came a break, wherein everybody else introduced themselves. There was Rose's daughter Lisa; and Mary and Lottie, sisters to one another; and Carrie, who knew Cheryl from high school and had been married to Cheryl's high school sweetheart until two years ago when he had left Carrie, the city and the Lord. Both Cheryl and Carrie piously insisted they prayed daily for him. Yet they laughed when I wondered what exactly they prayed their God should do with one such as he.

"You are *bad*," said Carrie, and Cheryl gave my forearm a gentle slap and shifted so her shoulder rested against mine. I felt a pang — for was I not a guest of Ruman, who had introduced me to these women? It is true that he had a wife in the old country, was bound to her in the ways of our people, and so he could lay no claim to any of these women here. Yet in the riot of our lusts, how often do we heed reason and ignore that deeper voice, speaking to us as it does through the ages?

The pang lasted an instant. Looking past Lottie, I noticed that Ruman was gone. Seeing my confusion, Lottie pointed to the pulpit.

"Ah," I said. Ruman had made his way there with some two-dozen others. There was no music playing, but he and they seemed to be dancing, or their shoulders were moving like dancers. The pastor stepped onto the low stage and reached down to help another up: this one an older woman in a long dress, her grey hair tied in a bun. The room dimmed as a cloud drifted past the sun. She held her hands up in the air, waggled her fingers, and began to sway. The pastor said nothing, but held his microphone to his chest, and swayed also. Around me, the congregation began to stand, and Carrie nudged me and Cheryl tugged my arm as she stood. Beside her, Lottie shut her eyes and began to hum.

A spotlight came on, illuminating the woman on the stage. She leaned her head back as though bathing in it. Then she too began to speak, to shout. She bunched her shoulders, as though coiling a spring there, and released, her arms spreading from her waist, and she did not just shout — she screamed. The pastor stepped back and held his arms out over her head, fingers spread as though he were preparing to catch her, should gravity fling her high.

I remember an impulse then, to wrap my own arms around myself. But I could not. Cheryl and Carrie had taken my hands, one each, and held my arms apart. I suppose I might have pulled away, forcefully drawn my arms in. But the fear passed as fast as it came. And like Cheryl, like Carrie — like Ruman, gyrating and babbling with the crowd in front of the pulpit...

I was swept up.

※⋅|⋅|⋅|⋅※

When it was finished, we all went for lunch at a pancake place on the other side of the motorway. It was crowded and noisy, and there was no hope of finding a table for all of us. We divided ourselves: Cheryl, myself, Lisa, and Lottie took a table near the window; Ruman, Carrie, Mary, and

Rose found a booth not too far off. Cheryl thought it important that no one who had come to church in the same car also sit at the same table.

"How else are we going to build community," she asked as we took our places in the sunlight, "if every time we worship, we all sit in our little tribes?"

"Amen," I said. I glanced over at the booth. Ruman's face was obscured by the menu.

"Aw," said Lottie, "you miss your friend?" She patted my arm.

"He seems to like it here," I said. It was true. We didn't speak much in the short drive over, but I had never seen Ruman seem so... nourished.

"He does at that," said Cheryl. "How 'bout you? You think you might join us?"

"Perhaps," I said. "I don't know about..." I waggled my fingers at my shoulders and swayed a bit in my chair. Lisa concealed a grin. Cheryl didn't bother. She laughed.

We ordered: me, a plate of bacon and scrambled eggs; Lottie, a platter of fresh fruit; Cheryl, an omelet. Lisa asked for a big plate of pancakes topped with stewed apples.

"Did you go to church with Ruman?" asked Lisa, as we waited for our meals. "Back in the old country?"

"No. Ruman came here just recently. I have been here two years more. I did not know Ruman. We have a job together."

"He said he didn't like church in the old country." I could see Lottie trying to shush Lisa, but she made as not to notice and pressed on. "He said he likes this one better. Do you like this one better?"

Cheryl cut in. "Well, I bet there's no dancing back in the old church, not like we have," she said. She waggled her fingers as I had.

"Oh, there can be dancing," I said. "They do all sorts of things in our churches."

"You see?" said Cheryl to Lottie, as though settling a long argument. "There's more we have in common than not, even across the wide ocean."

The food came, but not all at once. First, Lottie got her fruit, which she left untouched in front of her, sipping at her tea until my eggs and bacon arrived along with Cheryl's omelet, whereupon Lisa urged all of us to eat.

"I do like your church better," I said as I scooped egg onto a piece of toast. "But I did not spend much time inside our churches. We have a different... " I struggled for the word in the new language.

"Faith?" offered Cheryl, but I shook my head.

"Obligation," I said. "Nearer that. Our God demands different things than yours does."

"It's all one God," said Cheryl, and Lottie added: "Praise Be He."

"It's not all one God," said Lisa, "when you think about the Muslims and the Buddhists and the Hindus... the *things* they worship. Can't be. And how can you say God is He?"

"Oh cut that out. I'll tell your mother." Cheryl wagged her finger and laughed. "It's all one God," she said to me, "when you get right down to it."

"Okay," I said and nodded over Lisa's shoulder. "I think your food is coming."

The plate for pancakes was larger than any of ours, and I had to move aside to make room for it. The waitress smiled as Lottie made an oo-ing sound, and Cheryl said, "Better you than us, kiddo," to Lisa. "That'd go straight to my thighs."

"Enjoy," said the waitress, and moved off. Lisa just looked at it, hands in her lap.

"What is it, sweetheart?" asked Lottie. "Bigger than you expected?"

Lisa looked up at all of us.

"It's a miracle," she said quietly, and pointed to the top of her pancake stack.

We all looked. Cheryl said she didn't see anything at first, but she was the only one.

"It's the face of Jesus," said Lottie. Cheryl frowned and looked at it, and then at me. I nodded. There was a face, there, in the apples — strong cheekbones over deep-set eyes, brows of apple crescents, and the yellow sauce spilling down the edge of the pancakes in the unmistakable shape of a beard. It was a bright face, a Holy face — formed from apple on a young girl's plate.

Cheryl looked again and gasped.

"You're right, hon. It is a miracle." Cheryl waved at the booth. "Hey! Rose! Come look what the Lord made your daughter!"

Rose came over, and soon all from the other table were standing around, bearing witness to the miracle of the apple face on Lisa's plate. The waitress stopped by to see if everything was all right, and when Carrie explained to her, she looked and agreed. Mobile phones emerged from purses and recorded the miracle through their tiny lenses.

Lisa wondered what she should do with it, and it was finally Ruman who settled the matter.

"You should eat it," he said, "for God has delivered your Harvest, and it would be a sin to deny His bounty, yes?"

That made Lisa smile. "Well, I don't want to be sinning," she said, and I suppressed a gasp as she cut into the apparition's cheek with her fork.

⊹⊹⊹⊹

I didn't have opportunity to speak with Ruman again that day. As lunch finished, it transpired that Rose had offered to drive Ruman home. The offer created complications, displacing one from that car — either Cheryl or Carrie — and Cheryl wondered if she could take Ruman's place in mine. Of course I agreed.

When in Radejast, I did not only visit the cathedral and walk at night at solstice. I was there for two weeks time, on my own, and the nights were long. I visited the taverns, and one night in one of those, I met a woman. She was no virgin, but not a whore either. I think she may have hoped I would bring her back with me, as my bride. But no words were spoken to that effect as we quit the tavern arm in arm, slipped through a dark alcove and into her rooms. When I left, there were no tears. She kissed me on the cheek and touched her forehead to my shoulder and sent me away.

It was another matter with Cheryl.

She lived on the second floor of a low-rise apartment building that overlooked a deep ravine. When I started to pull toward the front doors where the taxis would come and go, she told me the visitor parking was in back. "If you want to," she said, and put her hand on mine. "It would be okay."

And so I came to Cheryl's apartment. It was not much larger than mine, but she had made it far more pleasant. The television, the sofa, even the pictures on the walls — everything seemed new. The window gave a tantalizing view of the ravine through tree-branches, and hid the view of the other high rises that grew from the far bank. It was as though she lived on the edge of a deep forest.

"You like?" she asked from behind me. I said that I did. She reached around and took my hand — and truly, I was not surprised when she placed it on her naked hip. I turned and saw that her dress was abandoned, sloughed off like a skin, on the floor behind her.

"You are very beautiful," I said as she withdrew, and she laughed — softly now — and for an instant turned away.

"You don't believe me?" I said, and she answered, "No. But you're a pretty liar," and the instant passed, and she kissed me once more.

"Oh God forgive me," she said as she reached down and fumbled with my belt buckle. I reached to help her, but she batted my hand away and finished the work, bent down and yanked my trousers to my knees. I stumbled a bit, and at that she laughed, and pushed, and I fell back, landing hard on my behind just short of the sofa.

Cheryl did not ask for my forgiveness. She laughed, fell to her hands, crawled forward so her face hung over mine, grinning like a mountain cat's. She moaned low. I kicked off my shoes, my trousers. She descended upon me. And in this way we copulated, swaying and growling as if to the rhythms of the old chants, on the thin carpet over her apartment's hard concrete floor.

⋙⋅⊺⋅⊺⋅⊺⋅⋘

I wrote down the number of my mobile before I left Cheryl's apartment that afternoon, but she told me not to expect a call.

"You got to go," she said, her voice flat, when she finally came out of the washroom. She had clothed herself, in light blue track pants and a sweater. Her feet, still bare, never lifted far off the floor as she led me to the door. I didn't hear her crying, not once that day, but her eyes were red and wet. Perhaps I should have apologized, although for what I could not fathom. So I said all I could think of—

"You are beautiful."

—which only enraged her. She shouted at me to get out, called me names, waved her fists, but I put my hands up in surrender and told her I would leave if that is what she wished. This placated her, and Cheryl stood, huffing and swallowing and glaring, as I gathered myself and hurried into the dim corridor.

⊹⫶⊹⫶⊹

I ate lunch with Ruman on Monday but we did not talk about very much. He did thank me for joining him at the congregation, or more properly, for the ride there, but he said he wouldn't need another; he'd made an arrangement with Rose. He didn't, thankfully, ask me if I'd enjoyed myself at the service or afterwards, and I didn't ask him. I made one feeble joke — biting into my apple, peering at the pulp I announced, "No face today." Ruman just shook his head and waved the little blasphemy away with the flat of his hand.

On Tuesday, Ruman brought a Bible with him and made it clear he preferred its company to mine. So I ate quietly, this one last time, at the same table as he, while he dipped his bread in soup as he thumbed the pages of his book. Did he smile as he read, or was I tricked by the way the overhead fluorescents cast shadows across his lips? I did not stay long enough, or look hard enough, to be sure. On Wednesday, I ate alone.

By Friday, the supervisors had responded to my request to join the evening shift.

⊹⫶⊹⫶⊹

In the beginning, the sun set an hour after I started work, and as the nights lengthened, darkness encompassed all my days.

Viktor was glad to see me.

"We should work the night all the time!" he said. "It's cool in the summer, and just as warm as day in the winter. And leaving that aside — it suits us, yes? — this peaceful time."

Viktor was right. There was work to be done, and we saw to it; but the urgency of the place... it was muted. When the trucks had pulled away, and one was moving the merchandise to and from its places... one might take a moment, listen to the sound of one's footsteps, and stop beneath high lights that only, at best, kept the shadows at bay. One might feel enveloped. Protected.

At home.

We ate together all the time, Viktor and I. And absent Ruman, we found we had things to say to one another. Viktor had once had a wife, and still had a son by her, a boy of fifteen, of whom he was very proud.

"His name is William," Viktor said as he showed me a photograph. William resembled Viktor inasmuch as he resembled any of us: thick black hair, a small mouth with lips bright red, on which formed a small and unpractised smile. The mark was on him too, but fainter than any of ours. "He is a wizard with machinery. And popular with the girls. The most important thing!"

That was the first time that I tried to talk with Viktor about that Sunday, the church, Cheryl. But I didn't want to seem boastful, comparing my prowess with that of a teenaged boy.

The second time was during the election that year, when Viktor and two other fellows were talking about one of the candidates — an unworldly woman who professed to have been saved by Jesus Christ, and during a debate had mispronounced the name of our homeland. Had it just been Viktor and I, perhaps I might have spoken of my afternoon with unworldly Christian women. But these other fellows... I couldn't even keep their names in my head. I didn't want them smirking at my adventures.

We finally spoke of it much later, when, during a break in late October, my mobile chirped, and answering it, I found myself talking with Cheryl's friend Carrie. Viktor asked me who calls at such an hour as this, and I shushed him.

"I got this number from Cheryl's kitchen," she said.

"Is Cheryl there now?"

"Cheryl doesn't know I'm calling you. She's... no, she's not here now."

Carrie's voice was tight. I didn't know her well enough to be sure, but in another woman I would suspect it indicated tears. Or perhaps anger.

"Where is she? What's wrong?"

"She's... she's at Rose's place. With the rest of them." And a pause, and a deep, sobbing breath. And then, sharper: "I just thought you should *know*."

And at that, she disconnected. Viktor raised his eyebrows. "Well," he said. "There is a story behind that."

And so I told Viktor the tale of my visit to the Good News Happening Congregation, and the pancake lunch, and the visit to Cheryl's apartment. He listened quietly the whole time, and sat still a moment when I finished.

"And you fucked," he said finally.

"And then — yes."

He held out his hand, and snapped his fingers. "Give me the phone."

I handed it over. After some fiddling, Viktor extracted Carrie's number. He leaned back in his plastic chair, crossed ankles, and when she picked up, didn't even pause to introduce himself before launching into questions:

"Where is Rose's house? Address please. Hold on." He pulled a pen from his shirt pocket, leaned forward in his chair. "And telephone number?" He scribbled on a napkin. "How long has he been there?... How many others?... And you?... I see... No, don't go yourself..." And finally, a longer pause, during which Viktor capped the pen, replaced it in his shirt pocket, and stood.

"Pray if you like," he said, and snapped the mobile shut, handing it back to me.

"Carrie asked me to apologize for being angry with you," he said. "She is under some strain. Our friend Ruman has moved in to Rose's house, and so has Cheryl now."

I could think of nothing to say.

"So tell me," he finally went on. "Is your terrible death-trap of a car still running well tonight?"

"It is," I said.

"Well." He looked at the break-room clock. "We finish in two hours. It can wait 'til then, but not much longer."

✦⊷╬⊷✦

In Radejast, Viktor explained to me, those who worship do so quietly.

"You can be forgiven for not knowing," said Viktor as we pulled from the parking lot into the deep morning dark, "for you are younger. Your parents... they would not have remembered the purges, the reform... they themselves would have been only small children, infants perhaps, through the worst of the Copper Revolution."

"They were not even that," I said. "Not even born."

Viktor rubbed his beard and nodded. "It's been many years," he said. "And more than lives were lost, hey?" He chuckled when I didn't answer. "It used to be that *everyone* worshipped. I remember my grandmother told me how at the Harvest, the whole of the land would wait, quiet as mice, as the sun vanished below the western mountains and the moon, new and dark, rose invisible over the fields. And then, we all would creep from our homes to the churches, and there in the pitch black of night-*whisper* our supplication. And then — and only then — under cover of the blackest piece of the night — would we dare celebrate the invincible shadow of our Lord."

We stopped a moment waiting for a traffic light to turn. Viktor shifted in his seat, so he leaned against the car door.

"What a temptation, though — for any man or woman — to look directly into the brightly-lit face of their God. Whatever God that may be. The people here seem to have no difficulty with it, by and by. But us? In the old days at least, we knew our God well enough to know better."

I touched the accelerator and the car lurched into the intersection some seconds before the light turned green. "Whoa whoa!" shouted Viktor, but it was safe. At this time of night, in this part of the world, we two Radejastians were the only souls in sight.

++*+*

Rose's house was in a neighbourhood not so different, indeed not so very far, from the one where Ruman had rented his room. The house, however, was larger, newer, and far better kept. The grass had been cut. Leaves were neatly raked and put at the end of the driveway, in a half-dozen orange bags made to look like pumpkins. An enormous spider-web spread over the front windows, and two figures — one a plastic skeleton, and another, a crude mannequin made from straw — flanked the front door.

Although it was just past three in the morning, the house blazed with light.

"What do you mean for us to do?" I asked as I pulled the car against the curb.

"You have done enough," Viktor said, and opened the car door. "Be prepared to drive off quickly when I return."

I did as I was told, but as Viktor strode up to the front of the house, I began to worry. For as he got out of the car, he had pulled something from his pocket, and I had heard a click! sound. And as I thought of it, the sound reminded me of the sound a board-cutting knife from the warehouse might make, as the blade extended. And didn't such a blade flash in the porch-light, as the front door opened and Viktor slipped inside?

So I tapped my fingers on the steering wheel, and thought, and thought again. And I got out of the car, and followed in Viktor's footsteps, up to the house.

The front door was not wide open but had not been properly shut either. I paused a moment, listening, and what I heard put me at ease: women's voices, talking at a reasonable level and even showing some cheer.

And so: inside, I stepped.

First, a vestibule. On one side, a coat rack, and a closet. On the other, a small dark-wooden table beneath a hat-rack.

And there, I saw a thing which made me less at ease: a twelve-inch high doll swaddled in bright red cloth, its venerable face carved from a dried apple. Tiny black-headed pins were its eyes.

I hurried past, into a high room with a wide staircase curving to the second floor. Past the stairs: a brightly-lit kitchen. It was from there that the conversation came, still convivial. Was that Rose's voice? And that, Cheryl's?

I was set to go see, when a door I had not noticed opened at the base of the stairs.

"Trick'er treat? It's early for— Oh, it's you!"

It was Lisa. Her black hair was tied in a tight bun behind her head; her pale cheeks flushed red; she wore a bone-white blouse and long red skirt that fell to her calves. She stepped into the vestibule and turned an oddly graceless pirouette.

She recovered her balance and beamed at me.

"You like?" she said, eyes wide, and turned again, this time with more agility. And at the end of it, she was somehow closer, and her eyes were wider — and I could not but think of the forest beyond Cheryl's balcony, and Cheryl's own eyes as they stared down at me. I took two steps back, and Lisa laughed and raised her arms over her head, and turned and swayed and was at my side again and somehow she was holding both my hands in hers and then we two were turning in the bright light of the entry hall, under the black clouds over Radejast, she stumbling... both of us, finding our feet... dancing the dance of the virgins.

Lisa flew far from me and drew close, her eyes — so round now they seemed lidless — never leaving mine. She never stood close long. But we were entwined.

Behind her, behind me, figures gathered. First one coming from the kitchen: Rose perhaps? The hair was the right colour, but I remembered the dress too well. In its absence, how would I account this pale naked creature, swaying beneath the stairs, hands in the air, as she came toward us? Or that other, face pinched tight— open hands slapping against her breasts, red hair plastered over swollen cheeks? Who might she be?

Cheryl, now. She was unmistakable. I remembered the curve of her thighs, her breasts... her narrow wrists and long fingers, clawing at the air as she swayed. I didn't need to see her face. I couldn't see her face. For she wore a mask of woven straw, its eyes and mouths dark circles, its high crown making a giantess of her.

And we turned, and she was gone.

The women clapped in rhythm, and Lisa drew in close to me, and I bent closer to her, mouth hungry — but she whipped back from my lips, turning so hard and sharply that I feared her neck might have snapped. For an instant, I was looking at the tightly wound bun of hair at the back of her skull, even as her young breasts pressed hard against my ribs. As I wondered at this, her head finished the circle, and those mad, reeling eyes took hold of mine again. She did kiss me then. She tasted of smoke. Of the earth. Of soot.

The clapping stopped. The women looked up, eyes as round as the virgin's. And I felt a jolt — like a tiny tremor of the earth — up my spine.

Lisa let me go. The women were staring past me, and down, and up... and I put my hands out, palms-up. It seemed as though it were snowing.

But it wasn't snow. Plaster and paint were falling from the high ceiling above us. I half-turned and saw on the floor behind me: Viktor. The hair on his skull was matted with blood and torn scalp. His neck was bent at a deadly angle. His right hand, turned in, gripped in a tight fist. His back was covered in white plaster dust — the same that was falling now, from the long cracks in the high ceiling, where a man might have impacted.

He was not moving. If the first fall had not done the job, then the second had surely finished him.

Lisa knelt down and lifted his hand, unbent his fingers. She drew the box-cutter Viktor had brought, and lifted it high, turned to the stairway.

"Ruman," I gasped, unable to take my eyes off the creature that stood on the curving steps, "look at you."

He did not speak. Ruman raised his blackened arms, and he lifted off his mask, and there in his bright cathedral — he howled."

Lisa turned to me, but this time I looked away. And alone, I fled the house, and back to the bosom of the early-morning darkness.

❖❖❖

I went to work the next evening. The supervisors were uneasy; they could smell the changes, the same as everyone. Where was Viktor? they asked. He didn't call. Was he sick? Did you drive him home? Drunk perhaps?

I didn't answer their questions, the same way I didn't contact the police. What would I say? What good would it do?

The night after that, Ruman took Viktor's place on the night shift. He found me at the meal break, and grinned as he pulled the chair out, fell into it in a happy exhaustion.

"She's pretty, yes?" he said. "Little girls get big fast."

I didn't look at him. There were so many things I might have said. "You have a wife," was all I finally could muster.

"Several, in fact," he said, and laughed. "Praise Be He."

The next night, and every night thereafter, I stayed home.

❖❖❖

As the weeks drew on, the darkness grew. Snow, real snow, swirled in corners, and gathered, covering the smooth pavement and neatly-laid brickwork, thickening that darkness.

But sometimes, for hours at a time, that dark broke, and daylight intervened.

It was at one of these times, three weeks before the solstice, that I ventured out of my apartment, and took my car to the Good News Happening Congregation.

The cross still climbed high over the motorway, but someone had rolled the sign away. This time, I was able to find a space in the parking lot. Indeed, there were barely a dozen other vehicles there, stopped at the end of wide curves of tire-tracks in the snow. All the doors in the wide glass bank of them were locked but one. I slipped inside.

The last time I had been in the Good News Happening Congregation, the hall's wide floor was covered in rows of folding chairs, and those chairs were filled with happy, fervent worshipers.

The Congregation was long gone. As I crossed the vast, dark floor, empty but for scuffed pamphlets and, here and there, shallow puddles, I wondered at where those people had found themselves. Did they gather their money together, flee to somewhere brighter, one or two of them at first, then once established slowly draw their kin in tow?

Or were they nearer? Huddled in their homes, blinds drawn, waiting for the shadow to draw over the land, to make it safe to worship?

I stopped at the foot of the pulpit, and looked up at the crucifix, climbing two full storeys high, the cool winter daylight striking the crown of thorns, setting it alight.

But the sun was an interloper here, and soon it too fled. In the ancient Radejastian gloom, the only soul in sight, I danced.

● ●

Toronto author and journalist David Nickle's stories have appeared in the *Year's Best Fantasy and Horror*, *Northern Frights*, *Queer Fear*, and *Tesseracts* anthologies; and magazines including *On Spec* and *Cemetery Dance*. His novel *The Claus Effect* (with Karl Schroeder) is available from Edge Science Fiction and Fantasy Publishing; his story collection, *Monstrous Affections*, from ChiZine Publications. His website is: *http://davidnickle.googlepages.com*

● ●

The Woods

by Michael Kelly

It had been snowing for days. Icy needles of teeth tumbled from the ash-flecked sky, clotting the woods.

The thick shroud of snow shifted, moved with the weeping wind, and pushed against a cabin. A bug-bright snowmobile rested near a leaning woodshed like some alien invader, its engine cooling, ticking, though the two men inside the cabin could not hear this. They could hear nothing of the outside world but the wind and its ceaseless winter lament.

Inside, logs crackled and smoldered in a fireplace. A black cast-iron pot hung above the small fire. A spicy tang permeated the cabin.

The old man in the old rocking-chair, who had a face like tree bark, blinked crusty eyes, looked up at the younger man (who nonetheless was near retirement himself but was still much younger than the old man in the chair) and gestured to the only other chair in the cabin. "Have a seat, Officer Creed."

The younger man grinned weakly. "How many times I have to tell you, Jack? You don't have to call me that. It's just the two of us. We go back a long way."

The old man blinked again, nodded, and stared at the younger man's uniform: the gold badge on the parka, the gun holstered at his side. "Well, Ned," croaked the old man, "it looks like you're out here on business, so it's only proper."

Ned clutched a small, furry, dead animal, fingers digging deep. He sat on the proffered chair and laid the dead thing

on the floor, where it resembled a hat. "We go back a long
way," he repeated, wistful.

They were silent for a time. The old man rocked slowly,
and the pine floor creaked. Ned stared at his wet boots,
glanced out the window at the swirling sheets of grey-
white.

Jack stopped rocking. "Get you some coffee, Ned?"

"No, thanks. Can't stay long. Need to get back before
the storm comes full on."

A sad chuckle from the old man. "You may be too late."

"I fear I am, Jack."

Another brief silence. Jack rocked slowly, and Ned
brushed wet snow from his pants.

"You still trapping?" Ned asked. "Still getting out?"

Jack paused, as if carefully considering his words.
"Course I am. I'm old, not dead." Another brief pause,
then, "Man's got to eat."

"That's why I'm here."

"I see."

"We go back a long way, don't we, Jack?"

The old man blinked and nodded.

"I mean, you'd tell me if you needed anything,
wouldn't you? You'd tell me if anything was wrong?"

The old man leaned forward. "Checking up on me,
Ned?"

"You might be snowbound awhile, is all. Just doing
my job. You're like a ghost out here."

Jack eased back into the rocker. "Pantry is stocked.
Plenty of rabbit in the woodshed."

Ned grimaced. "You were always a good trapper."

"Been here a long, long time, Ned. You do something
often enough you get good at it."

"True enough."

"You learn about things," Jack said. "By necessity. You
learn how the world works. The good. The bad. All of
it."

"Hmm, yes."

"I know things," Jack said. He was staring hard at
Ned. "But... tell me, what do *you* know, Ned?"

Ned fidgeted, returned Jack's look. "Not as much as you, Jack. That's the gospel. I know certain things, that's all. And other stuff I'm not so certain about. Trying to figure things out, is all."

"Oh, you're a sly one, aren't you, Ned?"

Ned turned away, sighed, gazed at the window. "Not so much. No."

"What do you see?" Jack asked.

"I can just make out a few trees. Nothing else. The woods and nothing."

"I know these woods like the back of my hand."

"I bet you do," Ned said.

Gusts of blowing snow swept past the window. The cabin door groaned. Each man sat, staring at the other, stealing glances at the window, then the door, expectant, as if waiting for a visitor.

Ned broke the silence. "Tom Brightman's got a spot of trouble."

Jack's face creased into a sneer. "You don't say."

"Wendigo," Ned whispered, as if afraid to say it aloud.

Jack sniggered. "That old saw again?"

"I'm afraid so." Ned scratched his head. "Every year. The same old superstitions. We've heard them all, me and you. We go back some ways."

"Stop saying that."

"It's true, though. There's not much between us. Is there, Jack? No secrets in these parts."

"Yes," Jack said.

Ned stretched his legs out, crossed them, uncrossed them. A log in the fireplace popped. The room smelled of spice and meat and wet fur. He turned toward the fire.

Jack followed Ned's gaze. "Get you something to eat? To tide you over?"

"No." Ned squirmed. "You hungry, Jack?"

"All the time. Seems the older I get, the hungrier I get." Jack stared off into a far corner. "It's not something I can explain. Not something you'd understand."

Ned gestured to the pot. "Don't mind me. Help yourself."

Jack smirked, swung his gaze around to Ned. "It's okay, I'll wait. I've some manners still."

"You've got a nice little set up out here, Jack. All by yourself. No one around for miles. Must get mighty lonely at times, I imagine."

The old man shrugged. "Not really. A man can find plenty of things to occupy his time. Idle hands and all that."

"That's what worries me, Jack. This place, this solitude, this... *nothingness*. It does things to people." Ned leaned forward, nodded toward the window. "You ever spot anything out there, in the woods? Anything... *strange*?"

"Ha." Jack's tree-bark face glowed orange from the fire, a winter pumpkin. "Stealthy man-eating beasts, Ned? Slavering cannibals? Wendigo?"

Ned blinked, watched Jack, said nothing.

"Tom Brightman is a damn fool," Jack said. "Every year it's the same damn thing. Can't control his dogs so he blames everyone else. Myths. Legends. Old wives' tales. Easier for some men to cast blame than take responsibility."

"What do you know about such things, Jack?"

"How many, Ned? How many of his sled dogs have gone missing this year?"

"None." Ned straightened and leaned forward. Rigid and intent. "It's the youngest boy. Johnny. Been gone a week now."

Jack was quiet. He began to rock slowly. Then, "He's a damn fool."

"May very well be." Ned scratched his chin. "You positive there's nothing I can get you, Jack? Nothing you need?"

"Nothing."

"Don't suppose," Ned asked, "at this point it'd make a lick of difference if I peeked into the woodshed on my way out? To make sure?"

"Not a lick, Ned. Not at this point."

Ned picked up his hat, stood, let out a heavy breath. "That's what I thought." He pulled the hat over his head, went to the door, opened it a crack, and peered into the gathering white nothingness. "I'll try and swing by later in the week, Jack. Watch yourself." He shoved through the gap, into the outside, pulled the door shut.

The old man rose from the rocking chair and scuttled across the worn pine floor. He went to the window, pressed his face against the frost-veined pane, and spied the younger man, a blurry black smudge, trudging through the blizzard. The younger man stopped at the woodshed, pulled open the door, and slipped inside.

Jack watched. Waited. It had been snowing forever. Glassy shards struck the ground, formed an icy shell. He thought surely that the world would crack, that *something* would crack.

Ned exited the shed, paused, gazed back at the cabin, and shambled over to his snowmobile. Soon, the white swallowed him.

Jack turned, walked to the cupboards, grabbed a chipped bowl and a spoon, and went over to the fireplace and the pot. Stew bubbled and simmered in the pot. His stomach grumbled, empty, always empty. It wasn't something he could explain. Wasn't something that he understood. A vast emptiness inside him. Nothingness.

He ladled stew into the bowl, spooned the hot meal into his mouth. Chewed. Swallowed. His thoughts turned to Tom Brightman, his dogs, his son... and his daughters.

Jack ate. The emptiness abated. Then he didn't think about anything except the woods.

The woods and nothing.

• •

Michael Kelly was born in Charlottetown, and raised in Toronto. He currently resides in Pickering, Ontario. His fiction has appeared in *Carleton Arts Review*, *Flesh & Blood*, *Nossa Morte*, and *Space & Time*. His books include the collections *Scratching the Surface* and *Undertow*, a co-written novel *Ouroboros* and, as editor, *Apparitions* and *Songs from Dead Singers*.

• •

The Language
of Crows

By Mary E. Choo

I told Min a thousand times not to feed the damn birds.

Rubbing a clear spot in the grimy pane, I watch her from the upstairs hall window as she tramps around the front yard. Her soiled dress clings to her, and wisps of her mousey hair drift about her head. I can see the end of her long, sharp nose as she turns this way and that, scattering crumbs and whatever else is on that revolting platter she's carrying. She's indulging the crows today, though she knows how much I hate them.

Min keeps the garden immaculate, like some sort of shrine for the birds. She's supposed to maintain the house too, but you'd never know it. The place is a pigsty. Like her, it needs a bloody good scrubbing, from top to bottom.

My hand tightens around the bottle of medication. I can hear a plaintive sound, then a sliding, clacking crackle. It's Jeremy's pet crow, Fidel, calling approval from his cage by the front hall window, downstairs. There's a flock of crows in the yard now, squabbling, shifting their glossy wings as they close in on the feast. Min's murmuring and cooing at them. Min's Jeremy's cousin, and they've always been close. If it wasn't for that, I'd throw her out on...

A soft moan from down the hall claims my attention. Of course. I forget myself.

"Coming," I call out, though I know Jeremy probably doesn't hear. The floor boards squeak as I move. It's a terrible old house — poky little rooms and a narrow, difficult staircase. I can just see Fidel past the stairwell. He cocks his head, studying me with a malevolent, glittering eye. Jeremy's passionately fond of him, and I'd swear the bloody bird takes advantage.

I push the door to the bedroom wide, approaching the bed. Jeremy's worse today. It's hard to believe he's the man I married three years ago. His illness has taken a terrible toll.

I pour a spoonful of morphine and brace his head and shoulders while he takes it. Pills are too difficult for him to swallow, now. I can hear Fidel squawking from the hallway below, and the screen door closing. Min has come inside.

"Susie... Susan..." Jeremy's eyes struggle to find me. His voice is coarse, beleaguered. "I must know how everything..."

"Jeremy, love... everything's fine," I interject. "Min's round and about, Fidel has been fed, and Edward is coming today, with the papers you wanted."

Edward, Jeremy's solicitor, has been back and forth with his secretary a lot lately, regarding Jeremy's will. Edward did tell me, last time, that he's getting concerned, in view of Jeremy's extreme medication and state of mind. Most of the estate and the house go to me, but... well... after... I'd rather not stay.

Jeremy seems satisfied with my explanation; either that, or the medicine's taking hold, as his eyes glaze over and his lids close. When I leave him, his breathing is shallow and even.

Fidel eyes me stonily as I tramp downstairs, my shoulders knotted with tension. I glare back at him. I didn't mind him that much when Jeremy and I first married and I came here. But with what's happening now, Fidel seems to be watching — no; almost enjoying what's going on. I stopped hauling the cage into Jeremy's bedroom for visits when the doctor objected. Besides, Fidel appeared to relish Jeremy's distress, his head cocked in curiosity and expectation with every moan of pain.

A small boy is coming up the front steps. It's Rollie, a neighbour's child. Imaginative, charming, he's my one

delight, these days. We talk and play games often.
"Missus...," he says through the screen, the perennial
question in his blue eyes.

"Later," I promise. "If you're quiet, we'll play ball out
back." Rollie smiles his radiant smile. He's a bittersweet
reminder that I'll never have Jeremy's child. My fingers
contact his through the screen, and his little leather bracelet slips down his wrist. Then he's gone, running down
the path.

Min is in the kitchen, washing dishes with a grubby
cloth and water that looks and smells like day-old tea.

"You're such a young, pretty thing, with those green
eyes," she says after a moment, making no effort to hide
the spite in her voice. "Pity you have to go through all
this."

"Jeremy's the one to be pitied."

"Some things are meant," she replies, turning to stare
at me with her colourless eyes. I'm furious at the plati-
tude.

"Min, for God's sake change the dishwater and get
a decent cloth — and rinse off the hard bits and the soap!"

She's supposed to help. That's why Jeremy asked her
to come here, when he returned from hospital. He thought
he'd recover, but I knew better.

Gritting my teeth, I bundle the garbage into one bag
and struggle outside to the back. I'm angry to find that
Min has made a scrap pile by the garbage bins, likely for
the birds. I glance up and around to see crows, on the
ridge of the roof, the chimney, all eyeing me.

"Wish you'd do something about that."

The voice of our neighbour, at the fence, startles me.
He's part of a contingent that's taken up residence in the
luxury homes that have gone up in the area. He frowns,
indicating the scrap pile. Mr. Russell's a good sort, really, and I can't blame him. I'm sure Min's violating some
bylaw, and anyway, scraps can attract rodents. The
Russells' house is some distance from ours, but still...

"Sorry," I mumble. "It's Min. I'll get rid of it."

His face softens. I don't think he likes Min any more
than I do.

"Damn crows." He looks up at our house. "They're all over. Even my air rifle doesn't bother them much. Neighbours have been complaining about them, lately. We're thinking of approaching Council. How's Jerry?" he adds.

"Fair." I muster a smile. He looks uncomfortable.

"Give him my regards." Mr. Russell waves and retreats, defeated by what he sees in my face.

On the way back to the house, I'm aware of sudden movement above, of a rolling shadow and a fluttering sound. I squint against the sunlight. A huge crow is hovering directly over me. I move on, and he follows, almost lazily, keeping himself between me and the light. I begin to run, but he maintains a precise distance between us. Suddenly he swoops, and there's a stabbing sensation at my temple. I swat him away and rush through the back doorway, slamming the screen shut. The crow retreats to the trees, and the others gather about him. A muted cackling starts up among them, as though they're discussing some manoeuvre. There's a report that can only come from Mr. Russell's gun, and they scatter. Min's been after Russell a lot, about that. Blood trickles from my temple.

"Small Rollie down the road's gone missing," Min says, handing me a towel that's more-or-less clean. She looks almost pleased. She makes no comment about the crow, and gets annoyed when I fetch a bottle of peroxide and begin cleaning my wound.

"How can that be, Min? I just saw him!" I'm shaken by the attack, scarcely paying attention.

A loud cawing from Fidel distracts me. I look through the kitchen doorway and down the hall. Edward, Jeremy's solicitor, is at the front screen, briefcase in hand.

⁑⋅⋇⋅⋇⋅⁑

"Edward, if Rollie *is* missing, I should help look for him," I protest, holding the towel to my head. We're sitting by Jeremy's bedside, waiting for him to waken. My rickety chair creaks every time I move. As I glance out the window at the Russells' and the other splendid houses nearby, I make the inevitable comparison before I dismiss it as unworthy.

"Everything looked normal on the street when I came in — we'll ask Minerva about it, later. This is important, Susan." Edward taps his briefcase. "Besides, I don't like what happened with that damn bird!"

Edward needed an explanation. He's a reassuring person, the kind that seems to have no doubts about himself or the world. He and I were going together when he introduced me to Jeremy. They were long-time friends. There was no animosity when I broke it off, and we've remained close.

"You know, Edward," I say softly, "The crows reigned supreme around here, before the developers bulldozed so many wild areas. I think they talk to each other — as if they have some strange kind of language — it's like they're discussing, judging me..."

Jeremy stirs, opening his eyes. He struggles to sit up, and I reach over to help him, plumping the pillows. His breath sounds like wind blowing through reeds.

"Ed," he says with a ghastly smile. Something twists inside me. That smile, once so beautiful, had first won me over to him. Now it's a travesty, more like a grimace.

"I think it's time, especially as your strength is so limited, just now," Edward says pointedly. Puzzled, I look from one man to the other. Edward opens his briefcase and takes out a long document, and as I glance at it, I realize it's Jeremy's will.

"Susan, I insisted we explain to you," Edward begins. Jeremy fumbles for, and finds, my hand. His fingers are so cold, I want to wrap him in a myriad blankets to keep what's left of him warm. Edward drones on, and as I listen, chill realization creeps in.

There are a few extra things — bequests, a trust for a distant cousin. While he talks, Edward hands me a list of Jeremy's assets, and I'm amazed to find out how wealthy my husband is. I was a practising accountant before we married, but even so, it takes a moment for me to absorb it all...

There are recent changes which are, in a word, bizarre. The house is still mine, provided that I don't try to sell it, or his other properties — part of Jeremy's fortune will go to maintaining them. The rest is split between Min and me — we'll both be well off. The catch is, I get nothing if I violate any part of the bequest. Min gets to stay.

So does Fidel.

I feel like a guilty child, reprimanded for taking what isn't mine. Jeremy knows I don't like Min. Before he got so ill, we used to joke about it. He's certainly aware of my feelings for Fidel, though I keep them as much to myself as I can. Jeremy was always a little eccentric. Now, my husband presses my hand with tentative strength. He looks at me, appealing. For a moment, painfully, I see the old Jeremy.

"Promise me you'll keep the house, set up place... in the lot... for the birds..."

I'm not sure what he means, but I'd do anything to ease his distress. A white lie can't hurt, and I nod.

"Take care of Min, Fidel... promise... I want to see Fidel," he adds, then, to my relief, sinks back. I nod again.

I sense there's more to his plea, something hidden and uneasy. Edward has set aside other changes Jeremy wanted. I glance at them, taking in some request about setting up a bird sanctuary, then thrust the papers away, too upset to read more. Jeremy is sleeping in that shallow manner I've come to dread. I motion to Edward, and we go downstairs. Once in the hall, I can't contain my anger.

"*Bitch!*" My voice startles Fidel, who shifts in his cage. I think back over all the time Min has spent with Jeremy, these past months... comforting him, I thought. "She must have planned this, Edward, from the first! I don't begrudge her the money, but the rest — it's impossible, insane. I understand — if I stretch it — about Fidel, but being saddled with the house, and *her* — Jeremy would never have made those demands, in his right mind! As for a bird sanctuary, after what happened with that crow...

"It's all right," Edward says quietly, trying to calm me — I'm shaking with shock and rage. "I've no intention of letting it stand — several people have noticed Min's undue influence on him."

It's true. Our friends said nothing, but most stopped coming around soon after Min arrived, and a few showed their dislike of her openly. I'm very aware of Edward, his solid masculine presence, exuding health and confidence. I'm so tired, I lean against him, and before I know it his arms are around me, and I'm kissing him, the way I used to kiss Jeremy. For a moment, I have the two men confused.

"No!" I pull back, ashamed. "Please..."

Edward is unabashed. "Just know I'm here, Susie," he says. "Now and... later. My feelings for you haven't changed."

I clasp my arms across my chest, and he leaves, closing the screen quietly. The tears come hot and fast. Suddenly, I see Min at the end of the hall, standing in the kitchen doorway. Her figure is shadowed, almost spectral, and I realize that she may well have heard, and certainly seen, everything.

This time my rage is consummate. I seem to float down the hall, stopping to confront her. I could strike her, if I chose.

"You... *you*..." I choke on the words. "You may think you've won, Minerva!" I never use her full name, and my tone is savage. "You and your bloody birds! One way or another, when all's said — and done — you're all out of here, do you hear? *Gone*!"

The last word ends in a sob. I stalk back down the hall, past a wary Fidel and into the sitting room, slamming the door.

✦❖✦❖✦

Pacing accomplishes nothing; in fact it increases my anger and my sense of panic. I had an unprepossessing childhood, with an evasive father and an alcoholic mother; an experience which left me with a passion for order, for control. In Jeremy, at least at first, I found stability and freedom, the delight I'd never had as a child. Now, it appears, I'm losing it all.

The sitting room is small and cluttered, dirty too, though I turned it out last week. Min again, with her filthy habits. Papers cover the small table by the window — accounts I'd taken in to help pay the bills. When I think of this, and how much money Jeremy has, I repress the urge to laugh hysterically. I've been paying for Min — her food, the stuff she feeds the birds, and some of Jeremy's medicine...

Bile rises in my throat. I don't want any of the estate, now, but if I don't contest it, Min gets far beyond what she deserves, and with the conditions... well, there's something vile, unnatural about it all.

My eyes go to the bookshelves. They stretch from floor to ceiling, and are the only decent furniture in the room. They're crammed with books that Jeremy and I used to read. My vision blurs as I recall our long walks along the shore nearby, often discussing some poem or novel. I can still see his wonderful, craggy face, his high colour as he laughs and slips his arm through mine...

The slant of sun is long as I collect myself. I thought I heard a noise a few moments ago, and suddenly it seems important. I yank the door open to find Fidel's cage and stand missing. There are creaks and muffled crow noises from upstairs, followed by a wracking, coughing laugh from Jeremy. I race up the steps and across the landing, bursting into Jeremy's room.

"Enough!" I keep my voice low, hoping Jeremy, who's lying sideways, won't notice too much. One of his hands is uplifted. He's stroking the side of Fidel's cage, which Min holds, steadying the stand, next to his bed. "Enough!" This last, though ferocious, doesn't rise above a whisper. For once, Min, who never responds much to anything I say to her, looks startled.

"Didn't mean any harm!" Min backs away, the cage tottering. Jeremy turns dazed eyes to me and speaks, but I can't hear, as in the next moment the cage clatters to the floor.

"The hell you didn't! Get that thing out of here!"

Matters threaten to turn ugly as Min, looking more disconcerted than frightened, stands her ground. Then I see Jeremy has a glass in his other hand, with the dregs of something discolouring the side and bottom. In the next instant, Fidel has opened his cage and flies, squawking, from the room.

I yell and gesture at Min, accusing her of all kinds of things. The medicine bottles on Jeremy's bedside table have been moved around. Min slides past me, muttering about finding Fidel, who's cackling in delight and malice somewhere below. In the midst of this, the front door bell begins a static ringing. After securing Jeremy, I hurry down the stairs.

It's the police on the front porch. Rattled, shaking, I open the screen, barely hearing the names of the two officers. They want to know about Rollie, as he's definitely missing, and it seems I was the last to see him.

"I don't recall exactly — but it was a lot earlier when he came over," I say. My voice is high-pitched, and I'm breathing hard. The officers stare at me.

"A neighbour said you asked the boy in," one of them says.

"No — no! That isn't true. Anyway, how could any of them see the front door, with all the trees..." God, I sound guilty! Why? I had nothing to do with the boy's disappearance; the thought of anything happening to dear little Rollie makes my heart lurch.

"Look, I've told you all I can," I finish, cross now, and anxious about Rollie. "My husband is ill..." Min comes up behind me. I stand there, agitated, while they question her. In a minute, the police are done, though they glance back at me with suspicion as they leave.

I'm about to start in on Min when I see movement down the hall. It's Fidel. He flaps towards us, grazing and reopening my wound, then flies through the open screen door, cawing triumphantly.

"Damn stupid..." I start onto the porch. Unused to flying, Fidel lands half way down the lawn, hopping and preening, cocking his head at me malevolently. I pause, wary of startling him.

"Fidel... birdie..." I inch down the steps, and he hops further away. There's a movement among the hollyhocks,

and a darkish blur streaks across the lawn, pouncing on
Fidel. It's Mr. Russell's grey tabby. Pandemonium reigns,
with Fidel shrieking and flapping as the cat struggles
to gain a secure hold. Fidel is a large crow, and I'm surprised by the cat's audacity. I can't seem to move. In the
back of my mind, there's a thought that if I wait just a
heartbeat longer...

No, I decide, this isn't right — it's cruel, horrible. It
would break Jeremy's heart! I begin to run. Something
flashes past me, and in a second it's the cat who's shrieking in pain, not Fidel. The tabby rolls over on its back,
a pair of scissors sticking in its side.

I look back to see Min, poised like an Olympic ath-
lete on the porch, her arm still in throwing position.
Plainly, she has talents I'd never have suspected.

"Go after Fidel!" she commands me.

I'm too appalled to argue. There's blood all over the
lawn. The demon Fidel is hopping away across the grass,
dragging one wing and grousing pathetically — there's
a certain gleam in his eye, as he turns his head, which
tells me it's a bit of an act.

I almost catch him as he reaches the fence to the wild,
vacant lot next door. My hand swoops down to grab him,
but he slips through a fence hole. There's no help for it.
With one foot on the rail, I swing my leg over the boards.
As I come down amidst the thistles on the other side, I
see the cat has stopped moving. The crows are perched
along the ridge of the roof — is it me, or are they actually
talking...?

The lot is densely wooded, almost two acres, on the
opposite side to the Russells. It belongs to Jeremy, and
he told me once he'd never sell it. It occurs to me that
this is the lot he meant, when we were talking about his
will; he wants the sanctuary here.

Night is bearing down as I press through brush and
bramble. Great, old trees tower overhead, and there are
heaps of fallen fir and pine needles everywhere. Through
the gap on my right I can just see the shore, then the bay
and the peninsula that's divided by the American border.

Fidel is warbling spitefully a way ahead. He's moving fast, for a wounded creature. The colours of wood and brush look strange, but I attribute that to the failing light. The smell of evergreen and earth is intense, measurably different. I'm sweating, feverish, I think, and it comes to me that I should have gone to hospital after the damned bird attack, for a tetanus booster shot and checkup. The reopened wound throbs, seems to reach into my skull; Fidel has really made it worse.

"Birdie..." I pant. Shadows press down all about me. Daylight is failing, and the air is thick, as if ready for storm. I can't see bloody Fidel anywhere, though I keep hearing him. I must be sick, because his garble sounds like words, and though I think I half understand them they're not in any tongue I know. My breathing is awful, pneumonic. I glance up to see a full moon climbing behind the trees, and the spaces between look like radiant tunnels of light. Insects fly everywhere on iridescent wings.

I stumble and fall to my knees, exhausted. I must have backtracked, because I can see the lights of our house a way in front of me, through the trees. Collapsing, I roll on my back in a bed of evergreen needles to catch my breath. I turn my head. There's a child's torn T-shirt crumpled next to me. Beside it is what's left of a small leather bracelet.

Rollie's...

I scream and struggle to a sitting position. Fidel, whom moments ago I willed to die, is at my feet, both wings tucked against his body. As he cocks his head at me, his eyes gleam with a demonic ruby color. He clacks his tongue.

Too late, I see my peril, their dark, powerful bird shapes silent in the dead branches of a tree above, visible against the moon. As I try to stand, the first of them, their evident leader, swoops. His beak and claws strike me on the head. I fall. Another bears down on me, then another and another. They peck savagely at my face, throat and hands, and then start on the rest of me. They're so strong. Blood runs into my eyes, the scent hot, the taste coppery as it reaches my mouth. I'm making pathetic sounds.

"Please... sorry about Fidel... stop please..."

They begin to answer me now, and I understand them better... theirs are the words of warriors, of predators, alien and pitiless and dark. As my body is ravaged and torn, I realize how much I am losing, and the least of it is control. One last blink before it all goes, and I see Fidel, who led me to this, dancing triumphant among the trees.

⋙•⫶•⫶•⋘

At some point, I have a sense of being dragged brutally through the woods. When I wake, I don't know my surroundings at first. Countless insects thrum about, some settling on me. Attempts to sit up, to swat at them are futile. My head and body feel like fire. As my vision clears a little, the moonlight is brilliant, luminous in a way I've never seen it before. I'm lying beside our garden shed, a shadowed figure standing at my side.

Min.

I try to talk to her, but find no words — my throat feels strange. Then I see she's bundling some of my clothing, badly torn, into a garbage bag.

"Min..." Her name sounds faint when I finally manage to speak.

"It's all right, Susan." Her tone is soothing, friendly. She shifts the garbage bag to one hand and helps me up. I say helps, because standing is a paramount effort. She loops one arm about my head and shoulders and hauls me along.

I wonder frantically about what's happened to Rollie. I'm sickened by Min's smell, her grubby clothing. My feet drag at first. Then I feel nothing. There are thudding sounds behind us as we move, but I can't see all that well. Min is talking to me, her voice reverberating. We cross the garden and enter the house. She manoeuvres me up the staircase and into Jeremy's room, easing me onto a chair beside him.

"... *hate* what you've done!" I try to yell, steadying myself as something falls away from my face. Hag. God, I despise her.

"That's all right, let it all out — such a young, pretty thing," she says, smiling. "Jeremy." She shakes his shoulder. He's sleeping on his side, facing me. He stirs and struggles up on one elbow, with an effort Min makes no attempt to ease. He stares at me blankly. Only then do I turn and look into the cracked mirror on the wall.

My reaction is extraordinary. I'm beyond panic. I survey the damage, then the changes. I no longer hurt, though bits of my former self cling to me — a piece of shoulder flesh hangs from my new neck. Most everything else is gone, except a scrap of foot sticking to one claw, and a few shreds of clothing. My eyes are still green, which is a bit of an anomaly, and my glossy black head and body, my wings and beak, are quite splendid, really.

"Why?" I demand hoarsely. I suspect most of it, but I need to hear what Min has to say.

"Oh, shoosh," she says. "*They'll* explain." She's breathing hard, looking pleased with herself. Jeremy's eyes flicker. He holds out one hand.

"You... ," he says in a whistling breath.

Is it recognition I see in his face, or confusion? I can't bear to think he planned any of this. Surely it was Min and Fidel, deceiving him, dragging him down into their ghastly, primeval morass.

"Come now," Min says, businesslike. She brushes away the last of my ravaged flesh and lifts me, struggling, from the chair. I protest, but my words sound odd. My memory of them appears strong enough, but my ability to speak seems to be altering. "They're waiting."

I see a couple of crow heads peering at me from the open dormer window at the front, the silver landscape bright behind them. Min pushes me through, and I scramble for a hold on the roof.

The crows are waiting as I pull myself up and cling to the shingles. The two beside me nudge me upward, and though I'm bewildered and frightened, I don't resist. More of them sidle down the roof towards us, eyeing me as they draw alongside. Shifting my weight from wing to wing, flapping, I gradually gain the lower ridge, the one right over Jeremy's window.

The crow leader looks across at me as the rest of the Clan — that's what they call themselves, rather than the more accepted 'murder of crows' — begins talking. It seems Jeremy's house and lot is their last foothold around here. They have plans to preserve the place, and I'm smart, useful. I'm to take part, to help bring in others, like me. Still, it's a tenuous beginning.

The Clan head has a smaller bird under one wing — they say it's Rollie, and the eyes do look light, perhaps blue, from here. I can tell he's horribly frightened. He's there for my benefit, so I don't get any rebellious ideas. I *must* find some way to protect, to free him.

Min emerges from the house to clean up any telltale remains, then goes back inside. The light is growing, and someone is coming up the walk. It's Edward. How splendid he is, how tall and straight. He's a threat, too. He'll ask questions, make trouble.

The Clan leader croaks at me and tightens his wing around Rollie, who lets out a pitiful squeak. Time to pull my weight, to recruit; I need to attract Edward.

I call out in my soft, novel rasp, but Edward bolts through the front door, slamming it. The house vibrates with his tread on the stairs. It comes to me, then.

Jeremy is dying.

Ignoring the others, I claw my way to the peak of the roof over the window. The pane is just beneath, and I peer down, my breast heaving.

Edward has propped up Jeremy and is yelling at Min. Fidel is back in the room, in his cage, and Edward tells her to take him away, demanding to know where I am. I see Jeremy breathe, then stop, breathe... then stop....

I feel so very human again for this, the last. Whatever my heart is, it seems ripped from my body, and my pain is hot, physical, absolute. Jeremy told me that crows mate for life; I make several attempts to let the Clan leader know that Jeremy is, was my mate. I do not know if the crows understand, but they all let me be.

I raise my head and take a deep breath. The unbearably beautiful moon is fading into the brightening sky. It's dawn, and Jeremy loved this time of day.

In the language of crows, I slowly start mourning my loss.

•••••••••••••••••••••••••••••••••

Living amidst the spectacular natural beauty and cultural diversity of the Lower Mainland of British Columbia has had a profound and lasting influence on Mary Choo's writing. Much of her poetry and fiction reflects this background, including "The Language of Crows". She had stories in two of the acclaimed Canadian *Northern Frights* anthologies, and her work has been published in a wide variety of magazines, anthologies and online publications. Her poems and stories have also appeared on preliminary and final ballots of the Bram Stoker, Nebula and Aurora Awards.

•••••••••••••••••••••••••••••••••

Lost In a Field of Paper Flowers

By Gord Rollo

Whenever evil befalls us, we ought to ask ourselves,
after the first suffering, how we can turn it into good.
So shall we take occasion,
from one bitter root, to raise perhaps many flowers.
— *Leigh Hunt (1784 - 1859)*

❖❘❖❘❖❘❖

A teenage boy lies in a coma.
Fell down the stairs, bumped his head.
Ask his father, standing by his bedside. He's telling
everyone that's what happened.
Don't ask the poor boy's mother, though. No, not
her. She's far too busy crying.

Existence #1: Dreamland

"Hello?"
"Can anyone hear me?"
There's fear in your voice. No panic, yet, but definitely
a hint of alarm. At first, this strange dream had been thrill-
ing, horsing around in this massive field of orange-red
dirt; something you'd never have been able to do from
the seat of the wheelchair in real life. The euphoric freedom of standing, of actually *running* on your own legs
is a joy you'd nearly forgotten. Two years have passed
since the accident left your spine twisted, legs withered

and useless. But in the dream you're going full throttle, pumping arms, chasing your shadow across the unusual colored soil with the exuberance and energy of youth. It feels great to be healthy again, to be *whole*.

It isn't until your feet slip, and you roll, laughing, to a stop in a swirling cloud of dust that you begin to wonder about your surroundings. What kind of place is this, anyway? A farmer's field, by the looks of it, the soil cared for and plowed in even, parallel grooves. But if this is a farm, where are the barns, crops, animals, or the farmer for that matter? Standing up, you spin slowly around, trying to spot something familiar. Surely there's a fence line, a pond, or a nearby road. There's nothing, just an endless expanse of flat, copper-tinted dirt.

You strain to hear any of the normal everyday sounds like birds, airplanes, insects, wind, laughter, but this field is void of those things — a dead place that despite its vastness begins to close in on you, the dusty air tickling your throat, making you dry swallow your first taste of fear.

"Is anyone out there?"

"Where am I? Please...somebody answer me!"

Inside your head you hear a woman's voice, tiny and faint, as if spoken across a great distance. You can't make out the words.

"Momma?" you ask, confused.

No, boy, I'm not your mother. I'm a friend.

"A friend? What do you want?"

To help you get back home.

"I don't know what you mean. Where are you?"

A long way off, but closer than you think. Don't worry about it. Stick out your right arm, then turn and walk in that direction. I've brought you something.

You're more confused than ever, but at least you aren't feeling as scared. Even a phantom voice is welcome in this desolate place. Better than being alone. You do as instructed and are soon heading in a new direction. You walk for ten minutes, not at all sure why you're doing this.

"Where am I supposed to be going?" you finally ask, but there's no reply. "Hello? Are you still there?"

Silence, inside and out.

You stop, unsure what to do next, consider retracing your steps—

Something green stands out in the distance.

"What's that? Is this what you brought me?"

A whisper: *Yes*.

You run, excitement and curiosity propelling you toward the small green dot on the horizon. Slowing your pace, you stroll the last thirty feet. It's a flower, a light green carnation growing out of the otherwise barren soil. Its stem reaches up past your knees, its blossom round, symmetrical, and full. Beautiful, sure, but it looks so strange and out of place growing on its own in this massive field.

"You brought me a flower? Why?"

Silence.

Existence #2: Reality

"Stay cool, Sally. I told you ten times already, I've got it covered. You don't need to say squat to anyone."

The tall man spoke quietly, checking over his shoulder down the corridor as he led his wife firmly by the arm into their son's private room.

"But, Paul, I'm just—"

"But nothin', Sally. Let me do the talking and everything will be fine. Understand?"

Sally nodded her head, but Paul wasn't looking at her anymore. She followed his gaze over to the foot of their son's bed, where a small woman stood leaning on a wooden cane. Even before the woman turned to face them, Sally could tell she was old and frail. Her left eye was opaque, a blank with no visible iris or pupil, her vision clouded by a thick, milky cataract. When she lifted the corners of her mouth to smile, it took a Herculean effort, depleting her limited energy. Sally felt pity for the poor woman.

"Who are you?" Paul asked, his tone sharp, confrontational. "What are you doing in Robbie's room? This is a private suite."

"Is it? Forgive me, Mr. Moore. I just came to see how Robbie was doing and bring him a little flower to cheer up the room. I meant no harm."

Sally pulled her eyes away from the diminutive woman to look at the blossom lying on the bedspread at her son's feet and noticed that it wasn't a real flower, but rather a paper one intricately folded using several layers of thin green onion paper.

Paul, not even noticing the flower, continued on. "You a nurse or something?"

This caused the old woman to smile, her face lighting up and revealing some of the beauty she'd possessed in her youth.

"Good Lord, at *my* age, I sure hope not!"

"Who are you, then?" Sally asked gently, trying to diffuse her husband's anger.

"The doctors and nurses all call me Aggie."

"Yeah, well, nice to meet you, but my wife and I would appreciate it if—"

"Did you make that flower, Aggie?" Sally interrupted.

"Why yes, I did." Aggie said. "It's called Origami. Learned how in craft class down on the ground floor."

"The assisted living center?" Sally asked.

"Yep. That's where I live. Been there...well, seems like forever."

"Then maybe you'd best get back," Paul said, annoyed. "Robbie needs rest, and I'm sure the nurses will be wondering where you are."

"Heavens! You're probably right," Aggie nodded and shuffled toward the door, leaning heavily on her cane for support. "Can I come for another visit tomorrow? Don't like to brag, but everyone says I have a special way with children. Maybe I can help?"

Paul was about to object, but Sally beat him to the punch. "No problem, Aggie. Just make sure the people on your floor know where you are, okay?"

"Sure will. Thanks."

Halfway out the door, Aggie stopped. "Hospitals are strange places. Buildings made of concrete, glass, brick, and steel; built strong enough to withstand years of pounding from wind and rain, but they're helpless to contain the flood of pain and suffering generated daily

within their walls. All that suffering...it has to go somewhere, don't you think?"

The tiny old woman left without another word, leaving Paul and Sally staring after her in stunned silence.

"What was that all about?" Sally asked.

"Nothin'. Just a crazy old fool who likes to hear herself
talk. Probably out of her freakin' mind, and *you're* gonna
let her visit Robbie."

"She's harmless."

"I don't care. Tell the nurses that Robbie has no other
visitors — none, especially nutty old bats from downstairs!"

Existence #1: Dreamland

"Are you still there?"

You wait a long time for the phantom voice to answer,
standing ramrod straight, eyes closed, ears open, hoping
the woman will talk and not leave you alone in this bleak
place. Well, you aren't completely alone. You have the
flower.

Frustrated and lonely, you sit down in the dirt to study
the flower. It looks like a normal, everyday carnation,
only slightly bigger. Leaning in, your nose almost touches
the delicate petals. You inhale deeply, and again, savoring
the sweet fragrance. It smells wonderful, reminding you
of your mother and the small garden she lovingly tends
in the yard back home.

Back home—

You shut that thought off immediately, not willing,
or able to go down that dark road just yet. A tear runs
down your cheek, a tiny drop of loneliness that escapes
the raging river of self-pity building within you. The tear
curls around your lip, dangles from your chin, and then
drops silently into the center of the flower.

The carnation begins to grow.

Jumping to your feet, you watch in awe as the flower
expands, the stalk as well as the bloom enlarging in front
of your eyes. The story of Jack and the Beanstalk pops
into your head, and for a moment you think this is how

the mysterious woman plans on helping. Unfortunately, before you can envision the carnation extending up through the clouds and climbing it to find your way back to your family, the flower stops, leveling off just under the height of your chin, the bloom a full eight inches in diameter. A huge flower, the biggest you've ever seen, but still no help as far as you can see.

Disappointed and angry, you reach to rip the mutant flower out of the ground. You grip your right hand around the thick stalk and...

≫┼∙┼∙┼≪

...you're looking down upon yourself. Not here and now. Has to be several years back. You're younger, smaller, dressed in a blue baseball uniform; knee-high socks, cap, and glove. You're hot and sweaty, the uniform stained with dirt, a huge contented grin on your face—

You shudder, realizing there is no wheelchair... yet.

Your father's shiny new Mazda RX-7 roars into the scene, skidding to a stop in a shower of dust and gravel. From above, you can easily see how drunk he is as he climbs out of the car and waves for you to hurry up and get in. Back then you hadn't been able to tell, hadn't had a clue your father had taken the afternoon off work to tie one on with a few buddies down at the local pool hall. Now, you know better. Horrified, you watch yourself climb into the car, fully trusting your father to take care of you and get you home, safe.

Wasn't going to happen.

You watch the Mazda squeal out of sight, knowing that three intersections away your father will run a red light and a yellow Ryder rental truck will t-bone the car on the passenger side, tearing the small foreign car nearly in half, ending your baseball playing days forever...

≫┼∙┼∙┼≪

The strange vision fades slowly from sight, water down a semi-clogged drain, and you stare at the green flower gripped in your closed fist. Your hand is sore, fingers cramping, so you let go of the carnation, only then noticing the thin ribbon of blood running the length of your palm. Seeing the blood triggers pain and your hand begins to burn. Examining the hand closer, it doesn't appear to be much of a wound, hardly a scratch in fact, more like a superficial paper cut, but it hurts badly and bleeds as if it were a gash cutting right to the bone. You reach for the flower again, to check for hidden thorns on the stem. Your finger barely caresses the smooth stalk when you wince in pain and pull your hand back to find yet another paper-thin cut. Blood runs freely from both wounds now, and no matter how hard you think about it, you can't understand why touching the flower cuts you. It's as if invisible razor blades coat the flower.

Trying not to panic, you remove your t-shirt and attempt to wrap your injured hand when something incredible happens. The bleeding stops on its own. The thin wounds begin to heal, the torn skin re-knitting back together as the pain fades away. Within seconds, your right hand fully heals and the only sign that you've ever bled are the scattered crimson splashes that stain the ground at your feet.

You don't understand what has just happened; don't comprehend any of this. Where are you and why is all this crazy stuff happening? The only certainty right now is that you desperately want to go home.

For hours, you roam the barren field, at times calling out for the phantom woman to speak again, sulking around depressed and afraid you'll be left in this awful place forever. No matter how far you walk, or which direction you choose to step, you never allow yourself to lose sight of the green carnation — your anchor in this wasteland.

The sky begins to darken. Spending the night alone in this field is a terrifying prospect, but staying near the mysterious flower gives you some comfort, some sense of protection, even if it's only in your head. You lie down on the ground, curling around the base of the giant carnation and soon fall asleep, oblivious to the field coming alive around you, the flowers finally starting to grow.

⊷•┝•┃•┝•⊶

Existence #2: Reality

Paul and Sally Moore made good time returning home from the hospital. Paul had bitched about the traffic regardless of their progress, but that was just the way he was, and Sally was used to it. Climbing out of the car, she stood by the front of their two-story Cape Cod home, waiting for Paul to unlock the door. For some reason, he still sat in the car. When she went back to check on him, she found him wiping tears from red-rimmed eyes.

"Why are you crying?" Sally asked.

"I'm not," Paul shot back, defensive. "I'm just, you know, upset about Robbie. He looked so small in that bed. So...*fragile*. Is he gonna die, Sally?"

Tears stung the edges of Sally's eyes too; she felt thrilled and shocked at her husband's unexpected show of emotion.

"I don't know, honey. The doctor said it could go either way. Come on in. Let's have a nice supper, and we can talk about it, okay?"

When he finally came up the stairs onto the porch, Sally noticed a red stain on the collar of his shirt.

"Jesus, you're bleeding, Paul. What happened?"

"Where?" Paul asked, glancing at both his hands and then down at the rest of his body. "I don't see anything."

"Your neck. Come here. You must have scratched yourself."

Paul looked down at his hands again, saw no blood under any of his nails, but shrugged and let his wife take care of him.

Sally removed a tissue from her purse and tried to clean up the mess. Fortunately, there were only two small wounds: one long thin cut and one not more than a scratch, neither very deep. As she dabbed at the cuts, a tiny brown spider dropped onto the shoulder of Paul's shirt, startling her and making her pull her hand back.

"What's the matter?" Paul asked.

"Nothing. Just a little spider on your—"

"Where?" Paul cried, using his hands to beat his head, chest, and back.

Sally knew about her husband's lifelong fear of spiders. "Relax, Paul, it's long gone," she said, trying to calm him.

Sally returned to checking his cuts, but Paul pushed her hands away and stomped into the house. Two band-aids later, the matter was forgotten and Sally went to fix Paul's dinner. He wasn't the kind of guy that liked to be kept waiting, especially after his little freak-out on the porch. He'd be angry with himself, feeling silly, and Sally knew from experience he'd be looking for any opportunity to prove his manhood.

⊁⊹⊺⊹⊺⊹⊹

Back at the hospital, Aggie spent the rest of the day in her room, refusing to eat dinner. She busied herself making flowers, dozens of them, her knotted old hands twisting and folding the thin colorful paper hour after hour, carnation after carnation, until the nurses came to shut off her light and gently force her into bed.

Exhausted, she quickly fell into a deep but troubled sleep. Aggie dreamed about a horrible car accident and of a young boy dressed in a blood-drenched baseball uniform, trapped and screaming within the wreckage. The dream replayed relentlessly, the boy's pain-filled screams haunting her throughout the long night.

When she finally woke, covered in a sheen of sweat, the digital clock beside her bed read 4:58 a.m. The sun wouldn't be up for at least another hour, but Aggie didn't care. She couldn't stay in bed another minute. She swung her feeble legs off the bed and placed her feet down onto the floor, using her wooden cane to climb shakily to her feet. Middle of the night or not, work needed to be done.

Existence #1: Dreamland

Wake up.

You stir, hearing the voice but ignoring it.

Come on; time to open your eyes.

This time you recognize the woman's voice and bolt to your feet, your heart trip-hammering inside of your chest.

"You came—"

Your words are lost as you open your eyes to something truly amazing. Flowers are everywhere! An entire field, no an entire *world* filled with huge carnations — a kaleidoscope of color spreading out from the small circular clearing you've slept in for as far as your eyes can see. It's an incredible sight, literally taking your breath away.

Are you with me?

"Yeah, I'm here. Where did all these flowers come from? Did you do bring them?"

You hear chuckling.

Heavens, no! Some of them, sure, but I think your mind did a lot of this planting on its own. That's good; it means you're ready.

"Ready for what?"

To come home, of course.

"But how?" you ask. "I don't even know where I am, never mind how to get home! What good is a field of flowers for finding—?"

Run, boy, the voice interrupts. *Trust me. Trust yourself.*

You look out across the endless expanse of flowers, not sure what to do. Then you remember what happened last night when you touched the original green carnation. Twice you'd come into contact with the flower, and both times it slashed you open and made you bleed. Would these flowers hurt you as well?

Run!

"I can't!" you cry back. "I'm scared. They're going to cut me. Please, I don't want to hurt anymore."

I don't want you to hurt anymore, either. That's why I'm here to help you.

"How?" you ask, frightened. "How can you stop the flowers from hurting me?"

There's a pause, then: *I can't. The flowers are made of paper...and they will cut you. They'll cut you bad!*

"Then why would you want me to run? Who are—?"

Shhhhhhhhh, listen. Think about what happened to your wounds?

"They healed."

No. They didn't heal; they just went somewhere else.

"I don't understand."

In the real world, pain has to be suffered by those who receive it. Not here. Here, pain can open doorways all on its own, and can be shared by those who truly deserve it.

"My father?" you ask, hesitant, tiny flames of hope igniting within you.

Silence.

Tears run freely down your face. You let them come this time; let your emotions pour out of you in twin torrents.

"I hate him. Always have. And not just because of the car accident. Not just because of my legs. He... he still hurts me. Me and momma both."

You break down completely, sobbing into your hands for several minutes, but not for a moment are you ashamed of your tears. No, the tears give you strength, give you courage; help wash away the wall of fear your abusive father has built within you.

And this last time?

"I was listening to my stereo up in my room. I didn't know he was sleeping, didn't even know he was home. He came upstairs, and he was so damn mad. I tried to say I was sorry...tried to explain, but he had this insane look on his face. He smashed my radio, then grabbed my wheelchair and shoved me out into the hall over to the stairs. Then he... he—"

I know what he did, boy, knew as soon as they brought you in. Bottom line is you don't deserve to suffer anymore. Neither does your mother. That's why I want you to run, boy. It's going to hurt, but you need to run anyway.

Your tears are gone now. So is your fear: Your mind made up.

"Bastard!" you yell, and with just that one word, you're gone, sprinting like you have winged feet.

The flowers make you bleed with every step, the stems, leaves, and pretty colored blooms slicing and ripping open your tender flesh as easily as barbed wire. Not all the carnations have grown to the same height. Some tear at your knees, others at your thighs, hips, throat, ankles, chest, and face. It's like being attacked by a nest of angry hornets, with no way to avoid their single-minded fury. The pain is excruciating, a monstrous all-consuming inferno, and you run open-mouthed, screaming in agony, but it doesn't slow you down. Your clothes tatter and shred, your momentum flaying the red-soaked rags free of your body, taking away strips of your skin too, but still you rush on. Nothing can stop you now.

The blood drains down your forehead, stinging your eyes like pepper spray, threatening to blind you, to force you to stop, but it's through this red-blurred vision of the field that you finally spot the portal. It's just a dance of light in the shape of a doorframe, a slight shimmer of motion like the heat haze coming off the road on a hot summer day, but you recognize it for what it is. You lower your head, pump your arms, and race flat out, fully aware you're likely using your legs for the last time. You don't care. All you want is one thing: to go home.

Existence #2: Reality

Sally would have preferred to skip breakfast and hurry to the hospital, but she knew better than to suggest such a thing. Paul steadfastly refused to leave the house without being fed. No, it was better to just put on some coffee, scramble a few eggs, and be done with it. The sooner her husband ate, the sooner she could go visit Robbie again.

"Your eggs are ready, Hon!" she shouted from the foot of the stairs, knowing Paul was shaving up in the bathroom. "Best eat them while they're hot!"

It was as close as she dared tell him to hurry up.

Paul responded with a series of escalating screams.

Before Sally could react, her husband appeared at the top of the stairs, naked, his body bathed in blood. Shrieking in agony with his eyes tightly closed, Paul's crimson-streaked arms flailed around in panic. Sally screamed too, grabbing the banister for support, her legs threatening to collapse From where she stood, she couldn't see the myriad cuts on her husband's ravaged body, but she didn't need to in order to understand the grievous nature of Paul's injuries. She nearly went to him but hesitated, instinctively knowing her husband was already beyond help.

Paul stumbled, rolling head over heels down the staircase, blood splashing everywhere. Sally backed out of the way, but Paul's progression, as well as his screams came to a sudden, nauseating stop when his head connected with a brutal *thud* on the thick newel post at the bottom of the staircase.

Sally couldn't bring herself to take a close look at her husband's body, much less touch him to see if he might be okay. Instead, she took a moment to compose herself, then went to the phone and dialed 911. When the paramedics reached the house, Paul was still alive, but in critical condition with a massive dent in his forehead where he'd struck the post. They found no cuts anywhere on his body, nor any trace of blood inside the house.

At the hospital, Robbie woke up gasping for breath, fragments of a bad dream lingering in his sleepy thoughts. He ached all over, fatigue overwhelming the boy as if he'd just run a—

Run! The echo of a familiar voice drummed in his head.

His eyes snapped open, a collision of thoughts, sensations, and vivid memories invading his consciousness, remembering everything at once.

Robbie immediately noticed the old woman standing at the foot of his bed, but then his eyes moved down to take in the colorful paper flowers strewn at his feet. Peripherally, he saw his wheelchair leaning against the far wall, but instead of looking at that old enemy, his eyes were drawn back to the woman. She hadn't spoken a word to confirm it, but Robbie already realized this frail little woman's identity.

"Thank you," he said. The "how" and "why" questions could be dealt with later.

"You're welcome, sweetie," Aggie said. "Everything should be okay now."

"Is my father dead?" Robbie asked.

"No. Not fully."

"He's in the field, isn't he?"

Aggie looked at her feet, neither confirming nor denying, shifting her weight onto the wooden cane. "Your father can't hurt you anymore."

Robbie thought about that for a moment, his eyes roaming the room and finding his wheelchair again. A dark and vengeful anger began to build within him, then an idea so sweet it brought a smile to his pallid face.

"These flowers you made me," Robbie swept his hand across the pile at his feet. "Can you teach me how to make them? How to *deliver* them?"

Aggie followed the boy's gaze to the wheelchair.

"You want to send your father flowers?" she asked.

"No...something else."

→·‡·‡·‡·←

A middle-aged man lies in a coma.

Fell down the stairs, bumped his head.

Ask his wife, standing by his bedside. She's telling everyone that's what happened.

Don't ask his son, though. No, not him. He's far too busy making giant paper spiders.

• •

Gord Rollo lives in Dunnville, Ontario. His shorter work has appeared throughout the genre, and his first two mass market novels, *The Jigsaw Man* and *Crimson* have been published by Leisure Books. Gord edited the acclaimed anthologies, *Unnatural Selection: A Collection of Darwinian Nightmares* and *Dreaming of Angels*. He can be reached through his website at: *www.gordqrollo.com*

• •

The Night
Before the Storm

by Jean-Louis Trudel

Kassim had made night his friend. The older he got, the more he forgot to sleep, as if it were an old habit that needed discarding. Instead, he would keep watch over his house late into the dark hours, seated in the inner courtyard, his frail hands clutching a cup of tea as it grew cold.

The quiet collapsed in upon him, as if he'd become the center of attraction of all the silences of the city, the lulls, the awkward pauses, the peaceful rests, the random breaks in the city's noises, all that was calm and tranquil amid life's bustle. Each sip of tea lasted a bit longer, the cupful staying impossibly warm. Time itself slowed down, and the sky's crystal spheres whirled slower and slower, obeying his unspoken fear of what the morrow would bring.

Each time he looked up, he wanted the motion to last forever. His gaze brushed past the shadowy mass of the wall before shooting up into the indigo expanse of the Syrian night. He watched the star-nailed sky revolve past the zenith, the heaven's ether driven by its passion for the perfection of the empyrean beyond any earthly sight.

At times, the darkness was cut open by a luminous bolt, but it wasn't the Moon's crystal sphere cracking open, it was a breath of elemental fire rising to find the fiery sphere, beyond the shell of air. Everything had a place in Aristotle's universe: men, women, beasts, elements... When a jolt of the earth beneath freed some long-trapped flame, it rose in a rush, all the way to the heights just below the sublunary shell.

Kassim had sometimes wondered if there were mountains so high that their peaks furrowed the underbelly of the sphere that was home to fire, the lightest and most subtle of all elements, and the most vital. There were alchemists who believed that fire in its purest state was the very essence of life. A man who climbed the world's tallest mountain might immerse himself in the flows of the fiery sea above and imbibe through his pores such a store of fire that he would live forever. Others believed that it was possible to blend the igneous element into the elixir of long life. But Kassim had never encountered anyone able to mix such a potion, and it was too late for him now.

When the night got too cool, Kassim would get up. Like a lion in a pit, he paced within the quadrangle, berating his friend. Why was it so cold? He shivered, his bones aching. He'd lean on a sturdy staff that he'd use as a weapon if anybody tried to break in. As long as he lived, no one would harm his daughter and son-in-law, or his grandchildren! Not that he'd ever needed to face down an intruder while the night watchmen walked the streets, clacking their clubs together to mark their progress.

When the night was warm, Kassim did not get up, for he knew he was no longer alone in the open air. All over the city, families oppressed by the heat climbed on the rooftops. The old man heard his next-door neighbours unroll mats for the night. Their patriarch, Hagop, was always the last one up, wheezing from the climb. Kassim listened to his friend's rasping breath with silent concern. Would Hagop's heart finally burst from the strain, like an overripe grape?

Snatches of faraway conversations reached him. And the tart smell of the aromatic rushes burnt to keep away mosquitoes. From other roofs, occupied by other families... The night-time beloved of Kassim was unfaithful then and, like a houri, shared her favours with others — those unable to sleep like him, kept awake by heat, age, infirmity, grief, or one of the many torments inflicted by love.

And then came the final night.

Day by day, Kassim had become so used to hunger that he'd forgotten what a full stomach felt like, or the pleasant stupor that followed a true feast. Ever since the beginning of the city's siege, cold meats had been more common fare than fresh cuts, and chick peas served more often than any meat. His daughter Fatima gave him more than his share, but it wasn't enough. His strength was failing like the fading flames in a fire when the ash-white wood is on the point of crumbling.

The evenings seemed cooler than ever before, even when he wrapped himself in a blanket. And there was no tea to drink. Water had become scarce, and the bundles of dried leaves from the Island of Jewels no longer entered the city.

Yet, the night before everything ended, Kassim found the strength to do more.

He'd insisted on spending the night outside, in the very heart of the house that might no longer belong to him the next day. The siege was ending, but not in the way they had all hoped for. The doors of the city would open and let in the infidel army, after letting out the governor's soldiery. The citizens would be left defenceless.

Mirroring Kassim's mood, the night was sulky, perhaps even hostile. Just before dusk, the clouds swept the skies in a furious charge, hiding all the stars above. He could not remember a darker night.

Kassim stared long and hard at the wall's plaster. He knew its cracks by heart. He no longer needed to see its dips and bumps. In spite of the darkness, he could read the pattern like a palmist able to tell the future from a hand's lines. It spoke to him of futility and impotence.

The old man had been sure that Fatima's future was safe in the hands of her husband. With the birth of his grand-children, he had believed his seed would live on. They weren't his own, not the way the children of a son would have been, but they were his flesh and blood.

Yet, it was all going to crumble in a single night. Man is small, God is great. His certainties meant nothing. He had been so sure, but then many a youth leaves school, thinking he knows everything.

As he despaired, it seemed to him that the contours
of the wall came into focus, not as clear as in the full light
of day but still outlined by a dim glow. The more he
peered, the more he felt blurry letters were spelling out
words that he might be able to decipher with one more
effort. For a moment, he let the task engross him, until a cold draft chilled him suddenly.

When he turned, he saw that the door was open.

"Fatima!"

How could she have forgotten to close it on such a
night?

His daughter did not answer, and Kassim did not try
calling again. He moved towards the opening. He could
now see it was the source of the glow he had perceived.

The man who lives long enough to reach the brink
of a second childhood is often tempted to leave just to
show that he still can. In his youth, he might have left
to prove that he had come of age, but now it would be
to convince himself that he can still escape, that there
is still an exit, a way out, even as he hears the soft footsteps of death catching up to him.

Kassim went out into the street, forsaking the familiar
walls. There was nothing to fear. The night watch no
longer made the rounds. It would have been pointless;
all of the city's troublemakers had been drafted to help
repair the ramparts or assist the governor's soldiers. As
for the animals that used to roam the streets, pigs, dogs,
cats, and chicken, all had been caught and eaten long
ago.

The streets were perfectly safe. The real enemy, the
only enemy, was a tangible presence still held at a distance. The infidel troops waited by the fires on the other
side of the ramparts. Tomorrow, the garrison would
surrender, the enemy would march in, and there was no
telling what would happen to the townspeople once the
Christian dogs slipped their leash.

Yet, Kassim wasn't alone in the streets. He grew aware
of shadows like his own, clinging to the walls and stumbling forward in the dark. He recognized the girth and
rasping breath of the fourth one he passed.

"Hagop! I'm so glad to see you out and about."

"You too, Kassim?"

Unable to understand the question's meaning, the old man tried to interpret Hagop's expression. Much to his surprise, his neighbour's face resolved into shadowy blotches, enough to know that it was Hagop though not to guess at his thoughts.

Was he recovering his eyesight of old, when he studied the Ancients, puzzling over Euclid's demonstrations and Aristotle's reasoning? Kassim was aware of many more darkened figures gliding along the public road, streaming by him, brushing by in silence. Were all of the city's townsmen taking a midnight stroll on this fateful night?

"What do you mean?" he asked, seized by a nameless dread.

"Haven't you guessed, *Hajji*? You suspect nothing? Oh, my friend! Were you perhaps in your courtyard and did you dream that you left by the door?"

"I'm not dreaming!"

"Not anymore."

Old age had taught him when to set aside his curiosity and wait for things to become clear. Kassim followed his friend and both came quickly to the ramparts, joining the throng as others filed up the stairs. He assumed that, like him, they wished to look at the enemy encampment and ponder their future masters. Wasn't that his own intent when he'd left his home's courtyard?

The truth emerged slowly, like a dancer throwing away her veils one by one. The clues accumulated.

That floating feeling as he moved...

The absence of all aches and pains, as if his worn-out flesh had regained the blissful obliviousness of youth...

There was also the old black slave who marched past without seeing them, bowed under the weight of such a small pack that it must have held a fortune in gold its owner was sending away from the infidels. And, more telling yet, Hagop's head was suddenly lit up by the glow of an oil lamp set in the wall, the small flame shining *through* his skull.

When he looked more closely, Kassim noticed that his companions gave off a light of their own, just enough to reveal the transparency of their limbs. They were becoming ethereal, exposing their share of elemental fire, shorn of its gross material raiment, reduced to a pure form that was the image of their ideal being. In short...

"We're ghosts!" he cried out.

"Do you remember dying? Me neither. And I've recognized people I've seen this last couple of days, who were still alive. Did we all die in a few days, in a few hours even, without noticing it or hearing about it? Hunger was not yet so dire."

"Then what is this?"

"What do you know of spectres, *Hajji*?"

"All that is told about them — and that the imams call rank superstitions."

"Maybe they are superstitions. Me, I think that the dead *haunt* the world they lived in *before* they die, and not after."

"How is that possible?"

Hagop shrugged and then invited him to follow to the top of the ramparts. Along the battlements bathed in moonlight, Kassim recognized old friends, distant relatives, neighbours, business partners... The old, the very young, and the women were numerous. There was Esther, the Circassian slave, and Khadija, and... He looked among them for Fatima, his son-in-law, and his grandchildren, but he did not find them.

Still, he stretched a hand out towards Esther, hurt to see her in the long line of ghosts. Sometimes, he'd seen the fair-skinned slave walking back from the fountain, a jar on her shoulder. But he had never seen her without a veil.

She faced the Moon as she untied her red hair, bleached by the savage Syrian sun, and she let the night breeze slip its fingers through the long locks. The night was warm, the wind remembering still the day's heat and blowing on their chilled flesh like a faithful dog's hot breath as it looks for signs of life before howling.

Below, enemy fires burned, within a single bowshot from the walls. Kassim wondered if any shades wandered among them, freed by imminent death from the bonds of fleshly life. Few, if any, he thought. A city's sack rarely took the lives of the looters and maddened soldiers. The ones who paid the price were among the weak, the old, the infirm. The ones worth nothing to the slave traders.

Kassim faced the truth. He was one of those. He would not survive past the end of the siege.

The night was giving herself to him for one last time, like a solicitous lover able to chase away his weariness and sustain him until daybreak. She was telling him to enjoy the stones rough and cold to the touch, the wind's aimless rustling, the constellations twinkling above and ruling the cloudless sky. Prim and kind, the night's darkness hid their sorrows from each other.

Hagop stopped in front of a guard asleep in a stone niche. The man had found a narrow ledge to sit on and leaned on his pike to keep from falling over as he snored.

"He's failed us, and yet he'll live," the trader snarled. "We paid well for his petty pleasures, and we gave till it hurt. But we're going to die."

"Would you like to know how?"

"I've thought about it. I wouldn't want to be slaughtered like sheep, *Hajji*. If I'm going to die, I intend to fight to defend my loved ones. I'd like to think there's an infidel shade wandering unseen through his camp, right now, because I'm going to kill him tomorrow."

"But is our death already written, Hagop? If I choose to submit, would I be spared? How can you know this isn't a mere dream? If I'm killed tomorrow because I attack an infidel dog, my family may suffer."

"I know. I've asked myself the same question and it may hold me back at the last, but I want to be ready to strike when they come. What I most fear, *Hajji*, is that I'll forget all of this when I wake up. I'll act and die blindly. Have you ever heard of men who were certain of their appointed hour?"

"Often enough, but it doesn't prove anything. Even those who are certain may say nothing to comfort the ones they love. I see only one way of turning this to advantage."

"Which one? If we fight back tomorrow, we condemn our families to slavery. If we don't fight and are killed out of hand, our deaths will have been shameful. And we don't even know if we'll remember this premonition we've been granted."

"That's why we must act tonight!"

"What?"

"Let's make a sortie. If we rush outside the walls by all available exits, the infidels will be taken unawares. Let's jump from the towers, let's burst out from the postern, let's open the doors and charge. If we're dead anyway, let's die fighting, in the open field. There's still a chance we can save our families from slavery and its evils."

"What's the use, Kassim? Look."

Hagop slapped his hand down on the spear held by the sleeping soldier. The iron spearhead stabbed through his palm, light flashing briefly, but the shaft hardly stirred in the soldier's grip. As for the trader, he grimaced and withdrew his hand.

"We can touch the world of the living, but its objects are hardly aware of our touch. I should have torn my hand open, but it feels like nothing more than a bad scratch."

"We could scare them," Kassim insisted.

"They can't see us. And I don't know if they can hear us. How do you propose scaring them?"

Kassim turned his back on the plain pocked with campfires. He considered the city he had so often walked in the light of day and listened to at night. Love and horror struggled in his breast, the way lightning and rain fight in the midst of a storm, and the flashes would chase away the darkness inside, showing him the faces of those he wished to see one last time. His fists tightened and released, but the anger roused by the massacre to come was overwhelmed by another force. He no longer wished to kill.

He had seen the elemental fire burning inside them all. It would not be quenched. If the body, that pitiful vessel, was broken, the fiery breath inside would rise to join the fiery layer within reach of the sublunary sphere. It was enough.

"Good-bye, Hagop."

"God guard you, *Hajji*."

Kassim had been to Mecca, but he bit back the answer expected by his friend. In a single night, he had abandoned many of his former beliefs, like the tree parts with the leaves torn away by the gale. Whatever the imams said, God, Blessed be His Name, God the Infinitely Great, God the Compassionate, would not let His creatures die so wretchedly.

He headed back, through streets that seemed even darker without the company of other shades, and he found himself once again in his courtyard, sitting in front of a wall that he couldn't see. Hagop had been right.

He had likely dreamt his exit from the courtyard, but he was sure that he hadn't imagined the scene on the battlements. When he went in, Fatima greeted him. She was cradling little Ahmed in her arms and whispering a song to soothe his fears. Or her own.

"Are you going to bed, father?"

"Yes, my daughter. Some things we should not try to postpone."

"You're trembling, *Hajji*. Don't tell me you saw a ghost out there?"

"Not yet. And I didn't see you either."

"Father... you're scaring me."

"I'm scaring myself. For I am a dead man speaking to a slave."

And what he spoke by night became truth by day.

• •

Born in Toronto, Jean-Louis Trudel holds degrees in physics, astronomy, and history. Since 1994, he has authored, in French, a couple of novels, two fiction collections, and twenty-four young adult books. His short stories, in French and English, have appeared in various magazines and anthologies around the world. He now lives in Montreal.

• •

End in Ice

By Alison Baird

Fire we might have fought. You have a chance with fire. Hoses or water bombers can contain it, even a spell of rainy weather can help defeat it. New houses and seedlings then rise from the ashes, and life continues as before. Or floods, now. Rising water will ruin all it touches, but it always retreats in the end. Rivers return to their beds, the sea to its former boundaries, and the drowned land dries and lives again. These elemental incursions are savage, but never lasting. Come back in ten years' time, and you'll hardly know a disaster took place.

Ice is another matter. When ice seizes territory, it does so to conquer and reign.

I remember studying the Ice Age in school. There was a book with a picture of spear-wielding cavemen in bear-skins, stalking shaggy mammoths on the Pleistocene plains — and, in the background, mighty cliffs of blue-white ice that reared up high as mountains. In this paint-ing, the cavemen weren't even looking at the glacier: to them it was just a part of their primeval world, familiar and unremarkable. But I was haunted by that picture as a child, imagining those white cliffs inexorably advanc-ing, until their crushing weight covered the fields where the cavemen and mammoths now stood. I imagined them grinding down hills and gouging out valleys. Later, in high school, I would learn the names of the geographical features of glaciation: eskers, drumlins, moraines. The ancient ice had, it seemed, inflicted perpetual scars and welts on our landscape, mute witness to its mastery. One day, our teacher said, those vanished glaciers might return. But that latter-day Ice Age would be in some inconceivably distant future.

Or so we then believed.

❧•❧•❧•❧

Of course there were signs and warnings early on, but most of us knew nothing about them. Full knowledge was kept from us: months passed before it began to seep through the government's carefully-erected barriers of concealment. For me, it all began with the owl. There it was, on a fine July morning, perching on the arch of the national war memorial. At a distance, I couldn't think what the small white blob was. It looked incongruous, like a patch of snow lingering into summer — which even for Ottawa was clearly impossible. When I drew closer, I saw it was a snowy owl, a beautiful white-plumed creature with eyes the colour of citrine. As I stood a moment to marvel at it, I heard a man (some amateur bird enthusiast he must have been) holding forth to his two companions as they also stared up at the bird. A snowy owl shouldn't be here, he said, not at this time of the year. They migrate south only if the arctic winter is unusually severe. I can still see his lean bony face, his wiry grey hair, and hear the almost disapproving tone in his voice. I was tempted to say, "Write the Prime Minister's office," but decided against it and just walked on. Meanwhile the owl went on perching where it had no business to be, upright and arrogant as an emperor surveying his rightful domain.

What strains credulity as much as the Phenomenon itself is, I suppose, the notion that our government should be able to hide from the public anything so immense and catastrophic. But it does make a kind of sense if you think about it. So few of us living up there in the arctic, even fewer go there to visit. A region that's almost never in the news. Hardly anyone Down Here really knows what's going on Up There: that's the government's job. So they could just feed a few stories to the media about hunger and poverty sweeping through Inuit communities, and so explain the evacuations and the large number of these people suddenly turning up on the streets of our southern cities. There was one aged Inuit man, his face a crag of wrinkles, who sat on the granite bench outside my office building and mumbled fantastical nonsense about ice demons taking over the North. It was instantly dismissed by all who heard. Poor delusional old man, addicted no doubt to drugs or alcohol until the old superstitions of his people took over his enfeebled mind. How could we have known, then, that he was trying to warn us? Had we stopped to hear his whole tale, we would not have believed it anyway.

But before long it would cease to be a matter of belief.

We were all still arguing around the office water cooler about why the polar ice caps were shrinking — global warming or act of nature — when, after millennia of slumber, or perhaps after its own protracted internal debate, the ice made up its mind. It stirred, roused, shook off a few icebergs that drifted slowly out to sea; and then it began to move. Not quickly, not by human standards, but with unusual speed for a glacier: the pace of a man walking, strolling along on a pleasant summer's day, knowing that he has all the time in the world. The first warning came from the weather station at the appropriately-named Alert on Ellesmere Island. Soon scientists were scrambling to come up with explanations. "Glacial surge" is the only one I recall now. It *is* possible, apparently, for a glacier suddenly and unexpectedly to travel at up to a hundred times its normal pace — perhaps due to melt-water at its base, or earth tremors, or other causes. But an entire polar cap? The debate raged on as the ice fields continued to advance... to *grow*. I can picture the increasing terror of the government as the situation became clear. There would be secret meetings, consultations with climatologists and with the military. Until finally it became necessary to inform the rest of us.

And all chaos broke loose.

Every rational explanation was abandoned within days, the debate veering from science to philosophy. Maybe there were, indeed, demons in the ice. Or maybe God was angry. Or Nature itself might be punishing us for past misdeeds. But though Mother Nature might want to eliminate humanity, what wrong had her other creatures done her? The animals? The trees? Perhaps it was not punishment, but merely an accident — like an elephant rolling over in its sleep and flattening a mouse. Its sleeping brain doesn't know about the mouse, and wouldn't really care much even if it did. There's no malice involved at all. The unthinking and unfeeling Earth might have twitched in its slumber, as it sometimes does: and somewhere a volcano erupts, or a mudslide comes crashing down on a village, or a tsunami wipes out thousands of people in a coastal area. Just a little twitch. Sorry folks, nothing personal.

But to me it all seemed too deliberate and purposeful for that. Perhaps it was all the methane that Earth's plant and animal life were producing, warming the atmosphere, threatening the Ice — and so it had decided in its slow cold way that anything organic must go.

Over the next few weeks, the ice field advanced, inexorable, an army no one could face or defeat. It covered the land as glaciers, the ocean as pack ice. The northern cities that stood in its way were flattened or entombed: Moscow, Tromso, Reykjavik. Here in Canada, we lost White Horse and Iqaluit and Yellowknife first, then Edmonton, Winnipeg, Quebec. I recall watching the first aerial footage of the northern forests being engulfed. There it was, the vast glittering whiteness crushing its way through hectares of dark green: my childhood nightmare come to life. I stared in fascination at doomed fir trees, some of them high as a three-storey building, dwarfed by the giant ice-face. They toppled before it like blades of grass before a mower. And then the helicopter pilot flew up higher, to reveal a sight more dreadful still: the upper surface of the glacial field, the long tumbled plain of living and moving ice stretching away unbroken to the far horizon. *This* was what would replace the world we knew, once the great march was over and done with: this endless waste of white.

The astronauts on the international space station beamed pictures down to us too, before they returned to Earth and their families. They showed us the growing blank whiteness of the expanding ice caps where once there had been the blue of sea, the green and brown of land. There were still some people who refused to believe the TV coverage, who babbled wild-eyed about hoaxes and conspiracies, and had to make the journey in order to see for themselves. They came back grim-faced and silent. Here in Ottawa my coworkers and I just soldiered on with our jobs. Amazingly, there were even some feeble attempts at humour. Ottawa would surely be spared, some said, because the hot air from the politicians would create its own microclimate. Then the jokes grew blacker and blacker, before they finally ceased.

I did not join in the gallows humour, or in the philosophical discussions. I had nothing to say. I did not wish the world to end, but there was no denying I had less to lose than most. Only my own life, and that life had never truly been *lived*. I was a minor assistant to a minor civil servant: bespectacled, dowdy, unmarried, aging. Everyone I'd cared about was already gone.

For a while, there was no major change to our daily routines. More snowy owls, and other arctic birds: these came first, being winged and swifter to flee; later the earth-bound animals followed. Whole herds of caribou streamed across the empty highways, and there were musk oxen grazing in the parks. I've travelled to all of the other borders, the extreme points where Canada crumbles away into islands: Pelee and Middle Island in Lake Erie, the southernmost points of the nation; Newfoundland and PEI and the Magdalenes down east; and to the forested sanctuaries of the Queen Charlottes out west. But the high arctic I've never seen, and its islands have always seemed vague and nebulous to me. I knew the names of the bigger ones, Baffin and Ellesmere and Victoria; but the others appeared to be no more individualized than scattered clods of earth. I'd go and see the high arctic, I always used to say — someday, I didn't know when. Maybe I'd take a cruise. But other places were higher priorities. The North would wait, I thought, till I was ready. Now it had come to me instead.

There were arctic wolves too, and polar bears. They infiltrated the urban areas and roamed the streets, hungry and hostile. Soon it was no longer safe for people to venture outside unless they were armed, although there were plenty of prey animals for the carnivores to feed on. The creatures were only fleeing the ice field, of course, but they seemed almost like its vanguard, spreading terror and violence in advance of its onslaught.

I kept on going to work, despite the danger. We all needed to feel that we were supporting a still-functioning government — or maybe it just calmed our nerves to keep busy. This was in the beginning, you see, when many still believed the crisis was temporary and the glaciers would recede, or else that some plan would be devised to defeat them. What plan, we never really considered. Had we done so, we would all have realized there could be no effective strategy against what we faced. Nuclear weapons were no use. A large number of thermonuclear explosions would render our planet as uninhabitable as any Ice Age. And nothing else was strong enough to challenge the Ice.

The next part's a bit blurry to me. We heard that the federal government was relocating down south, to Toronto — I think they were taking over the provincial legislature building — and after that it's all just fear and confusion, and people fleeing. Why *would* they flee? you might well ask, and I have no answer. The Ice wasn't moving fast enough to overtake them in their swift cars and airplanes. And it would have us all in the end, whether we moved fast or slow: time was on its side and always had been. But the government sent as many of its bureaucrats as possible down south. My boss packed his wife and kids and belongings in his van, and headed for the airport. After he went most of the office staff left too, and the place shut down. But I stayed behind, to see the last of Ottawa. I went to university here — landed my first job here — spent most of my life in this city. I wanted to witness its end, to make a final farewell.

Before long, I could see the Ice coming, like the foam-white top of a gigantic tidal wave descending on the towers of Parliament and the Chateau Laurier. I remember it was visible from my apartment window. But we not only saw it, those of us who stayed: we felt its deathly chill in the air, and heard it too. Yes, the Ice had a voice. As it advanced it sighed and groaned and hissed, as glaciers do. Some people went and hurled things in frustration at its blank white face: rocks, bricks, curses. It paid no heed. It just kept on creaking and moaning — and advancing, metre by slow metre. It devoured homes, offices, monuments: it would swallow the whole city in time, and any who remained would be swallowed along with it, buried and frozen. I remember thinking that perhaps some day an alien species might visit this planet and find these bodies, cryogenically preserved. It seemed a contradiction that the Ice, having decided to annihilate us, would not destroy us utterly but instead grant us this strange form of immortality. Fire and flood would not have done that.

The few of us from the civil service who remained — the unnecessary ones, unneeded by the government — went to the parliamentary library one day to salvage all the books and records of importance. An ultimately futile gesture, but I suppose we felt a need to *do* something, to keep ourselves busy at all costs. It staved off, at least for a time, the fear and purposelessness. I have a vague rec-ollection of volunteers hauling away stacked volumes on dollies and wheelbarrows. The electric lights finally went out while we were there, but we'd had the foresight to bring flashlights and candles. At last the shelves were emptied, and only the marble statue of Queen Victoria, a pallid ghost in the gloom, gazed down on the desolate scene. I glanced back through the door as I left with my load of books, wanting to see the interior one more time, recalling so many childhood field trips to that vast circular chamber. A store-house of knowledge. To think it had survived the fire that destroyed the first Parliament buildings, standing lonely yet triumphant amid the embers, only to be abandoned now...

After that, I was on my own. Someone offered me a lift south in their car, but I declined. I have no family, I explained, and nowhere to go. This is my home. After they'd all gone, I walked back, alone, to the houses of Parliament. They were cold as caves. In the dim light of the senate chamber, I went straight up to the carved wooden throne where all the governors general had sat, and the monarchs when they were visiting. I seated myself on its royal red cushion, gazing out on the rows of vacant chairs. For a moment I felt almost giddy. *Look at me! I'm queen of the castle!* But of course there was no real power here now. The Ice — vast, implacable, disdainful of authority — had driven it out. And it never had been anything but illusion, I realized. The illusion that we controlled this world, through ballots, through committees, through words weighted with pomp and ceremony. This huge stone building, once a hub of government, was now a shell emptied of grandeur and pretense, and the throne was just a chair. I rose and departed the chamber and the building, walking out through the great door still guarded by its vigilant stone lion and unicorn. Like the marble Victoria, they were emblems of an empire not only impotent now, but forever lost along with everything else.

I wandered aimlessly about the city after that, finally ending up at the National Gallery. The Ice had moved right up against the glass walls and tower of the Great Hall, shattering some panes and pressing against others so that you could go right up and look through them at the blue-white mass enveloping the building, with its layered patterns of accumulated debris. There was no electricity in this building either, of course, and the bitter cold of the glacier filled the granite halls. Some people had brought in lamps and candles, to look at the artworks that remained, and then left them behind on the floor like votive offerings for others to relight. But most of the valuable works were gone. Newman's Voice of Fire remained, its great size having made it too hard to transport: its one red abstract stripe still blazing on its dark background, its title a sad irony as it awaited its frigid fate. I saw no other people, though I heard voices in distant galleries, seemingly disembodied like ghosts, and somewhere a lone musician was playing a violin. The thin, thready music echoed through the glassy space like a dirge.

I walked across the frozen river to the Museum of Civilization in Hull, where a large crowd had gathered. The museum too was gripped in outstretched claws of ice. This should really have been a solemn time, as we all watched our heritage being swept away before our eyes. But the long unlit halls within rang with yells and laughter as gangs of drunken youths caroused through them. Some of them had smashed or vandalized the exhibits. Though I deplored the destruction, I felt I could not blame them. These young people had been deprived of the future that should have been their right. What respect did they owe the past? A heritage they could neither use nor pass on to a new generation? A society that had raised them, yet failed to defend them? This was not mere mischief, but a venting of their rage and despair. The laughter I'd heard was not merriment, but a kind of ghastly mockery. The surviving artifacts had a forlorn look in my flashlight's failing glow: the immense totem poles and sculptures, too heavy to move, abandoned along with the distinctive structure that housed them.

I could take no more. I left the museum to its destroyers and went back out into the daylight.

I confess I gave in to temptation myself once, and defaced a public monument. But I did not do it in anger: I only wrote my name on it. I can see my scrawl now, etched in white on grey stone: *Catherine Hanson*. Put there so something of *me* would remain behind in this place, this world on which I'd never left my mark in any other way. And never would, now. But my effort at a statement brought me no real comfort. In keeping with all else in my life, it seemed small and pathetic, and ultimately futile: like the fir trees before the wall of ice.

✦┼✦┼✦

In the end I too fled. I went to the Turks and Caicos
Islands, taking one of the last boats to go. Planes of course
had long since stopped flying, due to the shortage of fuel.
We docked at Providenciales to find it overrun. Even the
uninhabited islands, with their mangrove forests and salt
flats, thronged with terrified refugees. But most had gone
to Provo or Middle Caicos. I heard that some people were
hiding in the latter's network of limestone caverns. As if
that would make any difference. The Ice would find them
there, reach in its freezing fingers to crush them.

There were lovely long-tailed tropicbirds and seagulls
everywhere, retreating inland as they do before a storm,
huddling beside the native flamingoes and egrets. But there
were many other birds too, species never before seen in
these latitudes: refugees from northern climes, like us. I
spied a snowy owl perched on the nearly horizontal trunk
of a drooping palm — the very same bird, perhaps, that
I had seen on the war memorial? Who could say? It still
had the air of an emperor enthroned — but an old and sad
emperor, come to the end of an inglorious reign. In the
ocean hoary walruses mingled with dolphins and sailfish.
And on land the haggard faces of homeless northerners
contrasted strangely with the mostly darker-visaged
natives. The Phenomenon had forced a false unity upon
us, once-separate nations bound together now not by trea-
ties but by fear.

I left crowded Provo and took a little fishing boat headed
for Grand Turk, because of my good memories of the place
from my one vacation there — the only really happy memories I have. Once there I made my way slowly through the
capital, south towards the sea where the main crowds had
gathered. And there I stopped at last. Can you imagine it?
I'm standing on the southern shore of the island, on the
beach, amid these hushed throngs. It's still the picture of
a tropical paradise: turquoise seas lap at pale sands above
gardens of coral. But the breeze that rustles the palm-leaves
high over my head is *cold*. And here, at last, the illusion
of further escape is extinguished: for there *it* is, beyond
the distant blue outline of Salt Cay, beyond the sea, but

still too near... too near. It rises against the sky like a dazzling bank of low-lying white cloud: the antipodean ice field, advancing from the South Pole to meet that of the North. There is nowhere to run now, and no plane or boat to take me there. I just stand with the others. There's no talking, and no more sound from the small transistor radios people are clutching. All broadcasting's long since been replaced by a crackling static that no one can bear to listen to. There is just an eerie silence. We're all... waiting. For the jaws of the Ice finally to come together, to close upon us and the world...and then...

And then, as they say in the stories, I woke up.

✦•I•I•I•✦

What a heavenly waking, to the old familiar flat I had thought so dismal! And to a world still sane and unspoiled. To find everything so splendidly dull and normal — to feel wind and sun on my face — to be *warm*. To see traffic in the streets again, and people busily going about their lives. To hear so much blessed noise! Nothing was mundane to me any more. I felt this morning that I'd been given my life again — not the best of lives, perhaps, but one that might still be worth living all the same. And a mere dream — albeit one stranger and more detailed than any I'd ever experienced — had restored it all to me. So I thought in that moment.

I wouldn't have told you any of this, if I hadn't felt that I owed you an explanation for my behaviour. I'm grateful for your kindness, and regret that I made a scene. I hope you understand now why I reacted as I did. It's helped me a great deal to talk about it, and just to sit with you here in the café. But you see why I lost my composure just now, when we caught sight of that snowy owl perching on the war memorial.

So: it will all happen again, but in the real world this time rather than in my slumbering brain. I will stand again on the shore of that tropical island, gazing on the encroaching calamity. I will not, however, go public now with what I know and I urge you not to, either. What use is there in playing Cassandra? What difference could it make? It can't change the outcome, and in any case the government must already know about the Phenomenon. So for what purpose, you might ask, was I granted that vision last night? Not to give a futile warning, it seems, not to save myself or anybody else. Still, I refuse to see my glimpse of the future as a random cruelty. It may yet prove to be an act of mercy.

Because *you* were not in the dream. And I have told you now, not to warn you or to fill you with despair, but merely so that neither one of us need face what is coming on our own. This time there may be a hand in mine as I stand on that distant shore — a voice at my ear — a shoulder on which to slumber while I wait. Perhaps the end will not then seem so cold.

• •

Alison Baird was born in Montreal, Quebec, and now resides in Oakville, Ontario. She is the author of numerous fantasy novels for both young adult and adult readers, including *The Dragon's Egg* (Scholastic Canada), *The Hidden World*, *The Wolves of Woden*, and *The Willowmere Chronicles* (Penguin), *White as the Waves* (Tuckamore Books), and the *Dragon Throne* trilogy (Warner Aspect) which was recently translated into Russian. Her short fiction has been published in *On Spec* magazine and in various anthologies.
• •

HISTORY

Out of the Barrens:

Two Centuries of Canadian Dark Fantasy & Horror

By Robert Knowlton

Searching for Canadian dark fantasy is akin to peering into a dark wood; the foreground is densely foliated, but the background recedes into darkness. Admittedly, most of the undergrowth is scrub, written to please the passing fancies of distant markets and readers. The deep background descends far into the national psyche, and from these recesses emerge the legends and literature in which the peculiarly Canadian is revealed and we glimpse, fleetingly, the face of the boreal darkness. Insights may be gleaned, patterns discerned among a select few works of dark fantasy over the past two centuries. This is an exploration, nothing more or less; it is not a chronology, nor is it a comprehensive survey. It reflects back upon some fearful pleasures of a heritage largely unknown, and forth to a present teeming with bright promise, albeit of dark matters.

Our aboriginal cultures nurtured a rich tradition of fantastic myths and legends over millennia, nor were our ancestors utterly ignorant of same. Anna Jameson's *Winter Sketches and Summer Rambles* (1838) includes a legend of Mishosha the Magician, whose cunning sorceries rebound upon him, "the metamorphosis of the old man into a maple tree...related with a spirit and accuracy worthy of Ovid himself." Alas, Mrs. Jameson's appreciation of the Ojibway tale-tellers was not shared by her contemporaries, and Catherine Parr Traill best expressed the prevalent view in

her *Backwoods of Canada* (1836), stating "Fancy would starve
for lack of marvellous food to keep her alive in the backwoods. We have neither fay nor fairy, ghost nor bogle, satyr
nor wood-nymph: our very forests disdain to shelter dryad
or hamadryad." With these rueful words, she lamented
the absence of a Canadian mythology, whilst failing to
discern that this absence was a disturbing presence. A place
without a past, unsettled and unsettling, to the colonists
its very newness precluded the familiarity of ancient monuments to eyes unaccustomed. Rather, it unfolded before
the immigrant's gaze in an unbroken monotony of timeless,
trackless wilderness, inhuman in its vast scale — an
immense void unresponsive to human needs, whether for
physical or spiritual succour. And the very human response
to their awful insignificance in such a landscape? Northrop
Frye discerned in our literature "a tone of deep terror in
regard to nature.... It is not a terror of the dangers or dis-
comforts or even the mysteries of nature, but a terror of
the soul at something that these things manifest" (*The Bush
Garden*, 1971).

Therein perhaps lies a clue as to why there has seemed
such a dearth of dark fantasy in Canada down through the
years, given that the metaphysical terror aforementioned
does not readily lend itself to the traditional Gothic for-
mulae or old-fashioned ghost stories told 'round a chimney
corner. In any event our "enlightened" forbearers disdained
dark imaginings nor could they accord any value to savage
superstitions, so dwelling on the margins of terra incognita
they mapped away its mysteries. Where a civilizing hand
could survey and subdue the landscape, they prevailed;
boundaries were set, on the ground and in the mind. And
yet there remained wastes no hand could tame, and depths
no light could penetrate.

Charles G. D. Roberts's "The Perdu" (1895) is a bottomless "backwater of opaline opaqueness", a death-trap of
icy film in the winter, yet "on the new snow...human
footmarks run right across it," without footfall on either
shore. The Perdu at last draws a young girl to its depths,
her pale dead hand rising to beckon the living. Nigh on

a century later, in Margaret Atwood's contemporary ghost story, "Death by Landscape" (1989), a young girl walks into the bush and simply vanishes, with a shout "like a cry of surprise, cut off too soon." The devouring wilderness is viewed not as a landscape "in the old, truly European sense.... Instead there's a tangle, a receding maze, in which you can become lost almost as soon as your step off the path."

An enduring Canadian (indeed colonial) fear was that, in entering a wilderness, it entered *you*. "Going bush", a body can lose oneself. A remarkable continuity of Northern sensibility, as it were, is revealed in two of our most compelling legends: that of the Wendigo, which obsessed our Algonkian predecessors; and that of the Franklin Expedition, whose vanishment fascinated and haunted their English successors unto our own generation. The former were hunters for game, the latter for glory, both lost and wandering, windswept in the frozen wastes, their humanity stripped away by starvation, exposing the cannibal within eager to feed on nearest and dearest. Their transgression reduced them to mere skeletons, wraiths of ice — and hunger. Perhaps the most terrible part of these legends, other than their essential truth, is the utter absence of hope, either for survival or redemption. Atwood addresses both in *Strange Things* (1995), and her take on the Franklin legend regards Northern space as a *femme fatale*, cold and voracious. Perhaps Kipling spoke truly when he named Canada "Our Lady of the Snows."

Oddly, Canadian poetry and fiction have rarely addressed these themes, with occasional exceptions: W. H. Drummond's "The Windigo" (1901), Algernon Blackwood's "The Windigo" (1910), Alan Sullivan's "The Essence of a Man" (1913), W. H. Blake's "A Tale of the Grand Jardin" (1915) and more recently Gemma Files' "Words Written Backwards" (2007) and Graham McNamee's *Bone Chiller* (2008) all effectively tread the path of the wind-walker. As well, there is Laureate George Bowering's lengthy poem "Windigo" (1965), cataloguing its gruesome attributes, Paulette Jiles's more sympathetic "Windigo" (1984) and Ann Tracy's feminist interpretation *Winter Hunger* (1990).

The Franklin Expedition has inspired Gwendolyn MacEwen's verse play "Erebus and Terror" (1965) and David Solway's poem *Franklin's Passage* (2003), but for novels we must look abroad, to Briton Robert Edric's *The Broken* Lands (1992), and American Dan Simmons's *The Terror* (2007).

The loup-garou, however, has sired many whelps, often sharing traits with the wendigo. Notable exemplars are Wilfred Campbell's "The Were-wolves" (1893), cursed souls condemned to roam the Arctic Circle; Henry Beaugrand's "The Wer-wolves" (1898), assuming lupine form in the midst of cannibal celebrations; Alan Sullivan's "The Eyes of Sebastien" (1926), burning yellow with hunger for sweet Marie among the logging camps of the Laurentians; and H. Bedford-Jones's "The Wolf Woman" (1938), a legend of the first were-wolf. Robert Arthur Smith's *The Prey* (1977), Galad Elflandsson's *The Black Wolf* (1979), Douglas Smith's remarkable Cree myth/SF fusion "Spirit Dance" (1997) and Kelley Armstrong's *Bitten* (2001) are among the best of the recent brood, which have lately loped into the YA market with Edo van Belkom's Silver Birch series, *Wolf Pack* (2004), *Lone Wolf* (2005), *Cry Wolf* (2007) and *Wolf Man* (2008). Finally, mention should be made of the *Ginger Snaps* trilogy of films (2003-2004), beginning with suburban Goths in heat, then passing through the booby hatch way-back to a besieged forest/fort straight out of Frye. Those girls are sassy and sanguinary, in keeping with their situation.

Mrs. Traill may have found Canada a poor soil for fabulation, but her predecessors in Québec did not. The original Norman and Breton *habitants* imported an oral tradition of devils, witches, and ghosts, to which the *voyageurs* added the marvellous exploits of Indian shamans, and peculiar hybrids such as *Chasse-Galerie*, i.e. the Flying Canoe, and the aforementioned loup-garou. A good selection of these early narratives, many in essence 'tall tales', can be found in Aurélien Boivin's *Anthologie du conte fantastique québécois au XIX siècle* (1987).

In time this source material would inspire a revisionist response in the contes cruel of Yves Thériault, in *Contes pour un homme seul* (1944), and later still his daughter Marie-

Jose's florid, blasphemous tales of vampires, witches and demons in *The Ceremony* (1978). Michel Tremblay's *Stories for Late Night Drinkers* (1966) reflects his youthful love of the supernatural tale in a series of absurdist vignettes that are nightmarish, yet oddly playful, alluding to Hoffmann and HP Lovecraft, among others. More recently Daniel Sernine, in *Légendes du vieux manoir* (1979), *Les contes de l'ombre* (1979) and *Manuscrit trouvé dans un secrétaire* (1994) has revived the old legends with affection and fidelity. In the last named, he even harks back to the first Québécois novel with supernatural elements, Philippe Aubert de Gaspe fils's *L'Influence d'un Livre* (1837).

Gothic elements percolated through historical romances such as *Le Chien d'Or* (in which the notorious La Corriveau adds witchcraft and sorcery to her resume), and even *Marie Chapdelaine* and *Séraphin*, with oppressed heroines in the wilderness, can be seen as rustic *romans noir* at an oblique angle. Québécois Gothic comes of age as the 'old' Québec comes under assault politically and culturally in the 60's. Marie-Claire Blais's *Mad Shadows* (1959) sounds the clarion, in a dark reimagining of the Narcissus myth on a decaying seigneurie. Doomed characters dwell in a corrupted Eden, cursed not to wander but to stay, struggling to ascend from sin and death, but as the opening quote from Baudelaire makes clear, "[m]ad shadows descend to hell infernal...your chastisement born of loveless fires". Those with physical beauty are mutilated, to match their surroundings, left seared and sterile. "Nature...is ethereal and volatile", but in this case the nature is all too human.

The culmination of Québécois Gothic can be found in the novels of Anne Hebert, starting with *Kamouraska* (1975), which reimagines the woman-in-jeopardy as Faustian *femme fatale*, surrendering to uncontrollable passion so utterly she enters into a compact with her sorcerous servant. Elizabeth's perceptions shift and alter, such that dream and reality become fluid, and the two men in her life, her lover and her husband, the killer and the slain, also blur, each by turns becoming the Byronic brute. Wilder still is *Children of the Black Sabbath* (1975), in which Sister Julie of the Trinity's waking visions imagine a traumatic childhood of backwoods diabolism and ritual abuse erupting into the present as 'demonic possession', her hallucinations infecting her fellow nuns. Just as the Sabbat inverts the Catholic offices, reality and delusion become confused, as Julie's immaculate conception brings forth a tumescent monster, "a son of Satan" consigned to snowy death. The exultant sorceress, having shed her nun's habit like a snake's skin, descends the convent walls to seek her Master below, satisfied that "Evil is in them now. Mission accomplished."

Héloise (1980) is elegantly elegiac, a wry reverie on the ambivalent attraction of the *ancien régime*, even in the new Québec. A visiting young couple fall prey to vampires that prowl the underworld of the Paris Metro, albeit Bernard was clearly foredoomed to Héloise's hungry embrace, too erotically enamoured of her old world delights and terrors, too estranged from his sweet, sensible wife and their sterile Montréal home, termed "a blank page", like the modern apartment he rejects as "primeval nudity. Limbo. Nothingness...I cannot live in this white box. It has... no past! Could you make love here? It would be like trying to fuck in a block of ice."

Snow-bound Montréal, cold grimy and depressing, is also the locale of Joël Champetier's *La peau blanche* (1997), where exchange student Thierry's inverted nostalgia leads him from the old France to the new, only to discover a *morte amoureuse moderne* in Claire, pale cold and crimson (haired), an unhuman *gamine* old beyond her years, yet another 'illegal alien' hiding in plain sight amidst the urban blight. The author termed this his "urban romantic post-modern SF-fantasy", and it crackles with tension like hydro wires in a snowstorm, riddled with colourful *joual* dialogue as his snow white succubus seeks her prey, diseased rather than deceased, evolving rather than undead.

Champetier's other dark fantasies both feature protagonists of questionable sanity who find themselves enmeshed in conflicts with ancient evils resurgent in the modern world. Maddened with grief for his drowned children, Daniel Verrier in *La mémoire du lac* (1994) is drawn to the Algonkian sacrificial site beneath the cellars of an old resort, and to what lies waiting beneath the placid surface of Lake Témiscamingue. *L'aile du papillon* (1999) takes place in a decrepit asylum looming above Shawinigan Bay, where depressive Michel Ferron discovers that his delusions are in fact perceptions, and the supernatural forces battling within its corridors very real indeed, as the walls of the Hospital Saint-Pacôme prove as porous as its patients' psyches. Champetier is renowned in Québec as a science-fiction/fantasy writer, and this novel explicitly melds epic elements into the dark fantasy, with mention of mythical principalities and parallel dimensions.

Natasha Beaulieu's *Cités Intérieures* trilogy, *L'ange écarlate* (2000), *L'eau noire* (2003) and *L'ambre pourpre* (2006) is an Urban Gothic epic reminiscent of China Mieville or Conrad Williams, in which "the black water" flows between over-lapping dimensions, providing passage to the cities of Montréal, Penlocke, and ancient Kaguesna. An arcane manuscript, *Bo Betchuk*, contains the saga of the cities, and the key to saving all from a rising tide of evil. Beaulieu juggles a large cast of characters with considerable *élan*, as citizens both mortal and magical walk between worlds, in search of family, answers, and common salvation.

Esther Rochon's *The Shell* (1990) is more fabulation than fantasy, and its imagery at once both beautiful and hor-rific. It is indisputably a monster story, for embedded within a small island in the St. Lawrence rests a vast, iridescent nautilus shell, in the depths of which dwells a massive sentient cephalopod. This hermaphroditic omnisexual 'Cthulhu', as it were, telepathically summons, then seduces and impregnates human lovers who reside in the upper chambers of its shell, physically and emotionally nurtured and pleasured by the myriad forms of their host, embracing rather than devouring their lovemaking juices, their bodily wastes and even their deliquescent corpses when the lovers, after spawning monstrous offspring, die adoring and adored. This "marvellous monster" finally bears its pas-sengers living and dead out to sea, away from "the concrete monsters...the monster machines of Clindis", a cold and ugly caricature of Montréal, towards some unknown apotheosis longingly desired.

Patrick Sénécal's *Aliss* (2000) is a fable without the fabulous, an ironic/erotic reimagining of Lewis Carroll in which the monsters are all too human, perverse pathetic and very dangerous. Alice, an innocent 18, travels from her small island birthplace to the big bad city, Montréal yet again, in search of the "real world", only to take a one-way subway trip, sans white rabbit, to a neighbourhood not found in the Perly guide, a "wonderland" of wounded grotesques without laws, or morals, or limits of any sort. Absurdist, yes; whimsical, far from. Written in a profane *joual*, and rife with all manner of debauchery and violence, *Aliss* is genuinely disturbing even to a hardened horror reader who, like Alice herself, may find it difficult to keep their bearings in a place where everything is permitted, no matter how appalling.

To date, *Aliss* is a unique *tour de force* in Sénécal's oeuvre. He is better known in Québec as their home-grown version of Stephen King, a compliment much belaboured by reviewers and bloggers alike. Where quality of writing is concerned, the comparison is apt, but as to treatment, Sénécal is consistently darker, and grottier, and his world more dangerous and cruel, rife with snares to trap the unwary. Lost traveller Yannick knocks on the door of *5150 rue des Ormes* (1994) to call for assistance, only to find his need greater than he knew as the psychotic Beaulieu clan take him captive, the better to instruct him in their private religion of punishments and "power". En route to his hometown after many years absence, Stephen picks up *Le passager* (1995), a strangely familiar hitchhiker whose small talk turns to sinister hints at his driver's "lost years", and the terrible events to which both may have been more than merely witnesses.

Sur le seuil (1999) is more ambitious, as a cynical therapist comes to realize that his catatonic patient Roy Thomas has anticipated actual atrocities in his bestselling horror novels, then attempted suicide fearing his words, worse yet, brought these horrors into being. His fears are well-founded, as Dr. Lacasse learns the terrible secret of Thomas's conception, consecrated to chaos at birth by a mad priest who came to believe disorder is the natural order. This writer's wishes prove horses indeed, bearing Four Horsemen. For beggars, we must visit *Oniria* (2004), an isolated villa offering overnight sanctuary to four felons on the run, who have escaped one prison only to enter another far worse, a subterranean labyrinth where their secret fears, and desires, are made flesh. This book references earlier novels and characters, and plays with genre conventions, e.g. don't go in the basement, don't open that door, etc. The suspense is Hitchcockian, in that the reader is let in on the house's hidden horrors early on, and introduced to the convict's inner demons that will draw each to destruction. In a sense *Oniria* is Sénécal's *Malpertuis*, transplanted and perverted, with a wickedly sharp sense of humour, sharp as a devil's pitchfork.

Much of his recent work is more dark suspense than *fantastique*, although *Sept jours de talion* (2002) may be his most gruesome horror novel to date. A police procedural frames a fierce revenge motif, as grief-crazed surgeon Bruno Hamel kidnaps his daughter's rapist/murderer and literally deconstructs him in a series of operations described in clinical, and nauseating, detail. The moral dilemmas inherent in the material are directly addressed, as the 'monstrous' child killer becomes ever more pitiable and his punisher ever more monstrous, while the pursuing police debate amongst themselves whose actions are more reprehensible. Sénécal's most ambitious work to date, *Le vide* (2007) is also couched in terms of an investigation, examining the 'void' at the heart of modern life, an absurd abyss of random violence, rampant corporate malfeasance, and moronic mass culture, reflecting our rapt gaze every hour of every day on screens everywhere. Although not entirely successful, his arid vision of sterile decaying cities and their blankly cruel and avaricious inhabitants is unsettling and thought-provoking.

A more antique dust, no less arid, rests heavily on Martine Desjardin's *A Covenant of Salt* (2008), Québécois Gothic with a Faulknerian flourish, wherein a mad heiress summons a stonemason to her ruinous estate, there to carve the abandoned salt mine into a family sepulchre. The desiccated liches do not rest easy in their niches, haunting the memories of the living, their dead secrets lingering to devastate those already damaged. The saline taste of blood ever reminds us that "the essential Saltes of humane Dust" are the stuff of life itself, and the fifth element.

Morton Teicher's respected study *Windigo Psychosis* (1962) states that the outstanding personality trait among the Algonkian peoples of Northeastern Canada was "a powerful pattern of emotional restraint and inhibition...and instant repression of any display of emotion," so like those dour Scots Calvinists who followed seeking fur. An early example, Duncan Campbell Scott's "Vengeance is Mine" (1896) is set on the gray barren shores of James Bay where Scottish trader Black Ian, perversely cruel to those he loves, is visited by supernatural retribution, seized by "the intense and awful cold" until his flesh is blanched with hoar frost, frozen "ice to the core, rigid and unchangeable," the crystalization of his death-in-life.

A morbid yet mystic thread runs through the fabric of life among the Scots-Irish immigrants to Canada, and nowhere more so than in the Maritimes. The further east, the darker the hues, shading to black on the Rock. The prototype for Newfoundland Gothic was Margaret Duley's *Cold Pastoral* (1939), whose changeling heroine Mary Immaculate Keilley was "held by the fairies" as a child, and returned with her inherited arcane powers enhanced, which is as well for she needs employ them when adopted by Lady Fitz-Henry, the doyenne of a ruinous estate, and must battle a venomous servant for her rightful place. Myth and mystery play an integral part in the lives of the islanders, and an old parish priest observes that "he had never been able to eradicate the Celtic folklore they mixed so strangely with religion". Duley's contemporary heir is Nicole Lundrigan, whose novel *Thaw* (2005) tells the story of Hazel Boone, another fey spirit, born in a blizzard to burn through a life of fiery appetites with a heart of ice within until at last she returns to the snows. Stella in *The Seary Line* (2008) is a lost daughter, seeking connexion to her family bloodline with the aid of her husband Leander's second sight, while facing ancestral ghosts in memory and in spirit who must be laid to rest. These Brontean outport tragedies each feature strong women who must slog through much *sturm und drang* to seek a safe harbour, but there's no safety to be found in the work of Kenneth J. Harvey, which veers from Gothic to gallows humour, and at times beyond the pale.

Harvey's tales of the outports, in such collections as *Directions for an Opened Body* (1990), *The Hole That Must be Filled* (1994) and *The Flesh so Close* (1999), often as not tell of commonplace tragedy and domestic disturbance, gruesome yet oddly compassionate for the suffering of those caught "somewhere between brittle happiness and damnation", too often tipping into the latter. His most recent collection, *Shack: the Outland Junction Stories* (2004) chronicles a different culture, that of the inland villages set deep amongst the dense forests, where old ghosts and bogies jostle with more contemporary disturbances.

Out of the trees and over the water, *Stalkers* (1994) is a tale of sexual obsession, told by a half-breed hitman who lingered too long in the darkest recesses of the Toronto sex trade, where snuff films are no urban myth, and the aphrodisiac thrill of blood on tape is a memory still savoured and not easily erased. *Skin Hound (There are No Words)* (2000) hews even closer to horror, as serial killer William Merriam slaughters his family, then steps out onto the streets of St. John's to slay others for their skins, all the while fashioning his own corrosive self-loathing into a flensing knife to lay his torments bare. The unnamed (and unreliable) narrator of *Nine-Tenths Unseen* (1996) similarly descends into a dark maelstrom of guilt over transgressions real and imagined, caught in an ice-choked and snow-covered Christmas landscape of unholy longings and perverse desires, seeking absolution from his Lady of Exquisite Agony, an icy presence recalling De Quincey's *Mater Lachrymarum* "that night and day raves and moans". Ironically, his death-obsessed wife's delusions are, like Merriam's, truly dangerous, finding charnel import even in their pregnant daughter, now come home to a hearth long cold with hate. Her mad father reflects in a rare moment of lucidity that "there's no physical way of stopping what ails us. It is the spirit that must be healed."

This spiritual malaise that afflicts this benighted outport community of Bareneed deepens further in *The Town That Forgot How to Breathe* (2003) where successive waves of technology have undermined the bonds that held the local folk to their traditional ways, leaving them so enervated they succumb to a literal loss of breath, preceded by irrational rage. As the outport culture recedes into the past, the past emerges into the present as the sea casts up its dead, incorporeal yet strangely corporeal, such that a nose "becomes a stumpy white fish,....his eyes two throbs of jellyfish, his top lip a succulent sea cucumber, his bottom lip a moray eel." There's something of an Innsmouth look to this, but only if Lovecraft took Raymond Carver as his model, and although the risen dead soon begin to bear away the living, Harvey's quiet horrors are more those of lost memory than found monstrosity.

The old Christian death-trip/trap, whether Catholic or Calvinist, wends its way downbound across both outer and inner landscapes of ice and earth. Repression released in transgression, and the wages of sin... Are there perhaps other responses to the dichotomy of flesh and spirit in our culture? As ice melts to water, there is transmutation. Metamorphosis, in the Ovidian sense. P. K. Page's *The Sun and the Moon* (1944) is a welcome curiosity in CanLit, a symbolist romance with a psychic vampire as its heroine.

Born under a lunar eclipse, the adolescent Kristin can project her hungry, inchoate soul into "the static reality of inanimate things". First love threatens catastrophe as her spontaneous merging with her artist lover Carl leave them both less than whole; rather there is a confusion of mind in which each diminishes and loses their individuality. Kristin regards herself as "a leech, a vampire, sucking his strength from him — the moon eclipsing the sun", her conflicted passions echoed in turbulent wind and wave.

Recalling the Daphne myth, on her wedding eve her soul flees into a storm-wracked tree, withstanding the northern gale to remain rooted to the shore, the rising sun touching flesh and spirit each in its now separate residence. Kristin's dead-eyed husk marries Carl, who too late comprehends that he has exchanged a vampire for a zombie, yet her true self survives, "a shifting pattern of scarlet, vermilion and burnt orange" reflected in the water. Scott and Page are both accomplished poets, as are the Roberts brothers and Atwood, Bowering and MacEwen, Campbell and Hebert. All have been touched by the authentic "northern shudder"; indeed, Northrop Frye considered "the evocation of stark terror" to be one of the outstanding achievements of Canadian poetry (*The Bush Garden*, 1971).

As to the prose, for all that Douglas LePan called Canada "a country without a mythology," a series of novels over the past century have endeavoured to recover old myths and discover new ones, gazing over the landscape in search of gods and monsters.

Theodore Roberts's *The Red Feathers* (1907) relates the linked episodes of an epic battle between the good shaman Wise-as-a-SheWolf, a Glooscap surrogate, and his evil nemesis Bright Robe for possession of two small crimson feathers, which bestow near divine powers upon their bearer. Although set among the ancient "Beothic" peoples of Newfoundland, the folklore is largely drawn from Rand's *Legends of the Micmacs* (1893), telling of stalwart warriors and cannibalistic wind-walkers, man-eating ogres and shape-shifting sorcerers. Bright Robe is "a master of magicians...thirsting for power and blood and mischief", sacrificing his own family to taste the waters of immortality, and from his first Mephistophelean appearance, emerging from the boreal darkness in a shower of sparks, his cynical machinations sow discord throughout the Algonkian tribes of the region. At length, vanquished by Wise-as-a-SheWolf and malice spent, he is borne on the winds to a Caribbean island where, not unlike another misguided magus, Prospero, he may "drink the waters of forgetfulness" and abjure his baneful sorceries.

Howard O'Hagan's *Tay John* (1939) is the towheaded embodiment of a Tsimshian hero myth, "The Dead Woman's Son". Conceived in rape, his lust-inflamed preacher father nailed to a tree and burnt for his sins, the posthumous son is interred unborn with his dead mother yet he pushes out of her womb and up through the earth to fulfill his destiny and lead his brethren west over the Rockies to their ancestral lands. The high mountains are a Gothic terrain of terror and awe where he is sorely tested, but it is a new Eve that will diminish this old Adam. A prophet disowned by his people, Tay John walks between worlds on into the snowy wastes, "moved in the wind...fierce and starved", seeking a churchyard for his dead woman. Returning at last to his charnel womb, "he walked down...under the snow and into the ground."

Sick Heart River (1941), Governor-General John Buchan's posthumous metaphysical thriller, depicts another hero, Sir Edward Leithen of *Greenmantle* and *Mr. Standfast*. (Yes, he was that GG, founder of our national literary awards). This Presbyterian Cavalier sets off in search of lost men who have succumbed to the awful glamour of the North, "leaking into the landscape". He finds them in an isolated river valley of terrible beauty, "a cold cathedral of the North", whose benighted inhabitants exist "in sufferance; the North had only to tighten its grip and they would disappear." Leithen applies his muscular Christianity as balm to the wounds, physical and spiritual, of a tubercular Yukon tribe beset by mortal terror. Though the body dieth, yet the soul shall live, and his sacrifice *is* his salvation. It also marks the place where "the White Man's Burden" becomes insupportable, for, to reference Kipling yet again, "a bit of the dark world came through, and pressed him to death"

Wayland Drew's *The Wabeno Feast* (1973) takes a markedly different view of the 'White Man's Burden' and the result is a Canadian *Heart of Darkness*. The narrative is framed by, perhaps formed in, the ravaged visions of Charlie Redbird abandoned by past, future and death itself. The alienated protagonists have fled a polluted, depopulated pulp-mill town up north, only to find Toronto "a vision of destruction...buildings of a human scale toppling; skeletal new spires dwarfing their creators." Windigos, perhaps, not of iced bone but glass-skinned steel. Below, the streets seethe with violence and despair, as an old historian gives a crumbling journal to one of them, Paul Henry, to take back north in search of answers, and perhaps absolution. Its author is 18th century Scots trader Drummond McKay, born in an Age of Reason, who pressed deep into the virgin wilderness and found it *pressed back*. Far up country, he turns his spy-glass upon the *wabeno wekoondewin*, "a nightmare wherein fiends of neither sex made a mockery of both," as the celebrants feed the fire with sacrificial flesh and blood, then embrace the flames in frenzied dance, burnt black, then white. Seared and castrated, they scatter to spread their madness abroad, like ashes on the wind. McKay, taunted by his Mephistophelean companion Elborn, is infected by what he has witnessed, unsettled by Redbird's terrible words of warning "[y]ou are all wabenos, you whites, maddened by fires. You flee the enemy within, and fleeing, burn the plains and woodlands." Wanderers past and present alike arrive at a barren lakeshore, "umber, and bleached ochre, and grey...whipped ragged by the wind. It was very cold...all night the loons cried like wolves." McKay destroys Elborn, but this Faust cannot outlive his devil; Paul does survive, by burning the journal and rejecting the way of the wabeno. Ancient Redbird, trapped in "a state that is neither life nor death," calls out over the water, but only darkness, and silence, and the drifting snow give answer.

Timothy Findley's *Headhunter* (1992), is a literate and ironic reimagining of *Heart of Darkness*, as Kurtz is transposed from the page to the streets of a plague-ravaged Toronto, through the medium of Lilah Kemp, an unbalanced spiritualist possessing "intense but undisciplined powers." Reality and delusion interflow as Dr. Kurtz, Psychiatrist-in-Chief of the Parkin Institute is absorbed in the Club of Men and their erotic/horrific Sadean fantasies. His deterioration leaves the proverbial lunatic in charge of the asylum as Kurtz again goes bush, this time in the urban wilderness, yet he may not be so out of tune with his times. Findley's vision of modern urban life merges humour and horror, as one character ruefully observes: "There is little beauty left — but much ugliness. Little wilderness — but much emptiness. No explorers — but many exploiters." Canada, it seems, has inverted from a wilderness of wood and stone to one of steel and concrete, and whereas nature once menaced us, we now menace nature.

Rural Ontario Gothic still lurks beyond the GTA in lives of quiet depredation, and small towns like Salem, in Matt Cohen's *Flowers of Darkness* (1981), are rife with puritan repressions, self-abnegation, and grotesque eruptions of domestic violence. Apropos of Poe, "[m]uch of madness, and more of sin, and horror the soul of the plot." In the past decade, Tony Burgess has forayed far deeper into this territory, twisting the CanLit grid into a box of bedsprings.

The Hellmounths of Bewdley (1997) is pastoral perverted, in which the lost and the lonely wander a wintry landscape, failing to communicate save through physical pain; "Home" and The Bewdley Torture Society" veer into flat out absurdist horror. In *Pontypool Changes Everything* (1998) a viral plague erodes language and speech, rapidly reducing its victims to babbling zombie cannibals shambling about a frozen rural waste, seeking contact by tooth and nail. *Caesarea* (1999) is home to a neighbouring small town apocalypse, only this time the hollow vicious citizens are themselves the virus, deconstructing their tidy little world from within. Language again is affected, and as the local poet loses his words becoming one with the chaos, he can only gibber "Eye j(US)t w(ant) to D(eye)."

In Canadian culture the coupling of desire and death as a transmuting process is epitomized by David Cronenberg's horror films, germain to this study as he is not only the auteur of his images but often the author of the script as well. Throughout his early films, from *Shivers* (1975) through *Scanners* (1980), the cold clinical landscape of modern architecture housed "big science" institutions that, from the most altruistic motives, spawn ravenous mutants, whether bacterial or bipedal, that invariably violate the safely ordered world without. Cronenberg views the body as in "a state of revolution" — this revolting flesh, as it were, ever seeking to overthrow the tyranny of reason or cast off the tyranny of death, much as fantasy and horror assault the realist paradigm.

Initially, sexually transmitted disease is the *agent provocateur* of choice, but *Videodrome* (1982) marks a transition, as the images spawn brain tumors that open physical reality to metaphysical change. "Word begets image and image is virus," as William S. Burroughs puts it in *Naked Lunch*, filmed by David Cronenberg in 1991 as a hallucinatory experience, in which reality and illusion fully interpenetrate until they become indistinguishable. In interviews, Cronenberg envisions mutations where "human beings could swap sexual organs...or develop different kinds of organs that would give pleasure. The distinction between male and female would diminish...sheer force of will could allow you to rearrange your physical self." Long live the New Flesh. In *eXistenZ* (1999), the New Flesh becomes Virtual Reality, as genetically engineered gaming modules plug into various body orifices not provided by nature, allowing role-playing gamers access to interpenetrating levels of...reality? Of course, the equipment resembles sexual organs, and the new orifices prove adaptable to the old carnal applications. VR would seem on one level to be an extended masturbatory experience, with an adrenaline chaser, but *eXistenZ* also addresses questions of knowing and being, of flesh and fabrication, albeit with a black humour more sly and ribald than previously seen in Cronenberg's work. A sense of play is not merely appropriate, it is essential to such material.

Nowhere is this more apparent than in the works of Eric McCormack, a transplanted Scot whose splendidly bizarre, gruesome, eccentric fictions have been compared to James Hogg, Franz Kafka, and Thomas Ligotti. They are however, uniquely his own. His collection *Inspecting the Vaults* (1982) is by the author's own admission steeped in "the good old Scottish tradition of...blood and guts." Nothing dour here, there's sex and absurdist humour aplenty in *The Paradise Motel* (1992), which opens with the tabloid Gothic scenario of a mad surgeon killing his wife, then implanting her body parts in their children, merely the first of many intersecting tales of peculiar pain. There are also patterns of recurrence, for the good doctor is first met in "Sad Stories in Patagonia", from the preceding collection, and we will meet him again in *The Dutch Wife*. *The Mysterium* (1992) is set in a plague-ridden town under quarantine, afflicted by extreme garrulousness, and a faint yet pervasive odour. The guarded, secretive survivors are verbally vomiting themselves to death. McCormack's third novel boasts the impressive title *First Blast of the Trumpet Against the Monstrous Regiment of Women* (1997), and the distinction of being a picaresque horror adventure romance, an avis rara to say the least. Its ill-fated protagonist suffers many tribulations, his 'weird' so persistent that he suspects a predestination to disaster. Interpolated vignettes of a grotesque and horrific nature are scattered about the narrative, many courtesy of an old sea salt, whose tall tales warm the cold grue nicely. *The Dutch Wife* (2002) is framed by an abandoned son's search for his lost father, who has roamed the world as an anthropologist gathering improbable, grotesque, disgusting and amusing narratives, now brought back to his remote Pacific archipelago. Such peripatetic Sinbads feature frequently in McCormack's oeuvre, which in richness of invention, diversity and literary craft is a veritable Scots/Canadian Arabian Nights, a Roc's egg of terrors and wonders.

Robertson Davies' *High Spirits* (1982) are much lighter in tone, indeed these ghost stories are *jeux d'esprit*, a don's whimsy. As if to put the lie to Earle Birney's well-known quote, "It's only by our lack of ghosts we're haunted", Davies throws Samuel Butler back at him, with "[w]here murthers and walking spirits meet, there is no other narrative can come near it", and takes this for the title of his final novel (1991), a wistful and playful *ave atque vale*. He returns to Salterton, setting of his early social comedies, where critic Gil Gilmartin finds himself thrust into a peculiar film festival, screening ghostly epics of the daily "hero-fights" his own ancestors waged as they progress from Scots reivers to respectability in only six centuries. The story veers between farce and tragedy and much besides, but ends with Gil's own demise, 'murthered' and gathered to his ancestors at last. His final dialogue is with Lady Death herself, not surprisingly "a dear companion", and so exuent for critic and creator both, although unlike Dunstan in *World of Wonders*, without a bear in pursuit.

Death herself also overlooks poet Patrick Lane's first novel, *Red Dog, Red Dog* (2008), in the person of Alice, the posthumous narrator of the Stark family saga. It is a harrowing record of cruel predatory men, sorrowing women and the secrets they keep from one another within their closed community in the Okanagan Valley, a "land of Cain". They congregate at the local dogfighting pit, a sacrament of blood where the dogs truly are red. Grim stuff, albeit beautifully written, but for the ultimate Western Canadian Gothic one must look to Sheila Watson's *The Double Hook* (1959), set amongst an isolated prairie community of sad, savage grotesques trapped in a Manichean waste-land of drought and despair. Fishing for salvation, if you "hook twice the glory, [you] hook twice the fear." And there is much to fear from the malefic tempter Coyote, an ever-lurking whisperer in darkness, and his agents corporeal and spectral, sowing misery in their wake and savouring the suffering of others. The writing is a richly allusive symbolist prose, classical and Christian myth deeply embedded in the text.

A contemporary novel, John Buell's *The Pyx* (1959) is also imbued with Christian symbolism, but otherwise could not be more different. Nominally a hard-boiled police procedural, it resonates at a deeper level as a metaphysical mystery, in which an ancient contest between good and evil is joined on the mean streets of Montréal. Elizabeth Lucy, like Sade's Justine, remains incorruptible in the depths of corruption, and her refusal to defile the titular object means her death, but also that of Keerson, a diabolist whose Satanic pride erupts into possession by the powers he presumed to rule. *The Pyx* was a harbinger that the literary thriller was not an oxymoron in CanLit, but acceptance was long in coming.

Another Canadian author found a congenial reception south of the border for well-crafted novels of dark suspense, some much darker than others. David Morrell's *Testament* (1975) charts the systematic destruction of a decent man, as everything he values and cherishes is stripped away until he is reduced to a near-bestial state. Notwithstanding, at the brink of the abyss he steps back. Although seared by savage cruelties, his heart's core was fired from a finer clay than his enemies. In *The Totem* (1979), however, the fall is absolute, as a hippie commune in the Wyoming wilderness, frozen and starved over a harsh winter, regress back millennia to a death-cult of troglodytes. Worse yet, they contract a rare form of rabies, now caught in a closed loop of death and resurrection, resembling old world vampires and new world wendigos, combining the worst of both. Their mad messiah keeps them in thrall, and in hiding, until he is sacrificed to his own dark god of the hunt, and the survivors go forth to be feral and multiply, their bite infecting all they encounter until a vast rabid pack descends upon the nearest small town, to hunt and to gather.

Morrell's short stories, collected in *Black Evening* (1999) and *Nightscape* (2004), are among his best work, genuinely frightening narratives of the lost and the found, seekers in pursuit of secrets better left so, on dark journeys to the edge of madness, and beyond. "The Dripping" is only milk, but what tragedy it portends for, as Freud rightly observed, dolls truly are fearful things. In "But at my Back I Always Hear", the insistent footfall of an insane student stalking her English professor follows him beyond all boundaries of decorum and restraint, at last beyond those of time and mortality as well. Darker secrets still lie beneath "The Beautiful Uncut Hair of Graves", loosely inspired by the gruesome "Butterbox Babies" scandal in Depression-era Nova Scotia. An estranged son, in settling his parent's estate, is unsettled to discover a past he never suspected, and a massacre of the innocents that enriched, and damned his birthplace. Dead infants weep beneath the flowing grass, yet "to die is different from what anyone supposed, and luckier," rather than live on after such knowledge.

"Orange is for Anguish, Blue for Insanity" is Morrell's strangest, most distinctive story to date, plunging into the rolling chaos of colour that are a mad artist's masterpieces, which on closer viewing reveal "tiny mouths and writhing bodies", perhaps his personal demons trapped in paint? But no, a misguided scholar pursues this art and mystery to its source, the secret place of "Cypresses in a Hollow", there peering into the depths of a piercing otherworldly beauty, the pain of which can only be alleviated in artistic creation. There are echoes of classic writers here, Machen, Blackwood, Lovecraft, but in the simple notion of inspiration as infection, and the sophisticated palette of revelation and imagery applied to convey this, "Orange is for Anguish..." achieves a classic status in its own right.

Forty years after *The Pyx*, Andrew Pyper's *Lost Girls* (1999) provided a literate hybrid of legal thriller, murder mystery and ghost story, albeit his colleagues had warned him "a thriller couldn't possibly be literary". He himself believes "as Canadian literary culture becomes more sophisticated,...these categories are going to dissolve." Certainly *Lost Girls* is a clever mix of John Grisham and Henry James, in which Tripp, a creepy lit teacher in a rundown Ontario backwater is suspected of killing his two prize pupils, but perhaps they drew too near to Fireweed Lake and the dark lady who haunts its depths. His cokehead lawyer Crane senses the dead girls, and the presence in the lake, but his addled wits cannot separate fact from fancy: "He turns, but there's nothing there... a lick of wind sounding as a whispered name." Even stone lions on the courthouse steps seem to watch him with their cold stone eyes. The lake at last draws defendant and defender into its embrace, but Crane swims free, having learned "there's evil in this world" beyond human law.

Pyper himself trained as a lawyer, something he shares in common with another successful writer, Michael Slade, whose Special X series of psycho thrillers chronicle an RCMP task force's pursuit of sundry serial killers, with emphasis on clever plotting, and CSI gory details. Several titles flirt with the supernatural, notably his first *Headhunter* (1984) and its sequel *Primal Scream* (1998), grounded in Indian myth and magic, and climaxing in the high Rockies where "the winter goes on forever"; *Ghoul* (1987), an explicit homage to H. P. Lovecraft, whose writings inform the title character's psychosis; *Bed of Nails* (2003) another serving of Cthulhu Mythos, with a side of Jack the Ripper; and *Evil Eye* (1996), adding voodoo and zombies to the mix, also briefly touched upon in the earlier *Headhunter*. Slade has occasionally been compared to Stephen King, but in truth 'he' is the Canada's Thomas Harris, (and something of a committee effort, the number of hands on the keyboard varying from book to book, with Jay Clarke mostly taking the lead).

Michael Hale produced unusual variants on the serial killer theme, character driven and tightly plotted. *The Other Child* (1986) involves an AI prototype infected by a mass murderer's consciousness, now loosed to roam the Information Highway in its infancy, while *A Fold in the Tent of the Sky* (1998) finds a rogue psychic probing past events by remote viewing, at first for profit, then to allay suspicions by eliminating the forbearers of the suspicious, who thus never were.

Garfield Reeves-Steven's *Bloodshift* (1981) was an intelligent techno-thriller take on vampirism, followed by *Dreamland* (1986); *Children of the Shroud* (1987) and *Dark Matter* (1990), where physics and metaphysics meet for a skull session under the knife of a mad scientist. "The Eddies", a Fortean nightmare atop the CN Tower, was featured in *Northern Frights 2* (1994) but unfortunately this has been his last work to date in the dark fantasy field. Reeves-Stevens has commented that the Canadian genre has "a strong moral grounding...and a clear sense of moral order is something you need in good horror." Whatever shifts occur in the genre, then, it would seem our moral compass remains true, ever pointing due north.

Scott Bakker is best known for his epic fantasy trilogy The Prince of Nothing, but in *Neuropath* (2008) he, too, explores the moral and spiritual consequences of a rogue neuroscientist's probing into "the black box of the soul", the human brain, and in so doing addresses some profound questions concerning the nature of consciousness and being.

More monstrous malpractice can be found in Gord Rollo's *The Jigsaw Man* (2008), where the "surplus flesh" of the homeless is harvested in a Sadean castle of horrors by a mad surgeon motivated by love. While no *Yeux sans visage*, Rollo's staccato rhythms and 42 jagged little chapters bear an intriguing correlation to the "jigsaw" of body parts on parade. Marcy Italiano's *The Pain Machine* (2003) harvests agony itself, passed from suffering patient to accepting physician, at a terrible cost to both.

Having discussed the werewolf at length long since, it is high time to give the undead their due, for vampires have drawn the interest of several talented Canadian writers in recent years, starting with Nancy Baker, whose novels *The Night Inside* (1993) and *Blood and Chrysanthemums* (1994) juxtapose 1990's 'Goth' sangfroid with robust sensuality, while conveying the abiding melancholy of immortality. Her prin and proper heroine Ardeth is metamorphosed by the vampire Rozonov's surprisingly tender 'gift' into a formidable, predator. "The way of the vampire," as explored over the course of two novels, increasingly becomes a meditation on the moral choices an immortal must make, in the knowledge that humanity is hard won, and too easily lost.

Nancy Kilpatrick has written a series of linked vampire novels over the past decade or so, collectively titled Power of the Blood, beginning with *Near Death* (1994) and continuing through *Child of the Night* (1996), *Reborn* (1998) and *Bloodlover* (2000), with a fifth in the works. Her undeads are not solitary predators, seeking companionship among their own kind and even forming familial bonds, struggling towards a rough sort of ascension, aspiring to more than mere survival from night unto night. A prolific short-story writer, some of Kilpatrick's best work has been collected in *Vampire Stories* (2000), such as "In Memory of" and the brief but haunting "Memories of *el Dia de los Muertos*", as well as "Metal Fatigue" in *Cold Comfort* (2001), showcasing a talent for erotic horror that manages to be both. Her more recent zombie stories are worth mentioning, in particular, "Going Down" from *Mondo Zombie* (2006), and "The Age of Sorrow" from *The Living Dead* (2007), much subtler and smarter than your typical brain-munching gore-fest.

Tanya Huff's successful series of Vicki Nelson/Henry Fitzroy novels began with *Blood Price* (1991), concluding with the fifth, and final instalment *Blood Debt* (1997), and a wrap-up story collection *Blood Bank* (2008). The books mix police procedural, vampiric romance and dark fantasy devices, with some sassy patter for spice, and begat a television series, *Blood Ties*, which unfortunately didn't survive its freshman year. Fitzroy's nocturnal investigations continued, however, in *Smoke and Shadows* (2004), *Smoke and Mirrors* (2005), and *Smoke and Ashes* (2006), now relocated from Toronto to Vancouver and partnered with Tony Foster , a tyro wizard.

An altogether different sort of vampire than the handsome and cultured Henry Fitzroy can be found driving a semi on the Trans-Canada Highway in Edo van Belkom's *Blood Road* (2004); any similarity ends with the title. Konrad is a mean little mutt with bad teeth, bad breath and a portable transfusion kit, giving a whole new meaning to the term 'road kill'. The novel has pedal-to-the-metal pulp pacing and an unpretentious grindhouse sensibility, showcasing Belkom's best as a master of the modern pot-boiler. Briefer bursts of high-octane horror can be found in his collection *Death Drives a Semi* (1998).

There was a Canadian 'pulp' horror tradition of sorts before Belkom, from the prolific pulp hack Thomas P. Kelley in the 30's and 40's, to the even more prolific Dan Ross in the 60's, many of whose formula Gothics bear covers of blue skinned girls (hardly surprising, clad only in a negligee) stumbling over blue crags beneath blue turrets out into a dark and stormy night. Dark blue, naturally. Still less inspired schlockmeisters appeared in the 70's and 80's, surprisingly too numerous to mention for a supposedly neglected genre, but among the many discords a few grace notes can be found. Robert Arthur Smith's *The Prey* (1977), *The Toymaker* (1984) and *Vampire Notes* (1989) competently cover traditional themes, while Stephen R. George specialized in "child-in-jeopardy" thrillers, notably *Grandmas' Little Darling* (1990) and *Torment* (1994). Sean Costello's work stands out, particularly *The Cartoonist* (1990) and *Captain Quad* (1991), both involving psychic abilities, precognition and astral projection respectively.

But the most impressive genre horror novelist to emerge towards the end of this period was Susie Moloney. An award-winning humour columnist, her first horror novel was *Bastion Falls* (1995) a blizzard-bound Northern Ontario town where winter comes early, and with it cackling "black entities" that roam the white darkness in search of prey. *A Dry Spell* (1997) shifts locale to the drought-parched prairies, where a rainmaker raises an old evil in Goodlands. Her last novel to date, *The Dwelling* (2003), is a haunted house in the Jacksonian tradition, seeking a soulmate and definitely more than the sum of its parts. Moloney's work presents well-defined characters, strong plotting and a wry sense of humour. Humour and horror not only juxtapose, they are oftimes complimentary in skilled hands.

Kelley Armstrong is the popular author of the Otherworld series, beginning with *Bitten* (2001) through *No Humans Involved* (2007), in which werewolves, vampires, witches and assorted supernatural creatures endeavour to pursue 'normal' lives as young urban professionals, while taking both 'real world' and Otherworld crises in stride. Rather as if the 'children of the night' walked down the dark streets of New York City in Carrie Bradshaw's shoes, which in part explains a loyal and growing readership. That, and some very capable writing.

Armstrong's work borders on the "paranormal romance", a growth area of the supernatural genre to which Canadians have contributed their share of fangs and spells. Donna Lea Simpson's best-selling werewolf novels are matched by Lynsay Sands's best-selling vampire novels, nor is she alone in swirling a mean cape. Michelle Rowen, Eve Silver and Stephanie Bedwell-Grime all have vampire

romances to their credit, while Naomi Bellis works the
demon lover theme into good old-fashioned Sabatini-style
adventures. Where kissing stops, biting starts, so descending from *eros* to *luxuria*, our northern climes generate a
fetishistic *frisson* in the work of Sephera Giron, starting with
Eternal Sunset (2000) on through *Borrowed Flesh* (2004) and
Mistress of the Dark (2005), the former melding their author's
occult and erotic interests with graphic horror while the
last mentioned follows the depredations of a female serial
killer. *Hungarian Rhapsody* (2007) is a full-blooded erotic
romance of vampirism and concupiscence, in about equal
measure, with most bodily humours explored, and exchanged, therein. Erotic horror has perhaps not strayed so
far from tradition, for even the ancient Balkan curse,
whereby the dead are laid and the undead rise, states "May
thou become in the grave like rigid wood." And by the ordinary miracle of decomposition, so they do.

Charles de Lint is highly regarded for his contemporary fantasies set in the Ottawa valley and the Laurentians,
in which magical worlds, usually drawn from Celtic and
Ameridian mythologies, interpenetrate with our reality,
often through dreams. One notes with some amusement
that he has managed to locate in such a quintessentially
Canadian setting every creature Traill summarily banished
over a century and a half ago, and quite a few more besides. Supernatural predators cast a darker hue over some
of these fantasies: in *Yarrow* (1986), Lysistrakes, "the Thief
of Dreams," feeds on creative imagination, whiles in *Jack
the Giant Killer* (1987) and its sequel, *Drink Down the Moon*
(1990), the evil Faerie host of the Unseelie Court menace
our world with their darkness, threatening to rob it of all
wonder and joy.

For de Lint, the worst evils are invoked by aggrieved
humans who summon powers of darkness to attack perceived enemies, and in so doing endanger themselves. In
his darkest fantasy to date, *Mulengro* (1985), a spirit hunts-
man, "He Who Walks With Ghosts", is summoned by a
malicious gypsy to set his ravening *mules* upon his own
people. De Lint chose a pseudonym, Samuel M. Key, for

a series of horror novels, *Angel of Darkness* (1990), *From a Whisper to a Scream* (1992), and *I'll Be Watching You* (1994) which mark a departure from his gentler Otherworld books, although the second is, in fact, the first Newford novel. Grim as they are, the protagonists discover that employing evil against itself is self-defeating; one can only vanquish darkness, within and without, by embracing the good.

Justine Musk's urban Gothic fantasies lean markedly to the darkside, chronicling the internecine conflicts amongst the nephelim, descendants of angels laying with humans. The Summoners seek to preserve the world as we know it, while those corrupted by demons seek to make it the devil's playground. "The devil's music" is prominent in both theme and in the lush and sensual prose rhythms, apt given that Asha, the nominal villain of the piece, is an underground rock goddess of genuinely semi-divine pedigree, although so maddened by pain and rage her songs are magical incantations to open a portal in the Dreamlines, letting a demon horde through to gambol and slay. The Dreamlines connect the disparate characters, artist Jess dreaming of fallen angel Ramsey, both pursued by Asha and her sister Kai to join in their battle. All these creatures are children of a lesser God in Musk's post-lapsarian world, damaged and diminished and desperately seeking healing. Two novels of the Summoners have thus far appeared, *Blood Angel* (2005) and *Lord of Bones* (2008), with a third projected to complete the trilogy.

Another genre of popular fiction that has produced Canadian dark fantasy of note is that written for a Young Adult readership. Such works as Janet Lunn's *Double Spell* (1968) and *Shadow on Hawthorn Bay* (1986); Margaret Buffies's *Who is Frances Rain?* (1987); *The Guardian Circle* (1989), *My Mother's Ghost* (1992) and *The Dark Garden* (1995); Michael Bedard's *A Darker Magic* (1987), *Redwork* (1990) and *Painted Devil* (1994); and most recently Arthur Slade's *Dust* (2006), one and all explore that borderland between dark and light, death and life where young protagonists and older mentors must confront and vanquish, supernatural evils that threaten to destroy them, a rite of passage much like adolescence itself.

As a process of recovering the lost tradition of Canadian fantasy began in the early 80's, reprint anthologies appeared beginning with John Robert Colombo and Michael Richardson's *Not to be Taken at Night* (1981) and John Bell's *Visions from the Edge* (1982). These freely mixed ghost-stories, fabulation and SF from various classic CanLit writers such as Roberts, L. M. Montgomery, as well as Canadian contributors to the early pulps. Colombo also issued an excellent selection of windigo fiction and articles, simply titled *Windigo* (1982). The best compilation of early material to date has been Alberto Manguel's *The Oxford Book of Canadian Ghost Stories* (1990), with a strong selection of works by Atwood, Findley, McCormack and others. Greg Ioannou edited *Shivers* (1990), an innovative mix of older fiction with new stories by Garfield Reeves-Stevens and Karen Wehrstein, intending to extend it to a series, but the imprint folded.

Given the steady rise of dark fantasy novels (of variable quality) through the 80's and 90's however, the emergence of a lasting market for original short fiction in the genre was inevitable, and when *Northern Frights* (1992) appeared, the response from readers, and contributors, was enthusiastic enough to sustain a continuing series through *Northern Frights 2* (1994), *Northern Frights 3* (1995), *Northern Frights 4* (1997), *Northern Frights 5* (1999), and a concluding retrospective volume, *Wild Things Live Here: the Best of Northern Frights* (2001). Editor Don Hutchison believed "what makes Canadian [dark fantasy] different is a sense of place...once you step outside the city...you feel all the time like there's something out there, or nothing out there...Canada has this huge untapped vein of darkness running through it." A touch of chill can be felt through many of the stories, a cold wind blowing through our Canadian memory and imagination. But diversity in setting, style, and tone is what most powerfully impresses the reader. From the lonely anguish of Karen Wehrstein's "Cold," to the rustic grue of Nancy Kilpatrick's "Farm Wife," to the unnerving reality-shift of Andrew Weiner's "The Map," to the menacing metascience of Robert Charles

Wilson's "The Perseids", to the sheer grotesque weirdness
of David Nickle's "The Sloan Men," the *Northern Frights*
series opened a vein in contemporary Canadian dark fantasy, and established a place where dark imaginings were
no longer shunned, but welcomed.

Michael Rowe contributed several deliciously creepy
tales of a night-side Milton, Ontario to the above series,
then went on to edit *Queer Fear* (2000) and *Queer Fear II*
(2003), gay-themed anthologies in which two 'outlaw'
genres are well-met, the horrific and the erotic interpenetrating across a new Canadian landscape, not of ice and
fire, but of brick and wire. The monsters, too, are diver-
gent, old creatures in new guises, and new boogens come
home to roost. Innovative rather than transgressive, these
collections stay focussed on the purpose of any good horror
fiction, to "makes your flesh creep," and that they do.

For transgressive, Derek McCormack's "underground"
fictions do nicely. His prose has been described as "what
A. M. Homes might write if she were a gay man." In short,
lean and mean as a junkyard dog. All killer, no filler.
McCormack's two vampire novels insolently shake together
high camp with horror tropes to pour forth a toxic cock-
tail of rebel celebrities long gone, and those who fed upon
them body and soul. *The Haunted Hillbilly* (2003) purports
to tell the 'secret' history of 50's Country & Western legend
Hank Williams and his relationship with "Nudie" Cohen,
bloodsucking costumer to the stars, whose rhinestone glitter
clad the likes of Elvis and Cher. *The Show that Smelled* (2008)
is set in a dark carnival a world removed from Bradbury,
framed by the conceit that this scenario unfolds as a "lost"
Tod Browning film from the 20's. Both works feature "walk-
ons" by such cult luminaries as Jimmie Rodgers, Hank
Snow, Lon Chaney, Elsa Schiaparelli and Coco Chanel. Only
here red is the new black, as one of McCormack's impossibly stylish villains hisses, "At my vampire carnival, I'll
pinken my popcorn with baby blood." 'Nuff said.

A seminal development in Canadian dark fantasy and
horror over the past decade has been the emergence of an
indigenous specialty press, now that we have a community

of genre authors to sustain it. Burning Effigy, founded in 2003 by Monica Kuebler has produced a series of horror chapbooks, both prose and poetry, notably Gemma Files' fine Wendigo tale *Words Written Backwards* (2007)and Richard Gavin's daemonic *Primeval Wood* (2009). Kelp Queen/ChiZine issue poetry and prose, respectively, 'tho the former is also responsible for the "Loonie Dreadful" series of chapbooks, featuring David Nickle and, again, Gemma Files. ChiZine has recently launched an ambitious publication program, beginning with Brett Hayward's dystopian "New Weird" novel *Filaria* (2008), set in a labyrinthine underworld of strange beauty and terror, an Escher print in four dimensions where gods and monsters ascend and descend with impunity, and the Red Plague holds illimitable dominion over all. Their latest publication is Robert Boyczuk's *Horror Story and Other Horror Stories* (2008) is largely free of ghosties and ghoulies, but with plenty of things that go bump, and leave marks. Love hurts, and these "horror" stories count the myriad ways. David Nickle's first collection, *Monstrous Affections* is now scheduled for the summer of 2009. Both presses are owned and operated by award-winning poet Sandra Kasturi and her husband Brett A. Savory, no mean horror writer himself as evinced by his novels *The Distance Travelled* (2000) and *In and Down* (2007), as well as his short story collection *No Further Messages* (2007). ChiZine's recent emergence in paper and boards follows a long-time presence as an online magazine of twisted delights, one of two such sites of note in Canada. The other is Cathy Buburuz' *Champagne Shivers*, offering an annual sampling of dark prose and verse, complemented by striking visuals.

Royal Sarcophagus Society, under the aegis of Lisa Ladouceur, produce exquisitely crafted limited editions reminiscent of Cheap Street editions in years gone by, with loving care taken in the choice of typography, materials and design. Their list includes Nancy Baker's short story collection *Discovering Japan* (2007), and *The Book of Ghosts* (1997, 2nd edition, 2006), eccentric vignettes of disturbing elegance created by the press's lead designer David Keyes.

Last but by no means least, mention must be made of Ash-Tree Press, relocated from England to British Columbia a decade ago, and dedicated to the reclamation of the classic supernatural tale. Although primarily a reprint house, it increasingly publishes new material, both single author collections and anthologies, and it is in the latter that Canadian contributions of interest can be found, such as Simon Strantzas' "When Sorrows Come" (*At Ease With the Dead*, 2007) and "Under the Overpass" (*Shades at Darkness*, 2008), Ian Rogers's "Leaves Brown" (also *Shades of Darkness*, 2008) and Barbara Roden's "Northwest Passage" (*Acquainted with the Night*, 2005), a fine modern update on the traditional theme of 'going bush', set in the British Columbia hinterland where "something tall and thin...[and] really old" watches, and waits outside an isolated cabin to embrace the unwary in its boreal mystery. It should be said that Mrs. Roden, with her husband Christopher, are founders/proprietors/editors of Ash-Tree Press, but where her short fiction to date is concerned, the quality precludes any question of vanity publishing, and a much-anticipated collection aptly titled *Northwest Passages* is scheduled for publication in Fall 2009 from Prime Press.

Awareness of the ancestral legacy the genre gifts its aficionados with brings a familiarity born of respect to the writings of several emerging Canadian authors, whose tales are thus enriched and invigorated by the association. The promise of Richard Gavin's first collection, *Charnel Wine* (2000) is more than fulfilled by his second *Omens* (2008), containing affectionate homages to Robert Aickman and Jonathan Carroll, among others, yet stepping out from the masters' shadows to cast his own, like a tenebrous star "which do ray out darkness upon the earth as the sun doth light". The former, "Strange Adventures", also crucially references Magritte's "Attempting the Impossible", as a young Canadian adrift encounters the enigmatic Sophia in "Venice's rotting landscape", only to find a love as fluid and ephemeral as the place itself. She is likened to a Black Madonna, "flawed...and fading away to darkness", for the beauty and the decay are inextricably entwined. The latter,

"Beneath the House of Life" explores arcane Qabalah lore unknowingly embedded in a children's book which, if read aright, opens the Gates of Death to "the dreaded abyss of the false creation... where all our nightmares come from." This tale also references, more obliquely, Kenneth Grant's peculiar theories regarding the "hidden truth" of Lovecraft's visions, so we know the protagonist who descends through the gateway in the cellar will ascend much altered, and not for the better. At his best, Gavin's stylish prose and striking imagery effectively convey, in his own words, "a terrible rush of awe-tinged dread", an aspiration well met.

The aforementioned Simon Strantzas is more reminiscent of Ligotti and his antecedants, but with a fascination for permutations of the flesh closer perhaps to Cronenberg. In his first collection *Beneath the Surface* (2008), "The Wound so Deep" festers within a hollow man, another sad helot serving in corporate hell until his baffled rage and bitterness brings forth "a long ropy protrusion of flesh...covered with hundreds of tiny suckers" to avenge his wrongs, only to break "free from the empty shell of its old life" and go naked into the world. "A Thing of Love" haunts an eccentric writer, a moist madonna/muse that sucks up his miseries, "every dark and unrecognized thing in the recessed parts of [his] soul", and with them his talent. His editor/unrequited lover rejects the creature's embrace, but in crushing it to free him, the fertile darkness rebounds and crushes the creator who can no longer bear his own burdens. Strantzas' second collection *Cold to the Touch* is scheduled for publication by Tartarus Press in the summer of 2009.

Michael Kelly's taut compact pieces, collected in *Scratching the Surface* (2007) are at times reminiscent of early Matheson and Beaumont, but he has an idiosyncratic mix of cruelty and compassion, and his memorable imagery lingers long after the covers are closed. A drug-addled narrator discovers "Warm Wet Circles" on the pavement, realizing that a hungry city devours its homeless, leaving only "small dark circular stains that glisten suggestively" on the pavement, and a few pitiful scraps of flesh that their finder preserves in a memory box, against the day he loses himself to the warm embrace of the cold asphalt. A second collection, *Undertow and Other Laments* has been announced for the fall of 2009 from Dark Regions Press.

A writer to watch is Ian Rogers, previously cited for his contribution to Ash-Tree's *Shades of Darkness* anthology, who has been producing a steady flow of innovative stories that freely range over genres in search of the authentic shudder. "Charlotte's Frequency" from *Horror Library 2* is a good example, spinning a web of electronic vampirism, while "Relaxed Best" in *Not One of Us #38* is a peculiar melding of hard-boiled noir with high finance and netherworld diabolism, deftly juggling its disparate parts into a satisfying whole. Rogers' novella *Temporary Monsters* is forthcoming from Burning Effigy in the fall of 2009.

A number of new talents have emerged from the burgeoning specialty press past the cusp of the millenium, and two merit special mention. The oft-cited Gemma Files issued a series of chapbooks under her Quantum Theology imprint, *Soaked in Light* (2000), *The Narrow World* (2001), and *Heart's Hole* (2001), in which her "monsters" are often not the protaganists, their moral connexion as relevant as the metaphysics of their condition, be they witch or werewolf, vampire or revenant. Monstrosity intensifies their humanity, rather than diminishing it. Her recent omnibus collections from Prime Press, *Kissing Carrion* (2003) and *The Worm in Every Heart* (2004) gather most of her stories to date, including "The Emperor's Old Bones", "Keepsake", "Skeleton Bitch", and "The Diarist", which number among the finest horror fictions produced by a contemporary Canadian writer.

Another Canadian author with Prime Press is Holly Phillips, whose first collection *In the Palace of Repose* (2005) announced the advent of a major new talent. Like Raymond Carver, she thinks "it is a good thing in fiction when the story and its characters appear to have...lives [that] stretch out before and beyond the current tale." Hence Phillips's fictions are mostly middle, born on the backs of characters "stalked by wonder," and impelled not least by the beauty of her prose. They simply stop, unresolved, leaving the reader not sated, but hungry for more. A true original, her take on vampirism, "One of the Hungry Ones", leads Sadie through a mirror world of masquerade, grimy reality and gilded fantasy bonded in blood. The Small Ones, an alien race of "scrapyard, trash-heap, back-alley beings" shamble through "The New Ecology" in search of their unwilling goddess Millenium, as lost and broken as they, in hope of a shared epiphany. Phillips' first novel *The Burning Girl* (2006) is also set in a grim and grimy urban landscape, constantly altering in a succession of dimensional shifts as Rye recovers her past in pieces, like shards of a broken mirror. Her work to date consistently chronicles the trials and tribulations of lost girls, sought and seeking, in a world where the extraordinary erupts constantly from interstices in the ordinary.

Immigration has ever introduced new voices, and fresh responses, to the Canadian landscape; Rohinton Mistry's excellent "The Ghost of Firozshah Baag" (*Tales of Firozshah Baag* 1987) to Nalo Hopkinson's novels and tales, using "Afro-Caribbean spirituality, culture and language... subverting the genre, which speaks so much about the experience of being alienated, but contains so little written by alienated people themselves". This is changing, and now a world of mythologies has settled here, without apologies to Mrs. Traill, and with them new dreams and nightmares infuse a terrain more brightly lit, yet where dark shadows still lurk. As cities continue to rise and sprawl, and open spaces recede and shrink, the outer darkness merges with the inner one, a sure sign that this new place is no longer so new. A multitude of voices in many tongues crash in upon those awful absences and silences now filling them with word and image, as our omnipresence now overlays and expands the landscape of the Canadian imagination.

The modern urban environment may at times press too close, the emergence of Canadian fantasy, light and dark, perhaps signifying a dissatisfaction with upright walls and orderly grids, in streets and cyberspace, and expressing an inchoate yearning for something lost, or never found. And yet those forests of concrete and steel and glass now call forth their own ghosts and monsters to assail us. The "old" northern shudder may at last have stilled for, as Atwood observes, "[t]he North is not endless — it is not vast and strong, and capable of devouring and digesting all the human dirt thrown its way" (*Strange Things*, 1995). It only seemed so, when it was bigger and we were smaller. The "new" northern shudder need not wander the snowy wastes nor the dark woods, it walks among us, the true North strong and free. Two solitudes have given way to, if not Cronenberg's polymorphous perversity, then a kaleidoscope of possibilities in a Canada endlessly reimagined, the womb of terrors and wonders beyond all measure.

● ●

Robert Knowlton has always listened for, in George Herbert's lovely words, the "music at midnight" which is the beauty found in dark places and sweet discords. He edited *Borderland*, a small-press periodical devoted to dark fantasy in the mid-80's, contributed a number of articles to the *Penguin Encyclopedia of Horror and the Supernatural* (1985), and some years back wrote an article on Canadian dark fantasy, "The Haunted Silences". He continues to hear "music at midnight", and hopes he ever shall.

Acknowledgements for invaluable assistance with the preparation of this article must go to Mary Cannings, of the Merril Collection of Science Fiction, Fantasy and Speculation, to Hugues Leblanc for correcting the French language errors, and to Peter Halasz, whose stimulating arguments improved the final result.

● ●

Our titles are available at major book stores and local independent resellers who support Science Fiction and Fantasy readers like you.

EDGE Science Fiction
and Fantasy Publishing

Tesseract Books

www.edgewebsite.com

Our titles are available at major book stores and local independent resellers who support Science Fiction and Fantasy readers like you.

Gaslight Grotesque: Horrific Tales of Sherlock Holmes
edited by Jeff Campbell & Charles Prepolec (pb)
- ISBN: 978-1-8964063-31-9
Green Music by Ursula Pflug (tp) - ISBN: 978-1-895836-75-2
Green Music by Ursula Pflug (hb) - ISBN: 978-1-895836-77-6

Healer, The (Children of the Panther Part One) by Amber Hayward (tp)
- ISBN: 978-1-895836-89-9
Healer, The (Children of the Panther Part One) by Amber Hayward (hb)
- ISBN: 978-1-895836-91-2
Hell Can Wait by Theodore Judson (tp) - ISBN: 978-1-978-1-894063-23-4
Hounds of Ash and other tales of Fool Wolf, The by Greg Keyes (pb)
- ISBN: 978-1-894063-09-8
Hydrogen Steel by K. A. Bedford (tp) - ISBN: 978-1-894063-20-3

i-ROBOT Poetry by Jason Christie (tp) - ISBN: 978-1-894063-24-1

Jackal Bird by Michael Barley (pb) - ISBN: 978-1-895836-07-3
Jackal Bird by Michael Barley (hb) - ISBN: 978-1-895836-11-0
JEMMA7729 by Phoebe Wray (tp) - ISBN: 978-1-894063-40-1

Keaen by Till Noever (tp) - ISBN: 978-1-894063-08-1
Keeper's Child by Leslie Davis (tp) - ISBN: 978-1-894063-01-2

Land/Space edited by Candas Jane Dorsey and Judy McCrosky (tp)
- ISBN: 978-1-895836-90-5
Land/Space edited by Candas Jane Dorsey and Judy McCrosky (hb)
- ISBN: 978-1-895836-92-9
Lyskarion: The Song of the Wind (Part One of The Chronicles of the Karionin)
by J.A. Cullum (tp) - ISBN: 978-1-894063-02-9

Machine Sex and other stories by Candas Jane Dorsey (tp)
- ISBN: 978-0-88878-278-6
Maërlande Chronicles, The by Élisabeth Vonarburg (pb)
- ISBN: 978-0-88878-294-6
Moonfall by Heather Spears (pb) - ISBN: 978-0-88878-306-6

Of Wind and Sand by Sylvie Bérard (translated by Sheryl Curtis) (pb)
- ISBN: 978-1-894063-19-7
On Spec: The First Five Years edited by On Spec (pb)
- ISBN: 978-1-895836-08-0
On Spec: The First Five Years edited by On Spec (hb)
- ISBN: 978-1-895836-12-7
Orbital Burn by K. A. Bedford (tp) - ISBN: 978-1-894063-10-4
Orbital Burn by K. A. Bedford (hb) - ISBN: 978-1-894063-12-8

Pallahaxi Tide by Michael Coney (pb) - ISBN: 978-0-88878-293-9
Passion Play by Sean Stewart (pb) - ISBN: 978-0-88878-314-1
Petrified World (Determine Your Destiny #1) by Piotr Brynczka (pb)
- ISBN: 978-1-894063-11-1
Plague Saint by Rita Donovan, The (tp) - ISBN: 978-1-895836-28-8
Plague Saint by Rita Donovan, The (hb) - ISBN: 978-1-895836-29-5

Pretenders (Part Three of the Okal Rel Saga) by Lynda Williams (pb)
- ISBN: 978-1-894063-13-5

Reluctant Voyagers by Élisabeth Vonarburg (pb) - ISBN: 978-1-895836-09-7
Reluctant Voyagers by Élisabeth Vonarburg (hb) - ISBN: 978-1-895836-15-8
Resisting Adonis by Timothy J. Anderson (tp) - ISBN: 978-1-895836-84-4
Resisting Adonis by Timothy J. Anderson (hb) - ISBN: 978-1-895836-83-7
Righteous Anger (Part Two of the Okal Rel Saga) by Lynda Williams (tp)
- ISBN: 897-1-894063-38-8

Silent City, The by Élisabeth Vonarburg (tp) - ISBN: 978-1-894063-07-4
Slow Engines of Time, The by Élisabeth Vonarburg (tp)
- ISBN: 978-1-895836-30-1
Slow Engines of Time, The by Élisabeth Vonarburg (hb)
- ISBN: 978-1-895836-31-8
Stealing Magic by Tanya Huff (tp) - ISBN: 978-1-894063-34-0
Strange Attractors by Tom Henighan (pb) - ISBN: 978-0-88878-312-7

Taming, The by Heather Spears (pb) - ISBN: 978-1-895836-23-3
Taming, The by Heather Spears (hb) - ISBN: 978-1-895836-24-0
Ten Monkeys, Ten Minutes by Peter Watts (tp) - ISBN: 978-1-895836-74-5
Ten Monkeys, Ten Minutes by Peter Watts (hb) - ISBN: 978-1-895836-76-9
Tesseracts 1 edited by Judith Merril (pb) - ISBN: 978-0-88878-279-3
Tesseracts 2 edited by Phyllis Gotlieb & Douglas Barbour (pb)
- ISBN: 978-0-88878-270-0
Tesseracts 3 edited by Candas Jane Dorsey & Gerry Truscott (pb)
- ISBN: 978-0-88878-290-8
Tesseracts 4 edited by Lorna Toolis & Michael Skeet (pb)
- ISBN: 978-0-88878-322-6
Tesseracts 5 edited by Robert Runté & Yves Maynard (pb)
- ISBN: 978-1-895836-25-7
Tesseracts 5 edited by Robert Runté & Yves Maynard (hb)
- ISBN: 978-1-895836-26-4
Tesseracts 6 edited by Robert J. Sawyer & Carolyn Clink (pb)
- ISBN: 978-1-895836-32-5
Tesseracts 6 edited by Robert J. Sawyer & Carolyn Clink (hb)
- ISBN: 978-1-895836-33-2
Tesseracts 7 edited by Paula Johanson & Jean-Louis Trudel (tp)
- ISBN: 978-1-895836-58-5
Tesseracts 7 edited by Paula Johanson & Jean-Louis Trudel (hb)
- ISBN: 978-1-895836-59-2
Tesseracts 8 edited by John Clute & Candas Jane Dorsey (tp)
- ISBN: 978-1-895836-61-5
Tesseracts 8 edited by John Clute & Candas Jane Dorsey (hb)
- ISBN: 978-1-895836-62-2
Tesseracts Nine edited by Nalo Hopkinson and Geoff Ryman (tp)
- ISBN: 978-1-894063-26-5
Tesseracts Ten: A Celebration of New Canadian Specuative Fiction
edited by Robert Charles Wilson and Edo van Belkom (tp)
- ISBN: 978-1-894063-36-4
Tesseracts Eleven: Amazing Canadian Speulative Fiction
edited by Cory Doctorow and Holly Phillips (tp)
- ISBN: 978-1-894063-03-6

Tesseracts Twelve: New Novellas of Canadian Fantastic Fiction
 edited by Claude Lalumière (pb)
 - ISBN: 978-1-894063-15-9

Tesseracts Thirteen: Chilling Tales from the Great White North
 edited by Nancy Kilpatrick and David Morrell (tp)
 - ISBN: 978-1-894063-25-8

Tesseracts Q edited by Élisabeth Vonarburg & Jane Brierley (pb)
 - ISBN: 978-1-895836-21-9

Tesseracts Q edited by Élisabeth Vonarburg & Jane Brierley (hb)
 - ISBN: 978-1-895836-22-6

Throne Price by Lynda Williams and Alison Sinclair (tp)
 - ISBN: 978-1-894063-06-7

Time Machines Repaired Whie-U-Wait by K. A. Bedford (tp)
 - ISBN: 978-1-894063-42-5